I0436130

REDFACE

RACE

PERFORMANCE

INDIGENEITY

PERFORMANCE AND AMERICAN CULTURES

General Editors: Stephanie Batiste, Robin Bernstein, and Brian Herrera

This book series harnesses American studies and performance studies and directs them toward each other, publishing books that use performance to think historically.

The Art of Confession: The Performance of Self from Robert Lowell to Reality TV
Christopher Grobe

Realist Ecstasy: Religion, Race, and Performance in American Literature
Lindsay V. Reckson

The Queer Nuyorican: Racialized Sexualities and Aesthetics in Loisaida
Karen Jaime

Black Patience: Performance, Civil Rights, and the Unfinished Project of Emancipation
Julius B. Fleming Jr.

*F*ck The Army!: How Soldiers and Civilians Staged the GI Movement to End the Vietnam War*
Lindsay Goss

Disability Works: Performance After Rehabilitation
Patrick McKelvey

Like Children: Black Prodigy and the Measure of the Human in America
Camille Owens

Redface: Race, Performance, and Indigeneity
Bethany Hughes

BETHANY HUGHES

REDFACE

RACE, PERFORMANCE, AND INDIGENEITY

NEW YORK UNIVERSITY PRESS New York

NEW YORK UNIVERSITY PRESS
New York
www.nyupress.org

© 2024 by New York University
All rights reserved

Please contact the Library of Congress for Cataloging-in-Publication data.
ISBN: 9781479829378 (hardcover)
ISBN: 9781479829392 (paperback)
ISBN: 9781479829408 (consumer ebook)
ISBN: 9781479829439 (library ebook)

This book is printed on acid-free paper, and its binding materials are chosen for strength and durability. We strive to use environmentally responsible suppliers and materials to the greatest extent possible in publishing our books.

Manufactured in the United States of America

10 9 8 7 6 5 4 3 2 1

Also available as an ebook

CONTENTS

LIST OF ILLUSTRATIONS

INTRODUCTION

Indian. The word is a blunt weapon: imprecise, versatile. It requires great force to deploy it effectively. It is also a tool used in cunning and subversive ways. This book does not shy away from the power and danger the word possesses and provokes. *Indian* is unwieldy, yet it has been wielded against and by Indigenous folks so often that it must be reckoned with. In this book, I deny the sometimes self-evident truth that Indians exist in quotidian life. Indians do not exist. Indigenous peoples exist. Peoples with national, tribal, band, or community belonging exist. Peoples with relationships and obligations to land, water, and nonhuman relatives exist. Peoples with history, kinship, governments, and futurity exist.[1] Indians do not. Indians are a theoretical and ideological construction, a construction possessing indisputable power that creates and explains undeniably material conditions for Indigenous and non-Indigenous peoples. However, it does not exist in the way water or oxygen does, independent of human influence or action. It is not an element. It is a synthetic compound. It enters the world as a tool or a weapon depending on its purposes, which range from beneficial to benign to devastating.

This book is therefore an exploration and articulation of how something that is not (Indians) comes to be something that is (Indians). It is an explanation of how a concept becomes enfleshed, embodied, vivacious. This book is about how skin is grown over bones. Red skin. Understanding this process demands traversing academic terrains of race, representation, performance, history, politics, sovereignty, and Indigeneity, while remaining grounded in the materiality and dramaturgy of popular theater in the United States. *Redface: Race, Performance, and Indigeneity* is an examination of redface praxis in popular American theater, an analysis of the relationship between art and politics, and an interrogation of how American culture constructs Indians as a race and consequently delimits Indigeneity.

Theater is an excellent location for interrogating the relationship between representation and Indigeneity. It typically comprises co-present and communicative bodies; it is an embodied human action of experiencing and understanding together. It is also often entertaining and enlightening, humans sharing stories that are pleasurable or meaningful or both. Importantly for this book's goals, theater has been exceptionally popular in the United States. Broad appeal, cultural saturation, and accessibility are excellent conditions to begin an inquiry into political ideology (settler colonialism), public perception (Indian as a race), and the material implications when the two combine in/on a body (redface). These reasons are more than what makes theater a vibrant and fecund location for interrogating connections between Indigeneity and Indians. They are also why theater is an embarrassingly opulent space to interrogate race. Where else are bodies that are on display so overtly and quickly assessed and labelled? What other human action contains glaring omissions, expressive gaps, and sonorous silences that scream meaning and beg for analysis? Where else could one locate interactions so clear and intentional, happening faster than the speed of life but familiarly ephemeral? Where else is suspended disbelief and temporarily deployed belief the foundation of human experience? Theater is a clutter-free microcosm of the race making, race experiencing, and race interpreting that occur in every day American life. It boils it down, cuts out the boring parts, and attempts to render it digestible for audiences, even as it participates in and shapes the complex, contested, and durational process of recognizing and interpreting human bodies. Theater is where race is clear and clearly fictive while materially and powerfully present.

Defining redface in American theater is both the end goal and starting point of this book. I approach redface as a theatrical repertoire, something that can be seen and heard repeatedly over time, that which occurs routinely and familiarly but not uniformly. It is also something that obviously belongs to the body—*repertoire* as explicated by Diana

Taylor and as conceptualized by Tracy C. Davis as "multiple circulating recombinative discourses of intelligibility."[2] Davis explains that by encountering these "discourses of intelligibility," audiences become used to them and draw on them to interpret new performance experiences, which in turn become incorporated and relied on for interpreting yet newer performances. According to Davis, repertoire "involves processes of reiteration, revision, citation and incorporation."[3] This book focuses on the construction and circulation of redface in the nineteenth- and twentieth-century United States. Redface (the theatrical praxis) is a collection of material markers such as makeup, costuming, and staging. But it is more than just those tangible markers. It is not just an act of appearing; it is also an act of recognizing.

In this book, I argue that redface is a collaborative, curatorial process by which audiences and artists construct a legible Indian body onstage, a Stage Indian. It is a complex configuration of embodied markers, dramaturgical techniques, and claims of authenticity that also work beyond the stage to racialize Indigenous peoples and reduce the political potency of Indigenous sovereignty. It is an attempt to contain and constrain Indigenous peoples within the logics of western European drama, American settler colonialism, and Euro-American law and society. To understand the twenty-first-century world, where redface theatrical praxis endures across professional and amateur performances and reaches into other performance-based events (e.g., Halloween, sports mascots) is to understand the current political climate that undermines Indigenous sovereignty, nationhood, and self-determination (e.g., construction of pipelines across treaty lands, ongoing challenges to tribal sovereignty, and the persistence of blood quantum as a tool of racial authentication). Redface is not a harmless performance practice, but neither is it just a racist costuming practice. Redface is *the* way American aesthetic culture works to define and delimit its idea of and relationship to Indigenous bodies. It is how the United States processes and enacts the materiality of what Thomas King calls the deeply "inconvenient Indian."[4]

In this book, I will refer to people indigenous to the continent of North America as *Indigenous* or *Native American* interchangeably. Both these designations are imprecise, and there is not universal agreement among Indigenous people whether they are accurate, useful, or helpful. However, they are the best, widely legible words I have at my disposal at the time of this writing. When at all possible, I will refer to people using their tribe/nation/band's name rather than by the generic term *Native American*. I will rarely, though occasionally, use *American Indian* as a synonym for *Native American*. *American Indian* was popularized in the twentieth century but is typically a less preferred term in the twenty-first century. I reserve the word *Indian* for a generic, racialized identity created by Europeans and Americans. Indians are a fiction, albeit a useful fiction for both Euro-Americans and Native Americans. And although many Native Americans, including myself, might use the term when referring to ourselves or our communities, I think of it more like an old fence than an identity. It keeps some people in. It keeps some people out. It has its uses. But somebody else built it. And someday, it will be gone, and we won't have to look at that eyesore ever again.

REDFACE

Redface as it developed in the United States in the early nineteenth century was not alone as a racializing popular entertainment form. A more prominent form of racial impersonation developed around the same time, blackface minstrelsy. While a much more widely discussed and interrogated phenomenon than redface, blackface is an instructive touchstone for the work of this book. Blackface as a theatrical praxis has deep roots in western European theatrical forms, such as the mystery cycles and commedia dell'arte of the sixteenth and seventeenth centuries.[5] However, the uniquely American form arose around the 1830s when the supposed progenitor of the form, T. D. Rice, first performed his dancing and singing act in blackface makeup and costume. In the decades that followed, blackface minstrelsy would develop into its own highly codified genre of American theater. Songs, dances, comedy, dramaturgical structure, costumes, and makeup all came together to form a nationally recognized and internationally beloved theatrical form. Blackface minstrels were, as Eric Lott's groundbreaking work in the field has shown, primarily not-quite-white (immigrant), working-class males who used it as a tool for assimilating into white American society, critiquing that society, and freely expressing themselves.[6] After the Civil War, Black men entered the profession, and troupes of African American performers, still donning black makeup and performing exaggerated caricatures, became dominant in performance venues. Blackface minstrelsy was a national pastime by the late nineteenth century and continued into the twentieth century, increasingly as an amateur entertainment form.

As Stephen Johnson has insisted, blackface "has never left us"; it persists into twenty-first-century entertainment.[7] However, the social acceptability of blackface has changed drastically over the centuries. In the nineteenth century, it was often perceived as harmless, racialized fun. By the early twentieth century, it was becoming outdated as a form of popular entertainment but persisted in several performance contexts. By the mid-twentieth century, it was less socially accepted in commercial entertainment and more acceptable in private theatrical spaces.[8] By the late twentieth century, blackface became both a performance practice acceptable in popular entertainment (only for specific reasons) and totally unacceptable in mainstream American culture. However, it persisted in informal and amateur spaces like costume parties and fundraising benefits. Blackface's long history and the robust body of scholarship surrounding it reveal the complexity, possibility, theft, and continued presence of this form of performance in the United States and beyond.[9] It is similar to redface in many ways, relying on theatrical conventions, racializing political projects, and insidious narrative structures. However, it is distinct because the population that blackface worked to delimit and control, African Americans in the United States, is different. Other forms of racial impersonation, like yellowface, were also nascently circulating in the nineteenth century, although they have a different temporal and political trajectory from blackface or redface.[10] However, racial impersonation as a racializing theatrical project with political and material consequences was and is ubiquitous within US cultural production.

Redface is like blackface, except when it isn't. Like blackface, it is obsessed with making Americans American, has had a global impact on the representation of its subject, and offers a nostalgic look at an imagined past. It also persists across the centuries, even as it morphs and adapts to new cultural formats and media forms. Unlike blackface, there is no structured theatrical genre of redface minstrelsy. There is no repertoire of redface minstrelsy scripts, songs, dances, dramaturgical structure, jokes, or characters, although all exist individually. Redface does not take up class formation, but it certainly speaks loudly on racial and national formation. Redface is conceptually and teleologically distinct from blackface.

While the project of blackface is affixing conceptual Blackness to bodies to perpetuate their oppression and subservience, the project of redface is to affix conceptual redness to bodies to perpetuate their disappearance. Redface constructs the category of the Stage Indian and then implies that the character is an accurate depiction of Indigenous peoples. The impossibility of fulfilling the expectations of the Stage Indian is precisely the goal of redface as a racializing and depoliticizing project of embodied performance. For (white) America to flourish and dominate, it must create conditions for its consolidation, expansion, and absolution. Blackness both bolstered (through slavery) and threatened (through miscegenation) that consolidation and expansion. Therefore, cultural conceptions and depictions of Blackness have presented it as that which should be contained through an imposed and often violently enforced cultural hierarchy. Blackface created an inherently inferior character that absolved white Americans of their acts of control and violence. In contrast, white Americans conceived of Indianness as that which could be subsumed or co-opted. It was therefore a minimal impediment to consolidation and domination but a significant challenge for expansion. The burning question about Indians was not "How do we keep them in their place?" but "Why are they still here?" In response, cultural conceptions of Indians, and the materialization of those conceptions through redface, have always demonstrated the Indian as that which disappears. That disappearance is both racialized and politicized. Redface is a material, embodied practice that asserts that Indian is a race that vanishes. Because of this, redface denies the perpetuity of Indigenous nationhood and sovereignty, two things that stand in the way of American expansion and absolution.

"REDFACE" IN BOOKS AND FILM

The history of the word *redface* encompasses far more than a specific theatrical practice developed in the nineteenth century and still circulating in the twenty-first. However, perhaps unsurprisingly, the word's history and usage reflect the basic processes and preoccupations of that theatrical practice. Locating the origin story of the word *redface* and identifying its every usage is not the concern of this book. However, a brief look at its usage will illuminate the necessity of this book at this moment in time. The word *redface* has been used as a racialized category, a proper name, a factual adjective, a derogatory adjective, a theatrical practice, and at times, even a verb.[11] Although only a thumbnail sketch, limited in scope to English-language books between the years 1500 and 2019, the Google Books Ngram Viewer hints at the infrequent and inconsistent usage of the word (figure 1.1).[12]

According to this dataset, the word *redface* was basically nonexistent before the 1790s, at least in published books. Even at the height of its usage (how often it appears in all the unigrams contained in the database), the percentage of use for *redface* was only 0.00000018 percent (compared to the height of blackface usage, 0.00003 percent; figure 2). It is used infrequently when at all. When it did appear in the nineteenth century, it was often as part of proper names (e.g., Mr. Redface) or sometimes as a descriptor (e.g., redface opencast in mining). By the twentieth century, the word was in print as a name for the category some might also call Indian (e.g., paleskin and redface) but was still used as a descriptor of other, nonracialized things (e.g., redface anger). Only after 2000 was there a marked increase in *redface* usage in print. At the same time, other racialized performance practice words, like *yellowface*, were gaining in usage. By 2008, *redface* had begun to appear in academic writings focused on racialized depiction, circulating as the word identifying a theatrical practice of representing Native Americans through reductive, visual markers. Frequently, it was connected with *blackface* as a point of reference.

Beyond book publishing and academia, *redface* also became common parlance for journalists and theater artists. For example, a 2018 review in the *New York Times* of Brandon Jacobs-Jenkins's play *The*

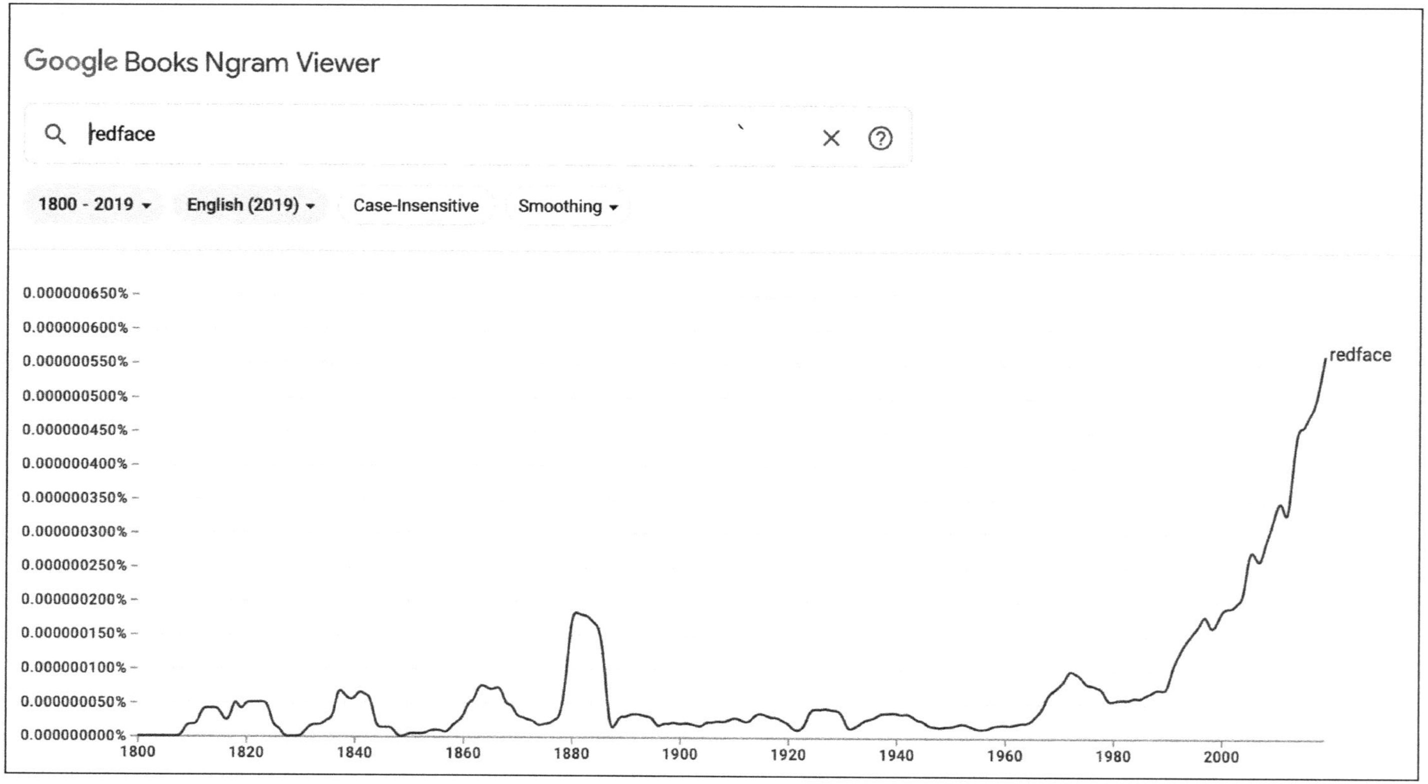

Figure 1.1. Google Books Ngram Viewer "redface." Image courtesy Google Books Ngram Viewer.

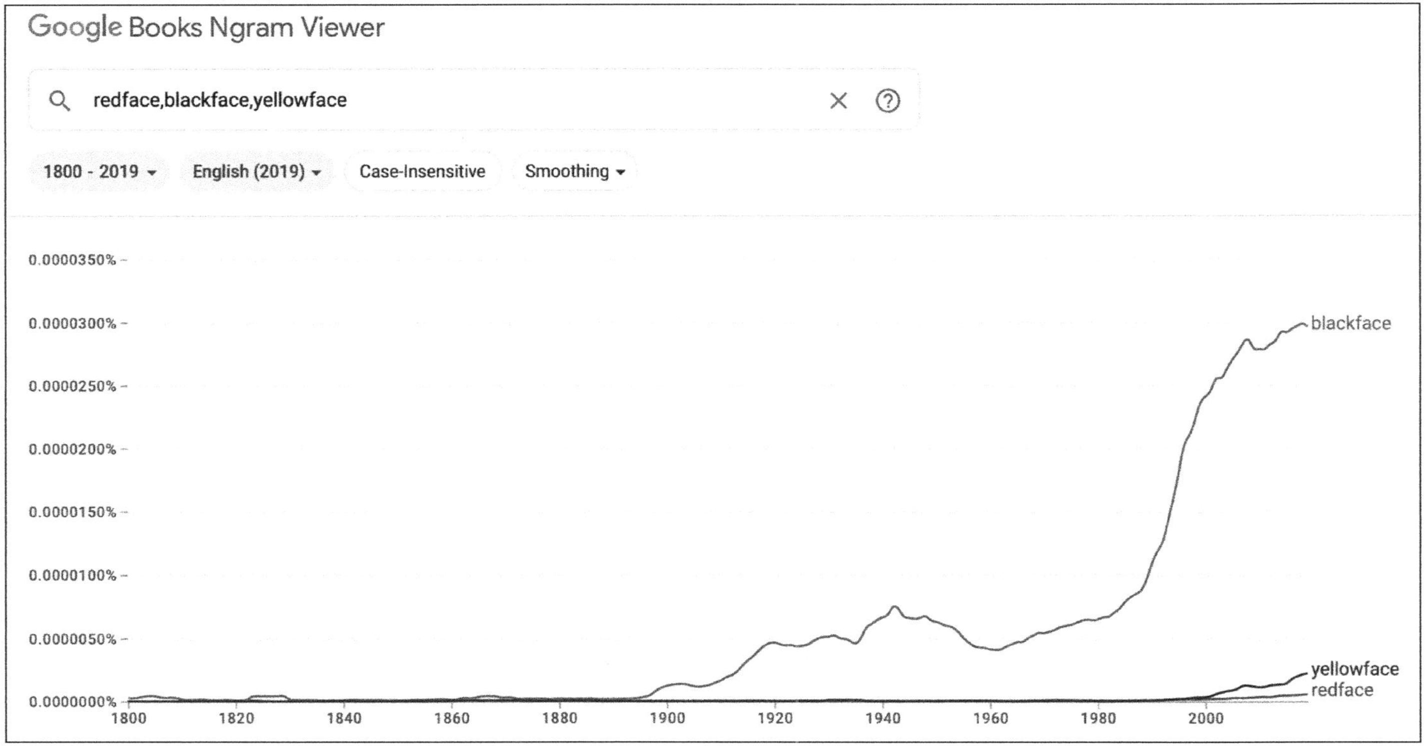

Figure I.2. Google Books Ngram Viewer "redface, blackface, yellowface." Image courtesy Google Books Ngram Viewer.

Octoroon discussed how one of the characters "applies redface" to play "the role of an Indian."[13] In 2018, the hashtag #InsteadOfRedface began circulating on what was then called Twitter and other social media platforms, as Native American theater artists used it to highlight plays and performances created by Native Americans. The increasing diversity of meaning and frequency of use for the word *redface* prompts this book's project. That project is to provide answers to the questions, What do we mean when we say redface? How is that different from any other racial representational practice? What is red/read about actors in redface? These questions shape the discussions in the following chapters and reveal the construction, persistence, and material consequences of Native American representation in US theater.

The concept and term *redface* have been to this point most robustly discussed in film and media studies, with little attention paid in theater and performance studies. Film and media scholars working in the mode of Native American studies have shed light on how stereotypical representations of Indians developed, were perpetuated, and caused harm to Native Americans.[14] These works bring to light the stereotypical Indian figure created by the film industry, as well as how Native American performers navigated the constraints of this racial caricature. From Jacquelyn Kilpatrick's concept of the "celluloid Indian," to Michelle Raheja's "Hollywood Indian," to Liza Black's "Movie Indian," film scholars have interrogated how the racialized figure of the Indian appears in American cinema.[15] Raheja's concept of *redfacing* is similar, though not identical, to *redface* as discussed in this book. Raheja thinks of the word in terms of its active use as a verb, a way of understanding a representation of Indians that can be and is wielded by Native and non-Native actors. While she defines *redfacing* as the "process and politics of playing Indian," a definition at home in this book's discussion of theatrical redface, she emphasizes the links between *redfacing* and "the traditional role of the trickster."[16] For Raheja, *redfacing* is the way Native American actors performed within the constraints placed on them by American culture and film studio expectations *and* how those performances opened up possibilities and suggested ambiguities rather than submission or complicity. Liza Black extends this emphasis on Native American actors in Hollywood in her work on mid-twentieth-century westerns. *Redface: Race, Performance, and Indigeneity* focuses on the construction of the Stage Indian and its perpetuation over almost two centuries of American theater.

"REDFACE" AND THEATER

Redface is deceptively simple. And a simple definition about makeup color would deceive us into thinking that it is a surface-level phenomenon. In twenty-first-century usage, it tends to mean non-Native actors playing Native characters. Sometimes it means stories about Native Americans told by non-Natives. It carries some of the negative cultural baggage of blackface but not nearly as much.[17] The hashtag #InsteadOfRedface condemns the practice while offering an alternative. This book contends that the locus of redface is neither makeup nor casting practices nor the identity of a playwright. Instead, I argue for understanding redface as a process artists and audiences undertake that results in a legible and racialized Indian body. The implied objective of redface performance is a kind of authenticity, but in practice and impact, it is revealed to be authority—authority over which bodies are and can be Indian. This book argues that redface is a collaborative, curatorial process through which a body is made legible as an Indian. It attaches racial meaning, forecloses Indigeneity and Indigenous sovereignty, and asserts settler-colonial authority over Indigenous peoples. It also has provided a mechanism for recognition, employment, and (constrained) agency for Indigenous peoples. It is a blunt weapon that has been used to attack and defend Indigenous peoples and nations.

Redface is a cultural phenomenon that makes meaning through curation, a process of accretion and subtraction. It layers text, narrative, materiality, history, performance, reception, interpretation, environment, language, humor, tragedy, and theatrical conventions to arrive at the solid though malleable figure introduced in chapter 1, the Stage Indian. However, redface is more than accretion; it is also subtraction. Redface leaves behind Indigenous sovereignty, culture, language, history, law, politics, and community to obscure that which would make the Indian fully human and therefore a threat to America. Understanding Indians as members of multiple nations ensures American innocence. If Indians are nations, then the United States rightfully owns and controls the land through treaty, war, and allyship. Understanding Indians as a race ensures American dominance. If Indians are inferior and doomed to vanish, the United States is not to blame for their disappearance or oppression. This relationship between innocence and dominance is fleshed out on the American stage in iterations of redface.

Redface as an iteration of the Indian is closely connected to the concept *playing Indian*, as so compelling explicated by Philip Deloria.[18] Deloria has thoroughly explained how the practice of non-Native Americans "playing Indian" supported the construction of an American identity. What has been given less attention is the embodied practice he names as its mechanism. Deloria declares, "Play was powerful, for it not only made meanings, it made them *real*," and he immediately explains how that play functions: "The donning of Indian clothes moved ideas from brains to bodies."[19] While Deloria conceives of "playing Indian" as "images of Indianness" being "translated into material forms" and specifically deploys the term *disguise*, I contend that his theorization is furthered by analysis of redface.[20] As Jodi Byrd has shown, empire "orients and replicates itself by transforming those to be colonized into 'Indians' through continual reiteration of pioneer logics."[21] Indianness is not then located in images first and bodies second; it is produced on and through bodies as a colonial act. It is an inherently embodied process that produces meaning for its target audience, those who wish to see an Indian. This is why playing Indian onstage is so powerful. It is also why theater is the space in which we can trace the genealogy of redface across shifting material practices and arrive not at a character but at the colonial structures and logics used to transform bodies into Indians. Redface turns colonized people into Indians for the benefit of a settler-colonial nation.

This book is invested in popular theatrical performance because I want to understand how the general public encountered and understood Indians through encounters with human bodies. I take *popular* to mean both its intended audience—something akin to mass media made for broad public consumption rather than for a specialized niche or elite public—and broad positive reception and familiarity with it. I turn to plays and theatrical performances that were popular in both senses—made for a broad audience and widely successful, often imitated, and well received. Because it focuses on the most frequent, widely accepted, and easily identified iterations of the Indian on the American stage, it spends less time on the outliers and exceptions, although the included essay "Hinushi Inla" (discussed shortly) focuses on what has been marked as outside the mainstream. Popular theater stands in for the average, the mean, and the most frequent mode of knowing the Stage Indian. The commercial aspect of popular theater, the price of that ticket and the profit made from it, are beyond the scope of this book. Nonetheless, the commodification of embodied Indianness, particularly in relationship to the myriad commodified images of Indianness that continue to circulate in the United States, is a subject in sore need of interrogation.

If frequency and saturation were this book's only concerns, it would make little sense to focus on theater. The reach of print, radio, film, and television is numerically far greater than theater. There is no limit to repetition and audience size for mediums whose technologies do not rely on the human body as conduit and location. Theater's embodiment is its limitation. It is also its superpower. Redface is about legible Indian bodies, not Indian images or ideas. Theatre's ability to tell a compelling story through human action is why it is the perfect location for understanding the mechanisms of racialization and their political impact. The narrative, material production, actors, audience, theater, social environment, political environment—all these and more interact, compete, and collaborate with each other in the simple act of putting on a play.[22] Theater is also a laboratory for how things might be and could have been.

The possibilities of performance, including theatrical performance, for rehearsing the future and the past have been well articulated by scholars of race and performance. Alberto Sandoval-Sánchez and Brian Eugenio Herrera have offered investigations into the specificity of Latine racialization and representation as well as how those minoritized communities respond to it.[23] Karen Shimakawa and Lucy Mae San Pablo Burns have worked to articulate and theorize the specificity of the legibly Asian body in US theater.[24] There is also a robust line of discussion, strongly resonant in queer studies, on the possibilities of performance in works like Jill Dolan's *Utopia in Performance*, José Esteban Muñoz's *Cruising Utopia*, and Joshua Chambers-Letson's *After the Party*.[25] Performance in general and theater specifically can invent the future through embodying its rehearsal. It can also invent the past. And if one power of performance is, as Dolan has declared, "to describe or capture fleeting intimations of a better world," the first question is, "A better world for whom?"[26] By understanding how redface is constructed, the power it wields, and the difficulty of excising it from our theatrical vocabulary, we can begin to see whose world redface improves. We can also begin to understand how it dismantles or denies forms of improvement that would support the vitality, complexity, and diversity of Indigenous peoples and nations. Redface might be utopian for certain segments of the US population, but this book explains why it is experienced and received as dystopian by many Indigenous peoples.

Beyond these compelling reasons to study theater, there is yet one more: the fundamentally human act of relating to other humans. This book takes as its foundation that human interactions are deeply and profoundly ethical acts, with implications and consequences for what some would call right and wrong. Rather than thinking of redface in terms of right and wrong, terms that invite simplistic determinations and can foreclose nuance, this book thinks in terms of human flourishing, which redface in so many ways serves to foreclose. While one might detect a Foucauldian echo in this project on the power of constructing race, it is not fundamentally concerned with an articulation of biopolitics under the footlights, nor does it discuss ethics directly. It is concerned with how actors and audiences interact with one another and how the rehearsal of those human interactions in a theater prepares the humans involved for interactions beyond the venue. It is to the concept of settler colonialism rather than biopolitics to which this book turns in questions of systemic governmental strategies and objectives. Settler colonialism, as compellingly defined by Patrick Wolfe, is a structure rather than an event.[27] A structure that "destroys to replace," and as J. Kehaulani Kauanui has shown, a structure to which "indigenous people are still subject."[28] It is settler colonialism's immanence and continuous presence vis-à-vis the United States that best shapes the questions this book poses and the answers it offers.

Theatrical performance makes clear the boundaries of its interactions and narratives. It cannot afford not to, otherwise the audience will leave confused or dissatisfied, and no more tickets will be sold. In the theater, there is a physical space marked off for performance, a cultural space marked off for observation and reflection, and a temporal space for beginnings and endings. There is also routinely a beginning, middle, and end of a story with clear characters whom the audience can identify and with whom they can perhaps identify. Theatrical performance offers a contained and complete system that mimics quotidian life, responds to it, and shapes it. Every experience in a theater is a real experience, and every experience in a theater is an imagined experience. It is this interplay between reality and imagination, between bodies in time and space together, and between rehearsing and experiencing that grounds the fecundity of theater as a site of interrogation and explication. In this book, I turn to theater to illuminate how people understand each other through the structures, narratives, and encounters in which they participate. I pay attention to these in order to understand how they shape the construction (the rehearsal) of and the experience (the performance) of race and Indigeneity.

PLAITING DISCIPLINES

This book narrows the space between theater studies, American studies, and Native American studies by drawing them into conversation with one another around the problem of Native American representation and the labor of racial legibility. Theater studies, and to slightly differing ends performance studies, has been interested in understanding race in performance and on the stage for decades. In works like E. Patrick Johnson's *Appropriating Blackness,* Susan Manning's *Modern Dance, Negro Dance,* Daphne Brooks's *Bodies in Dissent,* Robin Bernstein's *Racial Innocence,* Harvey Young's *Embodying Black Experience,* and Joshua Chambers-Letson's *A Race So Different,* theater and performance have been both a lens through which to see and the object to be seen in the quest for clarity and insight about race and racial formation in the United States.[29] *Redface: Race, Performance, and Indigeneity* adds to these conversations by focusing on the racialization of Native

Americans, an understudied and underarticulated subject in theater/performance studies. American studies, too, has been interested in how performance factors into questions of nationhood, race, and memory in books as diverse as Joseph Roach's *Cities of the Dead*, Tavia Nyong'o's *The Amalgamation Waltz*, and Su'ad Abdul Khabeer's *Muslim Cool: Race, Religion, and Hip Hop in the United States*.[30] This book thinks about the construction of the Indian as a social and political process of racialization and argues that race is both insufficient and harmful as a totalizing discourse for Indigeneity. These discussions of race and performance in theater/performance studies and American studies are increasingly in partnership with one another, feeding off and furthering debate and understanding in these fields.

Standing apart from these conversations, though with some connections to American studies, are lines of thought developed in Native American/Indigenous studies. Some of these lines of thought are on the creation of the Indian, the relationship between Indigeneity and sovereignty, and how Native American history is told and to what ends. From Robert Berkhofer's *The White Man's Indian* and Philip Deloria's *Playing Indian* to studies by psychologist Stephanie Fryberg, over the last fifty years, scholars of American/Native American studies have sought to understand the modes and mechanisms that make Indians so vital to America and so detrimental to Indigenous peoples.[31] The relationship between history, authenticity, and Indigeneity is routinely explored and explicated in works as diverse as Jean O'Brien's *Firsting and Lasting*, Jodi Byrd's *The Transit of Empire*, and Kim TallBear's *Native American DNA*.[32] Discussions of sovereignty have covered everything from the possibilities and limits of political action like Glen Coulthard's *Red Skin, White Masks* and Audra Simpson's *Mohawk Interruptus* to the facets of sovereignty at work and play in aesthetic and cultural production found in Robert Warrior's "intellectual sovereignty," Jolene Rickard's "visual sovereignty," Beverly Singer's "cultural sovereignty," and Dylan Robinson's "sensate sovereignty."[33] Coupled with Indigenous theories connecting actions, stories, and nationhood like *survivance*, theorized by Gerald Vizenor, and *tribalography*, by LeAnne Howe, Native American studies has looked expansively at how Native American and non-Native Americans propagate nations through creative acts of imagery, word, and embodiment.[34] This book expands these lines of thought to include theatrical representations of Native Americans, how theater remembers the past and embodies the future, and how Indigenous sovereignty is constrained by settler-colonial and racializing forces at work in American cultural production.

This book attempts the act of braiding heterogenous discourses because of its unwavering commitment to the results of this dexterous project. However, I do not braid for beauty's sake; the plait will be terrible and true. To understand the Indian onstage in the United States, one must understand how race and performance work in the American context. To understand *how* the Indian works on the US stage, one must understand how history, dramaturgy, and dramatic license work together in theatrical performance. To understand *why* the Indian is an insufficient metric for measuring Indigeneity, one must understand the stakes of Indigeneity beyond race. To understand redface as a theatrical technique is to understand it as a political attack on Indigeneity and Indigenous sovereignty. These are the stakes of playing Indian onstage. It is not just a racial stereotype or part of an embarrassing history of racism in the United States. It is the way that bodies are made legibly Indian with consequences reaching far beyond the footlights.

In drawing together these fields and inviting readers to follow, I will eschew a preferred relationship between questions and answers in academia, cause and effect. Instead, I follow the logic of a braid. It is not a series of events that precipitate one another. It is the interweaving of strands that intersect, react, and shape one another. Each strand is distinct and yet integral to an object called a plait. A strand is distinct *and* inseparable from the braid itself. In this way, *Redface* understands its goal as articulating a relationship among race, performance, and Indigeneity as kinship not causation. This book braids.

STRUCTURE AND PRAXIS, OR ARGUING THROUGH NOT IN A BOOK

Thus far, this introduction has prepared the reader of this book to anticipate questions like, How is the Stage Indian constructed? What are its components? How is redface connected to race and

Indigeneity? What are the stakes of redface? And why does redface persist? If the book stopped at answering these questions, it would satisfy most readers' curiosity and fill a too long empty gap in existing scholarship. Instead, it pushes outward to a larger question: Could knowing how Americans see Indians change their ability to see Indigenous people? In other words, by understanding how Indian legibility works, can Americans build a new, ethical Indigenous legibility? The aim of this book is to articulate the project of *Indigenous* legibility through explication *and* action.

This book explains how redface came to be what it is and interrogates the stakes of its continued performance in American theater. But what this book demonstrates is that redface is a praxis of legibility located in the labor of individual, systemic, aesthetic, and interpersonal choices. The problem for mainstream US culture is multipronged; Indians are still inconveniently around and reminding America of its failures, Indians are understood as a race, and Indians are denied Indigeneity and sovereignty through racialized representations. This book does not offer a solution but a rehearsal, an embodied praxis in how to read and see Indigenous peoples differently. *Redface* invites its readers to join in the praxis of unmaking redface through an embodied experience of rereading.

Interspersed throughout chapters 1–4 is a nonsequentially placed essay on Indigenous theater and performance titled "Hinushi Inla," which means a "different path" in Chahta Anumpa.[35] The essay's content focuses on the long history of Indigenous theater in the United States and illustrations of what redface obscures. It is spaced nonsequentially because its inclusion is not primarily to transfer information from the author to the reader but to demonstrate the simultaneity and disruption of Indigenous theater and the labor that is necessary to fully engage with it. The content of the essay exists in temporal relation with the content of chapters 1–4 and in temporal relation to the reader of the book. When reading the book from front to back, readers will occasionally encounter pages of the essay. These will be easily identifiable by the use of distinct tint, font, and design. The first page of the essay follows the book's conclusion, so it will be at the physical end of the book. Essay pages will include instructions on where the next (sequential) page will be for those who want to read the essay "in order."

Readers will choose how to interact with the essay pages and will likely find that they disrupt the physical and mental flow of reading this book. I invite you to take time to meditate on how you handled the disruption at the conclusion of your reading experience. (A few potential directions for your contemplation include, How do genre conventions foreclose alternative constructions? Is using existing skills in new directions invigorating or draining? What is the relationship between thinking through and moving through an argument? How do we respond to knowledge production modes that require atypical labor? Hypothetically, what would have to change for the essay reading practice to become standard?)

The labor of reading nonsequentially enacts the fundamental argument of this book: Americans have been trained to read Indians through redface, and what Americans need now is to train to see and understand Indigenous people differently. Reading differently is still reading. "Hinushi Inla" puts into practice the kind of laborious reading practice that solving redface calls for. This book does not seek to throw out the culturally ingrained practice of reading humans as X, but it does insist that both the X and the reading have to change. The first four chapters challenge the ubiquity and the authority of redface (the X). The essay disrupts the ubiquity and authority of academic book structure (a specific kind of cultural reading) and invites the reader to labor unusually, distinctly but not utterly differently. If a reader can successfully read this book against (academic) cultural expectations, then they might recognize the ways in which they can contribute their own skill and labor to reading Indigenous peoples differently, against American expectations of race, inferiority, and disappearance.

However, this book is not a test; it is an invitation. The reader will make the choice to engage or disengage with the labor of reading differently on their own terms and to their own ends. The book is written with the understanding that readers will not read in homogenous ways or toward uniform goals. *Redface* uses this as a strength rather than a weakness. It invites readers to consider the labor of creating and perpetuating redface through the unsettling of their own reading labor. This is an experience that invites patience, reflection, effort, and persistence, the very attributes vital to addressing and abolishing redface in American theater and the Indian in American culture.

To remake American theater and American culture in a form that supports the flourishing of Indigenous peoples, dismantling the Stage Indian is imperative and difficult but not impossible. It will be laborious and tedious. It will be most assuredly discomfiting. But to do anything less would be to support a theatrical and cultural praxis that, as this book will illustrate, is injurious to Indigenous peoples and leaves non-Indigenous peoples unequipped to examine the world in which they live. To fixate on the Indian-shaped hole in America is to constantly reinscribe the failure of the American project. This book describes the hole as a way through to the whole, to a space/relationship in which Indigenous and non-Indigenous peoples can live differently and better. The way through is rough and discouraging, full of frustration. Nevertheless, it is also the only way worth going, because its destination is the only one worth reaching: flourishing for all humans.

CHAPTER SUMMARIES

Given this book's unusual structure, a word on possible pathways might be useful for readers. For those wishing to pursue the experience of authorial intent, read in the following order: chapters 1–4, provocation, and "Hinushi Inla." The essay begins at the physical end of the text and is interspersed nonsequentially throughout chapters 1–4. For those interested in redface development and implications, read chapters 1–4 in order and skip over the essay pages. For those focusing on Indigenous performances and Indigenous agency, read "Hinushi Inla" first, followed by any other sections that interest you. And for those who seek specific information about style, time period, title, artist, and so on, the following summaries will assist you in locating the chapters most suitable to your reading goals. I understand that each reader carefully weighs the decision to expend or conserve labor in their reading practice, and I welcome the diversity and multiplicity with which readers will enter this book and what they will carry with them on exiting.

Chapter 1 introduces the concept of the Stage Indian and illustrates its foundational appearances and components. It explains the construction of the Indian in American culture as a process of racialization that American theater in the nineteenth century was uniquely suited to produce. Articulating the process through which theatrical characters are made legible as Indians, it draws together ideas of repetition, standardization, modification, and interpretation. To do this, it relies on Indian plays, a well-established category of American plays written in the early nineteenth century about Indians. Indian plays were the earliest form of theatrical entertainment that popularized redface as a performance technique. This chapter argues that the Stage Indian in Indian plays set the standard for the Indian in subsequent theatrical performances and reveals its saturation, flexibility, and persistence.

Chapter 2 looks at how historical fact and dramatic license were deployed to create a gendered and raced Stage Indian in nineteenth-century plays about Pocahontas. Because of a reliance on European and American ideas of the noble savage or the vanishing Indian, the Stage Indian is indicative of political and social ideologies, not historic accuracy. However, the overt attempt to connect the Stage Indian to "real" Indians indicates its role in racializing Indigenous peoples and denying them nationhood. Therefore, this chapter also recounts moments in US law, jurisprudence, and recordkeeping in which the racial identity of Indigenous peoples has been used to determine access to resources, justice, and rights. It connects how Pocahontas was made a female Stage Indian with how those gendered and racialized criteria of legibility are activated and/or weaponized in US legal and governmental systems.

Chapter 3 is focused on the persistent claims of authenticity that surround redface performance. Drawing on Edwin Forrest's claims to knowledge of authentic Indianness in his famous portrayal of Indian chief Metamora and the loud announcements of authentic Indian performers in *Buffalo Bill's Wild West,* this chapter shows how strategies of authentication change over time but the desire to be perceived as authentic stays constant. The consistency of this desire for authenticity reveals how redface is not actually submitting to an objective standard of Indianness but rather asserting and enforcing criteria that deny Indigenous nations self-determination and sovereignty.

Chapter 4 makes the largest temporal jump, moving readers from the foundational nineteenth-century performances of the Stage Indian to mid- and late twentieth-century Broadway musicals. *Annie Get Your Gun,* a musical based loosely on the life of sharpshooter Annie Oakley, first opened on Broadway in 1946. Over fifty years later, in 1999, it opened again in revised form, a musical reworked for modern sensibilities on gender and race. This chapter argues that the changes made for the 1999 production reveal that fixing the material practices of redface is insufficient for solving its underlying racializing and depoliticizing project. Through a discussion of the dramaturgical and production elements, this chapter seeks to explain how good intentions mixed with culturally ingrained systems of knowledge production around Indianness result in the perpetuation and not the extinction of redface. Redface is not a surface-level phenomenon; it is a political and ideological practice intent on producing a legibly Indian body that controls and legislates that body's existence.

"Hinushi Inla" describes the broad history of Native American theater and performance, beginning in the 1970s but moving forward and backward in time to reach a fuller picture of its scope. It highlights the career of Cherokee entertainer Will Rogers, the travel writing of Ojibwe/Chippewa performer Maungwudaus, and the oratory of Pequot minister William Apess. Taken together, these various performers and theater artists demonstrate the range of Indigenous performances that have been circulating within American theater for centuries. It argues that what redface obscures is the rich historical and contemporary presence of Indigenous theater and the sophistication and creativity of Indigenous theater artists.

CONCLUSION

Redface offers a way into understanding how Indians became a race and how racialization denies Indigeneity and Indigenous sovereignty. It does so by forwarding the bodies that are racialized onstage and how that racialization impacts the lived experience of Native Americans. Crucially, it also reveals how the bodies performing are not the entire story. The audiences receiving and interpreting the performances are equally as creative and equally as responsible for the Stage Indian. The Stage Indian *repertoire* is both what is onstage and how the audience understands what is onstage. Although redface is one of several forms of American racial impersonation in theater, it possesses unique traits because it is a manifestation of colonization. It is intent on making an Indian in order to control who is and can be an Indian. In doing so, it denies Indigenous sovereignty, nationhood, and Indigeneity itself. Theater is a charged location to interrogate and critique this phenomenon. It is live, embodied, and full of interaction and copresence. It has also been popular and accessible. It is a place where audience members across time, age, gender, class, and location have been able to see and recognize Indians. By drawing together Native American studies, theater studies, and American studies, this book shows how seemingly frivolous phenomena like theatrical fads and amateur theatrics reveal the political, legal, and ethical stakes of racial representation. Redface is not just a collection of costume pieces. Nevertheless, it is material, and its presence is usually heralded by visual markers. So to begin understanding redface, let us begin by tracing some of those markers. We will begin with feathers and face paint.

CHAPTER ONE

FEATHERS AND FACE PAINT

In August 2018, I attended the Association for Theatre in Higher Education's annual conference in Boston, Massachusetts. As part of the multiday event, local excursions were available to conference attendees. One of them went to the Boston Tea Party Ships & Museum just a short walk from the conference hotel.[1] Although the name "museum" might lead one to believe that this was a civic or state-owned property or even run by a nonprofit organization dedicated to Boston history, it is in fact a for-profit, historically based tourist attraction owned by Historic Tours of America.[2] I had been apprised of the interactive and reenactive elements of the museum tour, which included throwing boxes of "tea" over the side of the replica ship into Boston Harbor, just like those proto-Americans protesting the British tea tax centuries ago. I had also been cautioned that museum goers were invited to do this reenactment in Indian costume—wearing feathers.[3] As a recent PhD graduate and burgeoning scholar of Native American representation and performance, I was eager to witness this costumed (this redface!) performance by casual tourists desiring some history with their leisure. I imagined that it would be a Plains tribe headdress that people could put on before they threw the tea over. I was unprepared, however, for what I encountered.

As our group was called to begin the tour experience, I followed a small crowd toward double doors, held open by a period-costumed (eighteenth century), smiling young man. In his left hand was a satchel full of brown feathers. He offered each museum guest one in case we "needed to disguise ourselves later" (figure 1.1). I followed about a dozen others into the "Meeting House" room and looked down the rows of benches to find that a few other tourists had already chosen to "disguise" themselves by tucking their feather into the back of their hair or ballcap. I physically recoiled and backed away from the seats at the sight of this easy and nonchalant display of "playing Indian," gripping the hand of a friend and repeatedly whispering, "I'm not ready for this."[4]

I was surprised by my visceral reaction to a simple feather when I had been expecting someone to don a headdress, but I soon collected myself and chose a seat. I looked at the card I had been handed by another costumed reenactor that offered me context and a historical figure to play if I wanted to join in the reenactment spirit. I listened to a rousing speech about tyranny and freedom, setting the scene for our experience as a Tea Party-er, which included a brief nod to the feathers most of us held in our hands or laps. We were informed that we would be disguising ourselves as Mohawk. Our midnight protest in the harbor would be strengthened by the admirable qualities of those Native Americans. After that attempt to allay our contemporary consciences of any fear that wearing these feathers might be construed as racist, our group proceeded through the rest of the museum. Our last stop was aboard the replica ship to toss over some "tea." Those who wanted (I did not) could lift a small box and throw it over the side into the water. The rope attached to the box made this an easily repeatable action and ensured that no actual loss of "tea" was possible. Again, we were invited to disguise ourselves if we wished before throwing over the "tea." Those I saw throw the box over did not wear their feather. In fact, most of the people in our tour group, some of whom were conference attendees, never put their feather on.[5] Shortly thereafter, we were funneled down a gangplank toward a café and then a gift shop full of various tea- and patriotism-themed objects to purchase. I witnessed a family having a snack in the café, the young girl wearing three feathers tucked into her barrette. For the environmentally minded among us, a barrel with slots had been conveniently placed for recycling the cards and feathers we received. However, at each step of the way, along the gangplank or in the gift shop or in a trash can, discarded and forgotten feathers lay about. This was an encounter with redface in its most basic form. A performer curated a selection of racialized markers and deployed them in embodied performance, resulting in a legibly Indian figure being perceived by an audience. But like every other instance of redface, there was more going on than the deceptively simple act of wearing a feather.

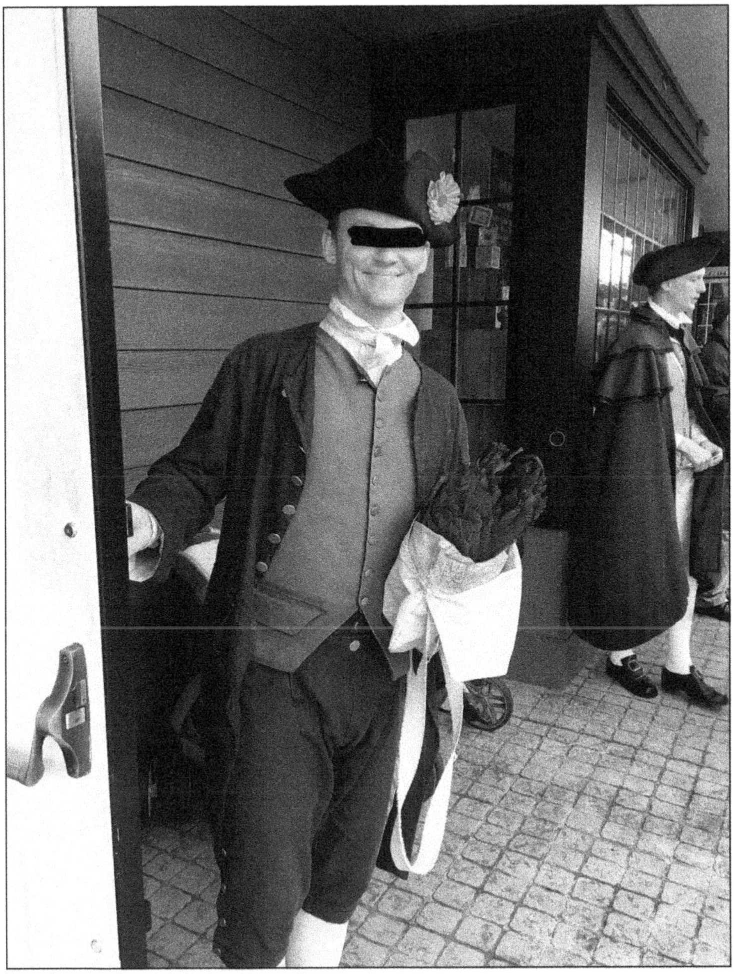

Figure 1.1. At the Boston Tea Party museum, 2018. Photo by author.

In attempting to process my own strong reaction to the experience, which felt something like a slap in the face—startling and with a sting that lingered—I arrived at a series of questions that shape this chapter. The feather was legible as a marker of Indianness. Why? We were provided minimal instructions on how to wear it, but all who wore them did so nearly identically. How did they know what to do? Feather wearing was introduced as a disguise and was specifically connected to the Mohawk nation. Was the justification/explanation part of legibility or was it revelatory of an underlying tension inherent in racial impersonation? Disguising oneself as "Mohawk" connected the reenactor with specific historical facts. What is the relationship between fact and Indian legibility in performance? These questions have helped me identify the practices, curatorial and collaborative, through which redface creates a legibly Indian character in performance. Racial legibility is the product, and the processes of legibility include racialization, repetition, standardization, modification, and interpretation.

Beyond these five processes that I contend are useful for identifying and analyzing redface performance in the United States, I recall my experience in Boston mostly for the unremarkableness of redface. It was the unnoteworthy quality that got to me. I was not surprised that someone would think dressing up like an Indian (whatever that means) was a good idea for a Boston Tea Party museum. It is a well-known fact that some of the Tea Partiers dressed up like Indians.[6] I was not shocked that it was feathers used to mark bodies as Indian. "Feathers equals Indians" has been ubiquitous for about five hundred years, and I had expected a feathered headdress, anyway.[7] The thing that disturbed me far more than I anticipated was how easy it was, how casual, and how it lived through embodiment not image. It was bodies not pictures that produced and presented the Indian, and it was amateur, impromptu performances drawing on centuries of redface repertoire that enacted legible Indianness. Anyone with a museum ticket could become a Stage Indian.

* * *

In this chapter, I explore the Stage Indian, an iteration of the Indian unique to American theatrical performance, though with much overlap and resonance with other Indians in American culture, such as those found in literature, advertising, film, and sports.[8] The Stage Indian is the result of specific historical practices within US theater, which combined to create a material, dramaturgical, and sensorial vocabulary that audiences have come to identify as Indian. It is not a static image but an embodied figure whose legibility as an Indian is co-constructed with its (copresent and embodied) audience. Its vocabulary has been, is currently, and will be picked up by various theatrical artists to produce the embodied, racialized performance practice called redface. As I will show in this chapter, the Stage Indian is *the* embodied instantiation of the Indian in American culture and reveals the saturation, flexibility, and persistence of redface in American theater.

RACIALIZING

Redface performance is fundamentally a cultural project of assigning racial meaning to markers of difference that results in a racially identifiable body onstage. It is a process of what influential scholars of race Omi and Winant call racialization, "the extension of racial meaning" to something, some group, or some practice that previously was not associated with a race.[9] Onstage, it is the making of a character and a character type. However, the most salient category it makes,—race,—extends far beyond the footlights. Redface presents characters whose lives, identities, and actions are bound by their race. While occasionally identified with a certain tribe, theatrical depictions of Native Americans repeatedly and routinely flatten Indigenous identity into a single racialized category, the Indian. Redface participates in a larger cultural project of racialization in a way that creates and confirms notions of homogenous Indianness. This book's critique of redface lies not in any inaccuracy in depicting Native Americans (i.e., "that's a racist stereotype"), which has been suitably articulated in academic and popular conversations, but in the racializing project and process of redface (i.e., "that's racializing"). This project and process subverts Indigenous self-determination in defining and enacting sovereign rights to peoplehood, nationhood, and livelihood, which will be discussed further in chapter 2.

That Indigenous nations have the inherent rights that come with sovereignty is not a controversial statement within the field of Native American/Indigenous studies. It is widely accepted that Native Americans are best considered as members of sovereign nations with longstanding relationships and obligations to other nations, land, water, and other-than-human relations.[10] This seemingly self-evident fact, backed up by centuries of treaties and legal decisions alongside contemporary tribal governments, hinges on the word *best*. Native Americans have been and are categorized by the US government as nations, as polities with governments and leaders and inherent rights to rule themselves. Native Americans have been and are also categorized by the US government and its citizens as members of a single race. This is the paradoxical condition of being Native American in the United States. Native Americans are configured as one race, Indian, and live their lives as members of many nations, with all the variety, complexity, and diversity one would expect across hundreds of nations.[11] It is in this paradox that the power of redface is most clear. Redface racializes, and in making the Indian legible as a race, it forecloses an articulation of Indigenous sovereignty and nationhood. As will be articulated soon, this is a feature not a bug of an imperial/colonial project. According to Omi and Winant, race "is strategic; race does ideological and political work."[12] The ideological work of the racialized Indian has been explored by numerous scholars, most forcibly by Philip Deloria in his incisive work on playing Indian and the formation of a national and individual American identity. The political work of the racialized Indian is to obstruct if not obliterate the ongoing political power of hundreds of Native American nations, tribes, and bands. The stakes of the Stage Indian are high, then. A racialized, embodied character is not just a representation of the Indian but an assertion of Indian bodies as raced and not as citizens of Indigenous nations. This claim will be unfolded and expounded on in chapters 2 and 3, while this chapter will focus on how the Stage Indian came to be on the American commercial stage.

That the Stage Indian is, in fact, an Indian is overt, explicit, and indisputable. European theater, from which American theater in its Western theatrical mode evolved, had been labelling characters indigenous to North and South America as Indians/Indios/Sauvages for decades before the United States was even formed. In the early seventeenth century, Spanish playwright Lope de Vega wrote *El Nuevo Mundo descubierto por Cristóbal Colón*, a comedic telling of Christopher Columbus's "discovery" of the "New World," with "Indios" first appearing and speaking in act 2.[13] In 1613, Inigo Jones and George Chapman staged *The Memorable Masque of the Two Honorable Houses of Inns of Court, the Middle Temple and Lincoln's Inn* at White-Hall for English royalty. This masque included maskers "in Indian habits . . . like the Virginian princes they presented" costumed in silver cloth embroidered with

(*Continued from page 76*)

they are current and existential threats to Indigenous nations and the United States. He recalls instances in his own life when racist and prejudicial opinions of Indians led to his mistreatment.[90] Apess explains that not only do past racist understandings of Indians continue to persist but also that their persistence allows for the continuation of unjust actions and attacks on Indian sovereignty. Apess calls for white "men to act as though they were going to war with those corrupt and degrading principles that robs one of all rights, merely because he is ignorant, and of a little different color."[91] Apess asks his white audience members to combat the racist prejudices of white Americans and therefore the political practices that deny Indigenous rights. He believes that doing so will save Indigenous peoples and nations, as well as the United States. He calls the destructive relationship white Americans have with Indians an undeniable "fire, a canker, created by the pilgrims" and perpetuated by Americans' actions denying Indians nationhood, self-governance, suffrage, and legal rights.[92] He calls on white Americans to "seize the mantle of Liberty" and extinguish the damaging fire lit so long ago by the savage colonists.[93] He implores them to advocate for Indian rights and challenges them to begin the work "here first, in New England."[94]

Apess was not just eulogizing King Philip. He was arguing for a complex and complete understanding of what it meant to live as an Indian within a colonial nation. Understanding Indians as a race and a polity, a race and nations, is not an invention of twentieth- or twenty-first-century activism or scholarship. Instead, it has been articulated for centuries by Indians who live through the racializing and politicizing experience of existing in the United States. In response to this, Apess importantly denied the fundamental project of redface, racializing Indians, by repeatedly connecting the past to the present and advocating for specific, national, and legal goals for Indigenous peoples in America. He calls his audience to action, recruiting them to create a better future for Native Americans and white settlers. He ties their futures together in a way starkly different from *Metamora's* project of disentangling an imagined Indian past with a solely white American future. He performs oratory to call for political change and an end to racism.

90 Apess, *Eulogy on King Philip*, 50–51.
91 Apess, *Eulogy on King Philip*, 55
92 Apess, *Eulogy on King Philip*, 53
93 Apess, *Eulogy on King Philip*, 55
94 Apess, *Eulogy on King Philip*, 59

(*Continued on page 100*)

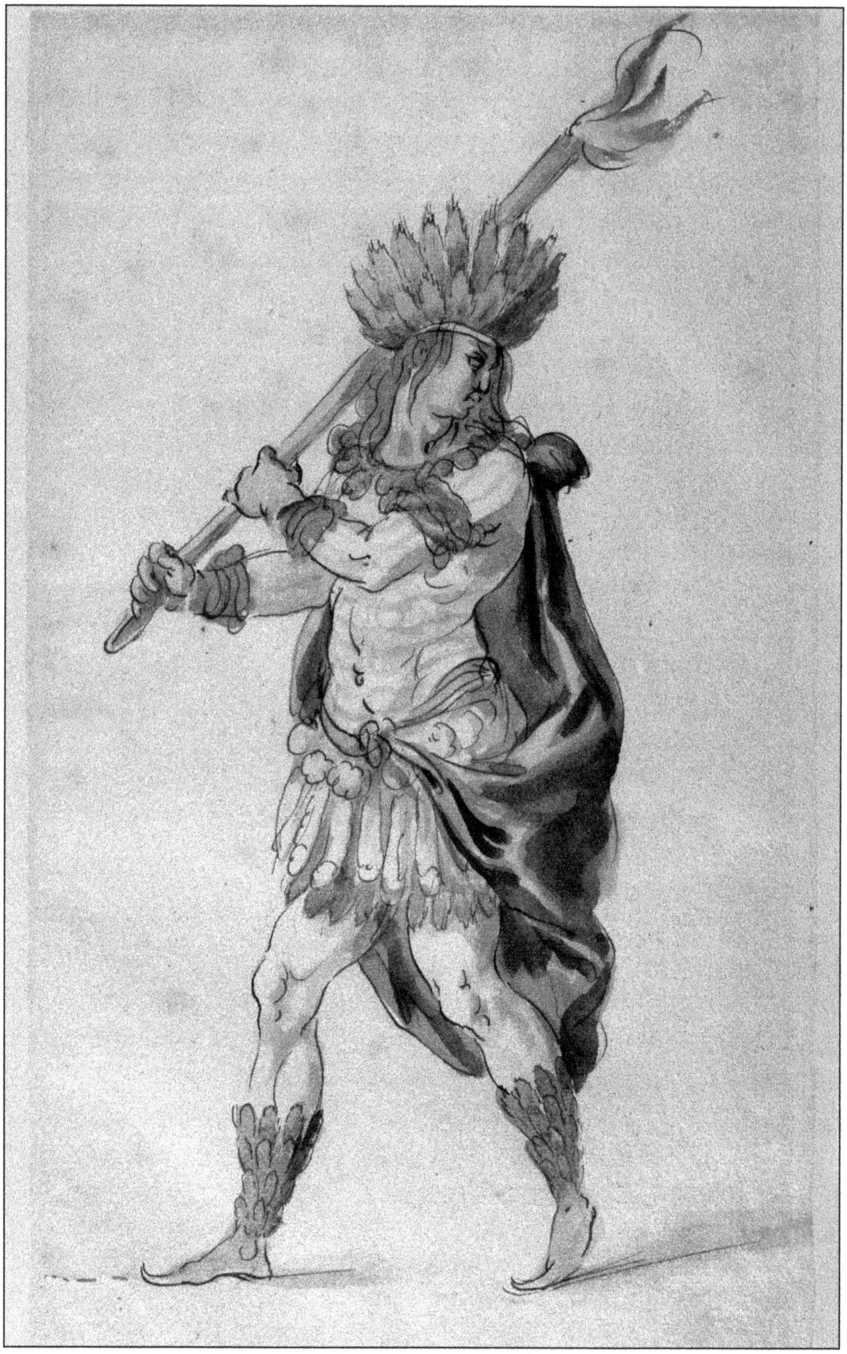

Figure 1.2. "Torchbearer: An Indian." Costume design by Inigo Jones. Image courtesy Chatsworth House and Bridgeman Images.

golden suns that imitated "Indian worke" and between "euery pane of embroidery, went a rowe of white Estridge feathers" mixed with gold.[14] To early modern England, Indians were from the North American colonies, wore silver and gold clothing, and were ornamented with embroidery and ostrich feathers. They also wore feathers around their necks and "on their heads" mixed with gold and pearls, while on their legs, they wore white stockings. The accompanying torchbearers "were likewise of the Indian garb," and while less extravagantly costumed, they were "showfully garnish[ed] with seueral-hewd fethers" (figure 1.2).[15] Elite English audiences by 1613 encountered actors in feathers and read them as Indians.

William D'Avenant's *The Cruelty of the Spaniards in Peru*, which played in London at the Drury Lane in 1658, included "Natives, in featherd Habits and Bonnets, carrying, in Indian Baskets, Ingots of Gold and Wedges of Silver."[16] French composer Jean-Philipe Rameau created *Les Indes Galantes* in 1735, an opera ballet collecting four exotic tales of romance, including one set in North America called "Les sauvages" (the savages). A 1766 production of the *Les Indes Galantes* costumed the sauvages without feathers but with leaves, a weapon (club), and the implication if not the reality of bare skin that Inigo Jones had merely suggested with the white bodystockings over one hundred years prior (figure 1.3).

By 1787, when George Colman's *Inkle and Yarico* began its long life on the stage, one critic objected to the costuming of Inkle and contrasted it with the "highly fanciful and ornamental" dress "of some parts of America," which included "plumes of feather."[17] A few years later, in 1794, *The Cherokee* by James Cobb was playing at the Theatre Royal Drury Lane with many "Indians" in it. This brief collection of European theatrical works demonstrates that people indigenous to North and South America were lumped together into a coherent-to-Europeans category of Indian centuries prior to the development of a uniquely American theater culture and practice. The Stage Indian in American theater is an Indian with all the colonial, ideological, and political baggage that comes with that term.

In North America, playwrights continued identifying characters as Indians/sauvages from at least the seventeenth century onward.

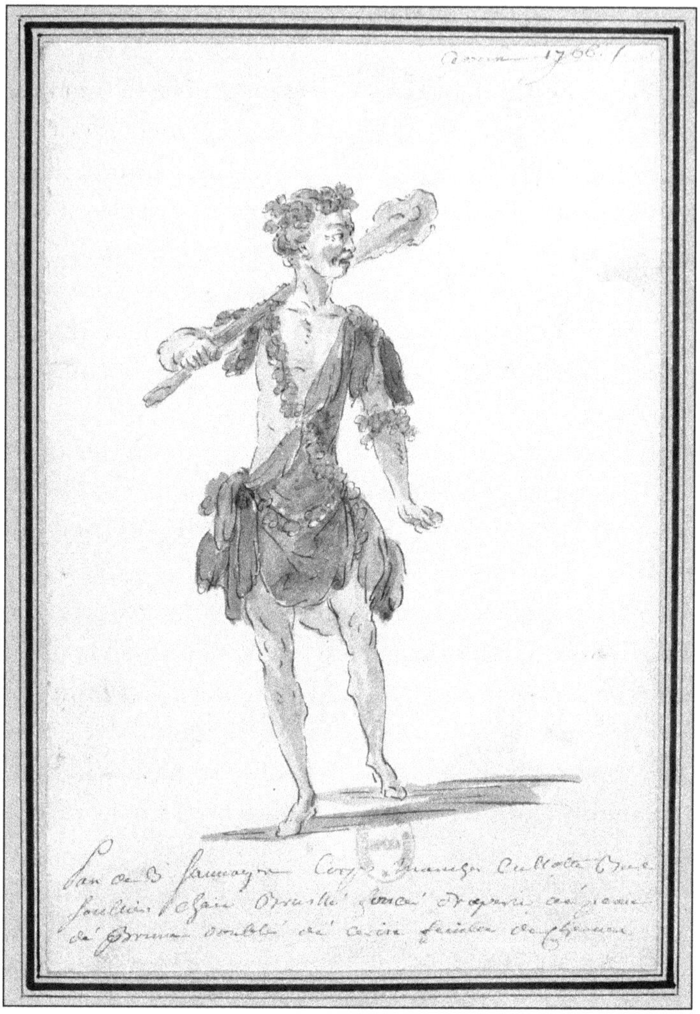

Figure 1.3. Sauvage costume design by Louis-René Boquet. Image courtesy Bibliothèque nationale de France.

In 1606, the French-language masque *Le Théâtre de Neptune en Nouvelle-France,* by Marc Lescarbot, was performed in present-day Nova Scotia, Canada. The masque included verses declaimed by "Neptune, his Tritons, and the attending savages" praising France.[18] Perhaps the first instance of redface on the continent, *Le Théâtre de Neptune* was performed by French colonists "in Native American costume who, bearing weapons and traditional ornaments, express their affection for and gratitude to their French 'hosts'."[19] About two hundred years later, in 1808, the operatic melodrama *The Indian Princess; or, La Belle Sauvage* appeared on the early American stage. A musical play about Pocahontas, the performance continued the centuries-long practice of identifying indigenous people of North America as Indians, despite or alongside acknowledgment of distinct tribal/national identities. The 1808 publication and reprints of the libretto for *The Indian Princess* also continued the practice of depicting Indians as carrying weapons, in this case a bow and arrows, and with feathers (figure 1.4).[20]

That the Stage Indian is an Indian is incontrovertible. But what exactly an Indian *is* is less self-evident. The Indian has been famously

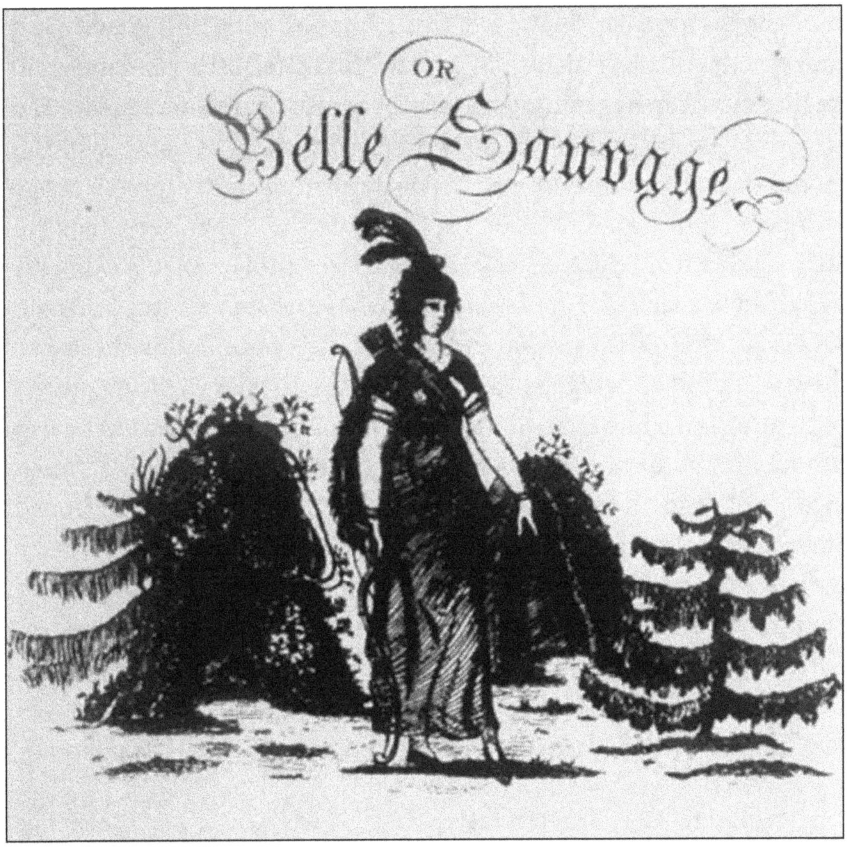

Figure 1.4. Title page image from Barker and Bray's *The Indian Princess*. Image public domain.

theorized by Robert Berkhofer as "the White man's Indian," a creation and fabrication of the European/White mind that combined nation, race, culture, identity, and morality.[21] It was an avenue through which Europeans could critique their own shortcomings or assert their own superiority. Europeans—or as Berkhofer refers to them, Whites—"primarily understood the Indian as an antithesis to themselves . . . because Indian was judged by what Whites were not."[22] This clear articulation of the Indian as a representational invention of Europeans has been deepened by scholars in Native American/Indigenous studies to fully articulate the stakes and the impact of the Indian for Indigenous peoples. Literary scholar Jodi Byrd (Chickasaw) has theorized Indianness as a "site through which U.S. Empire orients and replicates itself by transforming those to be colonized into 'Indians.'"[23] It is not an identity so much "as a transit" that a US preoccupation with "indigeneity and the reproduction of Indianness" uses to "facilitate, justify, and maintain Anglo-American hegemonic mastery over justice, democracy, law, and terror" to "make 'Indian' those peoples who stand in the way of U.S. military and economic desires."[24] For Byrd, the Indian is not an image Europeans and later Americans used to understand themselves and create meaning from difference. It is an imperial project that is explicitly deployed to materially control people whose existence rebukes Anglo-American desires for power and wealth. This book holds these two theories of Indianness together, one attentive to the racializing project of creating the white man's Indian, the other attentive to the political reproduction of domination and the accompanying disavowal of "ongoing colonization of Indigenous peoples that is necessary for the United States to exist."[25] The Stage Indian, as an embodied instantiation of the Indian, is both an engine and a repository for the racially and politically configured Indian, a body that is recognizable as a race and used, as Byrd insists all Indians are, to propagate the US settler-colonial order. The Stage Indian is a legible Indian body and a site of political power that has been wielded against and sometimes by Indigenous peoples.

REPETITION

To create a legible Stage Indian, actors and audiences must be trained to employ and interpret racializing markers, and that takes time and repetition. Nearly all theater needs the audience to recognize the performance and therefore to recognize the players of the performance, although some genres of theater would deny this statement. However, it is not enough for an audience to recognize a character on repeat viewing—that is, that person on the stage is an actor, not an audience member—over the course of a performance. They must also be able to "read" who/what that character is— that is, that actor is playing a hero. This reading is not passive but active. Together, the performer and the audience member are working to make sense of what is happening, what story is being told. Theatre historian Tracy C. Davis helps explain this collaborative process in her articulation of *repertoire*, "a semiotic of showing and a phenomenology of experience" through which "audiences are habituated to understanding . . . performative tropes and then recognize and interpret others that are unfamiliar, so that the new may be incorporated into repertoire."[26] The actor plays an Indian legibly. The audience members are trained to read the Indian as an Indian, and they use this training to interpret future, perhaps divergent, performances of the Indian. These new performances interrelate with past performances and shape the audience's understanding of what an Indian is onstage. This understanding informs future actors' choices in how to play a legible Indian. It is both the act of showing and the embodied reception of that showing, brought to bear on future showings, that make a thing recognizable, that make a Stage Indian. Repertoires, such as Stage Indians, are "multiple circulating recombinative discourses of intelligibility."[27] Simply seeing one play with one Indian character in one performance is not enough exposure to develop the multiplicity of encounters it takes to create a legible Stage Indian. Happily for repertoire's sake, American theater has never been without multiple iterations of the Stage Indian. The origins of the United States' Stage Indian can be found in the early nineteenth century, when an abundance of Indian characters graced commercial stages.

During the first half of the nineteenth century, Indians saturated American theater, so much so that the term *Indian plays* developed to account for this enthusiasm for Indians on the American stage.[28] Perhaps the first of these Indian plays was James Nelson Barker and John Bray's three-act "operatic melo-drame" *The Indian Princess, or La Belle Sauvage*.[29] First acted in 1808 in Philadelphia and then later that year in New York City, the play combined ballad opera with melodrama to tell the story of British exploration/colonization and romantic love through a narrative partially focused on Pocahontas, John Smith, and John Rolfe. The play has five romantic couples, cross-racial love affairs, intrigue, international diplomacy, several women disguised as men in search of their male romantic partners, and quite a lot of kissing. *The Indian Princess* was soon, at least according to the playwright, "frequently acted in . . . all the theaters of the United States."[30] It was followed by other popular works with Indian characters in both lead and supporting roles, such as *She Would Be a Soldier* (1819), *Logan: The Last of the Race of Shikellemus* (1823), *The Indian Prophecy, or Visions of Glory* (1827), *Metamora, or The Last of the Wampanoag* (1829), *The Fall of Tecumseh* (1830), *Pocahontas, or the Settlers of Virginia* (1830), *Oralloossa* (1832), *Pontiac* (1836), *Pocahontas* (1837), *Nick of the Woods* (1838), and *The Forest Princess, or Two Centuries Ago* (another play about Pocahontas, 1848). These plays' popularity waxed in the 1830s and waned by the mid-nineteenth century. A parody of the most famous Indian play, *Metamora*, titled *Met-A-Mora, or The Last of the Pollywogs,* and one spoofing the "numberless dramas that grew up around the character of Pocahontas," *Pocahontas, or The Gentle Savage,* heralded their fall from fashion and lampooned the star actor who originated and dominated the role of Metamora.[31] Generations of American theatergoers encountered Indians onstage in dozens of plays, illustrating the repetition vital to the creation and solidification of the Stage Indian.

Repetition of the Stage Indian on the American stage occurred in a burgeoning nineteenth-century theater industry marked by all the complexity, transformation, and ambiguity of the era. Although connected to histories of racial impersonation in Western European theater and performance since the sixteenth century, redface in the United States developed uniquely alongside and within the American theater system.[32] In the early nineteenth century, urban theatergoing was a pastime primarily for men.[33] American drama was marked by a clarity of structure and theme exemplified by melodrama. Melodrama is a sometimes maligned genre of theater that rests on clearly designated good and evil characters who receive morally appropriate reward or punishment. American drama also catered to both urban upper-class and lower/working-class audiences, with separate theaters taking up these diverse audiences' desires and needs.[34] A time when American artists and elites were preoccupied with creating a uniquely American identity in literature, drama, and music, the first half of the nineteenth century was fertile ground for the formation of theatrical forms and genres such as melodrama and blackface minstrelsy. Redface emerged in this masculinist, class conscious, aesthetically anxious, and ethnically/racially ambiguous era.

The routine use of different kinds of repetition, while specific to the American theater in the first half of the nineteenth century, is not unique to the American theater. Marvin Carlson has deftly shown how repetition and the meaning it makes and carries is ubiquitous across global theater cultures. His concept of *ghosting* most fully articulates the role of repetition in theater and how this repetition is connected to and constitutive of cultural memory.[35] His influential book *The Haunted Stage* illustrates how repeated viewings over time construct and solidify memories in the minds and bodies of performers and audience members. The conditions of repetition were especially pronounced during the early nineteenth century and created an environment in which redface began as a practice connected to character and body.

During the first half of the nineteenth century, theater management and business structures shifted from control by a single manager to a more entrepreneurial system of stock company and star actor. Theatre scholar Bruce McConachie has explained the intricate social and political forces that worked on the theater economy in this era, indicating that during the era in which managers controlled theater, "lines of business" were common. Inherited from the English theatrical tradition, "lines of business" was the permanent "assignment of specific kinds of roles to certain actors or actresses by the manager."[36] For example, an actress who specialized in ingenues would play ingenues until she retired. Her age was not a qualification or, more importantly for our understanding of redface, a disqualification for the kind of role she played. Certain actors specialized in certain types of roles for their entire career.

By the 1820s, this system was challenged and usurped by the stock company and burgeoning star system. However, actors could still play only a narrow range of roles. A stock company was a group of actors working together in a rotating play repertoire for a fixed period. The stock company continued the practice of casting actors in line with the kind of character they played (e.g., hero, soubrette, villain) but routinely added in another factor, the star. The star system, assisted by the expansion of the railroads, relied on incredibly popular actors traveling around the country to perform their most beloved roles. Stock companies would perform supporting roles in plays featuring these stars, ensuring employment for the stock company members and stars alike. Stars built their reputations and fame on playing beloved characters.

The repetition of specific actors in specific roles or specific kinds of roles was no accident. In fact, "the association of specific actors with specific types of roles was particularly clear" in nineteenth-century America, and playwrights "contributed significantly to this process."[37] Playwrights wrote character types, like the famous Yankee character, and with repetition, actors became attached to those types over time.[38] The theater culture of the first decades of the nineteenth century strongly connected certain kinds of characters with certain actors. The popularity of melodrama also meant that certain kinds of characters deserved certain kinds of actions and outcomes, a characteristic that would bolster the racist, negative qualities attached to Stage Indian characters.

The repetition found in "lines of business" and actors' specialization in specific character types was also echoed by the materiality of theater production. Material objects used in play production, from costumes to set pieces, were routinely reused during the early nineteenth century. Because the stock company performed a selection of plays for a set period, they developed and built a repertoire of set pieces. These pieces, for instance tables and chairs, would be used for multiple plays in the company's season. Costumes also were generally not changed for each play. It was not until the rise of naturalism and realism near the turn of the twentieth century that theater makers would insist on specific visual and material objects for each individual play. Like actors had for centuries before them in Europe, American actors in the first half of the nineteenth century provided their own costumes. Most costumes were contemporaneous, meaning that actors wore what was in fashion or typical at the time and only occasionally added a specific piece to signify a character. Actors might add a crown when playing royalty or, as theater historian Don Wilmeth has noted, "feather headdresses for Indians."[39] Theater audiences in the nineteenth century would see the same apparel on the same actors playing the same kinds of roles with the same set, even seeing the same star play the same role they already knew and loved. Repetition was everywhere in early American theater culture, and the Stage Indian came into existence through it.

Although the formation of a legible Stage Indian can be located in the Indian play fad of the 1830s and 40s, the Stage Indian did not begin or end in those decades. An extensive review of theater histories, copyright logs, and extant scholarship has revealed that the Stage Indian was significantly more prominent than American theater history has believed.[40] From the time that thirteen colonies declared independence from Britain to about 1820, some fifty to seventy plays with Indian characters were written and/or produced.[41] Between 1820 and 1840, there were approximately eighty new plays in America about Indians or in which Indian characters were significant to plot or setting, a marked increase from the first thirty-five years of American theater. These plays were performed primarily in urban theaters and toured smaller theaters around the country. However, rather than an abrupt decline in the production of plays with or about Indians, the next twenty years (1840–60) also saw about eighty new works.

(*Continued from page 123*)

* * *

Rogers was not the first Native American performer to offer an Indigenous perspective to his audiences. Fifty years before Rogers first took to the stage, an Ojibwe (also called Chippewa) man wrote a short book on his experiences traveling through Europe as part of an educational, ethnological tour. Maungwudaus, also known as George Henry, traveled Europe with American painter George Catlin's exhibition and published a short book in 1848 about his time abroad. Catlin had traveled for eight years in the 1830s to collect items from Indigenous tribes across North America and paint portraits of their members and eventually toured his collection and lectured alongside it.[63] He hired Indigenous people to perform in the tableaux vivant that accompanied his lectures and to provide cultural demonstrations. Maungwudaus belonged to a group of Ojibwe performers who had traveled to England on speculation and were hired by Catlin, forming a partnership of sorts for several years. After his return from Europe, Maungwudaus published an account of his travels explicitly for "the benefit of his youngest son, called Noodinokay, whose Mother died in England."[64] In the short description of his travels to England, France, Belgium, Ireland, and Scotland, he spends most of his time describing the sights, events, and experiences with minimal editorial comment, though also mentions the death of his wife as well as the loss of three of his children while oversees.

The moments in which he includes an anecdote or social commentary present tantalizing glimpses of Indigenous critique. In describing the inhabitants of London, he notes how many there were, "like musketoes [mosquitos] in America in the summer season," a folksy analogy. However, he continues this line of thought indicating that Londoners bite "one another to get a living." The analogy becomes subtly less folksy and more critical. London was filled with swarms of people, but people who live at the expense of one another. He recounts a dinner with English military officers and the female prostitutes the officers had invited to join them. He opens the paragraph with the statement, "They say

63 For more on the life and artistic accomplishments of Catlin, see McCracken, *George Catlin*.
64 All quotes in this section taken from Maungwudaus's account published in Henry, *An Account of the Chippewa Indians*.

that there are eighty thousand common wives in the City of London."[65] He describes the women as "very handsome" and the officers as "fine, noble, and dignified looking fellows" who also "have very big stomachs caused by drinking too much ale and porter." After dining together for two hours Maungwudaus's company began to leave, and an officer informed them that the "ladies would be glad to shake hands with you." After the men shook the women's hands, another officer said that the women felt that a kiss would show them more respect. So the Ojibwe men "kissed them according to our custom on both cheeks." Still unsatisfied, another officer said the women wanted "to be kissed on their mouths." After obliging the officers' wishes for the third time and kissing the women "on their mouths," there was a "great shout amongst the English war-chiefs." Say-say-gon, the war chief of the Ojibwe, admonished the women. However, Maungwudaus informs the reader that he purposefully mistranslated what Say-say-gon said when the women asked about it. He told them that Say-say-gon was telling the officers to invite them again so that he might "kiss the handsome ladies." In reality, he had made a dismissive comment about the women. After the faux compliment, the Ojibwe were given gold rings and pins before they left the dinner. His mistranslation in the moment and his forthright inclusion of the comment for his readers suggests that he carefully assessed the social and cultural dynamics he encountered and was savvy about his actions within them. It might also suggest that he agreed with his companion's critique of prostitution.

The critiques he does include in his account are often veiled. For example, while in Ireland, he explains, "The country people make fire of turf; many of them are very poor." And he follows this immediately with the terse statement, "The British government is over them." Is this a mere fact he is sharing for his readers' benefit, or is this an observation about occupying authorities and the poverty they allow? Does his obvious distaste for the social interaction with English prostitutes reveal his judgment against the women or a critique of the English officers who create business for them? His descriptive mode of writing seems to contain more than mere description. In one short section, he explains that the Ojibwe company lost three men to smallpox because they had refused a vaccine. Given the significant personal loss he experienced during his time in Europe, the inclusion of this extra information about

65 Henry, *An Account of the Chippewa Indians.*

(*Continued on page 197*)

In the period from 1860 to 1880, after the supposed end to the Indian play fad, new Indian plays still appeared approximately seventy times. This number does not account for the many combination companies circulating in this period, at least some of which were glued together by redface and Indian characters. Indian characters were also incorporated into blackface minstrelsy during this era and are not represented in these numbers either. The 1880s brought yet another live entertainment form to American audiences eager to see more Indians, the Wild West show. These shows purported to show the "real" Indian through their hiring of Native American performers to play Indian roles, but their outsized impact on the racialization and standardization of the Stage Indian belies that easy claim and will be further discussed in chapter 3. But even the rise of Wild West shows did not slow down Indians on the legitimate stage. During the 1880s, when Wild West shows were being birthed by men like William F. Cody, around sixty more Indian plays appeared. During the forty years between 1890 and 1930, the heyday of the Wild West shows' popularity, another theatrical entertainment form impacted the Stage Indian—vaudeville. Vaudeville, as Christine Bold has shown, contained around 350 "vaudeville Indians" played by Native American and non-Native American artists performing Indian acts across the domestic and international variety circuits.[42] And despite the glut of Stage Indians available for audience consumption in Wild West shows, blackface minstrelsy, combinations, and vaudeville, American theater churned out approximately three hundred more Indian plays between 1890 and 1930. To say that Indian plays were an 1830s–40s fad that did not impact American theater beyond 1850 is simply untrue. Indian plays appeared again and again for at least a century and a half with regularity, revealing that the Stage Indian was, if not always the most popular character, always repeated on the American stage.

STANDARDIZATION

All these Indian plays led to a standardization of redface praxis. Contributing to this was the modification of the production economy as mid-nineteenth century approached. As the stock system waned and after the Civil War, a number of new theaters were built, specialty houses formed to fill in the gap created by the absence of in-house costume and scenery shops.[43] These specialty houses built and maintained items available for rent that, thanks to the railroad, could be shipped across the country. The invention of the sewing machine further enabled these costume houses to efficiently create costume stock, available to professional and amateur theaters alike. The centralized model for costume rental likely contributed to the standardization of redface praxis as well, although its history is grossly under researched.[44]

A published costume list of Louisa Medina's 1838 play *Nick of the Woods* provides a glimpse at the standardization of the Stage Indian. Medina adapted the story from an 1837 novel of the same name by Robert Montgomery Bird, which was loosely based on real-life frontier figures. The play was popular with American audiences for decades. It follows two soon-to-be-married cousins, Roland and Edith, who are robbed of their inheritance, compelling them to travel west to start a new life. They meet a larger-than-life backwoodsman, Ralph, and a mysterious man called Nick of the Woods, who protects white people from Indians. Racial meaning accrues beyond visual markers, and in this play, as with many others, violence and savagery is marked as a distinctly Indian quality. The villain Braxley's men come to kill Roland and kidnap Edith but are foiled by Nick of the Woods, who defends her and kills the Indian attacking Roland. An Indian attack on a neighboring town causes Roland and Edith's friends and protectors to leave, and a young woman, Telie, who is secretly in love with Roland, guides them to safety. She takes them to the home of Nathan (secretly Nick of the Woods), an odd and unsettling man who reveals that Indians massacred his family on his wedding day. Indians attack, and Roland and Ralph fend them off. Shortly thereafter, another attack commences, this one interrupted by the Jibbenainosay (Nick of the Woods again), who, in a glorious spectacle, rides down a waterfall in a flaming canoe. Edith is kidnapped, and Roland joins with Nathan and Ralph to rescue her. She is found in an Indian village, held by the evil and cruel leader, Wenonga. The rescue is a success, although Nathan is captured. However, he reveals that his true identity is Reginald Ashburn and that he is the Jibbenainosay, the scourge of the Indians, before killing Wenonga. Telie is killed by taking a literal bullet from Braxley's gun meant for Roland. Braxley is killed by Ralph. Nathan/Nick/Jibbenainosay/Reginald declares his revenge on the Indians who ruined his life and dies. It is, as this brief synopsis suggests, a hair-raising and spectacle-filled tale, one that warranted standardized Indian costumes and likely Indian makeup, which had been refined since Inigo Jones put torchbearers in white bodystockings and blue feathers.

A costume list published in an 1868 edition of the play, over a decade after the first successful costume houses were founded, gives us an example of what had come to be legible Indian costumes.[45] Male Indians were expected to wear an "Indian shirt," "Indian headdress of feathers," leggings ("fringed and ornamented at sides"), moccasins, "Indian belt," tomahawk, and hunting knife.[46] The suggestions for women are, unfortunately, much less descriptive, mentioning only one female character, Telie, as "often dressed as an Indian girl."[47] Building on this basic uniform for Indian men were additional costume pieces that could be added to signal prestige or leadership among the Indians. Wenonga, the leader of the Indians in *Nick of the Woods*, has a shirt "garnished with silver brooches, tufts of hair, and several Spanish dollars."[48] He wears earrings of silver coins and a headdress with beaks, claws, and feathers on it, and wampum alongside his belt.[49] This costume list indicates that not only were there legible costume pieces that indicated "Indian" to an audience but that they were so widely standardized and recognizable that no specific instructions were necessary. Just what an "Indian shirt" was is undefined, although visual records of other performances from the same time period provide clues as to its shape, size, and identifying features (see the discussion of Edwin Forrest as Metamora below).

By the end of the nineteenth century, Indian makeup suitable for redface performance was so standardized and routinely required in American theater that special colors and styles of makeup application existed. In an 1898 how-to manual for actors titled *Hageman's Make-Up Book*, the author explains exactly what it takes to be made up as an Indian. Touted by its publisher, The Dramatic Publishing Company of Chicago, as "The only modern and complete treatise on the art of making up," the book is part instructional guide and part advertisement, with lists of makeup products available through the publisher.[50] In a chapter with the descriptive though lengthy title "Distinctive and Traditional Characteristics of different American, foreign, and character types, and what shades to use for their make-up and lining," the directions for "North American Indian" are succinct. They are also the first of the eighteen "American Types" included and the very first type of the forty-six total included.[51] This might suggest how frequently actors needed to apply this particular character makeup. The "Flesh Color" assigned to redface makeup is No. 17 and simply called "Indian":[52]

> No. 17 for groundtone. Aquiline nose. Wig with scalp lock and eagle's feather. Eyes reduced in size. Thin, compressed lips. Lines in combination shades of lake and dark gray with yellow high lights. If occasion demands it, warpaint in red, white, yellow and black.[53]

"Lake" refers to a shade of red derived from a particular pigment production process that was popular across the nineteenth century.[54] The instructions seem geared toward male actors playing male roles, which suggests how gender also shapes redface in American theater. I will more fully address gender in chapter 2, but for now, I would like to focus on the expectation that actors would need to know how to make themselves up as an Indian. There was enough demand that greasepaint manufacturers created a specific Indian shade. There was enough demand that an actor needed to know how to appear in redface. And there was an unspoken assurance that all Indians looked the same and that audiences would recognize an actor applying the redface "uniform" of Indian character identity.

The 1898 makeup guide indicates that redface did not just appear in the Indian play melodramas during the antebellum era. It was alive and well for decades following. It also seeped into other professional theatrical forms and amateur entertainment. Blackface minstrelsy, which began as a practice around the same time as the Indian plays of the 1830s, often participated in redface in a particularly complex racial form as white men played Black men playing red men. The progenitor of blackface minstrelsy is commonly understood to be T. D. Rice, the man who introduced American audiences to the song "Jump Jim Crow" and popularized blackface entertainment. Minstrel shows quickly evolved from a solo singing and dancing act that purported to demonstrate the singing and dancing popular among enslaved Africans. Soon, groups of performers such as the Virginia Minstrels and Christy's Minstrels worked together in performances full of songs, dances, skits, and comedy. While Indian plays are labeled a theatrical fad, blackface became entrenched in American theater in ways that differ from redface. Christy's Minstrels, who advertised their repertoire as "plantation melodies," played on Broadway for ten years.[55] Much of their most famous music was written by Stephen Foster and remains in the American songbook. Until well after the Civil War, most blackface minstrels were white men and, as Eric Lott has shown in his foundational work on minstrelsy, used blackface as a means of constructing their own white masculinity, participating in a performance practice that offered them the freedom to express themselves and to critique the social order.[56]

Within a decade of the Civil War, the popularity of blackface minstrelsy was such that numerous troupes toured the country and were exported from America to Europe and beyond. With this popularity came an increasingly codified version of minstrelsy that included characters (e.g., end men, interlocutor) and structure (e.g., grand entry, jokes, songs, olio, dances, one-act comedy) that would last into the twentieth century. In some cases, these well-defined elements, like the one-act, incorporated redface into blackface minstrelsy. For example, in 1873 in Cleveland, Ohio, Duprez & Benedict's Minstrels performed a comedic one-act called *Who's the Actor?*[57] In it, two men who want to be actors separately approach a theater manager, who has them dress as an "Indian Chief" for a rehearsal in which he tries to scare them away.[58] He does so by rehearsing a scene from *Nick of the Woods,* calling them Wenonga, and attacking them while he claims to be Reginald Ashburn (a.k.a. Nick of the Woods). Blackface as popular entertainment was relying on not just Medina's seemingly perennially popular play but audiences' residual knowledge of what makes a Stage Indian.

Redface, like blackface minstrelsy, circulated in professional and amateur performances, and the Stage Indian could be found far from prominent East Coast theaters. Redface was an accessible form of amateur entertainment popular in the second half of the nineteenth century. One 1868 guide to nonprofessional performance, *Parlor Tableaux and Amateur Theatricals,* included a tableau of a supposedly well-known story about an Indian attack in Wyoming. The guide suggests that the two men playing the Indians wear brightly colored tunics, shirts, skirts, buckskin leggings, fur-trimmed items, and "head-dress of feathers and beads."[59] Unlike the other characters in the tableau, both of the men's faces should be "stained copper-color."[60] While the availability of these costume pieces and makeup for the many amateur performers across the country is unclear, what can be ascertained is that the Stage Indian figure persisted and was legible on stages large and small to audiences used to professional, urban entertainment as well as to small-scale, rural audiences.

The legibility of the Stage Indian also continued to persist in amateur performances into the twentieth century. Rayna Green noted in her influential 1988 article "The Tribe Called Wannabee" that the "formal staged tableaux work[ed] themselves down to the schoolroom level, and these forms of playing Indian" became staples in classrooms seen in Thanksgiving school plays.[61] The subject of Indians was seen as suitable for children in both the nineteenth and twentieth century. In the February 1867 edition of *Oliver Optic's Magazine: Our Boys and Girls*, children could turn to the regular feature "The Orator" and find a brief text on "The American Indians" with instructions on gesture and declamation.[62] The text tells the story of a once vibrant people "blotted forever" from the land and usurped by "the anointed children of education," while "the tribes of the ignorant" were "a stricken few," "unlike their bold, untamed, untamable progenitors."[63] Fifty years later, in 1916, Indians remained a subject of interest for youth performances. A list of seven plays deemed "Indian plays" were among those included in the Drama League of America's guide to producing plays at the high school and college level. These included a few focused on well-known Indian subjects like Sitting Bull, Hiawatha, and Pocahontas.[64] The practice of children playing Indian in school plays continues into the twenty-first century, but now, teachers can find resources for those Thanksgiving plays online on websites such as Pinterest, in educational resource exchanges, and on blogs.[65] In the twenty-first century, redface in classroom settings is typically limited to early elementary school students, who might create construction-paper headbands with colorful feathers standing up in the back in preparation for Thanksgiving. However, even these Indian headdresses are growing less common as cultural values shift over redface.

The Stage Indian was standardized over the nineteenth century through costume and makeup in a visual repertoire that was portable across theatrical genres and theater spaces. Repeated appearances of the

Stage Indian resulted in a narrow range of costume pieces recognized as distinctly Indian, such as the "Indian shirt." It also resulted in a recognizable makeup application with "Indian" colored base and specific color expectations for highlights and war paint. These costume and makeup techniques were implemented in professional, commercial theater, imported into blackface minstrelsy, utilized in amateur theatrical performances, and deemed suitable for children. With the right costume pieces and a little makeup, the Stage Indian could appear on any stage.

MODIFICATION

With the many repeated iterations of the Stage Indian occurring on the nineteenth-century stage, there were, of course, modifications that occurred. These modifications were sometimes incorporated through the process of standardization, while others appeared only briefly. As has already been shown, the Stage Indian was not a static repertoire in European depictions, and the preponderance of redface in US theater provided further opportunity for change over time. While some markers of the Stage Indian remained consistent across centuries of Euro and Euro-American theater (feathers, always feathers), it was not the visual aspect of the Indian that was at the core of the process; it was the racializing project. As Rosemarie Bank has noted, the most famous Stage Indian character in the nineteenth century, Metamora, was played by nineteenth-century superstar actor Edwin Forrest and demonstrated modifications to his costume over the many decades he performed the role. His costume shifted from an eastern woodland Indian appearance, like the Wampanoag character he played, to one much more aligned with nations inhabiting the expansive plains, such as the Pawnee and the Oceti Sakowin (commonly called Sioux).[66] Indians onstage, their shifting and changing legible markers, reinforce their status as what Carlson calls a "repository of cultural memory," and like individual people's memory "[they are] also subject to continual adjustment and modification as the memory is recalled in new circumstances and contexts."[67] The perpetuation of a repertoire, such as the Stage Indian and the theatrical praxis of redface, demands continual performance and reperformance, new ways of doing and seeing that connect to the old and modify it. Modifications to the Stage Indian, which can be traced through Forrest's performances and beyond, were clear and continual.

The poster child for the Stage Indian in the Indian play era, and its longest practitioner, was superstar Edwin Forrest. Forrest rose to fame playing heroic figures full of bluster, action, nobility, and a kind of Jacksonian masculinity that endeared him to his largely working-class fan base. Known for his powerful voice (he wasn't lampooned as "Met-a-Roarer" for nothing), muscular figure, and physicality in performance, Forrest was the quintessential Indian figure of nineteenth-century Indian plays. He played the most famous Stage Indian of the era, Metamora, a character loosely based on Metacomet, the Wampanoag leader sometimes called Philip, who was the namesake of King Philip's War. Although there were plenty of other Indians at hand during the Indian play fad, none could compete with Forrest's superstar status or his portrayal of Metamora. Because Forrest would never allow the script to be published, no other actor offered a competing interpretation of *Metamora*.[68] It was the most popular and enduring of the Indian plays. In Philadelphia alone, it appeared in twenty-three out of twenty-five theater seasons beginning in 1830.[69] By 1855, over a million Americans had seen Forrest perform, although not necessarily in the role of Metamora.[70] He played the role for the duration of his career, and the beloved character became the namesake for towns in Indiana, Illinois, Michigan, and Ohio and for a steamboat, racehorse, fire engine, and locomotive.[71] If one wanted to find the most repeated Stage Indian, the most influential performance in redface of the early nineteenth century, look no further than Forrest as Metamora.

Metamora; or, The Last of the Wampanoag tells the story of the chief Metamora, whose conflict with the calumny of white colonists results in war, intertwined with another story that follows two young colonists who must fight against the opposition of the young woman's father to their marriage. Metamora is established by the young couple, Oceania and Walter, before he is even seen, as a noble and admirable warrior. He is provoked to war by a traitor whom he executes in front of the white colonists who were using the traitor as an informant. His wife, Nahmeokee, assists in the war by serving as an emissary to the Naragansetts, where her brother is chief, but she is captured by the colonists. Eventually freed, she is hunted, and their son is killed while she hides with him in the water. Metamora's forces overwhelmed and his son dead, he kills his wife (with her permission), preventing her capture, and then faces the final onslaught alone. He dies shouting curses at the white men who exterminated him and his people. Meanwhile, the lovers overcome the father's opposition by revealing that the suitor whom he has chosen for Oceania is a villain, while Walter's true noble (read, rich) identity becomes known. They unite by the end of the play and live.

Several images of Forrest in costume as Metamora exist, from portraits of the actor to commercial reproductions of the character's image. From these, it is possible to learn about Forrest in redface. For the role of Metamora, he employed the most obvious visual, namesake theatrical convention of redface: makeup. Nineteenth-century actors who "redded up" applied special makeup to change their skin tone. Lighter in color than the burnt cork used for African/blackface characters, Indian makeup used burnt umber.[72] Used before the advent of greasepaint by actors playing Indians, Romani, and mulattoes, it was "commonly called 'Bollamenia' by professionals."[73] When heated, the grayish brown pigment turned dark reddish brown and would then be mixed into a carrier oil or grease and applied to the actor's skin. Forrest employed redface makeup while playing Metamora (figure 1.5) along with other visual components, like costuming, as well as aural and kinetic markers such as grunts and, according to more than one Forrest biographer, even Indian breathing.[74] Around 1860, photographer Mathew Brady's studio created a series of images recording Forrest in his most famous roles, Metamora among them.[75] In the image of Metamora, Forrest is in full redface makeup and costume.

His skin tone is significantly darker in this photo than in the others of the series. He wears a form-fitting shirt that covers him to the wrist, likely to suggest skin without revealing it, just like the white bodystockings of Inigo Jones. His leggings have fringe down the outside, and his top half is covered with a tunic decorated with fringe and what appears to be beadwork. Returning to the *Nick of the Woods* costume list, we can begin checking items off. "Indian shirt" and "fringed" leggings. *Check.* His moccasins and sashes also appear covered in beadwork or embroidery. "Moccasins." *Check.* "Indian belt." *Check.* On his head, he wears a wig of long dark hair and a decorated headband with a handful of dark feathers sticking up from its back. "Indian headdress of feathers." *Check.* In his

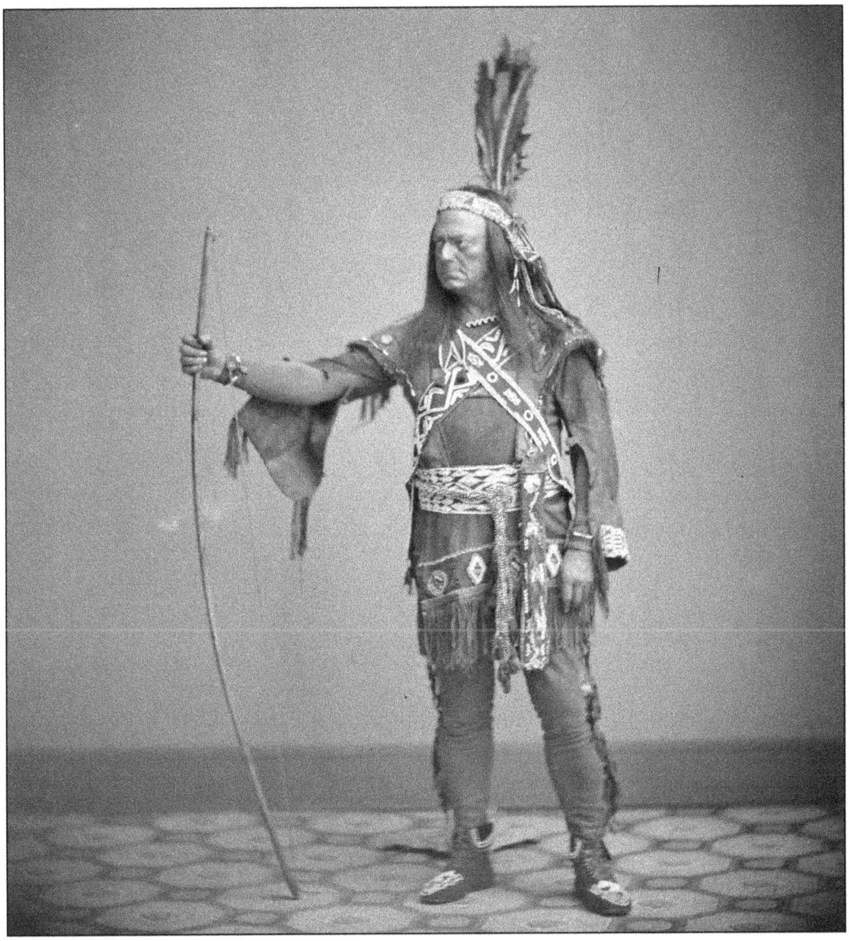

Figure 1.5. Mathew Brady. *Edwin Forrest as Metamora*. Collodion glass plate negative, 1861. Image courtesy Smithsonian National Portrait Gallery.

right hand he holds a bow that is only a few inches shorter than he is. His pose resembles one that he assumed in the final scene of the play.[76] The Brady photograph illustrates elements of the standardized Indian male costume and suggests that even if Forrest did not originate that particular collection of Indian markers, he participated in its circulation.

The photograph shows a markedly different costume from earlier visual images of Forrest as Metamora. The earliest visual recording of Forrest in his most famous role is by Frederick Styles Agate. Painted in 1832, the portrait shows Forrest from the chest to the head in a dimly lit location (figure 1.6).

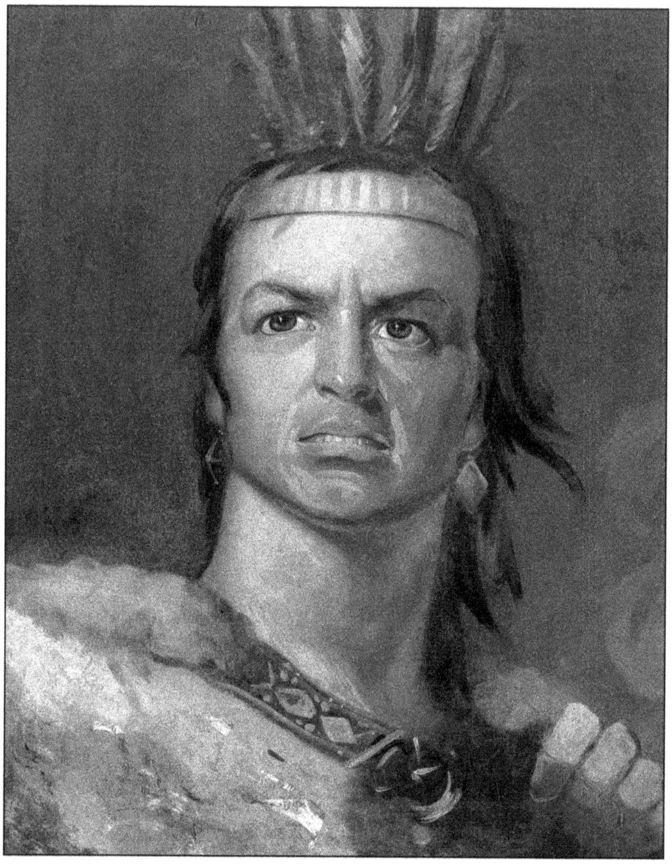

Figure 1.6. Frederick Styles Agate. ***Edwin Forrest in the Role of Metamora.*** **Oil on canvas, circa 1832. Image courtesy Smithsonian National Portrait Gallery.**

He wears a tan and gray animal-skin cloak with a strap decorated with red diamonds and small blue and red circles. It is unclear whether it is embroidered or beadwork.[77] On the top of his head, he wears a light-gray headband, a simple strap encircling the top of his head, covering his hairline. Unlike the one shown in the Brady photograph, it is undecorated. From the back of the headband rise brown and red and black feathers, at least eight, very similar to the Brady photograph.[78] He wears diamond-shaped earrings. No jewelry is visible in the Brady photograph.

The Agate portrait emphasizes the actor in the role, Forrest as Metamora. This emphasis is most clearly ascertained through his skin tone and the title of the painting. Unlike the Brady photograph, Forrest did not "red up" for this portrait. The placard next to this portrait, which hung in the National Portrait Gallery of the Smithsonian Institution during a 2015 visit by the author, read "Edwin Forrest 1806–1872 shown as Metamora . . . the Indian hero." This early portrait shows simple yet distinct visual markers of difference that the actor's performance racialized as Indian. The Brady photograph shows Forrest in more ornate and more standardized visual markers of Indianness, shifting away from the costume mentioned in the script (animal-skin cloak) to a costume widely legible and widely implemented as Indian. Forrest *as* Metamora or more precisely Forrest as *Indian* was what Brady captured in the photo.

Clearly, Forrest's Metamora participated in the circulation of a standardized Indian male costume. But what was standardized as Indian would continue to evolve across the late nineteenth century. A Broadway play from 1899 called *A Stranger in a Strange Land* offers insight into how standardization results in the condensation of redface markers as well. The play's script, by Sidney Wilmer and Walter Vincent, is currently lost, but a series of posters advertising a US tour circa 1902 reveals a few of the most salient plot points.[79] The play, set in Buffalo, New York, and England, included a man claiming to own a cattle ranch, a white man in disguise as an Indian, and a romance between the cattleman and a young woman. The Indian disguise is clearly a selling point for the play, since three of six extant posters for the tour refer to or illustrate it. In one, the self-proclaimed cattleman holds a blanket with geometric designs and a black wig with two wrapped braids and two feathers sticking up from the back (figure 1.7). He leans over a well-dressed and monocled man and says, "You'll look like an Indian when I get through with you!"

Abstracted from a body, a long dark wig with feathers and a blanket are sufficient to suggest an Indian to potential audience members viewing the poster. The blanket is an addition to the visual markers of the Stage Indian enumerated by the *Nick of the Woods* costume list and the Forrest photograph. It is an example of the process of modification that adds, subtracts, and rearranges over time but retains its purpose of creating a singular, racialized Indian character. While blanket, braids, and feathers were potent marker of Indianness, another poster shows that a convincingly embodied Stage Indian requires more (figure 1.8).

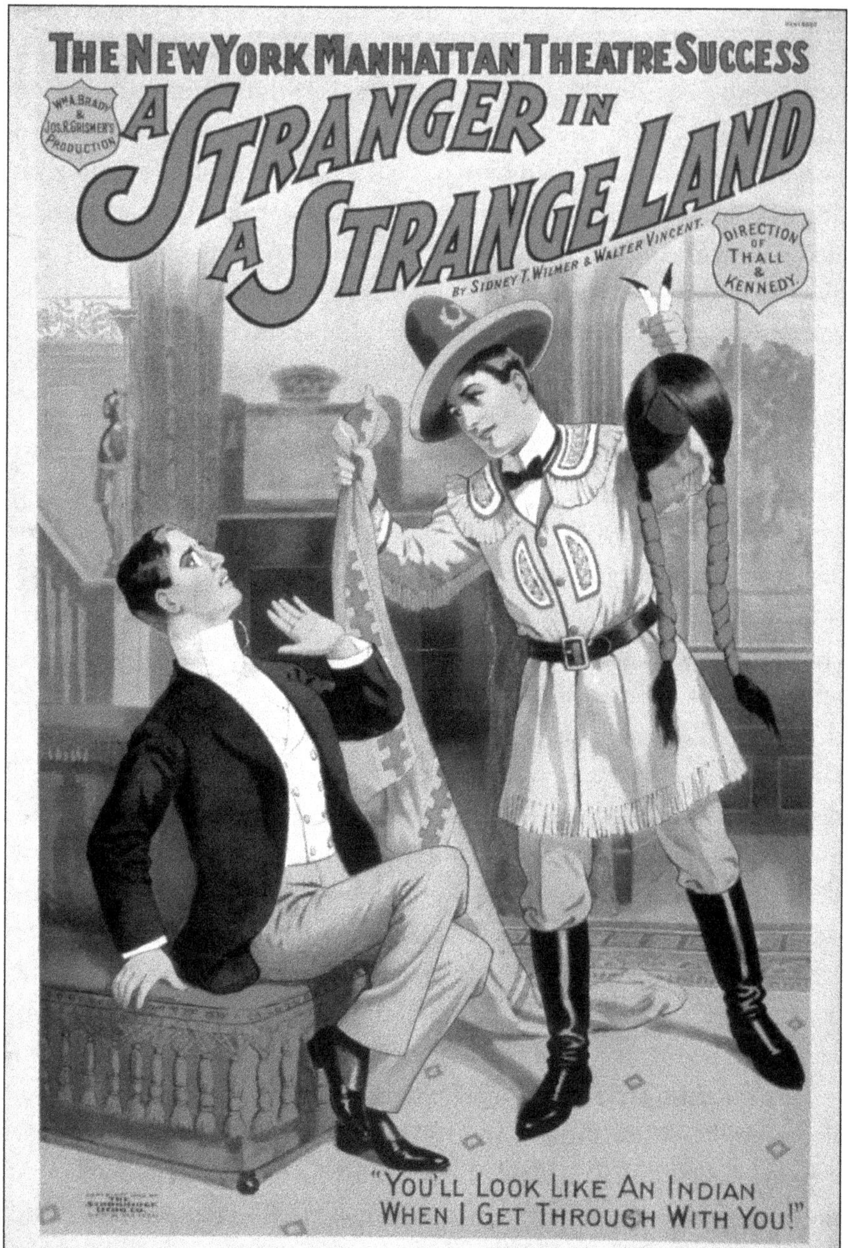

Figure 1.7. *Stranger in a Strange Land* poster. Image courtesy Library of Congress.

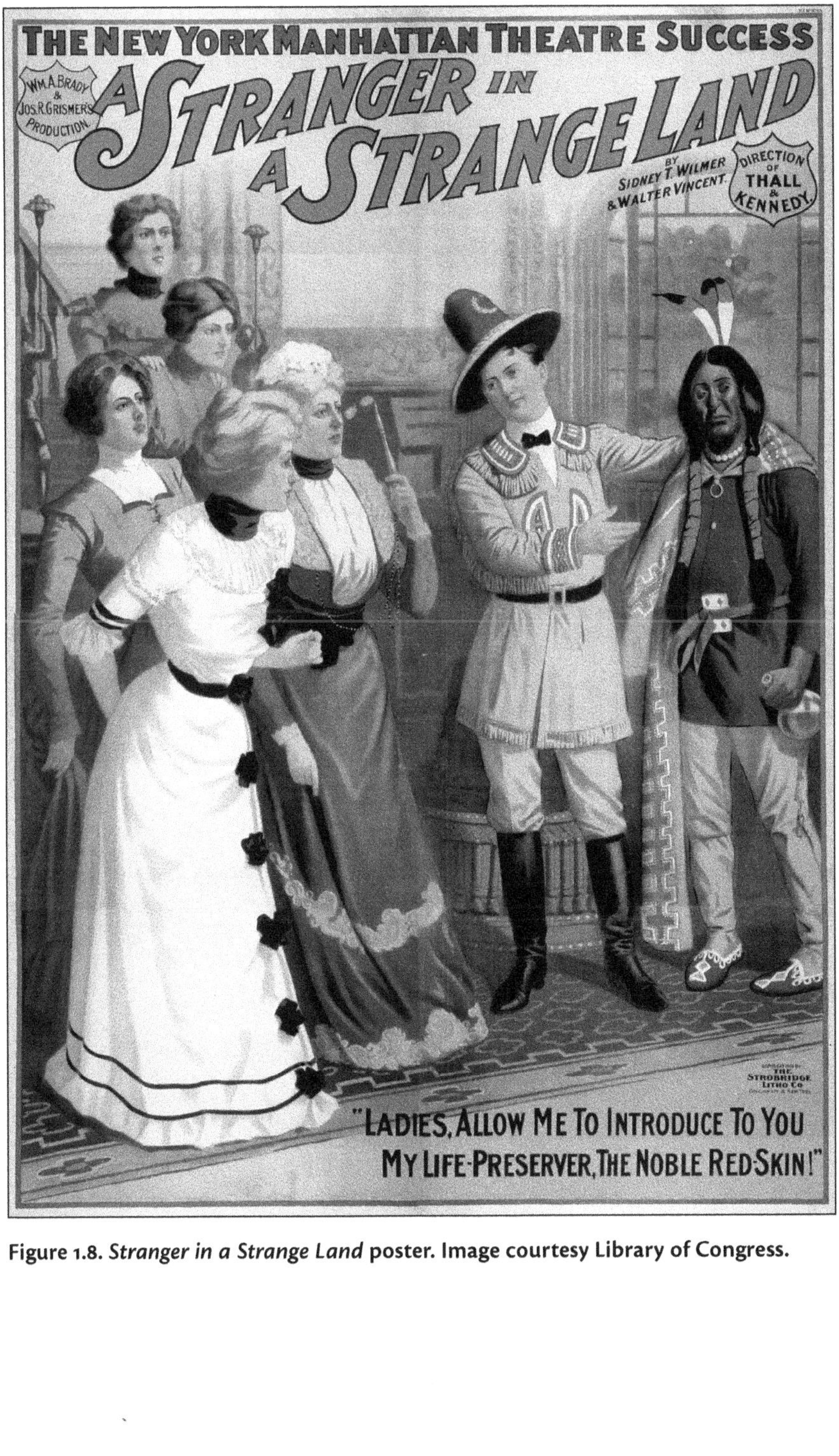

Figure 1.8. *Stranger in a Strange Land* poster. Image courtesy Library of Congress.

This second of six different poster designs for the play shows five women on a staircase expressing unease at being introduced to an "Indian" by the cattleman. "Ladies, allow me to introduce to you my life-preserver, the noble red-skin!," the poster's caption states. The cattleman stands next to the "Indian" with one arm around his shoulder gesturing to him with the other hand. The "Indian" wears the wig and the blanket seen in the first poster but to these has added a belted tunic, fringed leggings, beaded moccasins, dark (redface) makeup on his face and hands, and an open bottle of liquor. Most of these elements are recognizable from Forrest's photographed costume and the *Nick of the Woods* costume list. However, the bottle of liquor, like the blanket, is a newer addition. This suggests that new ideas of the Indian were circulating and modifying the Stage Indian. The term blanket Indian, widely used across the second half of the nineteenth century and into the first decades of the twentieth, referred in a derogatory manner to Native Americans who held onto traditional practices and lifestyles, explicitly refusing the ongoing American efforts toward their assimilation.[80] Similarly, the relationship between alcohol and Native Americans had been a source of concern, judgement, prejudice, and damage since early European settlement in North America. Recreational alcohol use was introduced by European colonists, traders, and settlers to Native Americans and sometimes used to coerce Native Americans in business and diplomatic dealings.[81] "Indian" became synonymous with "drunk" over the ensuing decades and centuries, and this association carried with it racialized and racist meaning about Indian inferiority and vice. This poster activated both the "drunk Indian" and the "blanket Indian" tropes, while relying on the Stage Indian repertoire previously developed. Without a copy of the script, it is difficult to say whether this disguised Indian character was perceived sympathetically, comedically, or derisively. Given the reductive visual markers the posters employ, it would not be surprising if the narrative employed other reductive, racialized markers of the Indian or what linguistic anthropologist Barbra Meek would call Hollywood Injun English.[82] This play traffics in the Stage Indian, highlighting how its repertoire changed over time and responded to cultural and historical contingencies that resulted in maintaining the racialized legibility of the Indian in the United States.

(*Continued from page 110*)

* * *

One such theater artist was Will Rogers (Cherokee), a phenomenally successful entertainer in the first decades of the twentieth century. His life and career never fit the mold of the Stage Indian, and consequently, his Indigeneity was largely illegible to mainstream American audiences. Rogers was adored nationally as America's "Poet Lariat," and writer Damon Runyon referred to him as "America's most complete document," but by the time of his death, his race was recorded as white.[20] Will Roger's career demonstrates how the Stage Indian not only constrains who the American public can recognize as an Indian but also renders the American public ill equipped to understand the Indigenous performers in front of them.

William Penn Adair Rogers was born near Claremore, Cherokee Nation, Indian Territory, on November 4, 1879, to a prominent and financially and politically successful Cherokee family.[21] At a young age, his disinterest in formal education was immediately apparent. Attending six schools before dropping out to work as a cowboy at the age of eighteen, Rogers did not thrive in educational settings.[22] After a brief stint as a cowhand, he returned home to Indian Territory and managed his father's ranch.[23] This, too, did not suit him, and he left in 1902 for Argentina to seek his fortune in the cattle industry.[24] When that proved unworkable, he sailed to South Africa to work on a horse ranch and by happenstance and because of his exceptional skill with a rope, he began his theatrical career as the Cherokee Kid in *Texas Jack's Wild West Show*.[25] While in South Africa, Rogers was also asked to play Stage Indian characters as well as characters in blackface and was eventually billed as America's Champion Mexican Cowboy when working in New Zealand.[26] The racial fluidity of his early performance career hints of the future challenges his racial ambiguity would present to the American public.

20 Rogers, *Will Rogers' Weekly Articles, vol. 5, The Hoover Years 1931–1933*, 620.
21 For brief biographies of Rogers's parents, see chapter 1 of Yagoda, *Will Rogers*.
22 Yagoda, *Will Rogers*, 28
23 Clem Rogers changed from cattle to the hotel business in 1898, at least in part as a result of the forthcoming allotment of the Cherokee land, which would drastically change the business and agricultural practices of the Cherokee. See Yagoda, *Will Rogers*, 35.
24 See Yagoda, *Will Rogers*, chapters 2 and 3.
25 B, Rogers, *Will Rogers*.
26 As quoted in B. Rogers, *Will Rogers*, 77. Yagoda, *Will Rogers*, 64.

By 1904, Will Rogers had returned to the United States and appeared at the St. Louis Exposition (a.k.a. the St. Louis World's Fair), this time working for *Mulhall's Congress of Rough Riders and Ropers* as a "lariat expert," or what modern audiences might call a cowboy.[27] Performing at the New York Horse Fair in Madison Square Garden in 1905, he was described as "a full blood Cherokee Indian, born on the Cherokee Strip, and educated at Notre Dame and Carlisle, Pa. His father is now chief of the Cherokee Indians."[28] While none of these descriptors are true, Rogers's roping act became successful, and he soon moved to the vaudeville circuit to display his skills with a horse and a rope.[29] He worked steadily for years, first earning $75 a week then later up to $250 a week.[30] Eventually, he performed his vaudeville act in Germany, England, and in the Keith and Orpheum vaudeville circuits in North America. In 1914 his roping act was picked up as a novelty act for the Broadway musical *The Wall Street Girl*. The show opened the night the Titanic sank, and Rogers had to deliver the news to the audience.[31] From his exposure on the theatrical stage, he was hired by Florenz Ziegfeld to perform in his *Midnight Frolic* and later the *Ziegfeld Follies*, performing in them from 1915 until 1925 when he moved to Hollywood to pursue a film career. As a star of the *Ziegfeld Follies*, he made $3,100 a week in 1924, which, according to the US Bureau of Labor Statistics CPI Inflation Calculator, is roughly equivalent to making $55,000 a week in 2023.[32] During his time on the New York stage, Rogers also began his writing career with a series of articles in 1916 that would eventually turn into syndicated weekly columns, daily telegram columns, special articles for magazines, and several books.[33] Having conquered vaudeville, Broadway, and print media, Rogers began work in film and radio. He appeared in about forty films spanning the silent and sound eras.[34] He even earned the distinction of being the top box office draw in Hollywood in 1933, beating out Joan Crawford, Mae West, and Clark Gable.[35] During these same years, he

27 Yagoda, *Will Rogers*, 76, 64. Undated program from Mulhall show titled "Cowboys' Carnival" in scrapbook held by Will Rogers Memorial Museum and Archive, Claremore, Oklahoma.
28 As quoted in Yagoda, *Will Rogers*, 83
29 Yagoda, *Will Rogers*, 91.
30 Yagoda, *Will Rogers*, 89, 95.
31 Yagoda, *Will Rogers*, 129.
32 Yagoda, *Will Rogers*, 209. The US Bureau of Labor Statistics inflation calculator is available online. "CPI Inflation Calculator," US Bureau of Labor Statistics, accessed November 22, 2023, www.bls.gov.
33 Yagoda, *Will Rogers*, 209.
34 See Yagoda, *Will Rogers*, chapters 8 and 11.
35 Yagoda, *Will Rogers*, 260.

(*Continued on page 150*)

From Inigo Jones's white stockings and feathers on legs, to male ballet dancers with leaf garlands on their heads, to Pocahontas with a bow and arrow and plumes, to the obviously ubiquitous Indian shirt, to an open bottle of liquor and a blanket, the Stage Indian has appeared in varying costume and makeup with varying props. But its identity as an Indian and the embodiment of that racialized, colonially invented, and colonially enforced figure remained steady—along with feathers, which are perennially present when the Stage Indian appears. But how audiences are supposed to interpret these variances and the steady presence of a legible Indian is answered not on the surface, through the visual, of the Stage Indian but in its contextual and narrative framing.

INTERPRETATION

Despite being explicitly about Indians, redface nearly always occurs within an interpretive lens that centers non-Indian characters and ideas. Unlike blackface minstrelsy, in which every actor onstage was in blackface and playing a selection of curated character types, redface has almost never been all encompassing. Even from the Indian plays phase of the 1830s, there are almost no extant plays that contain only Indian characters. *Metamora* contains many white English characters. All Pocahontas plays contain white English characters. *Nick of the Woods* contains white American characters. In fact, one scholar defines Indian plays, called Indian dramas in her book, as those that "feature Indian characters in plots centered on Indian-white relationships, as seen by American writers."[83] While this definition may well be too narrow to encompass all redface in American theater, I do believe that the emphasis on Indian-white relationships or dynamics is particularly salient.

Joseph Doddridge's 1823 play *Logan: The Last of the Race of Shikellemus Chief of the Cayuga Nation* displays this preoccupation with a white American perspective even as it features the actions of Indian characters. The play's first scene is an extensive discussion among British military officers about the wisdom of beginning a war against Indians. Two captains, transparently named Captain Pacificus and Captain Furioso, argue over whether the army should attack or show forbearance. Furioso claims that Indians do not own the land they live on, are akin to "a beast of prey," and are "doomed to utter extermination."[84] Pacificus urges caution and provides evidence that the gathering Indians are not preparing for war. When Furioso states that all Indians—men, women, and children—should be killed, Pacificus interjects that "would be not only inhuman, but dishonorable."[85] Furioso retorts, "I would kill all, nits will be lice. . . . No mercy ought to be shown them."[86] This back and forth continues the rest of the scene. Pacificus offers practical and ethical reasoning against attacking the Indians, while Furioso insists on Indian treachery, inhumanity, and taking his revenge. In the second scene, a vast majority of the soldiers vote to follow Furioso's plan of attack, and Pacificus has a short monologue in which he prays for God's protection and that God "witness that in the murderous deeds of this day, I have had no participation."[87] These white, male, military characters do not appear in the rest of the play. The following three acts, the rest of the entire play, focus on the actions and decisions of the Indians. Only two minor white male characters appear after the first act, a prisoner of war and a messenger from the royal governor of Virginia. In a play explicitly intended to commemorate the "bravery, talents, and misfortunes" of Cayuga chief Logan, the framing device of the play is an argument between white Americans over how to interact with Indians.[88] Clearly violence wins, but not without inducing considerable guilt. This moral quandary in the first moments of the play indicates to audiences how to understand what follows and that it is best understood as an inevitable though lamentable evil that shaped America.

Logan, the titular son of a chief, is faced with the loss of his entire family due to the preemptive attacks Furioso championed, but as he states, "he will not weep, he will think only of revenge."[89] Although he is a "friend of the white men [as] his great father Shikellemus taught him," he is bound to seek revenge for his losses because he "is still an Indian."[90] He spends a fair amount of time bemoaning the fact that he is "the last of a long race," which when he dies will "like the shooting star . . . leave no track behind," as will, for an unexplained reason, "all his race."[91] After several tribes (the Ottoways, Shawnees, and Wyandots) join Logan in exacting revenge, they are counterattacked and suffer losses, after which they come to the realization that "the white men are many in number; we are but few. They are rich; we are poor. They know everything; we know nothing—they can do everything; and we but little."[92] They accept their inevitable fate of being conquered in battle, so they decide to seek peace instead. Logan, after being magnanimous to his prisoner of war, declares that he has done his duty of revenge, and he does not stand in the way of peace. The final words in the play are Logan's message to the Virginian governor, reminding him of Logan's "love for the whites," the murders of his family that drove him to revenge, and how utterly alone he is. He also mentions that when he is dead, there will be no one left to mourn him, "not one."[93] Logan is admirable because he is a friend to whites and stops killing after he has reached a satisfactory state of revenge. However, he is lamentable because he has lost everything and everyone. Perhaps surprisingly, the play does not end in his death. The playwright noted in a section of the front matter to the published play titled "The Argument" that Logan "after the peace became melancholy and intemperate, and often wished for death" and was murdered "somewhere between Detroit and the Miami" but that no one knows why or by whom.[94] That Logan is honorable and had just cause for seeking revenge is signaled by the first act. The ethical quandary of American settlement—exterminate or honorably interact with Indians—is played out in a conversation. Then the Indians helpfully realize that they are just no match for white settler power and ingenuity, and they accept their fate. The settlers do not even have to seal the deal by murdering the title character, because he just fades away of his own volition. Logan's dramatic structure, dialogue, and character development interpret the title character as a noble, tragic figure. His hamartia, or tragic flaw, is simply being Indian.

Interpreting redface performance almost exclusively occurs within a larger conversation or question of white America. In *Logan*, the considerable time and focus spent on Indian actions, but truly just the discussion of Indian actions, is framed in terms of the internal tensions that white Americans feel about their dealings with Indians. No killing or fighting ever actually happens onstage. For *Metamora*, a play about noble savages dying to make way for virile young Americans, the Indian is necessary to demonstrate the location, the emplacement of English immigrants turning into Americans. The Pocahontas plays, discussed in chapter 2, are all concerned with Pocahontas's relationship with John Smith and her romantic relationship with John Rolfe, both of which demonstrate Indian support for English colonialist endeavors and are invested in bolstering American presence and nationhood. Later instantiations of redface continue this dialectic relationship between white America and red Indians. In *Buffalo Bill's Wild West,* which will be discussed in chapter 3, the Indians were pitted against white Americans in battle reenactments, races, and horseback-riding competitions. Indians in the Wild West shows illustrated the settlement of the West, the winning of the West. In the twentieth century, Indians continued to be a potent site for working through white American issues. Redface in the 1946 Broadway production of *Annie Get Your Gun,* which will be explored in chapter 4, showcased how a white American was bolstered professionally and personally through affiliation with Indians. Redface performance routinely and overtly shapes its own conditions of reception through framing the redface through the perspective of white America.

Use of Indian characters well into the twenty-first century, such as Tracy Letts's *August: Osage County* or the Broadway musical *Bloody Bloody Andrew Jackson,* continues this interpretive framework of helping make sense of white America. *August: Osage County* is a Tony- and Pulitzer Prize-winning play about a disintegrating white family in Oklahoma who are are physically and emotionally cared for by their newly hired live-in housekeeper, a Cheyenne woman named Johnna. Johnna is hired to literally clean the mess they have made of their lives, what the alcoholic father in the play calls the "cleaning of clothes or carpets or crappers," and she does "manifestly" refresh the home, resulting in a "transparent gleam of function."[95] However, she cannot stop the self-destruction the family enacts; she can be there only to clean up the mess afterward. In the final moments of the play, when the central matriarch of the family has been left alone by everyone in her family, she climbs into Johnna's lap, and Johnna holds her "head, smoothes her hair, rocks her . . . [and] quietly sings to [her]."[96] Johnna's unwavering presence in the play is the backdrop for the American family drama unfolding. *Bloody Bloody Andrew Jackson,* tells a loosely (very loosely) biographical story of Andrew Jackson with fictional Indian characters added to demonstrate Jackson's racist and violent character. One song, "Ten Little Indians," provides the backdrop for Jackson's atrocious actions toward and coercive treaty-making with Native Americans. It sings the death of the

Indians one by one, ending with the line "One little Indian nothing to be done. He went and hanged himself and then there were none."[97] Indigenous death exists in the show to illuminate Jackson's flaws. Indians are backdrops in these shows, present to reveal what is in the foreground, not to pull focus. As Phillip Deloria has shown, the Indian is a peculiarly American figure used by Americans to work through what being American means. And American theater's relationship with the Stage Indian is no different. However, the Stage Indian's relationship to Native Americans reveals that more than national identity is at stake.

LEGIBILITY

The Stage Indian became a racialized figure through a collaborative, curatorial process across the nineteenth and into the twentieth centuries. American actors and American audiences together explored, repeated, and refined a racially legible Indian. Redface appeared repeatedly on the American stage, was modified and standardized over time into specific material markers (e.g. feathers, face paint, Injun English), and was consistently interpreted through an American national lens. The Stage Indian persisted across these two centuries in part because of the flexibility it possesses, as demonstrated by the modifications made to it over time and the ways that Indianness was both antithetical and integral to Americanness at different times. Redface is both the result of and the pathway to a reductive, racialized identity called the Indian in American culture. It is the result of years of performances, and those years of performing and witnessing redface have created its legibility and ubiquity.

In the United States, the Indian, as a near-mythological creature, has appeared in arts and entertainment for the entire lifespan of the nation. Indians appear in, among other things, literature, music, sculpture, theater, film, painting, photography, comedy, drama, television, advertising, playing cards, and sports. I am hard pressed to find a single genre of cultural production that has not drawn on and reinforced the Indian in American culture. Redface on the theatrical stage participates in the American obsession with the Indian. While the Indian figure saturates American cultural production, redface focuses on that saturation in one of the few instances of embodied performance. The Indian in visual culture, on film or television, in books, and in the well-known cigar-store version, is often material but not embodied. The encounter, the audience's interaction with the redface performer, is unique and uniquely powerful. Seeing a human as an Indian and seeing an Indian as a human are reciprocal projects helped and hindered by redface performance. While we often use the word *humanizing* to draw attention to processes that create bonds of empathy, ethics, or identification between the audience and the observed, redface invites us to think of this term as a kind of physical embodiment of the capacious but constrained figure of the Indian. Redface is the culturally sanctioned method of encountering the Indian as a physicalized, racialized, and highly circumscribed human. It is the humanizing of the Indian, connecting abstract racial concepts to a body. But the enactment of these concepts occurs with almost no regard for the body doing the enactment.

This phenomenon, a non-Indian dressed like an Indian and playing an Indian character, is the most basic definition many people think of when they encounter the word *redface*. The name itself suggests putting red makeup on skin that is presumed not to be red. At its most fundamental, redface is the physical manifestation of appearing as an Indian. But that presupposes that redface is equivalent to or the distillation of Indianness. It suggests that there is a stable, definitive category or concept called the Indian that is actually translatable through material markers and embodied action to instantiate an Indian in the flesh. Redface, to paraphrase cultural historian Harvey Young, is enacting *an* Indian to call into being *the* Indian.[98]

But instead of magically conjuring the inherent quality called Indianness, what if we understood redface as a ritual of racial construction? It humanizes the Indian by putting the Indian on a human body, even as it reminds actor and audience of the space between that body and the character it portrays. This is the power of racial impersonation. It feels humanizing to enact a version of an Indian and can be received sympathetically by actor and audience alike, but through humanizing the Indian it dehumanizes Native Americans precisely because it racializes them. It denies the tribal/national specificity of a Native American. It flattens the linguistic, cultural, political, familial, ceremonial, cultural, and geographic differences that exist among

Indigenous peoples of North America. It recreates and reinforces the distance between the distilled Indian, an abstract concept of mythical proportions, and the actor, the body encountering other bodies through performance, even as it reinforces the distance between the Indian, a singular racialized figure, and a Native American, a member of a distinct tribe/nation/band.

CONCLUSION

Enacting redface rests on the ubiquity of its form and content in the broader culture. As a national audience, Americans have encountered redface characters routinely for centuries. And we/they know what to do with them. I turn to historian Robin Bernstein's concept of "scriptive things" to reveal how the enactment of redface, the knowing what to do, is a site itself of re-inscription and modification. Certain objects invite performances that are broadly structured "while allowing for agency and unleashing original, live variations that may not be individually predictable."[99] These live and perhaps improvisatory performances are grounded in the objects that inspire them, the things that script action and interpretation. And it is the importance of these performances to the creation and sustainment of race as a construct and a fact that demonstrates the stakes of redface. Bernstein notes that "performance is both part of racial projects and a set of practices by which racial projects connect with each other and with societal structures to create historical processes of racial formation."[100] Doing redface is one way the United States makes sense of the Indian and one way the United States makes the Indian.

A single feather at a Boston museum can be understood as a scriptive thing, just like red makeup, feathered headdresses, and long dark braids. These are the material objects that invite redface performances. Those performances in turn are received and understood as connecting the racial category of the Indian with a human body, even as they also distance the abstract from the experienced. Extending the concept of the scriptive thing, the object (redface) is also activated by other sensorial things (language, posture, music). In the 1830s, Edwin Forrest's rendition of Metamora inspired countless quotidian performances of redface, or more specifically red voice. A nineteenth-century Forrest biographer indicated that "the very boys in the streets were seen trying to imitate his posture and look, swelling their little throats to make the words sound big, as they repeated, 'Metamora cannot lie.'"[101] From this vignette of children in urban streets nearly two centuries before my feather in Boston, it becomes clear that redface is activated sensorially and materially. It is enacted and embodied. The casual instances of redface Alger describes do not rely on makeup, but they do rely on other sensorial markers that are kinetic and auditory. The markers used by the boys are directly related to the redface performance they mimic. However, I contend that they were not mimicking redface; they were enacting redface by participating in the production of a racialized Indian body. They did so by relying on sensorial, embodied markers drawn from the performance that inspired them.

Stage Indian characters during the early nineteenth century were marked by more than makeup and costuming. The construction of the characters as character types, in addition to the solidification of a visual repertoire of Indian markers, created a legible Stage Indian. These character types encompassed both what Indian characters did and how they did it. Actions of aggression or submission, qualities of vanishing or disappearance, and the representation of noble and savage qualities were constitutive of Indianness, just as much as burnt umber makeup or feathers in hair. The circulation of these visual, kinetic, and dramaturgical markers of Indianness was wide. Audiences across the country witnessed popular theatrical performances from stars like Edwin Forrest and lesser actors in nameless Indian roles. Together, the repetition of production and narrative constructed a legible Indian figure, one that could be solidified by the right makeup application and could be trusted to act in prescribed and appropriately vanishing ways. Through the continuous circulation of these redface performances, American audiences came to know what Indians looked like and what Indians did. They learned how to wear a feather and how to act like an Indian. This cultural knowledge has shifted somewhat over the decades, but the process through which audiences come to know it has not changed. Proof of the process's continued power is in a museum in Boston, where you can disguise yourself with a single feather.

CHAPTER TWO

INDIAN PRINCESSES AND THE STAKES OF LEGIBILITY

I was thirteen when Disney's animated retelling of the Pocahontas myth premiered in movie theaters, young enough to watch but not young enough to become attached to the newest Disney princess. High school, college, and adult life swept me far from the world of brave young women sick of swimming who paint with all the colors of the wind in poor provincial towns. But as with other institutions that shape American childhood, I was pulled back in when I became a mother. A family vacation in 2017 brought me to Disney World's Animal Kingdom, the global entertainment force's home for exotic (read, not native to the United States) animals, reproductions of Africa and Asia, dinosaurs, and occasional appearances by one famed Indian Princess.[1] Pocahontas is not ranked very highly in the hierarchy of Disney princesses. No ball gown. No magical powers. No getting the prince at the end. But she holds her own among the lower ranks, at least enough to warrant in-person character appearances at Disney World. As a vacationing mother of three, I took my kids to the most exciting and entertaining offerings of the Animal Kingdom. As a student of theater and Native American studies, I insisted on "meeting" Pocahontas. Our short moments together, thanks to the extremely efficient operations of Disney World, included my informing the young woman playing Pocahontas that I was writing a dissertation on Native American representation. She responded in character, as all Disney cast members are required to do, and expressed the interest her father, the chief, would have in my work. We stood together and smiled for a picture (figure 2.1).

I stood next to many Disney characters during our vacation: ants, spacemen, animals, princesses, and fairies. All but Pocahontas were based on purely fictive figures. Sometimes the human inside the costume was completely invisible and silent. Sometimes the human in-

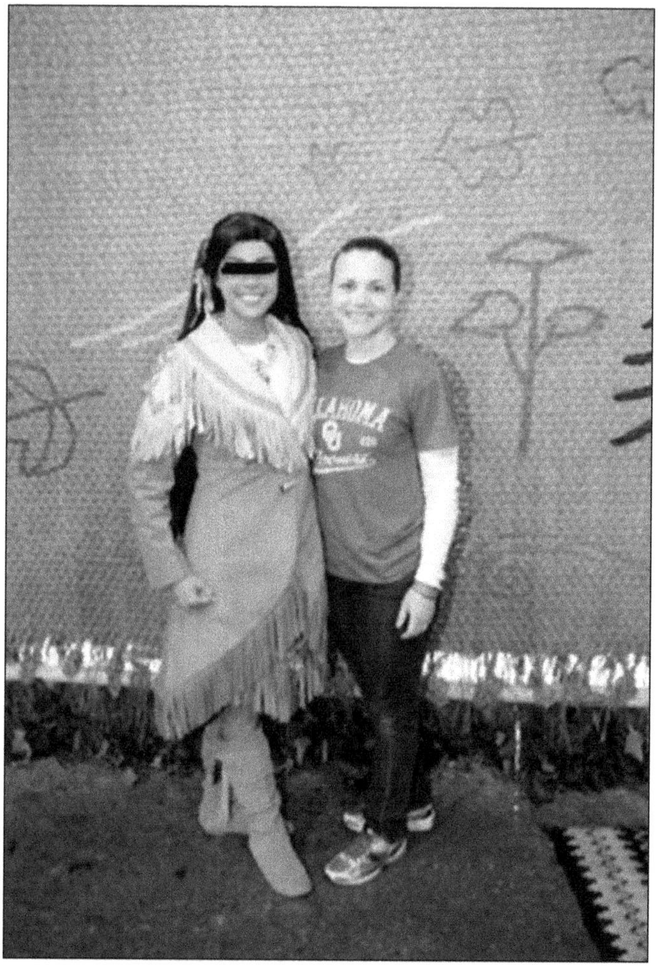

Figure 2.1. Author and Disney cast member. Photo from author's collection.

side the costume was revealed and communicative. All were intent on playing an iteration of a beloved and well-known character. There were many ways they could play the character wrongly and only a narrow set of criteria to playing it correctly. I wondered at the constraints on this young woman tasked with playing Pocahontas. First, she must look the part. But it was a cool January day in Florida, so she did not wear the one-shouldered, above-the-knee dress with blue necklace made famous in the animated film. Standing by me, she wore a tan, leather-looking coat with fringe over a white and tan dress decorated with fringe and colored stones, matching boots, flesh-colored tights, and a white and green stone or bead necklace. Perhaps most importantly for her legibility as Disney's Pocahontas was her hair. Wearing what I assume were extensions, her hair swept past her waist and was adorned with leather strips and shiny shell-like objects. (Sadly, it did not defy reality and gravity and get fuller as it got longer.) She had no feathers. No face paint. But she did have an ample number of beads and fringe. Even though she was not wearing the "right" Pocahontas dress, she still had to look like an Indian—but not too much like an Indian, or Disney would be accused of veering into racist caricature. Her outfit was distinguished only by the fabric and ornamentation: leather-like material with fringe, beads, antler-like clasp on the coat, and geometric border on her collar and extended epaulets. Were it not for these elements and the hair, it would be challenging to read who or what she was. Her legibility was also assisted by the prominent sign indicating Pocahontas's availability for interaction and photos. People walked into the space expecting Pocahontas, and the visual markers they took in were Indian enough to register her as Pocahontas.

Intensely curious about the performer's identity, I refrained from asking about it, knowing she could answer only in character. But I silently played through casting scenarios in my head. Was this woman Native American? Would she claim a Native American ancestor? Would she identify as a woman of color? If so, how did she specifically identify? If not, how did she approach cross-racial performance? Was she performing in redface? I have no answers to any except the last. And the answer to that is the question this chapter seeks to answer. Could any human playing Pocahontas, the mythic, American ideal of self-sacrificial Indian womanhood, ever do anything besides perform in redface? Or put differently, can the forces of historical fact (Pocahontas was real!) and gendered identification (Pocahontas was a princess!) overcome racialization (Pocahontas was an Indian!), or are they merely in service to it?

* * *

In this chapter, I explore the relationship among history, invention, race, and gender that interlocks fact and fiction through redface. It is important for the Stage Indian to be legible but also to be perceived as accurate or authentic in some form or fashion. Because of this desire for authenticity, explored in more depth in chapter 3, the Stage Indian is consistently and overtly connected to, for lack of a better word, "real" Native Americans. One of the most common and most effective ways to do so is through a reliance on historical fact or context to situate redface performance. Understanding the implications of presenting history as fact and the elision of history as a human-created narrative with cultural, ideological, and political impetus and outcomes is essential in distinguishing the political work the racialization of the Stage Indian does. For just as "real" Native Americans are brought into relationship with the Stage Indian, the Stage Indian is also brought into relationship with Native Americans. The Stage Indian impacts the lived experience of Native Americans in the United States through ideological, political, legal, and economic avenues. This chapter explains the extensive connection of Pocahontas, the Stage Indian Princess par excellence, to history, race, and gender, while also attending to how the creation of a legible, embodied, raced, and gendered Indian impacted Native Americans' political and legal lives. Through a careful look at how Pocahontas plays in the nineteenth century presented themselves as dependent on historical fact, participated in shaping a gendered female Stage Indian, and presented a "vanishing Indian," I argue that the legible Stage Indian was presented as distinctly "real." Because "real" Indians also had to contend with the expectation of racial legibility offstage, I highlight how these expectations for legibility were worked out in US law, jurisprudence, and census taking. Redface was the theatrical process of gendering and racializing Indians, but theater was not the only place Indians were racialized. The legible Stage Indian also became an expectation in nontheatrical spaces.

HISTORY AND DRAMATIC LICENSE

In the early decades of redface development during the Indian-play era of the nineteenth century, the drive to provide historical plays was nearly ubiquitous.[2] Plays about Metamora and Pocahontas were clearly and overtly linked to past events that had occurred in North America, King Philip's War and Pocahontas's life, respectively. South American Indigenous history was not forgotten, however, with several turn-of-the-nineteenth-century plays written about Pizarro's sixteenth-century conquest of Peru.[3] American playwrights during the Indian-play era consciously pointed to their historical sources and inspirations and were cognizant of their role in narrating American history. The many Pocahontas plays were no different. In fact, the space between history and dramatic interpretation was repeatedly narrowed and downplayed.

In an introductory essay to his 1837 play *Pocahontas*, Robert Dale Owen muses at length over the relationship between history and narrative fiction. He asserts that "by history, we live among our ancestors . . . come into contact with the mankind of former ages . . . travel among ancient nations, visit tribes long since extinct . . . are introduced to manners that have yielded."[4] He goes on to compare the "Historian" and the "Novelist," asking which of the two was more accurate or more attractive. Because a "book unread is but a bundle of waste paper," Owen takes seriously the creation of "attractive" stories imbued with meaningful truths readers can enjoy.[5] He claims that while the Historian must master facts, the Novelist must master the "unrecorded spirit of the age."[6] These are not just the musings of an artistic soul on why novelists are superior to historians, although that is a legitimate interpretation of Owen's essay. I draw attention to the importance and labor Owen describes as necessary for the Novelist to tell a historical story attractively and accurately. Histories must be true to their source material but more appealing than that material. Owen is naming the balancing act playwrights manage between the desirability of the Stage Indian and the accuracy of it. But he takes it one step further in articulating how to arrive at a play/character/narrative that is at once attractive and accurate.

The work of the Novelist is to obtain a level of knowledge and sensitivity to the past so its true essence can be distilled into the story. Owen explains that while a Historian must "make himself the master of facts," the "Historical Novelist must do more."[7] Factual accuracy is not the goal of the Novelist; faithful essence is. A Novelist must demonstrate the "accuracy of the portraiture" through mastery over the spirit or essence, the vibe of the time period.[8] When they have successfully done this, the Novelist can then "summon . . . images of the past" and bring them forth "in attractive succession."[9] The Novelist, through capturing faithful essence, can make a story more real than can the Historian, who serves and is bound by facts. The Novelist is bound by nothing and is in service only to a nearly inexpressible essence. Factual accuracy can be verified by the Historian. But what can verify faithful essence? Only the experience of it as truth, a kind of hyperreal reality. And the ultimate experience of the truth of faithful essence is live performance.

Moving from the Novelist to the "Dramatist," Owen insists that "the Drama . . . is yet one step nearer to reality, than the Novel."[10] And the expertise of actors on the stage brings us even "one step nearer."[11] To illustrate what he means by "nearer to reality," the hyperreality of "Historical Drama" in live performance, Owens asks a question about the famous eighteenth-century British actress Sarah Siddons. When Siddons, playing Catherine in Shakespeare's *Henry VIII*, stood onstage, "the living type . . . of the regal Catherine," had the "wheels of Old Time . . . been rolled back some three centuries" and the audience saw the "whole pageant, in its sad reality," would they "have felt it more, in the actual review, than in the scenic representation?"[12] His answer is simple and emphatic: "No."[13] The audience would not have felt the truthfulness of Catherine and Henry more if they had seen the actual Catherine and Henry perform the very same dialogue. Experiencing the "faithful essence" found in Siddons's living performance was resoundingly more real than experiencing factual accuracy. Owen attempts to capture faithful essence in his own historical drama, giving the audience an experience truer than real life even as he emphasizes factual accuracy. Pocahontas onstage is more real than the real Pocahontas. Owen's audiences' experience of the play

(*Continued from page 131*)

savages. And Philip is an honorable and noble leader." He does not shy away from confronting racist cultural expectations of Indians or challenging the foundations of what Jean O'Brien has termed the "firsting and lasting" stories that New Englanders told themselves to make sense of their presence and domination in the land.[80] Apess ends his introductory section with a simple statement pushing back on centuries of racist conceptions of Indians: "My image is of God, I am not a beast."[81] Equating Indian identity with humanity, Apess sets the scene for his coming critique.

Apess goes on to describe and critique specific incidents of cruelty and violence perpetrated against Indians during the British colonial era. These include kidnappings, enslavement, usurping Indian land and authority, massacres, treaty violations, grave defacement, massacres of sleeping Indians, unfair payments demanded of Indians, disease, and acts of war. Apess explains that cruel acts by white men permanently damaged the relationship between whites and Indians. While critiquing missionaries, Apess returns to these critiques of political actions perpetrated by whites who denied Indian humanity. He claims that missionaries have injured Indians "more than they have done us good, by degrading us as a people, in breaking up our governments, and leaving us without any suffrages whatever, or a legal right among men."[82] It is not a shift in spirituality or cultural practice Apess is most concerned by but a shift in legal rights to govern themselves. Missionaries dismantle Indigenous governance and are therefore one part of the violent and cruel attacks on Indians from colonial forces.

Apess is careful to remind his audience that self-professed Christians performed these heinous acts. As an ordained minister, Apess uses his spiritual authority to inform his audiences of the decidedly un-Christian-like conduct and motivation of their hypocritical religious ancestors. He calls out the contradictions in Christian mission work among the Indians, asking "how they could go to work to enslave a free people, and call it religion."[83] Furthermore, when Indians acted in a generous and kind manner, such as caring for sick colonists or providing food and supplies to colonists, they were still treated poorly. However, the

80 See O'Brien, *Firsting and Lasting* for a thorough look at stories New Englanders told themselves about how they came to be New Englanders.
81 Apess, *Eulogy on King Philip*, 7.
82 Apess, *Eulogy on King Philip*, 22.
83 Apess, *Eulogy on King Philip*, 9

poor treatment Apess highlights in these situations is not of ungratefulness or personal repulsion but political acts that constrained Indian nations. For example, Apess brings up Pilgrims landing at Plymouth. It is not that they landed that is an affront in Apess's mind but that they "possessed themselves of a portion of the country," built houses, made a treaty, and "commanded them [Indians] to accede to it."[84] It was not a personal offense but one that called Indians "to defend their country's rights."[85] Taking over land was not a racial project but a political one and an assault on a polity whose borders and rule were under attack.

Although Apess is intent on convincing his audience of the unfair treatment Indians had received at the hands of white people, he is also intent on correcting racist misconceptions white people hold about Indians. He repeatedly draws attention to Indian political equality with white people, as well as their human equality. He calls out people who "believe that Indians cannot feel and see, as well as white people," explaining that "their power of feeling and knowing is as quick as yours."[86] He insists that the belief of early Americans in Indian inferiority, "the seed of iniquity and prejudice," persists into his own time.[87] It "still remains" and has led to "a deep rooted popular opinion" that Indians' sole purpose is to be destroyed and "driven out by white Christians," who will "take their places."[88] Apess is describing, long before Wolfe's articulation of it, settler colonialism's quest to destroy in order to replace the Native alongside a racial hierarchy as the seeds that produced the flowers of prejudice and evil.[89] Apess argues that those in the nineteenth century who believe that the Indian should disappear from the United States are nothing more than the product of seventeenth-century colonial understandings of Indians as racially inferior and therefore, subject to violent domination. For Apess, racism begets unjust political actions that destroy Indigenous nationhood, sovereignty, and contemporary Indigenous relationship to the United States.

Also, Apess warns his audience that their connection to the sins of their forefathers, the persistence of degrading attitudes toward Indian people, and political actions against Indian nations are not just egregious sins;

84 Apess, *Eulogy on King Philip*, 10
85 Apess, *Eulogy on King Philip*, 11
86 Apess, *Eulogy on King Philip*, 18
87 Apess, *Eulogy on King Philip*, 21
88 Apess, *Eulogy on King Philip*, 21
89 Wolfe, "Settler Colonialism," 388.

(*Continued on page 31*)

becomes essential to its claim of faithful essence and reveals redface's deep need for embodiment. For Pocahontas to be more real than real, she has to exist near to reality, in other words, in a body. Furthermore, the audience also has to encounter this body and recognize it as Indian. The audience's interpretation of it as being more real than real is what demonstrates that it is Pocahontas's faithful Indian essence on stage. For the Indian to be fully experienced, identified, and appreciated, it must be an embodied version interpreted by an audience, the Stage Indian.

In taking on the story of Pocahontas, Owen understands himself to be practicing both the communication of historical fact and expression of historical truths. For Pocahontas "is intimately connected with the very first successful effort to colonize North America . . . [and] with the fates of a noble race, which is fast fading away from the earth."[14] He combines a nod to historical facts with an aesthetic interpretation of the race called Indian, which he offers as a historical truth. For he goes on to say that the Indian is "a race, the savage magnificence of whose character appears to me indifferently well adapted to dramatic effect."[15] In essence, he is arguing that everyone knows the story of Pocahontas and how the Indians are vanishing. ("Those Indians sure make great dramatic and tragic characters!") Owen asserts that the characters, "with two trifling exceptions, are strictly historical," and that "every principal event represented or alluded to" in his play is, "with very little variation," faithful to John Smith's own history.[16] Owen, unlike other Pocahontas playwrights of the nineteenth century, made sure to follow the historical record for the timeline and events of his play. Others shifted events around, even creating an ahistorical romance between Pocahontas and John Smith. Those playwrights chose dramatic strength over accuracy. This is never a choice Owen makes, to the detriment of his play, which is quite a bit duller than your average Pocahontas play.

Owen admitted the play's shortcomings in his introductory essay, pointing to his choice not to depart "from the recorded history," instead "making what I could out of the genuine materials before me."[17] However, Owen, like all playwrights who write in redface mode, allows himself room for dramatic license. He admits to not following history exactly in "a few unimportant details."[18] The dramatic license Owens turns to in explaining his artistic decisions is exactly what binds the fictive to the real through the power of embodied performance. It is the space through which an artist inserts their culturally, socially, historically, and aesthetically located ideas about what stories should be told and how. And as I will discuss in chapter 3, it introduces the dynamic of cultural and political power into what seems to be a simple decision not to depict "the manner in which Smith receives the wound."[19] These seemingly small choices to include, exclude, or modify, always justified by dramatic license, reveal the space through which the cultural and political projects of racialization inflect redface plays.

Despite his own admission of imperfection in not adhering to the unities of action, time, and place, so important to the French theater during the seventeenth and eighteenth centuries and influential into the nineteenth, Owen asserts that his project in writing the play was "to exhibit a faithful episode out of our early history."[20] He was untroubled by sacrificing the twenty-four-hour time period and some of the single location expectations of the unities.[21] But he did advocate for "an adherence to the spirit of this unity of time" in dramas, since asking the audience to believe that gaps in time were years rather than months or days would leave a chasm "too wide and frequent for the imagination to overleap, without being somewhat rudely awakened to the fact, that it is not reality which is passing before it."[22] Owen is pointing to the liminal space between reality and fantasy that is always at play in live performance. An audience not only sees real people doing things real people do (talking, standing, singing) but also is required to imagine that these people are part of something unreal/immaterial (the world of the play, a world where time works differently). Owen thinks of his disunities not as inaccuracies but as a kind of truth, not to Aristotelian inspired dramatic structure but to "early Colonial life."[23] Owen's defense for his disunities is that they are truer to history than to art, and he emphasized facts over a man-made dramatic structure. Owen includes substantial endnotes to his printed edition of *Pocahontas*, detailing and citing historical sources for everything from Indian language and customs to North American plants to historical events to excerpts from literary works from which he drew inspiration. These notes, he states, "may aid an opinion as to its [the play's] accuracy in regard to national portraiture and historical minutiae."[24] His endnotes demonstrate his commitment to his work being perceived as historically accurate and his dedication to a portrait of American history.

While Owen provides us the most explicit account of a playwright's concern with historical accuracy alongside a commitment to aesthetically pleasing narrative in Indian plays, he was not alone in his attention to history and dramatic license. Indian plays in the early nineteenth century were nearly always explicitly historical. In the 1808 published script of James Nelson Barker and John Bray's *The Indian Princess; or, La Belle Sauvage,* an advertisement for the play states:

> The principal materials that form this dramatic trifle are extracted from the General History of Virginia, written by Captain Smith, and printed London, folio, 1624; and as close an adherence to historic truth has been preserved as dramatic rules would allow of.[25]

Thirty years before Owen's lengthy musings over the relationship between drama and history, Barker and Bray's lighthearted ballad opera understood itself to be living in the tension between the two. George Washington Parke Custis's 1830 play *Pocahontas, or, The Settlers of Virginia* was noted for its ability to show "the resources for dramatic materials in the annals of American history."[26] The ease with which American playwrights held onto Pocahontas as part of American history rather than British history shows how strongly the Virginia colony was connected to America's lineage during the Early Republic and Jacksonian periods. Like the Plymouth Rock tale of Pilgrims and Indians, which would eventually be connected to a national holiday, Pocahontas and the Virginia colony were seen as an origin of America.[27]

Charlotte Barnes's 1848 contribution to the Pocahontas play genre, *The Forest Princess, or, Two Centuries Ago,* is explicitly subtitled "An

Historical Play, in Three Parts."[28] The introduction to Barnes's version of the Pocahontas tale details how Pocahontas is the exception to the historical rule in the United States that leaves "the early history of the red men imperfect."[29] Barnes notes how "prejudice and injustice" against Native Americans, along with their "disappearance," rendered knowledge of them incomplete or absent.[30] Against this frame of absence, Barnes notes that Pocahontas is known with "certainty and truth" and "all the particulars of her biography are confirmed by relatively distant and unimpeachable testimony."[31] She goes on to add another assurance of the accuracy of Pocahontas's known history: "the mere fact that some of the most worthy families in our land are the living descendants of Pocahontas."[32] Barnes's play, like the other Pocahontas plays mentioned here, is explicitly linked to history. She thanks the British Museum for allowing her to consult works, "at least twenty in number," as she wrote the play.[33] She understands herself as a playwright who does historical research, consults unimpeachable sources, and represents with certainty and truth the actual history of Pocahontas.

Despite a general haziness around Native American history writ large, Barnes is assured of the accuracy of her information about Pocahontas. Both the books recording history and the people descended from Pocahontas prove the accuracy of Pocahontas's life's story. Barnes knows that she could follow dramatic rules to "heighten" the romantic attraction in the story by representing love between Pocahontas and Smith.[34] She spurns this notion and insists that "this tale is no fiction."[35] Barnes's insistence on maintaining the historical accuracy of Pocahontas's marriage to John Rolfe, not John Smith, is not shared by centuries of playwrights, authors, and filmmakers.[36] Over the centuries, the pull of "perfecting the unity of the plot" by showing a Pocahontas/Smith romance has triumphed over the call of historical truth. Disney's 1995 cartoon version succumbed to that pull, as did the 2005 Terrence Malik Pocahontas film *The New World*.[37] However, Barnes's insistence on historical accuracy did not waver, even though she understood the structural problems that introduced to her play.[38] Barnes, like nearly all playwrights who write Stage Indians, was committed to understanding her work as true in some form to history. The Stage Indian was not just a character but a character grounded in historical fact that resulted in a figure nearer to reality than an average play character. The Stage Indian captured the truthful essence of the Indian as it communicated a legibly Indian figure. Race was made real through connecting redface and history, but it always did so with a healthy dose of dramatic license and attention to gender.

GENDERING RACE IN INDIAN PLAYS

In Pocahontas plays, the gender and race of the central character are highlighted and intertwined, deployed as markers that simultaneously speak to the American desire for a specifically female Stage Indian, one that aligns with America's own national and racial projects. In the 1808 Barker and Bray play, *The Indian Princess; or, La Belle Sauvage*, Indians are marked throughout as racially distinct by virtue of their skin color. In the first act, Indians are described as "black fiends" when an Indian attack on an English ship is described. Pocahontas's attendant and confidante, Nima, is described as a "little dark Diana" as she is about to shoot an arrow at a man she deems a threat.[39] Two lines later, the man she threatened to shoot calls her "my dusky dear."[40] The color of Indians' skin is represented as distinct from that of the English colonist characters. The frequency with which skin color is used as a tool to distinguish Indians suggests that color is a dramaturgical not an expository tool. To say it once is to describe a person; to say it repeatedly is to reveal something about that person, something the audience needs to make sense of what they are witnessing. Indians in the play are "black," "dark," and "dusky," which sets them off as different and connects them with the physical threat in the first act. The color distinction serves to clarify to the audience that Indians are identifiable through visual means.

Skin color as evidence of race is routinely employed in the show and not only in service of defining the female Indians. Pocahontas's Indian fiancé, Miami, whom she refuses upon falling in love with John Rolfe, offers a description of his best qualities when trying to convince Pocahontas to marry him. "In what do the red yield to the white men? And who among the red men is like Miami?" he begins. This may seem like an obvious point to make. Indians equal red skin. That is not new news in American culture. But the rest of the conversation between Pocahontas and Miami draws together race and gender in a way that complicates racialized understanding of the Indian. He tries to persuade Pocahontas of his superiority by highlighting his accurate shot, his skill and bravery, and the many hunting trophies he keeps in his "cabin."[41] In recommending himself to Pocahontas as the quintessential Indian *man*, Miami begins with his skin color and illustrates its import through connection to things recognizable as parts of Indian masculinity. Pocahontas rejects Miami by saying, "Thine eyes are as the panther's; thy voice like the voice of the wolf. Thou shouldst make my heart beat with joy; and I tremble before thee." He is like a panther to her, bringing to her heart fear not love. Because of repeated descriptions of her as angelic and pure in the show and her own virtuous reaction to killing a flamingo in her first entrance, it is clear that her affective response to Indian masculinity is morally upright. The violence of Indian men, what is sometimes more boldly called their savagery, is appropriately shunned by the pure woman, even when they are of the same race. Gender thus profoundly impacts how the Stage Indian is depicted and interpreted. Men extol and exercise physical power and prowess. Women do not. The Indian as a warrior is always male. So what is the Indian as a woman?

The five female characters in this play—two Indian and three European—are routinely connected with emotional and moral qualities. After she saves John Smith's life, he describes Pocahontas as being "like Heav'n's own angel-advocate, for mercy."[42] Kate, half of one of the five romantic couples followed in this play (Surprise! Pocahontas isn't actually the protagonist of this show!), reveals how European women are also recognized for their emotional qualities. Kate has disguised herself as a young man to follow her husband across the sea and talks with him before he discovers her true identity. They talk of the lovers, the women, they left behind in Ireland. Of the four qualities they mention, three are attractive facial features and one is a tender heart.[43] A heart that moves quickly to emotional response and attachment is forwarded as a desirable and admirable quality of womanhood. Pocahontas demonstrates this on her first interaction with her love interest. Immediately following John Rolfe's recognition of her "gentleness," "sweet simplicity," and "angel softness," he goes to her, and while other dialogue is happening, the stage directions indicate "*the princess discovers the first advances of love in a heart of perfect simplicity.*"[44] Her heart is exceedingly quick to emotional response, to love and devotion. Pocahontas has a woman's heart, which contrasts the Indian man's heart that was understood to be focused on revenge and loyalty.[45] Pocahontas's heart is focused on mercy and submission. Her heart is different because her gender is different.

Her actions are also different. Whereas the iconic marker of the male Indian was his power, seen in the quality of his movement (imposing, athletic) and actions (acts of violence such as hunting or war), the iconic kinetic marker of the female Indian is not an expression of physical power; it is an embodied act of self-sacrifice, protecting John Smith with her own body. All Pocahontas plays depict Pocahontas preventing the death of John Smith by protecting him with her own body. Note the similarity of the following stage directions from four different Pocahontas plays spanning five decades.

> the hatchets are lifted up: when the princess, shrieking, runs distractedly to the block, and presses Smith's head to her bosom. (Barker and Bray, 1808)[46]

> She rushes down from the throne, throws herself on the body of SMITH, raises her arms, and calls to the executioners to "Strike." (Custis, 1830)[47]

> POCAHONTAS rushes between them, and motions the Executioner away. . . . She throws herself down beside SMITH, folds his head in her arms, and lays hers upon it. (Owen, 1837)[48]

> Pocahontas rushes to Smith, and clasps his head in her arms, laying her own head upon his, as the Indians are in the act of striking the blow. (Barnes, 1848)[49]

While the male Indian of redface explodes, shouts, and fights, the female Indian of redface, exemplified by arguably the most prominent female Indian in American history, "rushes" to enfold the body of a white man in her arms and bosom. Male Indians reject. Female Indians protect.

These distinctly female qualities—sacrifice, protection, mercy, submission, and repulsion at violence—work with the explicitly racial label of Indian to construct Pocahontas as a character who is unlike any other female character in this play. These are not qualities ascribed to any of the male Indian characters. Nor are they all possessed by the white female characters. In fact, Pocahontas is the exemplary female in the show just as she is the exemplary Indian in the show. She is self-sacrificing, devoted, and merciful. She is innocent, pure, unassuming, without guile. And desirable. Pocahontas is gendered female and rendered sexually desirable.

When Pocahontas and Rolfe first meet in the play, they flirt with one another and speak about love, illustrating that she is a willing participant in the encounter and any future romantic/sexual relationship with him. Rolfe awakens Pocahontas to romantic love, or to be more precise, he teaches her what romantic love is. She tells him she likes looking at and listening to him, and when he presses her on why she does not call him brother, as she did John Smith, she says that that is not the name for him. "I feel the name thou art, but I cannot speak it." She does not have a word for what he is to her. Rolfe supplies the missing word: "I am thy lover, dear princess." Pocahontas accepts the label instantly, without fully knowing the definition of the word. She then presses him for reciprocity: "If thou feelest the name as I do, call me as I call thee: thou shalt be *my* lover; I will be *thy* lover."[50] But the love they speak of is more than emotional attachment. It is physical and erotic in nature, decidedly not platonic devotion. She speaks of her cheek burning and her heart beating. After kissing him, she asks if his heart beats like hers. He responds affirmatively, "Beat! O heaven!"[51] Clearly they are both in love after their first moments together, and the evidence is precisely their physiological arousal response.

Pocahontas's innocence is a comment on her state of being and maturity at the same time that it is a comment on her sexual desirability. Sexual innocence is not a characteristic noted for any of the European/white female characters in the play. Two of those women are already married, assumedly already sexually active; the other, an unmarried woman, disproves accusations of infidelity against her over the course of the play, which taints her with the idea of sexual promiscuity. Pocahontas is unknowing in the ways of love/sex. That unknowing is transformed through her relationship with a European/white man. Rolfe celebrates the "rapturous task to teach thee the difference" between pity and love, both emotional and affective responses in relation to other human beings. Obviously, Rolfe will be focusing his lessons on the response that excites arousal and presses for physical intimacy.

And only intimacy results in the procreation that is the true source of Pocahontas's deep meaning to Americans. Procreation, while not mentioned in this play, is assumed because the play is looking back toward colonial Virginia. It is precisely what connects the innocence and eroticism of Pocahontas to the politics and nationhood of America. Although Barker and Bray do not as overtly claim history as the goal of their play, it is most clearly a historical telling of what was identified as a precursor to the United States. The sexualization, gendering, and racialization of Pocahontas was and is deeply imbricated in the American national project. For only through Pocahontas's womb is it possible in the world of the play for white, European men to be the fathers of the "New World." Defining her as racialized elides her nation's specificity, sovereignty, and self-determination with visual markers reduced to skin color and feathers. Shaping her as a *her* distinguishes the social expectations, particularly around affect and action, of Indian women as different from Indian men. And sexualizing her positions her as a literal and figurative foundation for American nationhood and domination. Pocahontas shows us how visual markers of race are surrounded by historical markers of accuracy and connected to markers of gender. These elements, when encountered simultaneously in an embodied performance and read by an audience as legibly Indian, produce a female Stage Indian.

(*Continued from page 151*)

Cherokee citizen ever in question. At only seven months old, Rogers was listed in the Authenticated Rolls of 1880 for the Cherokee Nation within the Cooweescoowee District. His official number was 2340.[49] In 1900, his father enrolled him in the Cherokee Nation—his number on that roll was 11384.[50] Three years later, when allotment of Indian land occurred within the Cherokee Nation, Rogers was again recorded as Cherokee in what is commonly called the Dawes Rolls. His allotment was assigned in early 1903, with his father handling the paperwork because Rogers was working in South Africa.[51] He received a little over seventy-eight acres.[52] Again in 1907, Rogers was recorded as Cherokee in a roll of Eastern Cherokee descendants who claimed unpaid funds due them by the US government. Part of the enrollment process included explaining by what right he was entitled to a share of this money. He did so by listing five separate relatives, primarily maternal, from whom he descended.[53] These three documents make it clear that the Cherokee Nation considered him Cherokee, the US government considered him Cherokee, and he had extensive knowledge of his Cherokee family and their relationship to the Cherokee homelands. No matter what his billing said, Rogers was Cherokee.

Confoundingly, even as mainstream American audiences were unable to recognize his Indigeneity, Rogers routinely forwarded it. He regularly referred to himself as "Cherokee Indian," often followed by a phrase like "and very proud of it."[54] He took pleasure in communicating his relationships with other Native Americans, as evidenced by the stories he included in his print publications. For example, in 1924, he wrote about a lunch he had with some congressmen he described as "my fellow Cherokee Indian Representatives."[55] Similarly, he rooted himself in Oklahoma and most especially in Claremore, Oklahoma, the town nearest his boyhood home in Indian Territory. He often noted, "My home is Claremore, OK."[56] He frequently made trips back home.[57] Rogers fundamentally

49 Croy, *Our Will Rogers*, 7.
50 Rogers, *The Papers of Will Rogers*, 1:207.
51 Rogers had given his father power of attorney so that he could conduct his registration and allotment business while he was out of the country. Yagoda, *Will Rogers*, 67.
52 Yagoda, *Will Rogers*, 67.
53 Rogers, *The Papers of Will Rogers*, 2:346.
54 Rogers, *Will Rogers' Weekly Articles*, 1:169.
55 Rogers, *Will Rogers' Weekly Articles*, 1:225.
56 Rogers, *Will Rogers' Weekly Articles*, 1:181.
57 Sterling and Sterling, *A Will Rogers Treasury*, 46.

viewed himself as Cherokee and preferred being "among my people, my Cherokee people."[58] His connection to place, kinship, community, and nation shows that he was a Cherokee citizen and a member of a Cherokee community.

Beyond publicly identifying himself as Cherokee, Rogers regularly deployed Cherokee perspective, as evidenced in his writing. Several scholars have made a strong case for understanding Rogers's unique voice, particularly in his print work, as decidedly Cherokee in origin and format. Daniel Heath Justice explains how Rogers expressed "the realities of the enduring Cherokee presence in the modern age."[59] He quotes authors Jack Kilpatrick and Anna Kilpatrick to explain how Rogers's humorous and pointed observations were an example of "the crowning glory of Cherokee wit . . . a scintillating satire couched in dry understatement."[60] For example, when writing about the Pilgrims landing at Plymouth Rock, Rogers slyly highlighted the differences between Indians and Pilgrims:

> Now I hope my Cherokee blood is not making me prejudiced, I want to be broad-minded. But I am sure it was only the extreme generosity of the Indians that allowed the Pilgrims to land. Suppose we reverse the case. Do you reckon the pilgrims would ever let the Indians land? What a chance! Why, the Pilgrims wouldent [*sic*] even allow the Indians to live, after the Indians went to the trouble of letting 'em land . . . But they were very religious people that came over here from the old country. They were very human. They would shoot a couple of Indians on the way to every prayer meeting.[61]

Rogers wraps his critique of the genocide of Native Americans by European colonists within a folksy delivery and recognition of the connections between Pilgrims and piety. He also squarely frames his joke, and by extension his critique, within his Cherokee identity. This joke illustrates Tol Foster's assertion that Rogers's writings "utilize the counternarratives of their communities [his Cherokee community] as a theoretical base from which to conduct anticolonialist and cosmopolitan

58 B. Rogers, *Will Rogers*, 179.
59 Justice, *Our Fire Survives the Storm*, 121.
60 Justice, *Our Fire Survives the Storm*, 123.
61 Sterling, *The Best of Will Rogers*, 180, 181.

(*Continued on page 123*)

THE VANISHING INDIAN PRINCESS

While the male Indian of redface explodes, shouts, and fights, the female Indian of redface, exemplified by Pocahontas, "rushes" to enfold the body of a white man in her arms and bosom. By covering Smith's body (or part of it) with her own, by offering her body as a barrier and a haven, the Indian woman creates an alternative kinetic script for redface. Although the racial markers of redface might be the same, the gendered markers of redface are not. However, both the forceful rejection embodied by the male Indian and the self-sacrificing protection embodied by the female Indian reveal two sides of the same redface coin. They both participate in a widely circulating idea coming into focus during this period, that of the "vanishing Indian."

The vanishing Indian was a concept and a practice in the United States both artistically and politically. Materially, Indians vanished by leaving a place, dying, assimilating, or being "watered down." The vanishing Indian readily encompassed multiple settler-colonial logics of control over Indigenous peoples. Indians were forced off land to make way for "progress."[52] Indians were killed in war.[53] Indians were assimilated through religion and education.[54] Indians were "watered down" through intermarriage and the logic of blood quantum.[55] So convinced was the US government of the Indians' vanishing that they passed the Civilization Fund Act in 1819 "for the purpose of providing against the further decline and final extinction of the Indian tribes."[56] Before the Indian-play era had begun, the perceived state of affairs to Euro-Americans was that Indians were literally going extinct. Written into treaties was language such as "while they shall exist as a nation," which suggests that the US government did not actually anticipate that Indigenous nations would exist in perpetuity.[57]

The US political and governmental perception of the end of the Indian was mirrored in the aesthetic realm. James Fenimore Cooper popularized the mythic quality of the vanishing Indian with a book transparently titled *The Last of the Mohicans*. The last-of-something trope was not unique to literature, as seen in the plays mentioned previously: *Logan: The Last of the Race of Shikellemus* (1823) and *Metamora, or The Last of the Wampanoag* (1829). Historian Jean O'Brien's careful exegesis of what she calls "firsting" and "lasting" in New England history demonstrates how important the vanishing Indian was to American formations. In "firsting," New Englanders claimed to be the first to settle or the first to establish a town; in doing so, they declared themselves to be part of modernity and denied that opportunity to Indians. "Lasting" marked the end of a recognized Indian presence in the land and secured Euro-American ownership and belonging to the land even as it refused the obvious and ongoing lives of Native American peoples and nations in New England. Taken together, these processes reveal how the vanishing Indian was not a cultural, interpretive mistake about Native American populations' vigor but a politically, economically, and racially motivated choice that secured Euro-American dominance and denied Native American literal and figurative presence. Native Americans were understood as literally absent from New England and figuratively absent through the perceived diminishment of Indian blood through interracial marriages. Producing the absence of Indians and policing Indian identity through the creation of a legible Stage Indian occurred differently for male and female Indian characters but was always in service of the same result: removing Indians from America. Pocahontas plays offer a remarkably clear picture of the various ways female Indians vanish.

It is not generally Pocahontas's life that vanishes like that of the dying noble chief or the violent cruel chief; it is her Indianness. In Barker and Bray's *The Indian Princess,* Pocahontas's first entrance comes "from the wood, with bow and arrow, and a flamingo (red bird)."[58] These markers hark directly back to Indian Queen imagery and across the Indian Princess imagery, which was circulating concurrently with this play.[59] E. McClung Fleming's work on the Indian Queen details how it was a personification of the New World, used for hundreds of years in European art and thought, that was routinely depicted wearing feathers, holding weapons, surrounded by wealth, and accompanied by exotic (to Europeans) animals. It evolved into the Indian Princess in the eighteenth century and was closely associated with the thirteen British colonies that eventually declared independence from Britain and then later formed the United States. The Indian Princess was depicted sometimes with bow and arrow, a swarthy complexion, and long, dark hair, accompanied by an alligator or snake, in a skirt of feathers or tobacco leaves or fabric, but always with "one distinguishing detail . . . the feathered headdress."[60] The usage of Indian Princess/Queen iconography to identify Pocahontas to the audience elides the difference between Indigenous peoples and the nation/land of North America. Pocahontas, the redface character, is standing in for the historical figure Matoaka *and* the idea of America. She is, from her first moments onstage, already connecting a historical figure with a conceptual understanding of American history and place. The marker of violence that accompanied the Indian Princess, the bow and arrow, is quickly explained as the hunting tool that felled the exotic bird. The incongruity of a Virginian flamingo is unsurprising, given the history of exotic animals accompanying an Indian Queen or Indian Princess. These visual markers of both her Indianness and her royal status, bow and arrow and flamingo, quickly become opportunities to shed that same Indianness. Pocahontas arrives onstage with a dead bird. It is quickly admired by the other Indian women who have been awaiting her arrival, but Pocahontas uses the dead bird as motivation to stop hunting. "When the bird drops through the branches, tears come into mine eyes. I will no longer use my bow."[61] The marker of violence associated with the Indian race is overcome by her gendered affective response and feelings of pity for the marker of exotic Americanness. She chooses to divest herself of the act of hunting and its material markers and in the process becomes a less visibly Indian woman onstage.

In George Washington Parke Custis's *Pocahontas*, it is not Indian imagery that disappears but Indian spiritual beliefs. On seeing Pocahontas for the first time, with baskets of shells she has gathered, the audience learns that she is extremely impressed by the English ship's landing and its "gallant strangers."[62] But this infatuation with the appearance of the English ship and Englishmen is quickly placed in relationship to a less superficial preference for them. Pocahontas indicates in her conversation that she will refuse to wed the Indian "Prince" her father wants her to marry, because of her Christian faith. She admits to learning of God from a white settler and to being a practicing Christian: "To good father Barclay I owe the knowledge which I have acquir'd of the only true God, whose worship I in secret perform."[63] Although the audience does not witness her Christian worship, and her actions in the play are not labeled as specifically Christian, her statement removes the pagan quality so keenly connected to Indians in American culture. Pocahontas is a practicing Christian, so she is moving away from Indianness, a process overtly discussed later in the play.

In act 4, scene 1 of Owen's play, Pocahontas shares a conversation with her sister, in which she reveals sudden personal changes:

> POCAHONTAS: 'Tis autumn in my soul.
> From day to day my feelings change their hue
> Like to a seared leaf. Thoughts strange and new
> Crowd on my mind. Nomony! thinkest thou
> Woman was made to be the friend of man,
> To share man's confidence—win his respect—
> To be—to be—his EQUAL? That's the word.
> Are not these strange—strange thoughts?
> NOMONY: Alas! dear sister,
> It is not good for Indian maids to dwell
> Among these Yengeese.[64]

The autumnal change Pocahontas identifies within herself is that women should be equal to men. This confession is immediately followed by a warning from her sister that it is not good for "Indian maids" to be around the English, a.k.a. the Yengeese (Yankees). Pocahontas goes on to articulate that the equality of which she speaks is of partnership and deep love. "I am born to aid," she declares, "but not to slave: to stand beside not crouch behind . . . To be the object—not of his desire, in idle moment . . . [but] of his soul's affections."[65] Nomony replies that she is content to prepare food and care for a man's children and fields as their mother did for their father. The conversation abruptly ends there as Pocahontas spurs them on to hunt for deer, and Nomony calls Pocahontas's thoughts "strange and Yengeese phantasies."[66] Pocahontas's desires for equality and affection, for a life beyond servitude and being a man's "vain trinket," and for a place "in a warrior's heart" is specifically and repeatedly connected to proximity to the English.[67] Time spent with Smith and Rolfe and other English colonists is linked to the interior changes Pocahontas identifies. And these changes are in opposition to the gendered expectations of her tribe communicated by her sister. She is changing on the inside to have the thoughts and feelings of an Englishwoman rather than an Indian woman. The whiteness of Pocahontas's thoughts, the alignment with white, English culture, is markedly different from her sister's response to being among the same English. Pocahontas is a unique character in this. She is growing closer to whiteness, outside (saving Smith) and inside (changing religion and thoughts).

In the 1848 Barnes play *The Forest Princess, or Two Centuries Ago*, Pocahontas's Indianness does not vanish; she does. Written as "an historical play, in three parts," the play depicts Pocahontas literally vanishing through her onstage death.[68] In the final act of the play, set in England as Pocahontas is literally dying and figuratively dying to return to her homeland, Pocahontas positions her people as without political agency. When describing England with its "castles, palaces, and abbeys old: like fairy homes," she claims, "No classic lore adorns my native land; but rich redundant nature reigns alone."[69] In contrast to England's obvious history marked by architecture and buildings, Pocahontas claims no history for her own land and by extension her own people. This claim echoes her father's earlier prophetic vision of an extinct Indian race. Indians in Barnes's play came from nowhere with nothing—no history and no past. And they are going nowhere, only to extinction and oblivion.

In the final moments of the play, she falls asleep from exhaustion and has a prophetic vision. Her vision includes the ascension of Washington as father of a country and "by ties of love and language" peace cementing the relationship between England and the United States.[70] Moments later, Smith arrives to tell her that her husband has been proved innocent. She then gives him her thanks, declaring herself "one whose name and race will die Together!"[71] As she dies, Smith assures her that sculptors and painters will preserve her memory and that her story will be honored henceforth. Even though her life and her nation will become extinct, her "name will live for ever!"[72] Pocahontas dies in the last moments of the play, assuring her husband that they will "meet again—above!"[73] In contrast to earlier Pocahontas plays, in which Pocahontas's Indigeneity was reduced or denied, Barnes's play forwards Pocahontas as essentially different from the English and fundamentally unassimilable. Pocahontas's Indigeneity is not denied or constrained. Instead, it is highlighted as a marker of eventual decline and death.

Pocahontas does not survive Barnes's play; her Indigeneity connects her to the supposed fate of all Indians in America—disappearance. Pocahontas literally vanishes with her people.

Whether literal or figurative vanishing, Pocahontas's Indianness is prominent in these Indian (maiden) plays. Thus, disappearance was a marker of redface among male and female Indian characters in the early nineteenth century. The character itself is always in the process of vanishing, whether physically or culturally or racially. The vanishing Indian trope in nineteenth-century American cultural production is often connected to masculine depictions such as James Fenimore Cooper's *Last of the Mohicans* or Edward Curtis's well-known photographs. Pocahontas plays from the era of Indian plays shows us that vanishing, while often connected to masculine representations of violent and violently dying Indians (e.g., Metamora), can also be represented as vanishing identity or nationality and is connected to female gendered depictions. For Barker and Bray, Pocahontas's womanhood was fully developed only when Indigenous womanhood disappeared and was replaced by identifiably English/white womanhood. For Owen, Pocahontas was drawn to the perceived superiority of English/white gender roles, disowning her people's gender roles and therefore significant markers of her racial identity. For Barnes, noted as the most sympathetic and proto-feminist of all the era's Pocahontas playwrights, Pocahontas's Indigeneity was inseparable from her body and her people and therefore she herself vanished by the end of the play.[74] Vanishing Indianness in women is a quality of being Indian on the nineteenth-century stage. Even as Pocahontas always rushes to save John Smith, she is also always disappearing. She is at once hypervisible and invisible, standing in front of Smith while her Indianness becomes harder and harder to see.

POCAHONTAS FOR LAUGHS

In the second half of the nineteenth century, still more Pocahontas plays appeared, although fewer than would crop up around the tricentennial of Jamestown's founding celebrated in 1907. The later nineteenth-century Pocahontas plays were often more comedic and took themselves far less seriously as history plays. They were intent on parodying or spoofing earlier Pocahontas plays or merely using Pocahontas as a familiar vehicle to entertain audiences with topical and/or witty dialogue or songs. These are not serious dramas or even frothy melodramas. They are not intent on depicting History with a capital H. Nor are they thinking carefully about the relationship between the vanishing Indian and the ongoing American project. However, what they do offer is a Stage Indian who relies even more clearly on instant racial legibility within a distinctly historical context. In addition, the sustained use of dramatic license to create Pocahontas plays that serve the aesthetic needs of the moment continued to connect the historical and real figure of Matoaka to the imagined and mythic Pocahontas, who could then appear in a burlesque comedy, a serious history play, or eventually in a cartoon with a racoon for a best friend.

John Brougham's burlesque of the Pocahontas story premiered in 1855 at the Lyceum Theatre in New York City and successfully played in America and later in England with publications in 1856 and 1870 following these productions.[75] In the United States, it was titled *An Original Aboriginal Erratic Operatic Semi-Civilized and Demi-Savage Extravaganza, being a Per-Version of ye Trewe and Wonderrefulle Hystorie of ye Rennownned Princesse, Po-Ca-Hon-Tas: or, The Gentle Savage.*[76] Several years before, in 1847, Brougham's burlesque of *Metamora* also appeared onstage and later in print.[77] Brougham's Pocahontas, as a burlesque of Pocahontas plays, was explicitly and overtly disinterested in historical accuracy. Its dramatis personae included descriptions of Captain John Smith, who was "in love with Pocahontas, according to *this* story, though somewhat at variance with *his* story," and Mynheer Rolff, who was in this show German, as "the real Husband of Pocahontas, but dramatically divorced contrary to all law and fact."[78] Po-Ca-Hon-Tas was acknowledged to be "married, according to the ridiculous dictum of actual circumstance, to Master Rolff," but in his play, Brougham flattered himself that she was "much more advantageously disposed of."[79] In Brougham's play, historical fact was a constraint to free oneself from and to poke fun at.

Another way Brougham mocked history and expectations of historical accuracy was through his approach to naming characters. He described Pow-Ha-Tan, Pocahontas's father, as "King of the Tuscaroras," a decidedly different Native American nation from the Powhatan tribes that Pocahontas actually came from. Four "Medicine Men, of the Saultz and Senna-ca Tribe" are included in the character list, again connecting the Pocahontas story to the wrong nation. The Seneca, like the Tuscarora, are part of the Haudenosaunee confederation, often referred to as the Iroquois. Names for the minor Indian characters did not attempt to connect to reality and were all jokes. The four "Medicine Men" had names referring to medicinal substances like "Ip-pah-kak" (ipecac) and "Kod-liv-Royl" (cod liver oil). Po-Ca-Hon-Tas's female companions, fellow students at Tusacarora Finishing Institution (more Haudenosaunee references), had descriptive phrases for names: "Lum-Pa-Shuga" (lump of sugar), "Luv-lie-Kreeta" (lovely creature), "Oso-char-ming" (oh so charming). For Brougham, names were an opportunity to make a joke or to make unexpected connections. Accuracy was never the motivating force for his burlesques.

Brougham explicitly distanced his play from history in part to comment on the perceived relationship between history and myth in Pocahontas plays. Scholar Zoe Detsi-Dimanti contends that Brougham's play "exposes the emptiness of the romanticized version of the encounter between Pocahontas and the English colonizers . . . and the American playwrights' license to distort the facts in any way they pleased."[80] Creating a new, decidedly inaccurate, version of the Pocahontas story poked fun at the plays that took Pocahontas seriously, especially when they justified their own inaccuracies with aesthetic appeals to dramatic license. Brougham recognized that dramatic license and historical inaccuracy traveled together in redface. He openly mocked the tensions between historical accuracy and the dramatic myths of Pocahontas, explicitly naming the ongoing controversy over historical accuracy outside the theater and the melodramatic story inside the theater. In scene 2 of the first act, John Smith declares his love for Pocahontas, and in rhyming couplets, the standard language pattern for this play, he asks her to marry him. She believes that her father would not allow their marriage, but she also brings up another impediment:

> POCA. Stop! One doubt within my heart arises!
> A great historian before us stands,
> *Bancroft* himself, you know, forbid the *banns*!
> SMITH. *Bancroft* be *ban*ished from your memory's shelf,
> For spite of *fact* I'll marry you myself.[81]

The historical accuracy of the Pocahontas story, both her supposed rescue of John Smith and her supposed romantic relationship with him, were subjects of debate across the nineteenth-century. Early in the century, historians such as George Bancroft presented Smith's telling of the rescue as historically accurate but eventually modified their understanding of the historical record to raise significant suspicions of its accuracy.[82] In Brougham's play, Pocahontas brings up Bancroft as forbidding the marriage, or more precisely the banns, a practice of publicly announcing an upcoming wedding. This is a veiled reference to the settled historical fact of her marriage to John Rolfe. Smith dismisses the contemporaneous Bancroft reference and insists that he will marry her in spite of fact. Shortly after this exchange, the two sing a short duet that ends with the phrase "For *chang*ing the current of History would certainly be *divert*ing."[83] These characters knowingly engage with history as a series of fixed events that they are obliged to repeat in the story, but they also see history as an evolving and human-created understanding of the past. In telling a historical inaccurate story, or at least a story that holds loosely onto historical accuracy, the play highlights how facts are manipulated in service of the Stage Indian.

Brougham understood that the historical fact of Pocahontas's existence plus the dramatic license playwrights employed resulted in a culturally legible Stage Indian figure that was ripe to use for all sorts of aesthetic ends. Brougham's play illustrates how remarkably flexible the Stage Indian could be and how little connection to reality was required to make it legible as an Indian. Any nation would do; no history was needed, and individual identity existed for playwright punch lines, not for Indigenous humanity. However, even he could not create an Indian with no ties to reality. When he overtly divorced his character from historical accuracy, he still persisted in connecting that character to history and historical debates.

Pocahontas's story was made into another comic play thirty years later by playwright Welland Hendrick. His two-act burlesque operetta *Pocahontas* published in 1886 also contained "full directions for presentation, costumes, properties, etc., etc."[84] Hendrick's *Pocahontas* employs aesthetic and dramaturgical techniques similar to Brougham's work, such as humor, popular tunes with new lyrics, contemporary cultural references, and the interpolation of other ethnic and racial stereotypes. Just as Brougham included a German Rolff to include ethnic-humor jokes, Hendrick includes an African American servant to John Smith whose characterization, language, and banjo playing are taken directly out of blackface minstrelsy. Like Brougham, Hendrick creates distance between history and narrative and relies even more heavily on a legibly Indian figure to tell his story. The freedom with which American artists approach Pocahontas as raw material for their aesthetic and dramaturgical projects continues to connect historical reality with contemporary construction and circulation of a racialized Indian. This is most overtly seen in the costume suggestions provided for the play.

The costume list for the show and the included "hints for easily made scenery and costumes" offer a vivid picture of how generic the Stage Indian was by the late nineteenth century and how easy it was to communicate racial identity through a collection of visual markers. The costume list lumps all Indian characters into one category with slight distinctions for those who play leading and supporting roles, while still insisting on connection to historical facts:

> Indians.—Ideal costumes after styles shown in historic cuts; blankets when entering for second chorus in Act I; elaborate dress for Powhatan and Pocahontas; braves in full paint; Pocahontas slightly painted; in Act II, large fur cloak.[85]

Hendrick seemingly cannot conceive of the fictive Indian figure, the one he is co-constructing, as purely fictive. It must be connected, even tangentially, to actual Native Americans. Ideally, the Indian costumes will reflect actual and historical Indian dress. But in the absence of the ideal, the legible will suffice. The hints for making these legible if not historically accurate costumes offer a fuller picture of how the Stage Indian was deployed even as the names of Pocahontas and Powhatan were invoked. A brief discussion on Indian costuming brings to light how accessible these visible markers of Indianness were:

> Imitation buckskin can be made of flesh-colored underwear. Cut strips of black, orange and red calico four inches broad and slit for fringe. Place this fringe the length of sleeves and breeches. For cheap skirts for braves take

> burlap from twelve to twenty inches broad and ravel for fringe. Moccasins are easily found or imitated. Cover everything with beads, bright buttons, and anything gaudy. For head dress cut pasteboard crown piece to fit, sew outside, thickly, long feathers; cover with bright calico. Inside sew black yarn trimmed to hang down at right length for hair.[86]

There was no expectation of cultural expertise or craft-making to depict an accurate representation of a specific tribal/national dress. There was simply an invitation for a heavy-handed and reductive representation that would be easily read by audiences as racially Indian.

Buckskin with fringe covered Indian bodies. Braves wore loincloths. Moccasins were so easy as to be hardly worth mentioning. And everything Indian should be decorated with bright colors and ornamentation. The feathered headdress once again appears as extremely important to portraying a convincing Indian, worth devoting two sentences out of the total eight in this section, one quarter of the time allotted for Indian costume construction. This version of the feathered headdress was made to fit the specific actor, likely the Powhatan character, and had long, black hair built in. The costume list indicated that the braves should be in full paint, with Pocahontas only "slightly painted."[87] The reason Pocahontas was slightly painted is pivotal to the plot and openly discussed in the play.

In Hendrick's version of the play, Pocahontas is actually not the daughter of Powhatan. She is his niece. Her real parents are Powhatan's brother and a white woman left by "a tribe of whites" that had come "many years ago" across "the great waters."[88] When her parents died, leaving their infant daughter, named Rebecca, Powhatan stepped in and raised his niece as his own. The revelation of this story to John Smith by Powhatan is the setup for a joke, an explanation for her attraction to a white man, and the justification for a later plot point. After she is revealed as a "half-breed," the blackface character, Mahogany, jokes in stereotypical dialect about her being left to Powhatan's care, "Poked her on *you*, did dey? O, I see, dat's why you call her Pok-er-on-us."[89] Mahogany's aside to amuse the audience with wordplay is followed by John Smith's pronouncement, "It's not strange then that she likes the whites."[90] Having clarified why an Indian woman would marry a white man, the play is prepared for the disguised identity plot point. Rolfe works with Pocahontas and Smith's fiancée, Ann Elizabeth Brown, described in the character list as "a practical blonde," to change coats during the Indian engagement dance. The dance cements the parties to a future marriage, so when Smith dances with the woman in Pocahontas's fur cloak, he believes that he is set to wed Pocahontas. But the grand reveal of the women in coats shows that Pocahontas was dressed in Ann's and vice versa. This ensures that Pocahontas marries (the historically accurate) John Rolfe, and the frothy comedy ends with John Smith also delightfully married to a young woman.

Smith's inability to tell the difference between an Indian woman wearing a cloak and a white woman wearing a cloak is forgivable given that Pocahontas was understood to be half white, which is in part why she is to be only "slightly painted" and had already been noted as "the fairest of Indian girls" and more like "Spanish beauties" by John Smith himself.[91] Pocahontas is depicted by Hendricks as a mixed-race and nearly white-passing Indian, although she is still bound in some degree to historical fact. This fanciful and fictive Stage Indian is malleable for narrative and comedic purposes. Although she is shaped by dramatic license, she is never entirely inseparable from a real, historical person.

Both of these comedic Pocahontas plays illustrate how Pocahontas as *the* female Stage Indian persisted in circulation and modification throughout the nineteenth century. They demonstrate how redface connects race and gender in embodied instantiations of the Indian and how even when gendering and racializing the Indian, redface insists on historicizing. Seen through Pocahontas, the Stage Indian can move further and further away from attempts at (or sometimes just gestures toward) accuracy and in doing so move more deeply into a flattened, racial identity that relies on visual markers that are themselves disconnected from accuracy. Being legibly Pocahontas onstage was being legibly Indian and legibly historical, although not legibly Powhatan/Pumunkey. The preoccupation of redface with history is not just an aesthetic or ideological preference of American theater artists. Instead, it is the pathway through which the imagined Indian and the embodied Stage Indian are perceived as an actual Indian, a real Indian with a real body. To fully understand the stakes of redface, the stakes of bodies being legible as Indian, one must understand the stakes of being an Indian in the United States.

* * *

On the first day of the Native American Women's Theater conference in 1999, seven playwrights and three scholars gathered for an informal discussion.[95] They spoke about the writing process, Indigenous storytelling structure in light of continued expectations for Western theatrical conventions, themes and perspectives meaningful to the playwrights, the challenges of communicating the spirituality intrinsic to Indigenous theater, and goals for publication and production of the various artists involved. Toward the end of the conversation, several playwrights issued challenges to American theater and to its predominantly white theatergoing public:

> JudyLee Oliva: "It seems to me like everyone wants to print our plays in anthologies, but no one wants to do them. . . . I want to get up on stage so they can experience it, so we don't have to maybe come and define it and analyze it but just be there."[96]
>
> Vera Manuel: "I feel like white people have to work harder to understand, why should we have to . . . [define] ourselves in the white context.[?] Why don't they work harder to understand it?"[97]
>
> Marcie Rendon: "Instead of us having to do it, why don't the white people work harder to get it, and work harder to bring in Native performers, and educate audiences . . . [it would] become your [their] responsibility."[98]

The labor these Native American women ask for is challenging and resource intensive. It is disruptive to systems and individuals and deeply

95 Diane Glancy (Cherokee descent), LeAnne Howe (Choctaw), Victoria Kneubuhl (Hawaiian/Samoan), Vera Manuel (Secwepemc-Ktunaxa), Monique Mojica (Kuna/Rappahannock), JudyLee Oliva (Chickasaw descent), and Marcie Rendon (White Earth Anishinaabe) joined Shirley Hutson-Findley, Rebecca Howard, and Paul Jackson in the ranging conversation. The transcript of this discussion is available through the NAWPA digital collection at https://spec.lib.miamioh.edu/home/wp-content/uploads/2015/07/nawpa_roundtable.pdf.

96 Page 13 of discussion transcript found at "Roundtable," Native American Women Playwrights Archive, accessed November 3, 2023, https://spec.lib.miamioh.edu.

97 Page 11 of discussion transcript found at "Roundtable," Native American Women Playwrights Archive.

98 Page 14 of discussion transcript found at "Roundtable," Native American Women Playwrights Archive.

transformative. Fortunately, it is also not solitary; nor is it without beauty or discovery. Instead of *Metamora*, American audiences could have grappled with the legacy of war, colonization, and racism in Apess's oratory. Instead of watching a fictive Pocahontas, they could have been asking questions of the women who traveled and performed across the United States and Europe, like Maungwudaus's wife before her untimely death. Instead of a Wild West show demonstrating victory over Indian savages, they could have been watching the first known published play by a Native American woman, *Wep-Ton-No-Mah: The Indian Mail Carrier* (1892) by Go-won-go Mohawk and Charlie Charles.[99] Instead of looking for the Indian they recognized, they could have been learning to recognize Will Rogers as the Cherokee performer he told them he was. Instead of a fictive Sitting Bull next to a feminist(?) Annie Oakley, they could have been watching Indigenous feminist theater created by Spiderwoman Theater. There has always been an "instead" of redface. It is up to audiences to choose a *hinushi inla*.

99 Gowongo Mohawk and Charlie Charles, *Wep-Ton-Nno-Mah: The Indian Mail Carrier* (1892) is available in the Manuscript Plays Collection, Library of Congress Copyright Office drama deposits, 1863–1973 and digitized at thepeopleandthetext.ca. "Go-Won-Go Mohawk," The People and the Text, accessed November 22, 2023, https://thepeopleandthetext.ca.

LEGAL STAKES OF INDIANNESS

The Stage Indian is a racialized theatrical character used for centuries by American theater artists to communicate a generic Indian identity. However, theater is not the only or the sole realm in which Native Americans are racialized. The process by which the Stage Indian is racialized and Native Americans are racialized as members of a supposed Indian race are nearly identical. Native Americans' bodies are connected to ideas of a stable race, historical events/context/figures, gendered and raced categories, and vanishing Indianness. Additionally, legal rather than dramatic license is deployed to justify racial continuity rather than admit to racial formation. These mirror processes fold in on one another and are used by and against Native Americans to navigate the confounding but inescapable space of being labeled a race and nations.

Native Americans are and are not a race in the United States. The Bureau of Indian Affairs within the Department of the Interior serves "American Indians and Alaska Natives."[92] The nomenclature refers to geography (America or Alaska) and a racialized grouping of Indians/Natives. The United States Census Bureau tracks data on American Indians and Alaska Natives as a single race.[93] Countless forms where boxes are checked to self-identify with a race include "American Indian" or "Native American." Indian is a race. Cries of racism rightfully surround popular depictions of Native Americans from Chief Wahoo to Tonto.[94] But Indian is more than a race. It is also a political identity entrenched in US law from the Constitution onward. It is a history of treaties, government-to-government relationships, and (often severely constrained) sovereign nations.

Even as the United States Census Bureau counts Indians as a race, it also manages "Intergovernmental Affairs" with Indigenous nations.[95] Access to Indian Health Service services are limited to "members of federally recognized tribes," and the rights to these services "grew out of the special government-to-government relationship between the federal government and Indian tribes."[96] The US federal government interacts with Native Americans as individuals possessing a specific racial identity at the same time that it interacts with tribal governments as sovereign nations, thereby declaring that Indians are a race and comprise many (national) political identities. This is not a contradiction. It is a fact constructed, as many facts are, through cultural, social, and political praxis, coupled with ideological and intellectual interpretations.

The political identity of Native Americans has long troubled European and Euro-American people and organizations. If Indians are an inferior race, a view with widespread support among "civilized" people of European descent for centuries, then their presence on the continent could only imperil for a moment the imperial advancement of colonialism, settler colonialism, and Manifest Destiny so heartily enacted by generations of settlers and those whom Afro-Caribbean poet Kamau Brathwaite termed arrivants (i.e., enslaved peopled with far less agency in choosing their actions).[97] Indians were and continue to be racialized as part of a political project that interprets and shapes the world for the benefit of settler colonialism.

However, Indian as a political identity, based on membership to a sovereign nation with inherent legal, especially land-based, rights, has also furthered the American settler-colonial project. Creating treaties between sovereigns gave legitimacy to a fledgling country in the late eighteenth century and, perhaps more importantly, justified the morality of invading and ruling a land not their own. Indians are a polity because the United States has invited them to be, in the image of European sovereigns. The fact that Native American sovereignty is caught up and tainted by European conceptions of nationhood and rights is an ongoing concern within Native nations and the Native community and is beyond the scope of this book.[98] While this book takes on redface as a theatrical praxis of racialization, it also and equally asserts that redface is a political praxis precisely because it racializes Indigenous peoples, which is an imperative task for the US national conscience and national project.

Legibility as an Indian is an ongoing concern for Native Americans and is a double-edged sword. Being legibly racialized as an Indian can come with discrimination, racism, and oppression. However, it can also bring attention, access to resources, and legal rights. It is no wonder that so many Indigenous theater artists worked to accept or deny their Indigenous identity and that so many non-Indigenous artists saw achieving legibility as an Indian as an advantageous professional and personal goal. And it is no wonder that Native Americans for two centuries have found it essential to perform an Indian identity and appearance to successfully navigate the settler-colonial environment through which they move.

Even before the United States existed, being legibly Indian, that is being recognized by non-Natives as Indian, particularly though not exclusively because of visual appearance, was sometimes a benefit and sometimes a detriment to Native Americans. Historian Jenny Hale Pulsipher's account of John Wompas/White, a Nipmuc man from the Massachusetts area who moved between identifying as Indian and English in the mid-seventeenth century, provides a glimpse of the possibilities and limitations for Indigenous people at a moment when "skin color began to replace culture as the defining element in being an Indian."[99] Wompas's death in 1679 revealed a time when the world "began to demand that people who looked like Indians *be* Indians." While identifying as Indian allowed Wompas considerable freedom to sell land and profit from his real estate dealings, after King Philip's War he had to contend with significant, race-based constraints. After the war, those recognized as Indian by colonists were "confined to five, later three, Praying Towns."[100] They were also "prohibited from carrying guns in the presence of the English," which extended to disarming themselves when encountering English hunters in the woods, and they were "banned from English towns."[101] The economic and practical impact of these race-based policies were significant. Over time, when Indians began to be allowed back in cities like Boston, they were often servants, and by the end of the eighteenth century, after the United States was founded, they were prohibited from intermarrying with whites.[102] Access to land, the ability to freely move and engage in trade, and the opportunity to build family and kinship networks were drastically curtailed because of race. Looking like an Indian in the seventeenth century and beyond could come with high costs but also high value.

In 1806, the Virginia Supreme Court handed down a decision in *Hudgins v. Wrights* that affirmed that several generations of women in one family were in fact Indian and therefore not subject to slavery. This case, which scholars such as Ian F. Haney-López have written persuasively about, rests on evidence supporting the women's claims to Indian rather than Black ancestry.[103] The evidence was almost entirely their personal appearance. The youngest woman was noted to have "the characteristic features, the complexion, the hair and eyes . . . the same with those of whites."[104] Another one of the women was described as having "long black hair, was of the right Indian copper colour, and was generally called an Indian by the neighbours."[105] The judges decided that the women were indeed Indians and not African descended precisely because of their appearance. One of the judges declared that those of African descent possessed "two characteristic marks," the shape of nose and texture of hair, and that because the women in question had "long, straight, black hair of the native aborigines of this country," it proved they were not of African descent.[106] He went on to give a hypothetical in which someone with characteristic African features, another "copper-coloured person with long jetty black, straight hair," and a third "one with a fair complexion, brown hair" were before a judge and that judge had no other evidence as to racial identity other than the people themselves. In his view, in that situation, a judge should "judge from his own view."[107] The judge should use his own eyes and determine racial classification on the basis of visual markers of race each person displayed. For these Virginian women, looking like an Indian was the difference between a life of freedom and a life of enslavement. This judge's reasoning illustrates succinctly the way that identifying bodies as legibly Indian could greatly benefit individuals. Racial legibility could harm and help those recognized as Indian.

The nineteenth century brought contradictory forms of legal legibility to Native Americans. In 1823, the US Supreme Court decided in *Johnson v. McIntosh* that Indian nations could sell lands only to national governments and that no individual Indian had the right to sell land. This made complete sense to the court given "that discovery [by the 'great nations of Europe'] gave title to the government by whose subjects or by whose authority it [discovery] was made."[108] This reasoning, resting on the centuries-old Doctrine of Discovery, contended that

Indians did not own title to land in the same way Europeans did. They had the right to occupancy but not an absolute right to title after Europeans "discovered" the land. As Chief Justice John Marshall explained, "The character and religion" of Indians "afforded an apology" for European discoverers to consider the Indians "as a people over whom the superior genius of Europe might claim an ascendancy."[109] Simply put, Indians were historically understood as a race inferior to Europeans, so Europeans could discover and own the land.

Shortly after this decision, the Marshall court handed down another foundational decision to federal Indian law (Indian is the legal term) that rested not entirely on racial inferiority but on constrained sovereign nationhood. In *Cherokee v. Georgia*, decided in 1831, Chief Justice John Marshall wrote that Indian nations were "domestic dependent nations" and that the Cherokee nation named in the suit was in fact "a state . . . a distinct political society, separated from others, capable of managing its own affairs and governing itself."[110] Going further, he proclaimed that the Cherokee "have been uniformly treated as a state from the settlement of our country."[111] The Supreme Court again turned to history and precedent in determining how to approach the question at hand. Given that the Supreme Court of the United States and decades of case law has been invested in understanding the legal rights, responsibilities, and status of Indians, it might be surprising to learn that it was not until the 1879 case *Standing Bear v. Crook* that US courts finally and definitively decided that Indians were legally persons.[112] Throughout the nineteenth century, Native Americans had to navigate a legal system that recognized them as members of nations, as racially inferior, and, at least for several decades, as not legal persons, all while their present existence was routinely compared to the past.

As the Supreme Court and US case law were determining the legal and political implications of being an Indian, the federal government was also busy recording who was legibly Indian in a different sphere, the census. The United States' decennial census was a place that the government tried out, modified, and standardized the racial and gender logics that were (and are) in continuous formation. Beginning in 1790, the census did not originally count Indians, but by 1860, Indians who had renounced tribal authority and lived under state or territorial laws were enumerated, or counted. There were few instructions for census enumerators to determine the racial identity of the individuals they counted. In fact, until after the 1950 census, "the race of an individual was determined by the enumerator."[113] Occasionally, the government provided some direction, but it was inconsistent, sometimes contradictory, and difficult to enforce. In 1870, people "reported as 'Half-breeds'" when found living among "whites, adopting their habits of life and methods of industry," were to be counted as white.[114] Those living among Indian communities were to be counted as Indian. Instructions for the 1880 and 1890 censuses focused not just on Indians' living situation but also on whether they were "residing in white families, engaged as servants or laborers," or living "on the outskirts of towns or settlements."[115] By 1900, instructions for determining who was an Indian diminished, and only indications for what should be written in the "Color or race" column appeared, such as "Write 'W' for white . . . 'In' for Indian."[116] In the 1940 instructions for census enumerators, Indians were to include those of "mixed white and Indian blood" if they were "enrolled on an Indian Agency or Reservation roll," if their blood quantum was one-quarter or more, or if the community in which they lived regarded them as an Indian.[117] For those mixed-race individuals with both Indian and Black (the census used a different word) ancestors, the instructions indicated that they should be recorded as Black, "unless the Indian blood greatly predominates and he is universally accepted in the community as an Indian."[118] However, the abridged version of those instructions simply stated, "Any mixtures of white and nonwhite blood should be recorded according to the race of the nonwhite parent."[119] It is difficult to say just what criteria enumerators used when they determined what blood quantum an Indian did or did not possess, whether a person had white or nonwhite parents, whether they had adopted the "habits of life" of whites, and, in the case of people who were deemed mixed race with Indian and Black parentage, just how Indian blood might "predominate." In short, the US census demanded that enumerators be proficient in recognizing an Indian without fully and consistently defining what an Indian was. In the absence of clear instructions, enumerators, as the judge had a hundred years earlier, very likely judged simply from their own view. The Stage Indian was a rehearsal for just this skill of instant and authoritative recognition of an Indian. If the person looked like an Indian and the audience/enumerator interpreted them as an Indian, they likely were counted as an Indian.

As these race-judging enumerators worked across the decades recording people's races, they also recorded people's genders. The instructions for enumerators on how to record genders were far more straightforward than the sometimes complex racial ones. "Column 9. Sex.—Write 'M' for male and 'F' for female," declared the 1920 enumerator instructions.[120] Seventy years earlier, the 1850 enumerators received much the same instruction: "Insert the letter M for male, and F for female, opposite the name, in all cases, as the fact may be."[121] The 1880 enumerator instructions explained how seriously the US Census Bureau took the information on age, color, and sex, warning enumerators, "No returns will be accepted where these spaces are left blank."[122] For census enumerators, sex and gender were identical binary categories that all people, Indian or not, would fall into. This is an example of what literary scholar Mark Rifkin might call an effort to make Indians "straight," "to insert indigenous peoples into Anglo-American conceptions of family, home, desire, and personal identity."[123] Insisting on confining Indians to a binary understanding of gender denies the rich history of genders other than "male" and "female" within Native American nations.[124] Confining Indians to male or female was more than a gendering project; it was also a colonial project. As Rifkin explained, "The effort to insert American Indians into the ideological system of heterosexuality [and the gender confines it presupposes] imposes an alien social logic while also discounting the particular ways family and household formation are central to native peoples' functioning as polities."[125] Forcing Native Americans to subscribe to white American ideas of gender, sexuality, and family structures, all categories of information that were recorded on a census, enumerators participated in the dismantling of Indigenous nations.

A final example of Indian legibility in US governance and law shows the impact of racialized thinking to support white American investments in Indianness as a vanishing property and the continued importance of Pocahontas to American history. In 1924, the state of Virginia passed its Racial Integrity Act in an effort to more narrowly define the white race and more completely control marriages in the state.[126] The statute created a registration system in which each Virginian would register their race, marriage licenses would be issued only after assurance of the individuals' races, and white people could not marry nonwhite people.[127] The definition of "white person" was quite narrow and insisted on absolute racial purity, "the person who has no trace whatsoever of any blood other than Caucasian."[128] Yet the definition went on to carve out an exception: "Persons who have one-sixteenth or less of the blood of the American Indian and have no other non-Caucasian blood shall be deemed to be white persons."[129] This was what has come to be called the "Pocahontas Exception." This exception, as historians have insisted for decades, was specifically designed to "protect the racial status of Virginia's leading families who were the descendants of Pocahontas and John Rolfe and other early settler-Indian marriages from being categorized as blacks."[130] The pride Virginians took in being descended from Pocahontas was culturally meaningful, and legislators worked to protect the social status of those descendants, some of whom were within their own ranks. Without the Pocahontas Exception, the act "could have 'outed' no less than sixteen legislators who thought of themselves as White."[131] The Pocahontas Exception was not available to any other racial group and was explicitly denied to those of African ancestry. If a person had a Black ancestor, they were to be counted as Black, no matter the number or kind of other races they might also represent. Blackness was understood to persist indefinitely, while Indianness would be watered down through intermixture with whiteness and eventually become so insignificant as to no longer classify a person as Indian. According to the Racial Integrity Act, Indian blood vanished though intermixture, and what was left was white people who could claim status through a connection to a historical Indian woman. Race, gender, and history worked together to ensure that Indianness remained legible to white America, but only through a settler-colonial logic of elimination.[132] The logic of elimination and its imaginative iteration, the vanishing Indian, were more than an ideological experiment; they were also a material process in Virginia that denied Indigeneity to Indigenous peoples.

(*Continued from page 176*)

in their work by decolonizing and indigenizing Shakespeare. Many Native American theater artists are comfortable on both stage and screen, like Delanna Studi (Cherokee) and Lily Gladstone (Siksikaitsitapi/Blackfeet and Nimíipuu/Nez Perce descent). While not reaching parity with Euro-American theater artists, Native American theater in the twenty-first century is dynamic, active, and growing in visibility and impact. This is perhaps unsurprising, because its history actually began long before the 1970s.

The story of Native American theater history is not one of sudden birth in the fertile soil of the post–Vietnam War, post–American Indian Civil Rights Act, self-determination era. Although intimately connected to the significant shifts in US federal policy toward Indigenous peoples and nations that are beyond the scope of this book, the rise of Native American theater did not depend only on federal policy and changing social values. It also reflected decades of knowledge and practice by Indigenous theater artists across commercial theatrical stages and spaces. Cherokee author and playwright Lynn Riggs's play *Green Grow the Lilacs*, which hit the stage in January 1931, was the first known work of an Indigenous playwright produced on Broadway, over ninety years before Larissa FastHorse became the first known female Indigenous playwright there.[15] Despite a modest run of sixty-four performances, Riggs's play was adapted into the hit musical *Oklahoma!* a decade later.[16] In 1938, the opera *The Sun Dance*, cowritten by Zitkala-Ša (also known as Gertrude Bonin), was presented as the opera of the year by the New York Opera Guild.[17] Performers like Te Ata (also known as Mary Fisher) and Princess White Deer (also known as Esther Deer) were active on stages throughout the early decades of the twentieth century, appearing across the United States and Europe in events as ostentatious as the *Ziegfeld Follies*, as weighty as state dinners, and as streamlined as a one-woman show.[18] As historian Christine Bold has carefully detailed, many more Indigenous performers filled vaudeville circuits across the continent in the late nineteenth and early twentieth centuries.[19] Indigenous theater artists had already been contributing to American theater culture for decades before the rapid innovation of the 1970s.

15 Information on the production can be found at "Green Grow the Lilacs-Broadway Play—Original," IBDB, accessed November 21, 2023, https://www.ibdb.com.
16 *Oklahoma!* opened in March 1943 and ran on Broadway for five years. "Oklahoma!," *IBDB*, https://www.ibdb.com/broadway-production/oklahoma-1285.
17 Hafen, "A Cultural Duet."
18 "Musical Plays Monopolize Broadway Premieres Next Week," *Women's Wear* 22, no. 30 (February 5, 1921): 12.
19 For more see Bold, "*Vaudeville Indians*."

(*Continued on page 59*)

One of the statute's strongest proponents illustrates the impact of putting ideas of the vanishing Indian into action, of demanding that Indians be legible using criteria determined by white Americans. The Racial Integrity Act was championed by the Anglo-Saxon Clubs of America, eugenicist-minded clubs devoted to racial purity and not incidentally white supremacy. Mika Endo's excellent work on one of the Clubs' cofounders, Walter Plecker, has shown how he was in a position to enforce the statute after its passage. He served as Virginia's registrar of the Bureau of Vital Statistics from 1912 to 1945.[133] Both a strong supporter of eugenics and a Virginia state official, Plecker brought his particular disgust for interracial admixture to his work. Writing in the Virginia Department of Health's *Health Bulletin*, he explained the need for the new act on racial integrity. He estimated that "10,000 to 20,000 possibly more, near white people, who are known to possess an intermixture of colored blood" were pushing to "declare themselves" white, to demand "the admittance of their children into the white schools," and to intermarry "with white people."[134] But, he went on to caution, "these persons . . . are not white in reality."[135] He asserted that "racial measures" must be used "to prevent" this racial intermixture including making "impossible" marriage between whites and nonwhites, encouraging the public "to look with scorn and contempt upon" those that choose interracial marriages, and using "clerks who issue marriage licenses, and the school authorities" as barriers between the "danger" of racial intermixture and "the safety of the Commonwealth."[136] Plecker's deeply anti-Black beliefs led him to prevent "Indians from being categorized as white by denying their birth and marriage certificates" because he "assumed that all Indians had vanished through their mixture with blacks."[137] In a 1947 booklet he authored called *Virginia's Vanished Race*, he claimed that state, federal, war, and other records showed "that there is not now living a person of Virginia ancestry, claiming, or reputed, to be Indian, who is not" mixed with African descent also.[138]

Because of his deeply held belief that anyone with a drop of African-descended blood was Black and his deeply held belief that all Indians in Virginia had intermarried with people of African descent, Plecker believed that all Indians in Virginia were actually Black. The idea of the vanishing Indian supported both the Pocahontas Exception (that

Indian blood gets watered down until it does not even count as Indian anymore) and the denial of Indigeneity for those deemed mixed race (that Blackness overpowers Indianness until Indianness does not even count as Indian anymore). Plecker's unique position of power coupled with his deeply held racial and racist beliefs resulted in material consequences for Indigenous people in Virginia. As historian Mika Endo has noted, "Until he retired in 1946 Plecker continued to refuse any application that listed an applicant as Indian."[139] His actions "separated Indian families and tribes," caused Indigenous Virginians to leave Virginia, and "made it difficult for tribes in Virginia to gain state and federal tribal recognition."[140] Plecker's criteria for legitimate and legible Indianness was so restricted to a racial purity that existed only in the historical past that he refused any possibility of modern Indigenous peoples. In this way, Indian legibility became an impossible goal for Indigenous peoples. The racial, historical, and legal (though still dramatic) license that Plecker took ensured that the Indian and the Stage Indian were never far from one another. Both demanded those performing it to align with audience expectations and to modify those performances to obtain audience recognition, permission, and acceptance. Pocahontas onstage and Pocahontas as an authenticating ancestor are both filtered through a gendered, racialized, historicized lens that provides ample room for those in positions of power to employ dramatic and legal license in determining the appropriate way to assess an Indian. The Indian as an embodied figure in US entertainment (Stage Indian) and law (legal Indian) rests on its legibility as a race that is politicized and legalized in strict parameters that uphold settler-colonial nationhood.

CONCLUSION

This detour into a few hundred years of legal and political machinations of Indian identity provides a cursory overview of the sometimes paradoxical status of Indians in the United States as both race and polity. What it does not do is reflect a confusion or misunderstanding by governmental agencies, lawyers, judges, or even temporarily employed enumerators, for "the political and racial elements of Indianness are inseparable . . . and hopelessly intertwined."[141] These entities were simply articulating and enacting the racial regimes presupposed and demanded by the US as a settler-colonial nation intent on establishing its legitimacy and authority through its relationship to and dominance of Indigenous nations and land. Racializing Indians as Indian was and remains an essential project for American nationhood.[142] Enshrining into US law, jurisprudence, and even censuses the understanding of Indians as a race was a necessary step in transforming Indigenous nations into racialized individuals who are subsumed into a settler-colonial society. Enshrining Indians in embodied, live performance assists in this process, for making a legible Stage Indian means making the Indian legible in and through bodies.

Recognizing a Stage Indian demands that an audience and actor work together to communicate and interpret racialized information. Pocahontas shows us that racialized information is also gendered information. While the Indian in American culture is most widely recognized as a male, wearing a feathered headdress, perhaps on a horse, likely shirtless, maybe with a bow and arrow or gun, Pocahontas reminds us that this is only one version of the Indian. The Stage Indian is not a singular character but a collection of figures that have the same goal, to present and make legible racialized Indian bodies. These characters connect fact and fiction through their emplacement in historical tales and the dramatic license used to make those tales more exciting or more palatable to American audiences. They reveal that the goal of redface is the Stage Indian, an embodied Indian who is recognizable as such because of their race, gender, context, and characteristics. But American theater artists did more than just create a character type in creating and perpetuating the Stage Indian.

Redface racializes the Stage Indian as an Indian, and because the Indian is the inescapable expectation of the US nation, the Stage Indian became the inescapable expectation for legible Indianness. Historian Christine Bold's investigation of "vaudeville Indians" provides a pointed example of how the Stage Indian as racializing project of Indian legibility onstage creates legible Indianness offstage. Bold includes a litany of Indigenous and non-Indigenous performers, male and female, who wore feathered headdresses and other identifiably Indian visual markers as part of their acts. While feathered headdresses are worn in some Native American nations, they are not ubiquitous, and the most recognizably Indian version, the kind with feathers reaching perhaps to the ground, is particular to nations who inhabit the central plains region of the continent. To be seen as an Indian onstage, one often had to wear a feathered headdress. And sometimes, to be seen as an Indian in the offstage world, one also had to wear a headdress.

Bold notes the experience of Paul K. Diabo, a Mohawk ironworker whose 1928 court case upheld the 1794 Jay Treaty, allowing free passage between Canada and the United States for members of some Indigenous nations. In the Kanien'kehá:ka Onkwawén:na Raotitióhkwa Language and Culture Center (Kanien'kehá:ka/Mohawk of Kahnawà:ke), Bold witnessed an exhibition including the clothing Diabo wore to his important court case, a "fringed, beaded buckskin suit and big feathered headdress" that resembled the "pan-Indian style" of the Wild West shows rather than anything "particularly Iroquoian in design."[143] A librarian and cultural liaison at the center, Teiowí:sonte Thomas Deer, explained that "it was the only way to ensure he would be recognized as 'Indian'" in that time period.[144] Whether being counted in a census, recognized by a court, or identified by an audience, Indian legibility has haunted Native Americans. To be legibly Indian has repeatedly meant participating in the embodied enactment of raced, gendered, and historicized Indianness crystalized by the Stage Indian. This is how a theme-park employee on a winter's day in Florida can be recognized as both a historical figure and a fictional Indian Princess. We know what Indians look like. We know what Indianness is. And we can spot a Pocahontas a mile away. Just look for the long, straight, black hair and "judge from your own view."

CHAPTER THREE

AUTHENTIC INDIANS

"Do you have Native American ancestry?"
"Are you aboriginal?"
"Oh, I see it now, in your face."
"Do you have Native American blood in you?"
"How much are you?"

There is a dance of legibility Native Americans are invited to perform with partners not of their choosing. It has several variations but always the same theme: Are you Indian enough? The above remarks are some of the cues for this dance I have heard at various points in my life. The person who forwards themselves as my partner (more often demanding that I partner with them) is hesitant at first. This is because I look legibly white. My family has not engaged in decades of interracial romance to no effect. I am a byproduct of the whiteness, visible and intangible, that helped shape my family and my world. I can choose to be seen as a Native American woman or a white woman—it is rarely chosen for me. That is my privilege and luxury. It is also why I am a disappointment. I have seen the shoulders sink, the eyes look downward, and the hint of a frown when people hear my fraction. I know that the space between "not that much" and "not enough" is infinitesimal. One is the front door and one the back door, but the room is the same.

How much Indian I am, where I fall on the spectrum of authenticity, is connected to many things in the United States, but chief among them is blood. Ancestry, the suggestion of genetically inherited racial identity, and blood quantum, the suggestion of a substance that can be watered down or diminished, work together in US culture to define and delimit authentic Indianness. Having Native American ancestry is a necessary but not sufficient condition to authentic Indianness. It puts you on the right path, but it doesn't show how close you are to the end of the journey, the goal. Blood quantum is a tool to measure you. If you are full of Indian blood, then you are purely, authentically Indian. Anything less than full, and your authenticity fades as your fraction shrinks. Less than full is less than fully Indian.

Like most Native Americans in the United States, I can tell you my blood quantum in fraction form. For some reason, we do not use decimals or percentages; apparently, it is an inequivalent expression, which is not surprising. Blood quantum is how the United States and many Indigenous nations within US boundaries track the presence and persistence of Indianness. My blood quantum is tracked from what is termed an Original Enrollee in the Choctaw Nation of Oklahoma. My great-grandfather and great-great-grandparents were recorded as members of the Choctaw Nation around the turn of the twentieth century, in what is commonly known as the Dawes Rolls. Because of their names on that roll, I can be a member of our tribe and issued a Certificate Degree of Indian Blood card by the US government (figure 3.1).[1] The US government is, even into the twenty-first century, still in the business of issuing cards officially recording Indian blood, that ubiquitous and phantasmic substance.[2]

My fraction is what it is because of mixed-race relationships. For example, say a Native American man falls in love with and marries a white, Euro-American settler woman. He, as fully Native, sires children who are half Native American.[3] One of his daughters (a half) falls in love with and marries a white, Euro-American settler man. Her children are now one-quarter Native American.[4] You keep that up for a few more generations and the denominators get pretty big and the Indianness gets pretty small.

That is the logic of blood quantum, disappearance. While the desire to enslave people of African descent motivated the logic of Blackness and its persistence in the United States (see the "one-drop rule"), the logic of Indianness as a category is predicated on the anticipated disappearance of Indians. Indians, and therefore Indianness, can and will vanish. But just how much it vanishes can makes a big difference, so it is important to be able to record it. The right fraction is an admission ticket to a lot of

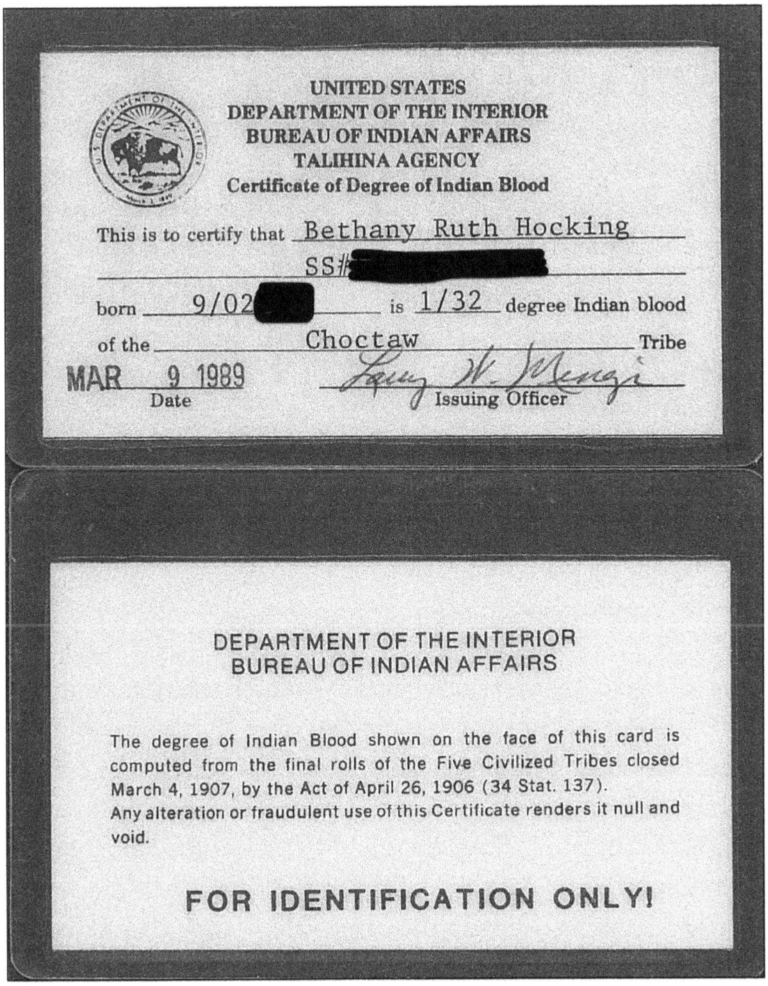

UNITED STATES
DEPARTMENT OF THE INTERIOR
BUREAU OF INDIAN AFFAIRS
TALIHINA AGENCY
Certificate of Degree of Indian Blood

This is to certify that Bethany Ruth Hocking
SS#
born 9/02 is 1/32 degree Indian blood
of the Choctaw Tribe
MAR 9 1989
Date
Issuing Officer

DEPARTMENT OF THE INTERIOR
BUREAU OF INDIAN AFFAIRS

The degree of Indian Blood shown on the face of this card is computed from the final rolls of the Five Civilized Tribes closed March 4, 1907, by the Act of April 26, 1906 (34 Stat. 137).
Any alteration or fraudulent use of this Certificate renders it null and void.

FOR IDENTIFICATION ONLY!

Figure 3.1. The author's Certificate of Degree of Indian Blood card issued to her by the Bureau of Indian Affairs, showing her maiden name, identifying information, tribe, and blood quantum. Image by author.

things. In the 1910s, it was the ticket to Indians' being marked as competent to own title to their own land, a high-stakes event.[5] In my nation, it is the ticket to whether a girl can compete in the Choctaw Nation Princess Pageant, a low-stakes event. For many nations, though not all, it is the ticket to enrollment and tribal citizenship and the rights and privileges that accompany it. It is a useful measurement, a shorthand, that can be used to quickly determine if someone is Indian enough.

But it is not the only measure of belonging, of enough-ness. In Native American communities, discussions over belonging encompass citizenship, kinship, cultural knowledge, language, tradition, location, politics, religion, and more. The supposed clarity of race and blood quantum breaks down in the minutiae of lived experience. The tension over who is Native enough extends far beyond who has the biggest slice of the fractional quantum pie. What does it mean to belong? What does it mean to participate in and contribute to the life of a nation? Of a people? These are questions for a different book. The pressing question now is, What does redface have to do with blood quantum? I return to the legibility dance.

> "Do you have Native American ancestry?"
> "Yes"
> "Oh, how much are you?"
> (Answers may vary)

Sometimes I give my partner what they want, a fraction. Sometimes I avoid the question and answer another one: "I'm a member of the Choctaw Nation of Oklahoma." Sometimes I explain why that question is not the best way to approach someone about their Indigeneity. Sometimes I talk about the failure and harm of blood quantum. No matter my response, I have not changed the dance, just the variation I perform. All my answers do the same thing: appeal to a marker of authenticity, assert that marker's legitimate authority over Indian identity, reveal my allegiance to that authority, and claim power through that authority. This is the rhythm of the legibility dance. The tempo may change, the steps may be simple or complex, but the rhythm stays the same.

* * *

In this chapter, I argue that claims supporting the Stage Indian's authenticity are best understood not as adherence to objective standards but as efforts to create and enforce legible and subjective standards. Attending to the ever-present quest for material or immaterial authenticity in redface allows us to clearly see the connection between racialization of Indigenous people and US settler-colonial assertions of power over Indigeneity. This chapter interrogates explicit and implicit claims to authenticity in redface performance in the nineteenth century, returning to *Metamora* as an example of ethnographic and essentialist interpretations of the Stage Indian and exploring *Buffalo Bill's Wild West* as a space of curatorial interpretation connecting Indigenous bodies with the Stage Indian. I do so to understand how strategies for authenticating Indianness have shifted over time and to demonstrate that authentication is inherent to redface.

By focusing on these extremely popular and influential iterations of the Stage Indian, I shift beyond representation as a subject of inquiry and into the mechanisms that undergird representation. These mechanisms secure authority over Indian identity and have been used by America and Americans across centuries to define, delimit, and police who is Indian, who can be Indian, and who will never be Indian enough. The Stage Indian always stands next to Indigenous people and asks, "How much are you?" Against the measure of redface, the only answer afforded to Indigenous people is, "Never enough."

EDWIN FORREST AND THE GENUINE/DISINGENUOUS INDIAN

Forrest's iconic role, Metamora, provides a vivid illustration of how the Stage Indian always claims to possess authenticity and therefore asserts authority over Indianness. Forrest's performance was understood, at least by some members of his audience, to be an authentic Indian portrayal. These claims to authenticity were routinely supported by evidence of his research into Native American life and lives. Several of his biographers claimed that he had worked to become an expert then implemented his expertise through his theatrical performance. Despite his now debunked claims to knowing Choctaw chief Pushmataha, Forrest could have possibly known *a* Native American.[6] Translating a relationship with a specific individual in a specific place to a different location, time, and tribe was perceived as a perfectly natural leap of logic. He knew one Indian; therefore, he knew them all. Through Metamora, Forrest linked the Stage Indian to both a specific Indigenous person and a generic racialized idea of the Indian. In doing so, he was legibly Indian to his audiences *and* legibly authentic. However, the actual criteria of authenticity clearly reveal Euro-American racial investments. Evidence presented to support Forrest's "authentic" Indian portrayal purports to demonstrate the accuracy and detail displayed in his performance. However, what it actually reveals is that the criteria for authentic Indianness was shaped far less by ethnographic accuracy and far more by racial essentialism and dedication to conceptions of the Indian as hypermasculine, noble, and utterly free.

That Forrest's performance of Metamora was accepted as authentically Indian is well documented by his biographers. William Alger, writing five years after Forrest's death in 1877 in the most detailed and hagiographic biography of Forrest, provides the fullest description of Forrest's Indian authenticity.[7]

> Never did an actor more thoroughly identify and merge himself with his part than Forrest did in Metamora. He was completely transformed from what he appeared in other characters, and seemed Indian in every particular, all through and all over, from the crown of his scalp to the sole of his foot.[8]

James Rees, writing a biography of Forrest a few years before Alger in 1874, noted that his readers would already be familiar with the play as well as Forrest's "aboriginal delineation" within it.[9] Gabriel Harrison, a self-described friend of Forrest and biographer, declared in 1889 that Forrest's portrayal of Metamora "did the work in accordance with all the marked characteristics of the purely native Indian of America."[10] Early twentieth-century biographer Montrose Moses announced that in his Indian chief role, Forrest stood "forth as a gorgeous figure of the red man" and that "he conjured into being all he had seen during his sojourn among the Louisiana Indians."[11] Forrest's biographers declare his performance accurate or authentic by referring to his expertise, developed by personal study, both in person with Indians and through books. They assert that he was convincingly Indian "all through and all over," support their interpretation of it due to authenticating evidence, and locate that evidence in a kind of academic expertise. They claim that thorough study, both intellectual and physical, was the source of Forrest's knowledge. Furthermore, they believed that Forrest could communicate that knowledge during theatrical performances. Understanding the accuracy of the evidence offered in support of Forrest is an essential first step in understanding why his performances were received as authentic. Nevertheless, what the evidence reveals is not whether Forrest was an actual expert on Indians but the allegiance of the evidence to American and western European ideologies, positive and negative, of racial essentialism. Tracing the evidence offered and analyzing the trail of evidence to arrive at its source of authority allows us to more fully understand the relationship among redface, racialization, and US settler-colonial projects of dominance over Indigenous peoples and nations.

In the case of Forrest, evidence presented to support his authentic Indian onstage was rooted in his personal experience with Indians. Alger connected the authenticity of Forrest's Stage Indian, his "seeming Indian," directly to Forrest's "observations while on his visit with Push-ma-ta-ha among the Choctaws, when he had adopted their habits, eaten their food, slept in their tents . . . and left the print of his moccasins on their hunting-grounds."[12] Forrest's expertise was established in embodied knowledge derived from living among the Choctaw. His expertise was authoritative, however, because more than living among them, he had lived *like* them. He knew Indians, and he had acted like an Indian. To supplement this participant observation, Alger also noted that Forrest "studied their [Indians'] characteristics from all other available sources."[13] Forrest's considerable personal library, impressive enough to warrant publication of its contents in 1863, contained Thomas Church's 1827 *History of Philip's War*, among other possible "available sources" at his disposal for study.[14] Experiential and textual research was the basis for his Indian portrayal. The crowning achievement of all this research was that when Forrest played Metamora, "it was the genuine Indian who was brought upon the stage, merely idealized a little in some of his moral features."[15] Forrest's convincing portrayal of an Indian chief was explicitly connected to intellectual and embodied knowledge based on intentional study. Evidence for his acting excellence was grounded in his knowledge of Indians.

Interestingly, Forrest's biographers rarely point to his appearance onstage as prime evidence of his legible Indianness. Instead, they point to accuracy in the physicality, emotion, and mind of the Indian as evidence of his performance's excellence. Even while forwarding the idea of Forrest's intellectual knowledge, they employ physical and essentialist descriptions of his performance. The characteristics of the "genuine Indian," as described by Alger, included "sudden muscular movements," "repressed emotion," a "peculiar mode of breathing," forceful guttural noises, and a "straight or slightly inward-pointing" walk.[16] For Alger, these characteristics made Forrest legibly and accurately Indian. Being legibly Indian was about not appearance but kinetic markers requiring an embodied representation of Indianness. Despite Alger's suggestion that "careless observers" might have overlooked these distinctly Indian attributes of action, he was not the only observer convinced of Forrest's Indianness onstage.

Other Forrest biographers also turned to tangible and intangible descriptions of his authentic Indian performances. Forrest biographer Gabriel Harrison looked to Forrest's breathing to provide evidence of his mastery of Indianness: "So accurate had been his observation that he even caught the very manner of their breathing," which for those who might be curious involved "the lifting and throwing out of the chest from the small ribs up to the collar bone."[17] The attention to detail in Forrest's performance was a marker not just of Indianness but of his own powers of observation. Had Forrest not been so good at observing how Indians breathed, he would have not been so good at being a Stage Indian. Harrison also implies that Forrest's excellence as an Indian was not limited to kinetic or tangible markers. "So deep and thorough was his study of the Indian mind and heart," Harrison informs us, "that he could not fail to present a perfect portraiture of the highest type of the native Indians."[18] In Harrison's estimation, Forrest's performance was a psychologically and emotionally accurate one. Alger, too, stated that Forrest's time with the Choctaw provided him "accurate knowledge of the American Indian, alike in his exterior and interior personality."[19] These biographers—and, one presumes, at least some of his audience members—understood Forrest to accurately portray the interior and exterior lives of an Indian. Forrest knew Indians inside and out. All this expertise based on personal experience and some textual study meant that until Forrest, "no

(*Continued from page 87*)

critique."[62] Despite his audiences' inability to understand the source of his wit, Rogers repeatedly offered them the chance to witness Indigenous political critique.

Rogers was a deeply loved American star whose Indigeneity was obscured by redface. American performance had created such a powerful figure in the Stage Indian that by the early twentieth century, an actual Indigenous man who forwarded his tribal citizenship, openly presented a biracial identity, and provided incisive critique of American colonialism and hypocrisy in support of Indigenous sovereignty was legible only as a folksy, white (though very tan) cowboy.

62 Foster, "Of One Blood."

(*Continued on page 42*)

other actor or author had ever presented the Indian character in such completeness for the stage before."[20] Forrest was not only convincing; he was complete. The evidence for this completely convincing and legible Stage Indian was a mixture of the intellectual knowledge he had obtained through study, his physicality in performance, and an expression of the intangible heart and mind of Indians.

Alger, always the Forrest fan, was invested in his readers' knowing that Forrest's performance was not just convincing to typical theatergoing audiences. Alger assured his readers that Forrest's portrayal "might have deceived nature herself."[21] A "large delegation of Western Indians" who attended a performance of *Metamora* were so moved that "in the closing scene they rose and chanted a dirge" for the death of the chief Metamora.[22] Clearly, Forrest's performance of Metamora was understood as a masterful one; he played Indian so well that he fooled the Indians themselves. But what seems to be a pejorative dig at Native American naivete about the differences between theatrical performance and reality is a piece of evidence presented to support Forrest's performance as authentically Indian. He was legibly Indian not just to white, urban audiences, but to "Western Indians," who saw in his performance a legible Indian. This does more than demonstrate the supposed impact of Forrest's acting; it secures the legitimacy of the criteria for Indianness used by Forrest's biographers and presumably Forrest's audiences. It explains that those who identified Forrest's Metamora as an Indian were correct. They did know how to recognize an Indian, because actual Indians agreed with them.

Forrest was perceived as thoroughly Indian when playing Metamora, and the material and immaterial evidence put forward by his biographers and presumably believed by his audiences proved it. He had researched Indians. His actions and physicality onstage were Indian-like. His speech was Indian-like. His psychological and emotional states were Indian-like. He was the "genuine Indian." But what exactly is a "genuine Indian"? As I will show in what follows, what Forrest offered audiences was in fact a counterfeit Indian, a Stage Indian. And the audiences and biographers who accepted and lauded his performance as authentic were actually collaborating with Forrest to construct the Stage Indian and solidify their implied claims to authority over Indianness.

That Forrest created a disingenuous Indian rather than a genuine one is certain because he fabricated evidence, paid allegiance to racializing and racist tropes, and amplified already circulating discourses about Indian disappearance. While his biographers claimed that it was studious research and careful attention to accuracy that created the impactful character of Metamora, the mechanisms actually at play were quite different. His assertions of expertise and accuracy are suspect given that he made demonstrably false claims. However, what is crystal clear is how he supported and relied on a racialized understanding of Indianness to portray a reductive and generic Indian identity. Furthermore, he enacted what was at that time a culturally diffuse understanding of Indians as inferior to white Euro-Americans and therefore destined to extinction. While maintaining the cover of authenticity, Forrest's performances actually worked to construct the Indian through the eyes of white America.

Forrest's proto-ethnographic research occurred during the summer of 1825, when he spent some weeks, possibly two months, among an Indigenous tribe near New Orleans, Louisiana. He was working as an actor at the American Theatre during 1824–25 when he suddenly left town to spend time with an Indian acquaintance.[23] Forrest's biographers give several reasons for his having left town, from unrequited love to conflict with theater management to desire to research Indians, but no one knows exactly why he left when he did.[24] Forrest claimed that he spent these weeks with his Choctaw friend, Chief Pushmataha, who was "just six years his senior."[25] This chief was supposedly the inspiration for Forrest's portrayal of Metamora. Several of Forrest's biographers included anecdotes or comments about his time with the man they call Pushmataha. An 1881 biography of Forrest describes that summer when "he betook himself to the wigwam of his Indian friend . . . Push-ma-ta-ha."[26] A 1960 biography explains that "for almost two months Forrest cast aside all connections with civilization . . ." with his friend "Push-ma-ta-ha."[27] Even some twenty-first-century scholarship on Forrest assumes "the fact that Forrest spent a significant amount of time getting to know Push-ma-ta-ha, the young Choctaw chief."[28] However, despite what about 150 years of assertions suggest, Forrest did not know Pushmataha.

The historical record indicates that while Forrest may have known an Indian man, he could not have known the Choctaw chief named

Pushmataha.[29] The first and most important reason is that Pushmataha died in 1824, the year before Forrest claims to have spent a summer with him.[30] An obituary in the Alexandria, Virginia, *Phoenix Gazette* (reprinted from the Washington, DC, *National Journal*) named his time of death as "about 12 o'clock" on December 30, 1824, in Washington, DC. Because of his status as a "great chief of his Nation" and his service to the United States as a military officer (brigadier general), he was buried "with military honors."[31] His funeral procession included "at least two thousand" people, and the funeral services included then general and soon-to-be president Andrew Jackson paying his "last respects."[32] Pushmataha was buried on December 25, 1824, and remains in the Washington Parish Burial Ground, now called the Congressional Cemetery.[33] Clearly, a man who died in Washington, DC, in December 1824 could not be alive and hunting during the summer of 1825.

Additionally, there is the discrepancy between Forrest's friend's age and Pushmataha's. Alger describes Forrest's friend in 1825 as "in the bloom of opening manhood."[34] Moody explains that "the Chief was just six years his [Forrest's] senior."[35] Forrest was born on March 6, 1806, which meant that his friend would have been born around 1800 and would have been about twenty-five at the time of their summer together.[36] Mid-twenties could certainly be described as the bloom of opening manhood, and a six-year age difference between the two men would not prevent a friendship from developing. Unfortunately for Forrest's reputation as an honest man, Pushmataha was not a young man in the 1820s. At the time of his death in 1824, Pushmataha was in "his sixtieth year."[37] Although his birth date does not appear in the historical record, his birth year is understood to be around 1764, several decades prior to the year Forrest's friend must have been born.[38] It is unlikely that Forrest mistook a sixty-year-old man for a twenty-five-year-old man. It is also unlikely that a man known to be "medium height, but portly" was the same as the person Forrest's biographers described as "erect as a column, graceful and sinewy as a stag."[39] It is much more likely that Forrest was friends with an Indian, perhaps though not assuredly a Choctaw man, and simply called him Pushmataha. Forrest likely chose the name Pushmataha purposefully rather than accidentally because Pushmataha was so well known and respected.

One Forrest biographer, Alger, does suggest that Forrest knew the son of Pushmataha, describing the father of Forrest's friend as the Choctaw chief who died in Washington, DC.[40] However, this is highly unlikely if not impossible. The best historical sources available indicate that Pushmataha had only one surviving son, who would have been a minor in 1825, not a twenty-five-year-old man.[41] Two biographers of Pushmataha, H. B. Cushman and Anna Lewis, indicate he had one son called Johnson Pushmataha.[42] If we take Forrest seriously as to the age of his friend, the archival record creates insurmountable challenges to Forrest's knowing the son of Pushmataha. A son of Pushmataha named Hachalahurtibbi is mentioned in a deed recording the sale of land by Pushmataha's widow to a Charles Land in 1834.[43] A guardian, Rene Logan, signed this document on his behalf, which would be unusual for a thirty-four-year-old man. A student enrolled in 1840 as J. Pushmataha is found in the records from the Choctaw Academy in Scott County, Kentucky.[44] It seems unlikely that a man of forty would be called an "Indian youth."[45] Additional evidence from baptismal records in Indian Territory place "Johnson Pushmataha" in Blue County, Choctaw Nation, in 1849, supporting both Lewis's and Cushman's claim that Pushmataha's lone son lived in Indian Territory. From these sources, it appears likely that Pushmataha's surviving son was not the age of the man Forrest claimed to know.

Given the fact that Pushmataha was dead before Forrest claimed to have known him and the young age of Pushmataha's surviving son, it becomes increasingly obvious that Forrest misidentified his Indian chief friend. He could have had many reasons for doing so. Perhaps he wanted the connection to a nationally known and respected Indian. Perhaps he misunderstood who his friend was, given that there is no evidence anywhere that Forrest spoke Chahta Anumpa (the Choctaw language). In contrast, there is evidence that Pushmataha used an interpreter because "he spoke no English."[46] While misrepresenting the identity of your inspiration for a role is not a criminal act, it is a dishonest one, a dishonesty that appears designed to bolster the reputation of Forrest both onstage and off. However, it did more than that. Forrest claimed authoritative knowledge of one Indian that allowed him to play another Indian convincingly. However, Forrest's false claim to knowing Pushmataha actually points to an exercise of a different kind of authenticity, an authenticity to the essence of Indianness, a racially determined, intangible substance supposedly belonging to every Indian.

In telling of Forrest's experiences with and expertise about Indians, several of his biographers include anecdotes that purport to demonstrate Forrest's proximity to Indians but in reality illuminate his understanding of authentic Indianness as essence. One such anecdote reveals Forrest's investment in being perceived as masculine by way of Indianness. One evening, Forrest and his friend were together by a fire. Forrest, as one who felt "that the best image of God we have is nude humanity in its perfection," asked his Indian friend to strip naked and "walk to and fro before him between the moonlight and the firelight."[47] The friend acquiesced and was like "a living statue of Apollo in glowing bronze."[48] Aside from the homoerotic undertones of this situation, the anecdote might show Forrest's appreciation for the human form and his intimacy with his friend, in addition to the apparently trusting and free-spirited nature of the young Indian man. In his 1960 biography of Forrest, Moody expressed discomfort with the story, likely due to its eroticism, suggesting that Forrest might not tell that story were he alive in the mid-twentieth century.[49] As historian Jill Lepore has noted, the Indian's nakedness "signaled virility and liberty" because Forrest admired him "for his primitiveness . . . [and] for his unfettered masculinity."[50] Forrest used this anecdote to connect himself with a kind of masculine liberty, which was desirable for his own reputation. Forrest's public persona was strongly connected to a muscular masculinity and Jacksonian politics.[51] Moody has noted that a defining feature of Forrest's public persona was his physique and a muscular, manly appearance.[52] Forrest reinforced his own masculinity through his appreciation for its appearance in an Indian. While his admiration of a naked Indian could be interpreted as erotic, it can also be read as an attempt to align himself with that which he admired, a physically perfect specimen of an utterly free man, the essence of an Indian. In his convincing portrayal of Metamora, Forrest was not accurately depicting a specific Native American but rather evoking the essences attached to Indianness in American culture, such as masculinity and freedom. And since those are racialized essences, it only stands to reason that Forrest believed that he could interchange one Choctaw man, Pushmataha, for one Wampanoag man, Metacomet. Forrest was compelled to be true not to his interpretation of a specific Indian but to the true essence of Indianness.

The assumption that Indians are interchangeable justifies Forrest's choices but also reveals Forrest's commitments. Refusing to distinguish between Wampanoag and Choctaw aligns Forrest with the many audience members and biographers who readily accepted his portrayal of an Indian chief as authentically Indian. He was committed to the already circulating and accepted idea that Indians are a singular category. Lumping all Indigenous nations and peoples together into one category flattens the distinctions and differences among them. This is not a neutral act and feeds into larger cultural projects of racialization and the depoliticization of Indigenous peoples. If Forrest had truly been invested in gaining expertise in Wampanoag life, he could have traveled from New York, where *Metamora* premiered, to Massachusetts, where the Wampanoag continued to live. For, in what should be no surprise to readers of this book, the subtitle of *Metamora, The Last of the Wampanoag,* was factually inaccurate. The Wampanoag continued to exist in the early nineteenth century, as they do in the twenty-first century.[53] In fact, the Mashpee Wampanoag (sometimes called Marshpee) had been advocating for their self-determination, sovereignty, and land rights since at least 1746 to the Massachusetts Assembly, General Court, the King of England, and later the state of Massachusetts and the United States.[54] With a millennia-long history, hundreds of years of political, diplomatic, and martial relationships with England and the United States, and an ongoing effort in the 1830s to promote their sovereignty, the Mashpee Wampanoag could have educated Forrest on the long-standing concerns of their nation as well as their linguistic, cultural, spiritual, and governing practices. During the early years of Forrest's great popularity as Metamora, he could have even taken to publicly supporting the Mashpee efforts to rid themselves of onerous and duplicitous management by the state of Massachusetts and Harvard College (now Harvard University).[55] Forrest did not avail himself of either of these opportunities. His dedication to the interchangeable Indian as one of racial essences overshadowed the actual ethnographic knowledge he could have obtained.

(*Continued from page 197*)

* * *

A decade before Maungwudaus published his travel account, another Indigenous man took to the stage in 1836 to tell American audiences his experience of the world and his own critique of it. Six years after Boston audiences watched Edwin Forrest declaim the death of the Indian in *Metamora*, they again had the opportunity to attend a performance retelling the story of King Philip. William Apess (sometimes spelled Apes), a Pequot minister and political activist, took to the stage of the Odeon Theatre as himself and orated an address titled *Eulogy on King Philip*.[66] His oratory provides an example of sophisticated Indigenous critiques through the mode of performance, critiques that engage with what we would now call racism, settler colonialism, and genocide. Apess presents a pointed indictment of American history, shows how historical failures are replicated in the present, and offers an alternative to audiences. Apess knows that American audiences could see the Indian differently, but must first root out the racist, colonialist assumptions that are the foundation for their interactions with Indigenous peoples.

Scholarship on Apess and his contributions to Native American political, religious, and cultural life has blossomed in recent years.[67] While his writings "received only scant public attention at their time of publication," they, according to literary scholar Drew Lopenzina, provide "one of the more persuasive reminders of the persistence of Native community and resistance in a time and place" that had committed itself to understanding Indigenous peoples and nations as extinct.[68] For a man "born into poverty in western Massachusetts," Apess endured the rupture of his family of origin, physical abuse, and indentured servanthood before reaching adulthood and eventually becoming a Methodist minister.[69] He held many odd jobs, traveled across New England and Canada, and spent years "addicted to drinking rum," according to his autobiography.[70] However, when he arrived in Mashpee, Massachusetts, in 1833, he found a place that welcomed his leadership, both spiritual and political.

---

66 Apess, *Eulogy on King Philip*. He first performed his *Eulogy* in Portsmouth, New Hampshire, in July 1835, before performing it in Boston and publishing it in 1836. Lopenzina, *Through an Indian's Looking-Glass*, 22.

67 See Lopenzina, *Through an Indian's Looking-Glass*; O'Brien, *Firsting and Lasting*; Brooks, *The Common Pot*; Gura, *The Life of William Apess*.

68 Lopenzina, *Through an Indian's Looking-Glass*, 2

69 O'Brien, *Firsting and Lasting*, 180.

70 Apess, *A Son of the Forest*, 67.

An ardent advocate for the rights of the Mashpee, a Wampanoag community, he worked, was jailed, and eventually published a book in support of what might now be called Indigenous self-determination.[71] By 1837, he had begun a series of lectures on "the Indian origin and character" using the stage name Gos-kuk-wa-na-kon-ni-di-yu, for the advertised purpose of creating a fund to establish an "Indian academy."[72] Two years later, in 1839, Apess died unexpectedly after a short illness.[73] Documents from an inquiry into his death reveal information consistent with appendicitis, a ruptured appendix, and inadequate nineteenth-century medicinal practices that exacerbated the problem.[74] A complex, intelligent, and talented man, Apess practiced and perfected the art of public performance as a rhetorical tool, as a Methodist preacher, political advocate, and multiracial Indigenous man.[75]

The *Eulogy* begins by declaring Apess will focus on Philip as an honored, accomplished martyr.[76] He aims to vindicate Philip's character and "melt the prejudice that exists in the hearts of those who are in the possession of his soil."[77] Immediately connecting land rights, Indigeneity, and colonialism, he clarifies that the possession of Philip's land is held by white Americans "only by the right of conquest."[78] Apess is building a case for understanding Indigenous history as race and polity intertwined. He quickly forces his audience members to reckon with their own history of bloodshed and war, not as the victim of English aggression but as the perpetrator of violent conquest. He identifies himself as an Indian, claiming "the blood of a denominated savage runs" in his veins.[79] His use of *denominated* occurs throughout the oratory and most closely resembles the descriptive term *so-called*. Apess's oratory tells his audience in essence, "You think I'm a savage. *You* are the descendants of

71 Apess had published a justification for the Mashpee Revolt in 1835. Apess, *Indian Nullification*.
72 Lopenzina, *Through an Indian's Looking-Glass*, 238.
73 Apess and O'Connell, *A Son of the Forest and Other Writings*, xxi.
74 For a discussion of his cause of death and the inquiry into it, see the "Conclusion" of Lopenzina, *Through an Indian's Looking-Glass*.
75 For a discussion of the likely white, Black, and Pequot ancestors Apess possessed, see Lopenzina, *Through an Indian's Looking-Glass*; and Apess and O'Connell, *A Son of the Forest*.
76 This analysis relies on Apess, *Eulogy on King Philip* (1836).
77 Apess, *Eulogy on King Philip*, 6.
78 Apess, *Eulogy on King Philip*, 6.
79 Apess, *Eulogy on King Philip*, 6.

(*Continued on page 75*)

Forrest's claim to masculinity through his appreciation of a fine Indian specimen shows his commitment to another essentialized conception of Indianness, the idea of the noble savage. As a conceit of European philosophers and culture, the noble savage is an idealized figure utterly free from the ruinous influence of society.[56] Unfettered by social institutions that attempt to control him, the noble savage can enact humanness in its unsullied and unconstrained form. That Forrest's portrayal of Metamora participated in the circulation of the noble savage is unquestioned. The character Metamora is noted for his nobility. In act 1, scene 1, Metamora is described by one character as "the noble sachem of a valiant race—the white man's dread, the Wampanoag's hope."[57] Metamora demonstrates superior moral virtue and impeccable (and admirable to Christian) spiritual sensibilities.

> Is justice goodly? Metamora's just. Is bravery virtue? Metamora's brave. If love of country, child and wife and home, be to deserve them all—he merits them . . . his worship though untaught and rude flows from his heart, and Heaven alone must judge of it.[58]

He is an excellent hunter and warrior and displays vigorous masculinity in direct defiance of Euro/Euro-American forces. He "stands between" English colonists "and extended sway, ready alike with words of power to urge, or gleaming weapon force his princely dues."[59] He was, as one character plainly stated, the "grandest model of a mighty man."[60] Forrest enacted the noble savage onstage as his contemporaries were creating it on the page, connecting the noble savage to the vanishing Indian.

Trafficking in ideas of Indians as a romanticized racial other while also asserting their inevitable demise, Forrest's Stage Indian connected already entrenched ideas of Indianness as an inferior race destined to die off with cultural tropes of Indianness as primitive. He likely did so in the service of his own reputation and social status. He claimed expertise about Indians through experience and study and was recognized as legibly Indian onstage. He enacted cultural assumptions about Indian inferiority by perpetuating and glorifying the vanishing Indian, and he was lauded as a "genuine Indian." Actively connecting himself to essences of masculinity and freedom by way of the Indian, he solidified his own reputation and masculinity. Furthermore, he strengthened circulating assumptions of Indians as a race by repeatedly demonstrating his understanding of Indians as interchangeable. By engaging in these uses of a racialized and essentialized Indian, he participated in racializing the Indian as a vanishing, noble savage, interchangeable across nations/time/space/language/culture. He did not acquiesce to objective criteria of Indianness; he helped draw the racialized boundaries around the Indian.

More importantly, Forrest's depiction of Metamora reveals criteria Forrest and those who wrote about him used to define what an Indian was and therefore what was legibly and authentically Indian onstage. More than an account of the research he did or did not undertake or the raced and gendered essences he did or did not exemplify, Forrest's "genuine Indian" reveals the social and cultural project of the Stage Indian—to determine the boundaries of Indianness and consequently control Indigenous life. The proof of Forrest's authenticity as an Indian chief is evidence of what was required to be read as Indian. Noble savage? Check. Vanishing Indian? Check. Unfettered masculinity? Check. Hunting? Check. Walking/breathing/standing like an Indian? Check. Talking like an Indian? Check. Being authentically Indian onstage? Indubitably.

These criteria for Indianness are not solely or even mostly about visual appearance, although visual appearance was definitely a factor in Forrest's legible Indianness. The Stage Indian as played by Forrest shows us that redface does not live on the surface of an actor. It is through the practice of curation and the collaborative process of recognition that the racial legibility of the Stage Indian is enacted. The authentic Indian is the one who activates and fulfills the criteria of Indianness. And that criteria must already exist and be circulating in order for the same actor in the same performance to be read as legibly Indian across a country and across decades. The audience could recognize these traits and behaviors as accurate and assess the quality of the authenticity precisely because they were not encountering it for the first time. To recognize a legibly Indian body is not simply to make a judgment about proximity to a standard but to affirm that standard. Legibility is not as much about accuracy as it is about the authority to decide who has authority and who wields it. To agree is to defer to criteria in making a judgment and to submit to the source of authority for that criteria. Forrest's claims to authentic Indian performance show where those sources of authority reside: European and Euro-American ideas of savagery, race, and Indian inferiority. The Stage Indian is legibly Indian when it affirms American expectations for Indianness as inferior through admirable, no longer present, and above all a racial category. These expectations, these criteria for legible Indianness, expose much more about the artists and audiences who rely on them than they do of the performances that depict them. Because the Stage Indian is a character of raced and gendered essence, not one of just feathers and face paint, it denies complexity, variety, and self-determination to Indigenous peoples. As such, the Stage Indian is an aggressive and disruptive act against Indigenous peoples and nations. In service to polities and people that would delimit and control Indigenous identity, redface is not merely a racist act but a colonial one as well.

The Stage Indian is one way the United States transforms members of Indigenous nations into Indians. It presents a legible Indian body and, as Forrest has shown us, proves its legibility by offering up evidence of ethnographic or academic expertise. But in actuality, it defers to criteria of Indianness imbued with racialized, gendered, and essentialized logics. By insisting on representing *an* Indian, redface calls into being *the* Indian.[61] Forrest's Indian performance onstage was supposedly rooted in his Indian friend in real life. Audiences witnessed this performance and read it as legibly Indian, as matching their expectations for what they already knew an Indian to be. Forrest's Indian friend in real life was legitimized as truly Indian, because he also met the expectations for what Forrest already assumed an Indian to be: unfettered, masculine, experiencing ultimate liberty, hunting, living outdoors, naked, smoking pipes. It is through theatrical performance that the Indian of European and later American ideology (noble savage, treacherous savage, Indian Princess, drunk Indian) is fleshed out through the body of a performer. The essence of Indianness is not on the surface but expressed through embodied actions that align with already circulating cultural expectations of an essentialized, racialized, and gendered identity.

The stakes of the creation of an authentic Indian, this enforcing of colonial boundaries around who and what is an Indian, are more than racial. The construction of a racial category called Indian is imperative to the US national project to dismantle its political obligations to Indigenous nations and to ensure a racialized (read, white) national identity. Creating a legible Indian character onstage, a Stage Indian, is part of the twin national US projects of making a nation and making a race. And ensuring that the Stage Indian is read as an authentic Indian is necessary for reinforcing the authority that the United States as a settler-colonial nation asserts over Indigenous people. If Forrest's performance is received as authentically Indian, then the actors and audience alike are collaboratively subscribing to a shared understanding of what makes an Indian. As I have demonstrated, these shared understandings rely not on ethnographic fact or intellectual knowledge but on racializing and gendering logics rooted in European and American conceptions of the Indian as racially inferior, on the road to extinction, and primitively free. Forrest and his audiences were not making Wampanoag or even Choctaw legible. They were making the Indian legible as an embodied instantiation of colonial ideas.

Perhaps this is why redface so eagerly and desperately points to its authenticity, either through historical fact or racial essence. To assert its own authority in settler-colonial projects, the Stage Indian must prove itself to be true and inevitable. The Indian must be real. And redface is a powerful mechanism for making the Indian real. It works, as Deloria might have explained, on brains and bodies, moving ideas "from the realm of abstraction to the physical world of concrete experience."[62] Playing Indian onstage, performing the Stage Indian, is "powerful, for it not only made meaning, it makes them [the racialized, generic Indian] *real*." And through making a "real Indian" and making the Indian "real," redface works on the level of race *and* of nation. It is an attack on Indigenous identity *and* polity.

BUFFALO BILL AND THE REALLY GENUINE INDIAN

As the Stage Indian evolved across the nineteenth century, the mechanisms to assure audiences of its authenticity and solidify American authority over the criteria of Indianness remained constant. Although the preferred criteria shifted across time to include the racial identity of the redface performer, the fundamental mode of redface, collaboratively curating a racially legible Indian body, remained the same. In the last fifteen years or so of the nineteenth century, a new kind of theatrical entertainment rose to popularity and grew to have remarkable influence on the Stage Indian: Wild West shows. The exemplar of this new form of live, mostly outdoor, episodic, and spectacular entertainment was *Buffalo Bill's Wild West*. Founded and led by William F. "Buffalo Bill" Cody, *Buffalo Bill's Wild West* ushered in a new criteria for authenticity in Stage Indians: an Indigenous actor. Although the requirement of fulfilling this criteria waxed and waned and waxed again throughout the twentieth century (as will be discussed further in chapter 4), it appeared as a robust and seemingly self-evident category for Native American representation in the late nineteenth century. *Buffalo Bill's Wild West* used the dramaturgical logic of progress, the casting of Indigenous performers, and assertions of educational impact to support its claims of authentic historical production. I will show how these practices fell short of historical accuracy and participated in the racialization of Native Americans and how despite hiring Native Americans, *Buffalo Bill's Wild West* steadfastly presented Stage Indians.

THE DRAMA OF CIVILIZATION

Buffalo Bill's Wild West trafficked in facts. The fact that Buffalo Bill Cody was famous for being a scout, Indian fighter, buffalo hunter, and entertainment personality.[63] The fact that the Deadwood Stagecoach reenactment used the (supposedly) actual Deadwood stagecoach.[64] The fact that real Indians were hired to play real Indians.[65] However, these facts were highly mediated. They were selected, arranged, and interpreted by a creative force. They were curated. The three men primarily responsible for this curation were William F. Cody (star and producer), Nate Salsbury (manager/director), and John M. Burke (publicity). Together, these three men created the Wild West show that Americans have come to know and love: the cowboys and Indians, rodeo and racing, spectacle, horses, and romance of western nostalgia. However, it was a fourth man who would solidify and clarify what the other three were doing over their decades producing *Buffalo Bill's Wild West*. Steele MacKaye was a director, playwright, actor, teacher, and inventor who became the creative force behind *Buffalo Bill's Wild West* during the winter of 1886–87. He took the disparate elements of the Wild West show and shaped them into an epic tale of the progress toward and obstacles to civilization, using the Native American performers as an essential component of this grand narrative of America.

While MacKaye's time as director of *Buffalo Bill's Wild West* was atypical, the unique nature of his contributions are worth considering. MacKaye's work unmistakably reveals the dramaturgical logic of progress as the show's particular avenue of mythologizing history, or historicizing myth. After a successful two-month summer season in 1886 at Erastina, an amusement grounds on Staten Island in New York, Cody decided to reconfigure his *Wild West* with the help of theater director Steele MacKaye for the winter season to draw repeat customers.[66] The new version of the *Buffalo Bill's Wild West,* called The Drama of Civilization, was performed indoors at Madison Square Garden in New York City and illustrated the relationship between "authentic" Indians and an epic myth of the American West.[67] The Drama of Civilization marked what historian Louis Warren called "the ascension of *Buffalo Bill's Wild West* to middle-class entertainment and respected cultural institution," even as it also marked the rise to international fame of the Oceti Sakowin Lakota peoples, the Sioux Indians.[68]

The popularity of *Buffalo Bill's Wild West* at Erastina and in Madison Square Garden can hardly be understated. The winter season was attended by one million people, on the heels of the million who saw the outdoor version at Erastina.[69] With the population of New York City proper at 1.5 million just three years later in 1890 and the region encompassing New York City, Brooklyn, and Jersey City at 3.6 million, nearly two-thirds of the New York City region could have seen *Buffalo Bill's Wild West* in one of its iterations within the span of nine months.[70] According to the 1890 census, there were only 325,464 Indians in the United States, while the total population of the country reached sixty-two million.[71] Put another way, there were about five times as many people in New York City as there were Native Americans in the United States. And millions of New Yorkers witnessed around a hundred Indians in The Drama of Civilization in less than a year.

This kind of widescale exposure was replicated over the *Buffalo Bill's Wild West*'s thirty-one-year history from 1882 to 1913, as tens of millions of people across the United States, Canada, and Europe witnessed one of its thrilling, spectacular, and Indian-filled entertainments. *Buffalo Bill's Wild West* was also widely imitated, with over eighty companies producing similar shows that looked to *Buffalo Bill's Wild West* as the "prototype of all Wild Wests and the longest running, most financially successful, most widely traveled, and best-known Wild West that ever performed."[72] The Wild West "Show Indian" became iconic in American (and global) culture and reset the standard for what Indians looked like, what they moved like, and how they could be understood as a part of American history.[73] Shifting from the prominent noble/vanishing savage so common among the Indian plays of the early nineteenth century, Wild West shows forwarded a violent/vanishing savage figure playing a supporting role to American settlers and military. The "Show Indian" performed its own spectacular defeat, which assured audiences of its paradoxical vanished status and thrilling visceral presence.

Before Steele MacKaye, *Buffalo Bill's Wild West* was a hodgepodge of various acts strung together in no particular order. Trick riding, steer roping, and bronco busting were among the acts audiences witnessed in its earliest iteration in 1882, when it was called the *Old Glory Blow-out*.[74] By 1884, it had morphed into *Buffalo Bill's Wild West, America's National Entertainment*, a name that would stick for decades.[75] Using his connections to hire a group of Pawnee to perform a race while riding bareback, Cody inaugurated real Indians on this outdoor stage.[76] The Pawnee also appeared as Indians in a battle scene between them and the government scouts, as well as in a scene where they attacked a stagecoach. These early experiments brought together what would become the iconic *Buffalo Bill's Wild West*, a cross between a rodeo, a circus, a melodrama, and a generously dramatized historical reenactment.[77] Indians played an integral role in *Buffalo Bill's Wild West*, both as featured acts, human set pieces communicating historical accuracy, and in the drama Cody brought to his dramatization of history.

In no other season did the dramatization of history become clearer and more explicit than in the winter of 1886–87, when Steele MacKaye was in charge. The Drama of Civilization unabashedly claimed that it

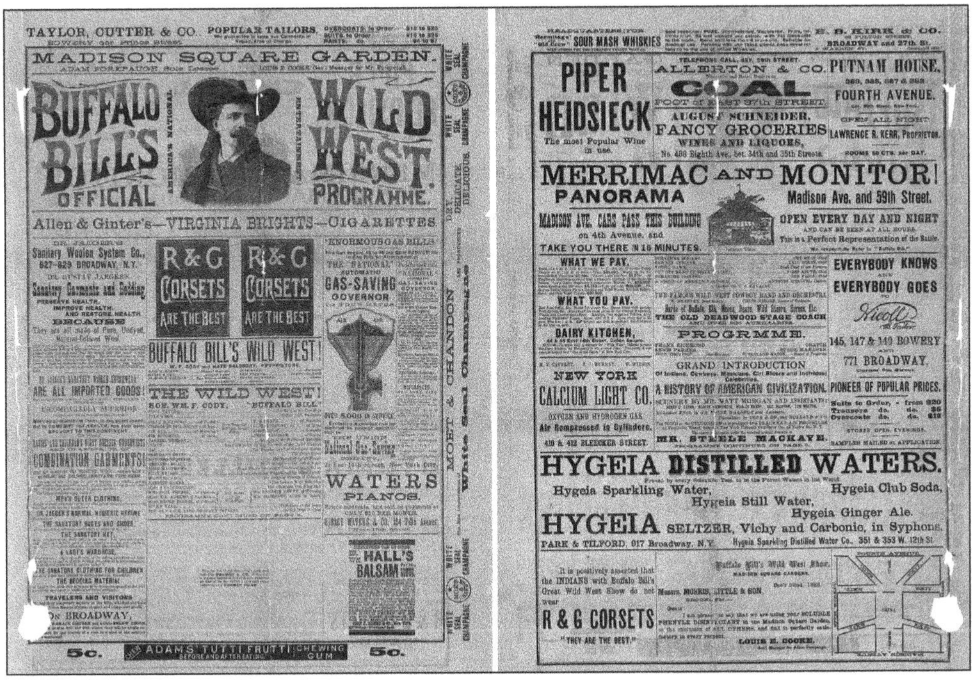

Figure 3.2. Winter 1887 Drama of Civilization program. Image courtesy McCracken Research Library.

retold history, events that had actually happened. It further highlighted that its performers were actual actors within these historical events. The cast list for the production includes Indian tribes and names of their chiefs, as well as "A Group of Mexican Vaqueros" and "A Troop of U.S. Cavalry." As historian L. G. Moses explained, "Indians who had fought Custer at the Greasy Grass also attacked him, twice a day, in the arena."[78] Real historical actors reenacted real history every day in *Buffalo Bill's Wild West.*

The Drama of Civilization was billed on its program's second page as "A History of American Civilization" (figure 3.2).[79] But this history mythologized events, concocted scenarios, and heavily shaded audience's interpretations of the historical record through its dramaturgy. As I will show, the facts in The Drama of Civilization were heavily manipulated by both MacKaye's narrative and the curation of performers, acts, and publicity by William F. Cody and Nate Salsbury and by John Burke's mediation of *Buffalo Bill's Wild West*'s public image. MacKaye envisioned four epochs structuring The Drama of Civilization: the Primeval Forest, the Prairie, the Cattle Ranch, and the Mining Camp (figure 3.3). Each epoch claimed to represent an era in the progressive settlement and expansion of the United States into the West. Illustrating what Anne McClintock calls panoptical time, "the image of global history consumed—at a glance—in a single spectacle from a point of privileged invisibility," The Drama of Civilization purported to give its audience members an epic scope and spectacular scale of their national history, within one evening's time.[80] Together, the epochs told a national story by recreating or imagining scenarios and vignettes representative of the challenges and pleasures of this westward conquest, complete with a spectacular animal stampede, working watering hole, prairie fire, and cyclone. During the run of the show, The Drama of Civilization changed only one scenario, adding a reenactment of the Battle of Greasy Grass (also known as the Battle of Little Big Horn) called "Custer's Last Rally," during January 1887.[81]

MacKaye's dramatic and dramaturgical contributions to the production were extensive. In total, MacKaye suggested seven new scenarios to Cody for The Drama of Civilization, including "the aboriginal savage in his garb of skins, and with the weapons used before the white man appeared," the Indian attack on the emigrant train, the prairie fire, the stampede, life at the mining camp, life at a fort, and the cyclone.[82] The only suggestion not produced was life at a fort. However, a western town and military were represented in "The Mining Camp" and "Custer's Last Rally." An Indian attack on a stagecoach had been a standard scenario since 1883.[83] Indian attacks on settlers and towns were added by MacKaye and became a standard part of the show's repertoire for decades.[84] MacKaye obviously grasped the "winning the West" ethos of *Buffalo Bill's Wild West* and pushed it forward in his imaginative, dramatic, and visually driven contributions to its long life.

One of MacKaye's unique contributions, never to be duplicated in other seasons, was its chronological and linear structure and dramaturgical logic. The real Indians, real horses, real soldiers, and real fire were all placed within a curated vision of civilization, progress, and chronological development. That development echoed a nineteenth-century

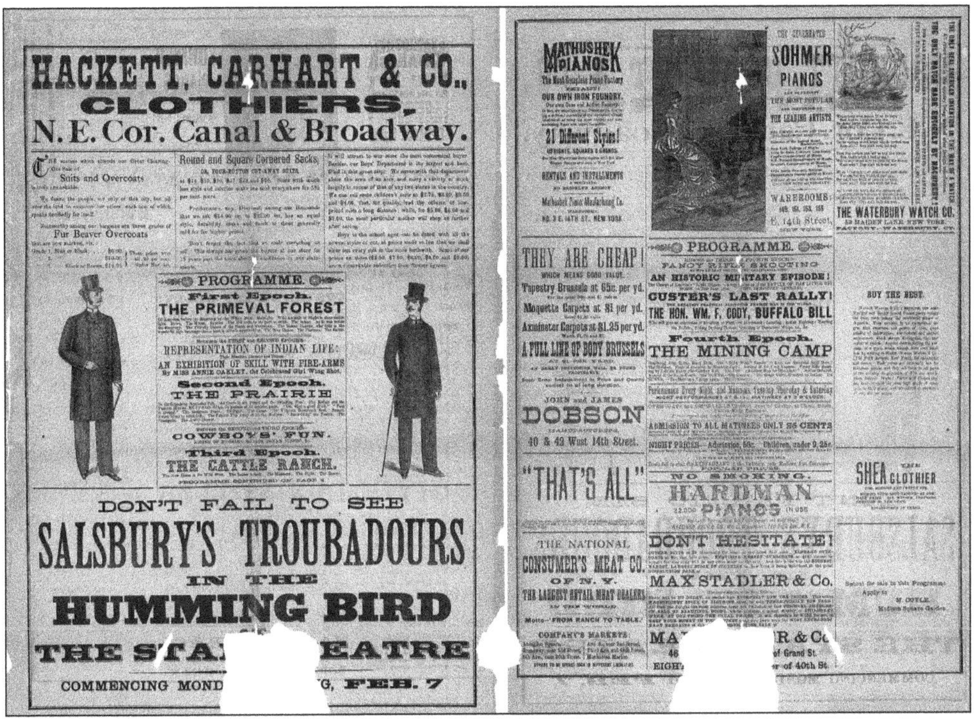

Figure 3.3. Winter 1887 Drama of Civilization program. Image courtesy McCracken Research Library.

understanding of cultural progress as linear and fixed. This popular thinking was most clearly articulated by anthropologist Lewis Henry Morgan, who claimed that all societies pass through three stages of social development: savagery, barbarism, and civilization.[85] Writing in 1887 as The Drama of Civilization unfolded in Madison Square Garden nightly, Morgan asserted that convincing evidence existed "that savagery preceded barbarism in all the tribes of mankind, as barbarism is known to have preceded civilization. The history of the human race is one in source, one in experience, and one in progress."[86] Lest Morgan be interpreted as an outlier or individual proponent of a kind of scientific racism, his view was widely held and espoused across the American population. "Friends of the Indians" associations, nineteenth-century organizations dedicated to aiding and advocating for Native Americans in social and political venues, also shared these rigid assumptions about cultural development. Many believed that the most highly developed form of civilization was "white Anglo-Saxon Protestants of the United States" and were motivated to encourage Native Americans to attain that particular form of civilization.[87]

MacKaye's artistic vision for The Drama of Civilization argued just as dramatically for the backwardness of the Indian, a savage tribe or perhaps a barbarous tribe consistently overwhelmed by the superior civilization brought by (white) Euro-American settlement of the West. For MacKaye, the best story to tell of American westward expansion began with primitive Indians, showed the violent encounters settlers had with (the losing) Indians, demonstrated the joys and dangers of cattle ranching in western towns, and depicted the adventures of miners. MacKaye employed the dramaturgical logic of linear human progress and showcased Indians as those stuck in savagery or barbarism. They are chronologically and dramaturgically arrested by the powerful force of American progress. Employing contemporary Native Americans to tell a story of Indian deficiency and defeat, MacKaye's vision for The Drama of Civilization explicitly states the dramaturgical foundations to *Buffalo Bill's Wild West*: Indians are primitive foes but have been overcome by American expansion and excellence.

Given the circulating ideas about Indian civilization and the answer to its supposed "problem," it is little wonder that the narrative structure and dramaturgical logic MacKaye employed in The Drama of Civilization was received as evidence of its authentic plot. Additionally, by hiring only "real" Indians to play Cody's version of the Stage Indian in The Drama of Civilization, *Buffalo Bill's Wild West* participated in an ongoing cultural conversation about the nature of race and civilization, a conversation in which Indians were understood as inherently inferior to white Americans. Racial science in the late nineteenth century was dominated by the newly embraced theory of Darwinian evolution, which was also influencing fields such as linguistics, archaeology, and the burgeoning field of anthropology. These fields were "scientifically" codifying what made an Indian an Indian. Historian Steven Conn has shown how nineteenth-century academics understood Native Americans as anthropological subjects, which drastically diminished interest in their languages, histories, and cultures. As peoples with a presumed past but without a presumed legitimate history or evidence of the technological progress valued by Euro-America, Native Americans were understood as socially and culturally inferior to Anglo-Europeans/Americans.[88] This inferiority was believed to be rooted in fundamental racial differences, which were also understood as obviously visible and biologically measurable.

Anthropologist Audra Simpson's (Mohawk) book *Mohawk Interruptus* explicates this racializing, deeply constraining, and damaging formation of the Indian in anthropology. In doing so, she might just as well be explaining the function of redface in American theater. She describes how the desire in early anthropological literature on the Iroquois was "for order, for purity, for fixity, and for cultural perfection that at once imagined an imminent disappearance immediately after or just within actual land dispossession."[89] Anthropologists wanted a legible and stable Indian, one that was already or nearly extinct; they wanted a Stage Indian. The realization of that anthropological desire was "found in the authenticating discourse on culture and history" that permeated anthropological literature.[90] Early anthropologists were invested in delimiting Haudenosaunee (Iroquois) and other Indian identity and did so by focusing on those Haudenosaunee they felt met their own standard for legibility and authenticity. Or as Simpson puts it, "things, people, and matters that could not be assimilated to the ethnologic eye and mind at certain times could not be apprehended, or were simply discounted because the eyes and ears that apprehended them were narrowed and tuned to see and hear certain things."[91] Embodied legibility was always preceded by ideological commitments to a racial Indian category.

Anthropologists and Wild West show audiences were looking for the Indian they already knew. For audiences in Madison Square Garden, the Indians were overtly labeled, played a clear role in the linear progression of the plot structure, demonstrated their savage/barbaric ways, and subscribed to racial stereotypes of violence, disappearance, and defeat. The evidence for authenticity offered by The Drama of Civilization was in part its narrative alignment with accepted cultural knowledge on the nature of history and human development. It was real history on display because it was how things really happened, reinforcing how cultures moved from savagery to barbarism to civilization. Those who have reached civilization naturally overcome those who have not. However, the dramaturgical logic of *Buffalo Bill's Wild West*, so clear in The Drama of Civilization, was not its only or most prominent method of proving that it was the real deal. The heavy lifting of its claims to authenticity was performed by its performers, or to be more precise, by their bodies.

SPECIFICALLY SIOUX

Although William F. Cody was not involved or invested in academic or popular deliberations on the articulation of race and the development of human civilization, he was an immensely popular and prolific creator of the understanding of Native Americans as a race rooted in biological and physical traits. He exclusively hired Indians to play Indians. The hiring practices of *Buffalo Bill's Wild West* have been well articulated for nearly 150 years. The show hired Native Americans to perform as themselves. There is virtually no evidence that *Buffalo Bill's Wild West* ever had non-Native Americans dress up and play Indian during performances. The considerable efforts to brand the entertainment as an educational and historical experience for audiences (discussed shortly), coupled with Buffalo Bill Cody's own commitment to hiring the "real deal," meant that his Wild West production (Cody declined to formally call his troupe a "show," eschewing that word in favor of words like "national entertainment," to emphasize its pleasurable qualities, factual focus, and national importance) worked to present itself as fact and not fiction.[92] Historian Paul Reddin has further clarified that Cody also claimed that his employees were not actors and quotes him as saying, "They simply appear just as they are; nothing more, nothing less. The work done here is not the result of rehearsal, it is not acting, it is nature itself."[93] It is this commitment to not just theatrical realism but "nature" that shaped *Buffalo Bill's Wild West* and was later reshaped by other Wild West shows.

By interrogating "the real" in the Stage Indian of *Buffalo Bill's Wild West*, the criteria for "realness" comes into focus. Those criteria maintain the same structural logic as the ones used for Forrest's portrayal of

Metamora. *Buffalo Bill's Wild West* presented the Stage Indian, accompanied by vociferous claims of its authenticity (Real Indians performing Indian roles!). The claims of authenticity were based on culturally informed logics of race and inferiority (Come see the primitive savages and how the West was won!). The commitment to those logics exposes actual commitments of *Buffalo Bill's Wild West,* not to ethnographic accuracy of Northern Plains tribes but to the American settler-colonial project and its desire for control over Native American land and lives. *Buffalo Bill's Wild West* helps us recognize that the stakes of redface are indeed appropriate and respectful representation, but more importantly, that they are Indigenous lifeways and futurity.

The Stage Indian of *Buffalo Bill's Wild West* was a collaboration among narrative, publicity, and the presence of the primarily Oglala Lakota performers hired to play the Indian roles. Their tribal, cultural, and social characteristics were the foundation of the show's Stage Indian. The skills, regalia, and way of life shown both onstage and off were rooted in Oceti Sakowin identity. The Oceti Sakowin, also known as the Great Sioux Nation or simply the Sioux, is a confederacy of seven councils, each council comprised of different bands. Speaking three different dialects—Dakota, Nakota, and Lakota—the Oceti Sakowin homelands are represented by their contemporary locations across the Northern Plains states, including North Dakota, South Dakota, Minnesota, Montana, and Nebraska.[94] The Oceti Sakowin were, at the time of The Drama of Civilization, antagonized by settler immigration and American military pressure, and violence and war had broken out across the Northern Plains. Forced to live on reservations and to report to Indian agents, such as the one at the Pine Ridge Agency, where most of Cody's Native American employees called home, the Oceti Sakowin experienced traumatic and difficult challenges in the latter part of the nineteenth century. For many, a job at *Buffalo Bill's Wild West* was a good way of addressing several of the challenges of being Oceti Sakowin, including maintaining traditional practices and cultural expression, making a fair wage to support their families, and escaping from often rigid and negative environments on reservations.[95]

Despite routinely hiring Pawnees for theater jobs over a dozen years, around 1886 Cody made the switch to hiring primarily Oglala

Lakota. The shift began in the 1885 season, when he hired Hunkpapa Oceti Sakowin leader Sitting Bull to appear in the show.[96] Originally denied the opportunity to hire Sitting Bull by the Indian agent at Standing Rock, where Sitting Bull lived, Cody went over his head to gain final approval. Because of his military and political connections, Cody successfully appealed to General William Sherman and Secretary of the Interior Henry Teller and gained approval for Sitting Bull's hire.[97] Sitting Bull received fair remuneration at $50 a week plus a $125 signing bonus.[98] In addition, he retained some creative control over his performance and image, including sole rights to sell his autograph and photograph along with his own silent moment onstage alone in a "heroic posture."[99] When Cody tried to rehire him for the 1886 season, he was prevented by Indian agent James McLaughlin.[100] However, he was able to hire twenty-nine men from the Pine Ridge Agency for the 1886 summer season at Erastina.[101] Many of these same performers stayed on to perform that winter in The Drama of Civilization.[102] The image below (figure 3.4) was taken circa 1886 and shows employees of *Buffalo Bill's Wild West*, perhaps the very group who performed at Erastina, with many appearing in The Drama of Civilization several months after this was taken.

Shortly after The Drama of Civilization closed, Cody began hiring almost exclusively Oglala Oceti Sakowin from the Pine Ridge Agency, despite increasing regulation by the US government.[103] For example, the 1887 tour of England included only Oceti Sakowin performers. Oceti Sakowin translator Luther Standing Bear traveled with the show on that tour and declared in his memoir that "all the Indians belonged to the Sioux tribe."[104] This group hiring was only possible under new terms created by the Bureau of Indian Affairs that required Cody to sign a contract stipulating that he would guard the Indians from immoral influences, hire married men whose wives would accompany them on any tour, provide food and clothing, and keep performers' salaries in escrow held by a religious figure who cared for their moral well-being while working on the show.[105] Cody also had to pay a $10,000 bond to ensure that he would follow through on all the contract's terms. Contractual arrangements like these became a regular part of Cody's hiring of Native American performers. The

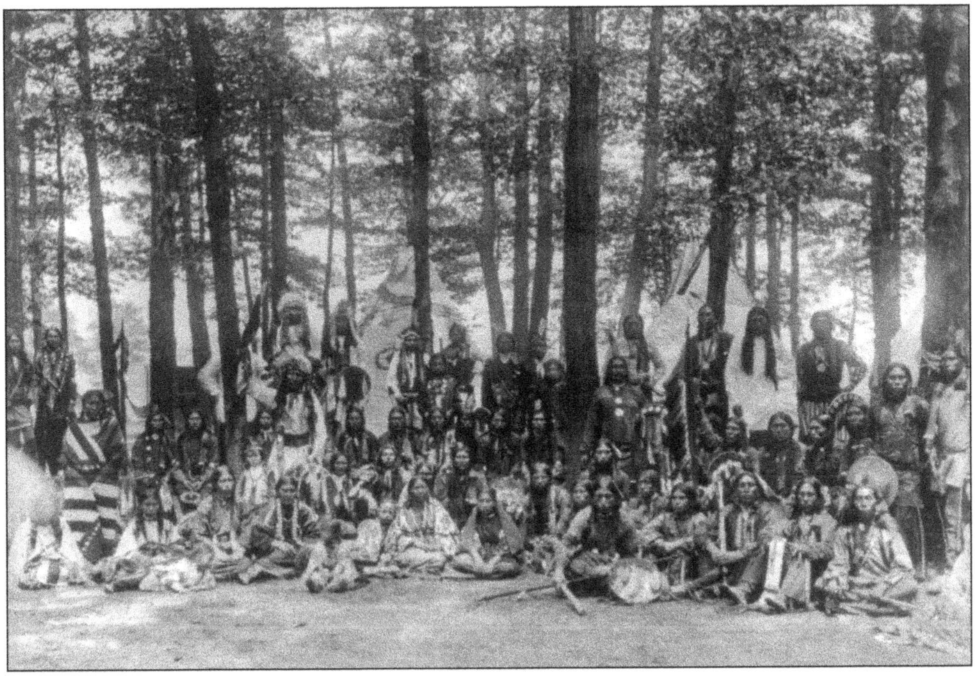

Figure 3.4. Napolean Sarony. *Buffalo Bill's Wild West,* circa 1886. Image courtesy Library of Congress.

Oglala Lakota were so desirable for Cody's narrative and aesthetic vision that he was willing to undergo significant challenges and possibly cumbersome administrative procedures to secure their employment. The results of that commitment to hiring Lakota performers had a lasting impact. As historian W. W. Moses puts it, "The Sioux became the most prized Show Indians." Given that "Cody's show inspired legions of imitators," including *Pawnee Bill's Wild West, Miller Brothers 101 Ranch Wild West,* and *Texas Jack's Wild West,* it is little wonder that the premiere western show's choice of Native American employees influenced other shows.[106] Sioux became synonymous with the Stage Indian and eventually with simply Indian.

In addition to a specific ethnic and national identity, Oceti Sakowin (Sioux), Cody also explicitly preferred hiring Oceti Sakowin with certain visible achievements and notable reputations. Concerned with how his Indians looked, Cody based his hiring decisions in part on the regalia each Lakota employee owned and brought with them to wear during the performances. One of Cody's assistants in the hiring process at Pine Ridge, Standing Bear, recounted his own experience "select[ing] those having the finest outfits and who were the best dancers."[107] Black Elk, an Oceti Sakowin performer in The Drama of Civilization, recorded providing his own clothing and regalia to use in performance: "We bought all the material we needed. I had some moccasins, buckskin clothes, war bonnet and everything."[108] When auditioning potential employees, Cody would watch as "Lakota aspirants in the hundreds would don regalia and audition for the season's tour."[109] Standing Bear's recollections of important hiring criteria included how they moved, how good a dancer they were, how they looked, and how fine their outfits appeared. To Standing Bear, they needed to move and look impressively Oceti Sakowin, but audiences recognized them only as impressively Indian.

The impressive Indians Cody hired soon became the standard Stage Indian for all Wild West shows and later for the Indian in American popular culture. Despite the specificity of Oceti Sakowin identity and citizenship in Cody's hiring practice, audiences noticed the visual and kinetic markers and began recognizing them as markers of Indianness. Those markers of Indianness were abstracted to racial makers and eventually were enough to mark any person wearing/possessing them legibly Indian. Other Wild West shows, like the *Miller Brothers 101 Ranch*, expected their Indian employees to be "as nearly as possible long haired or have good wigs and good costumes."[110] Undoubtedly, a "good costume" for a male employee would be a feathered headdress. One of the most iconic visual elements of the "Show Indian," the Indian popularized by the Wild West shows and adjacent performance genres, is the feathered headdress, like the one seen below in a production photo taken around 1905 as an advertisement for the *Buffalo Bill's Wild West* (figure 3.5).

Indians in headdresses are seen all over *Buffalo Bill's Wild West* publicity materials, from photographs to souvenirs to posters. By including headdresses in virtually all imagery advertising the Indian in the show, it is clear that the headdress was highly valued as an impressive

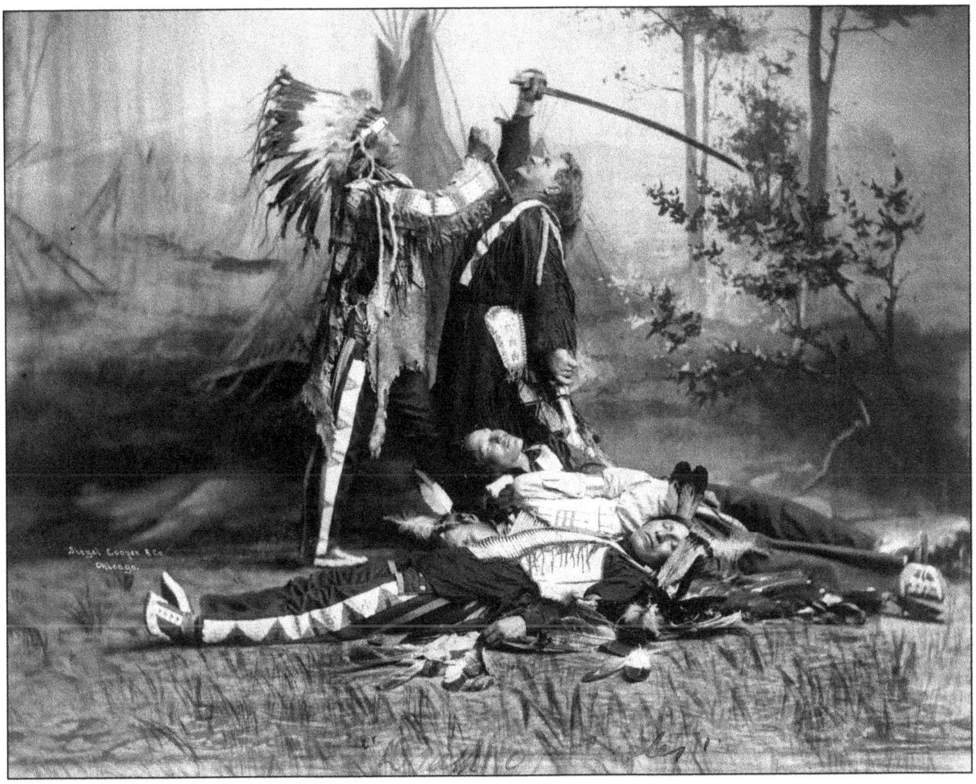

Figure 3.5. Death of Custer, circa 1905. Image courtesy Library of Congress.

marker of Indianness. As the National Museum of the American Indian explains, headdresses are extremely specific and significant apparel in Native American communities: "The right within a culture to don a headdress . . . depends first on the acquisition of cultural knowledge and second on the ability to use that knowledge for the benefit of the people."[111] Feathers that are used to make a headdress are earned individually for special, communally acknowledged acts, for example, for acts of bravery or strength. An Oceti Sakowin man demonstrated through wearing a feathered headdress his acknowledged feats on behalf of his community and nation. This nuanced information, however, is not translated in the publicity photo. Instead, those who buy the photo are reminded of or taught the appearance of the Indians in *Buffalo Bill's Wild West*: Indians wear feathers.

(Continued from page 60)

also toured the United States delivering lectures and had a weekly radio program.[36] In short, there was not a form of popular or mass media and entertainment that he did not enter or achieve success in during his career. By the time his career was cut short by a tragic plane crash in 1935, he had developed a folksy, of-the-moment style of commentary coupled with a self-effacing humor, or as biographer Ben Yagoda explains, he "embodied" old-time values through his "geniality and horse sense."[37] He was admired and respected for his humor across a wide spectrum of American society, meeting presidents, princes, elected officials, and everyday folks. Rogers was a star.

Rogers was also a mixed-race Cherokee citizen; his racial identity was variously and inconsistently interpretated throughout his lifetime. By tracking how his audiences understood him, Rogers draws attention to the power of audience interpretation as well as the negative impact the Stage Indian has on the accuracy of audience perception. When he began attending Scarritt College in southwestern Missouri in the fall of 1895 and was one of only four Cherokee boys at the school, he was given the nickname Wild Indian.[38] In 1897, he was attending Kemper Military School and called Swarthy.[39] Even in early adulthood when Rogers was gainfully employed as a performer in a Wild West show, Betty Blake, the young woman who would eventually become his wife, was still put off by his Indianness. She explained that "marriage to an Indian, even a wealthy and presentable quarter-blood Cherokee, couldn't be seen as anything other than a social step down."[40] Money and moving within white society were not enough. In the first few decades of his life, Rogers's race was perceived by non-Cherokees as Indian, and Indian was understood to be inferior.

Indianness was a primary but not the sole component in his professional persona early in his career. He was billed as the Cherokee Kid in South Africa, and newspaper coverage of his early performances in the United States described him with headlines like "Judge Lassoed by an Indian."[41] By the time he was a vaudeville regular in 1906, the

---

36 Yagoda, *Will Rogers*, 248–49, 307.
37 Yagoda, *Will Rogers*, 184
38 Yagoda, *Will Rogers*, 25.
39 Ware, "Unexpected Cowboy."
40 Yagoda, *Will Rogers*, 79.
41 Undated article titled "Horses Cut Up Lively Capers" in scrapbook held by Will Rogers Memorial Museum and Archive, Claremore, Oklahoma.

descriptions had changed, calling him the "Lasso King," a "Texas Cowboy" whose father was "born and raised among the Cherokee tribe of Indians, and ultimately became a member of their Senate," thus explaining the moniker "Cherokee Kid."[42] A feature article on Rogers's work in Keith's vaudeville circuit from September 12, 1906, goes straight to the matter of race: "Is he an Indian? Sure!"[43] The public advertisement of his Indian identity began to disappear as he shifted to state-based billing after Indian Territory became Oklahoma in 1907. So quickly did the coverage of his Indianness shift that in September 1907, just one year after he was surely an Indian, he was described as a "tanned-up, lean and richly witty cowboy."[44] His connections with Indian Territory were also presented differently. An article fetchingly titled "Rogers Roped His Mother's Turkey," describes him as living "among the Cherokee Indians" rather than being one of them.[45] The rapid shift from Indian racialized identity to vocational cowboy identity led to the eventual inability of mainstream American audiences to recognize his Indigeneity. His skin tone had not changed, but the accepted interpretation of its meaning had. Scholar Amy Ware has articulated the particular challenges Rogers's Indigeneity presented to American audiences. Ware explains that "Americans of the day expected a cowboy to appear a certain way; they expected an Indian man to look another way."[46] Because Rogers was billed as a "Lariat King," "genuine Oklahoma cowboy," "lasso expert," and "Cowboy comedian," American audiences were unable to see past the cowboy to the Cherokee man behind it. His "playing cowboy on the Wild West circuit limited Rogers's reception as an American Indian performer."[47] He "simply didn't act the part" of a Stage Indian, and audiences came to see only his "tan."[48]

Unlike the billing and publicity for Rogers that changed over time, his self-identification as Cherokee never wavered, nor was his status as a

42 Vaudeville program "The Palace Theatre of Varieties" labeled "Week of May 21 06" in scrapbook held by Will Rogers Memorial Museum and Archive, Claremore, Oklahoma.

43 W.E. Sage, no title, no publication, Wednesday, September 12, 1906, in scrapbook held by Will Rogers Memorial Museum and Archive, Claremore, Oklahoma.

44 Amy Leslie. "'Girl Rangers' Opens" from unnamed journal, Monday, September 2, 1907, in scrapbook held by Will Rogers Memorial Museum and Archive, Claremore, Oklahoma.

45 "Rogers Roped His Mother's Turkey" in scrapbook held by Will Rogers Memorial Museum and Archive, Claremore, Oklahoma.

46 Ware, *The Cherokee Kid*, 85.

47 Ware, *The Cherokee Kid*, 68, 66.

48 Ware, *The Cherokee Kid*, 1

(*Continued on page 86*)

In addition to looking impressive, potential Native American performers in *Buffalo Bill's Wild West* had to dance impressively. When auditioning hopeful Oceti Sakowin, Luther Standing Bear "watched their dancing very closely" and observed as Cody hired the "best dancers" and highlighted their dances in performance.[112] For example, in The Drama of Civilization, the first epoch, the Primeval Forest, included, according to a *New York Times* review, a "war dance."[113] The first interlude, "Representations of Indian Life," contained still more dances. Few descriptions exist of what these dances, primarily called "scalp and war dances" by the show's publicity materials, looked like.[114] Specific information about the dances, including their purpose and message, was not made available to audiences of The Drama of Civilization. For instance, one of the earliest American films was of Native American performers from *Buffalo Bill's Wild West* dancing, but for decades, it was erroneously labeled as a "buffalo dance," and only recently has dance studies scholar Tria Blu Wakpa revealed that it is actually a performance of an Omaha dance that incorporates North American hand talk.[115] But audiences did not need factual information about what they were seeing to be able to read the dances as authentically Indian. As dance studies scholar Jacqueline Shea Murphy has explained, "the show Indians were seen to be performing not just barbaric conjurings or enactments of war or healing practices, but real, exterior manifestations of their authentic Indian selves."[116] Dancing in *Buffalo Bill's Wild West* was not only an entertainment; it was also a kind of authentic communication of another kind of racial essence. The dances Native Americans performed in the show relied on the performers' identities "as 'real' Indians performing dances with 'real ferocity'" while also taming the inherent danger in these dances by framing them as "pretend by way of their public staging."[117] Although these dances undoubtedly carried cultural and social meaning to Oceti Sakowin performers and viewers, the average attendee saw only real Indians doing real Indian dances. Understanding Indian dances as Indian did not require audiences to understand the significance or meaning of the dance but did demand the audience read the performers as Indian.

In addition to hiring actors who looked and moved like an Indian and possessed the racial category of Indianness, Cody also hired based

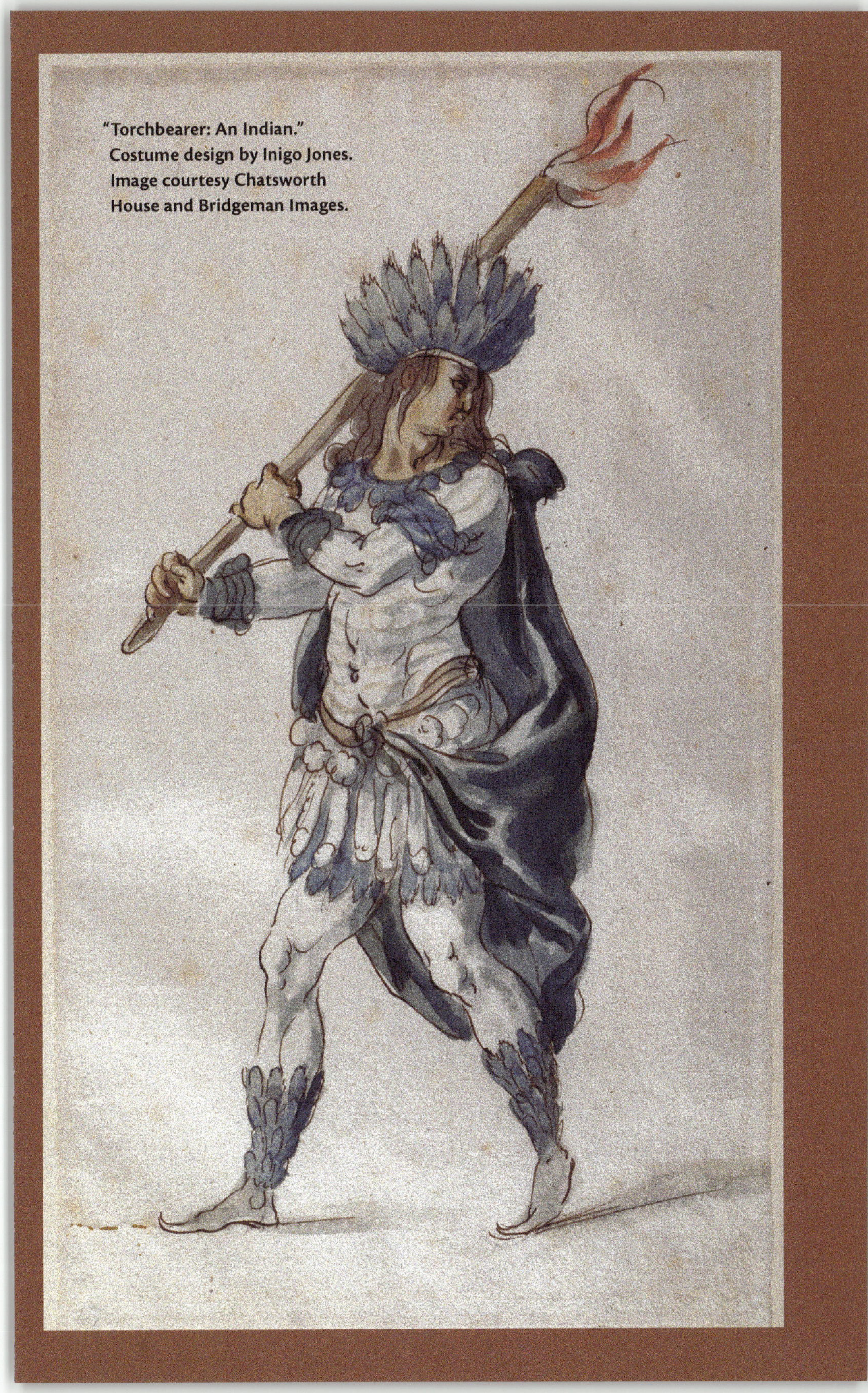

"Torchbearer: An Indian."
Costume design by Inigo Jones.
Image courtesy Chatsworth
House and Bridgeman Images.

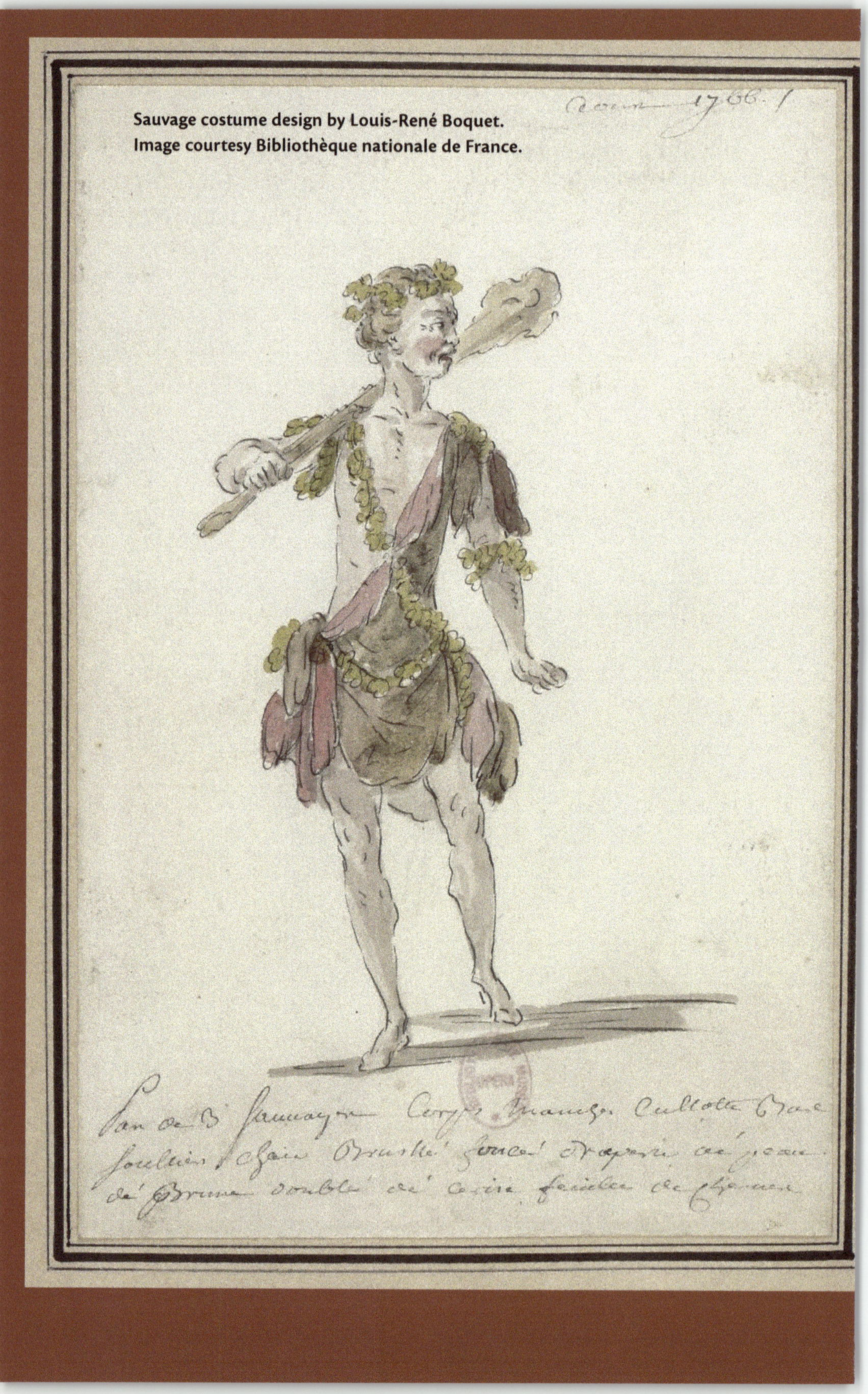

Sauvage costume design by Louis-René Boquet.
Image courtesy Bibliothèque nationale de France.

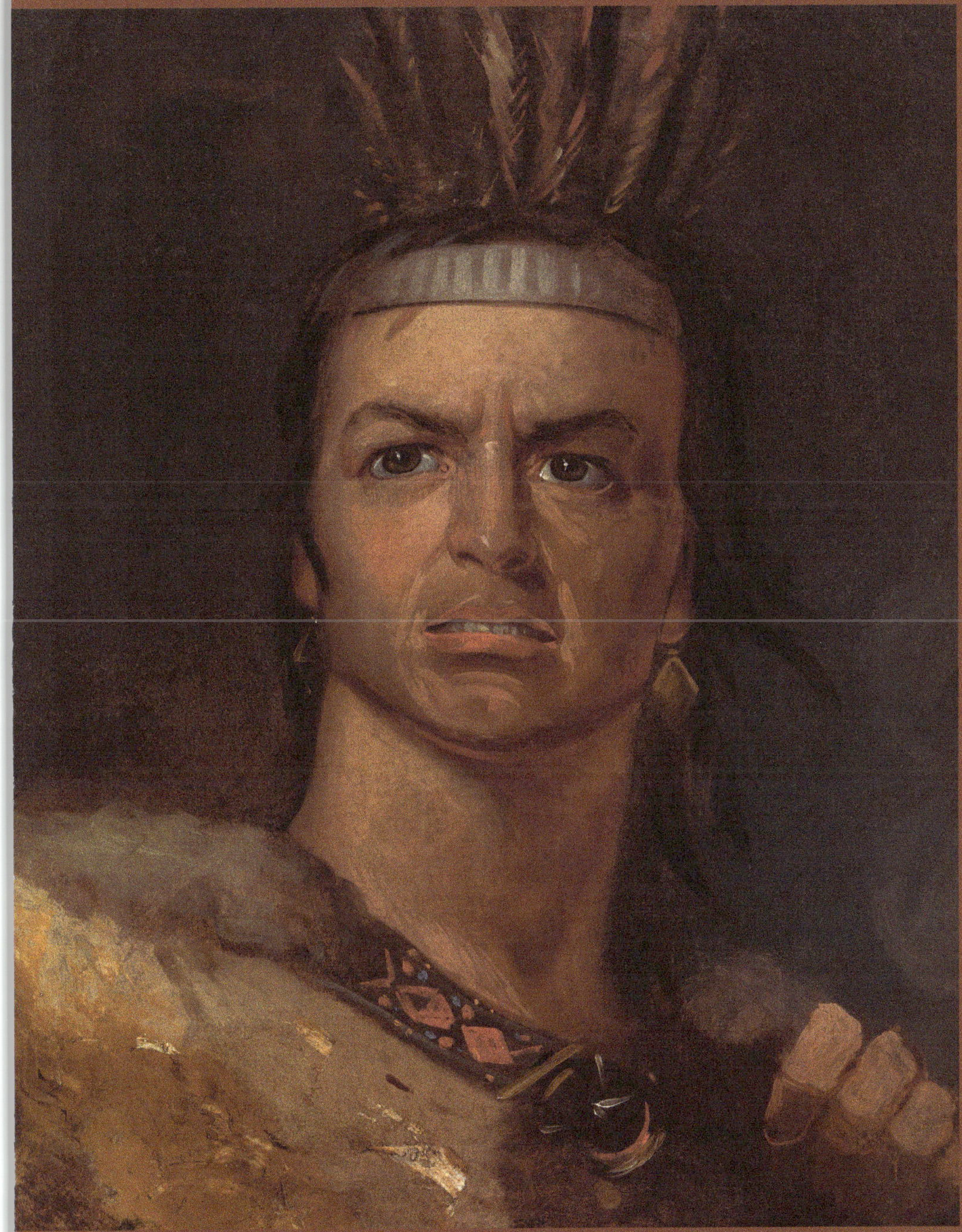

Frederick Styles Agate. *Edwin Forrest in the Role of Metamora.* Oil on canvas, circa 1832. Image courtesy Smithsonian National Portrait Gallery.

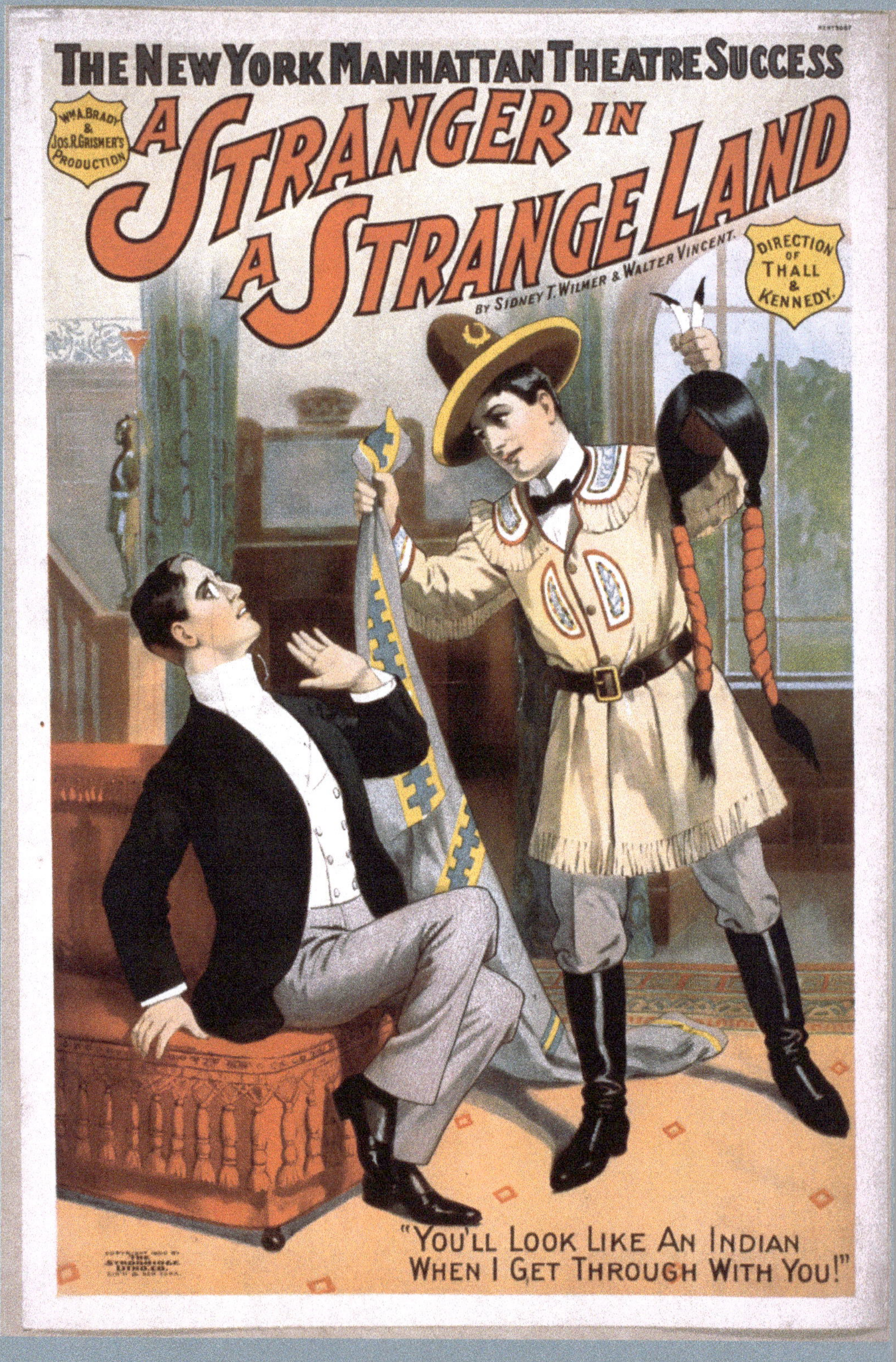

Stranger in a Strange Land poster. Image courtesy Library of Congress.

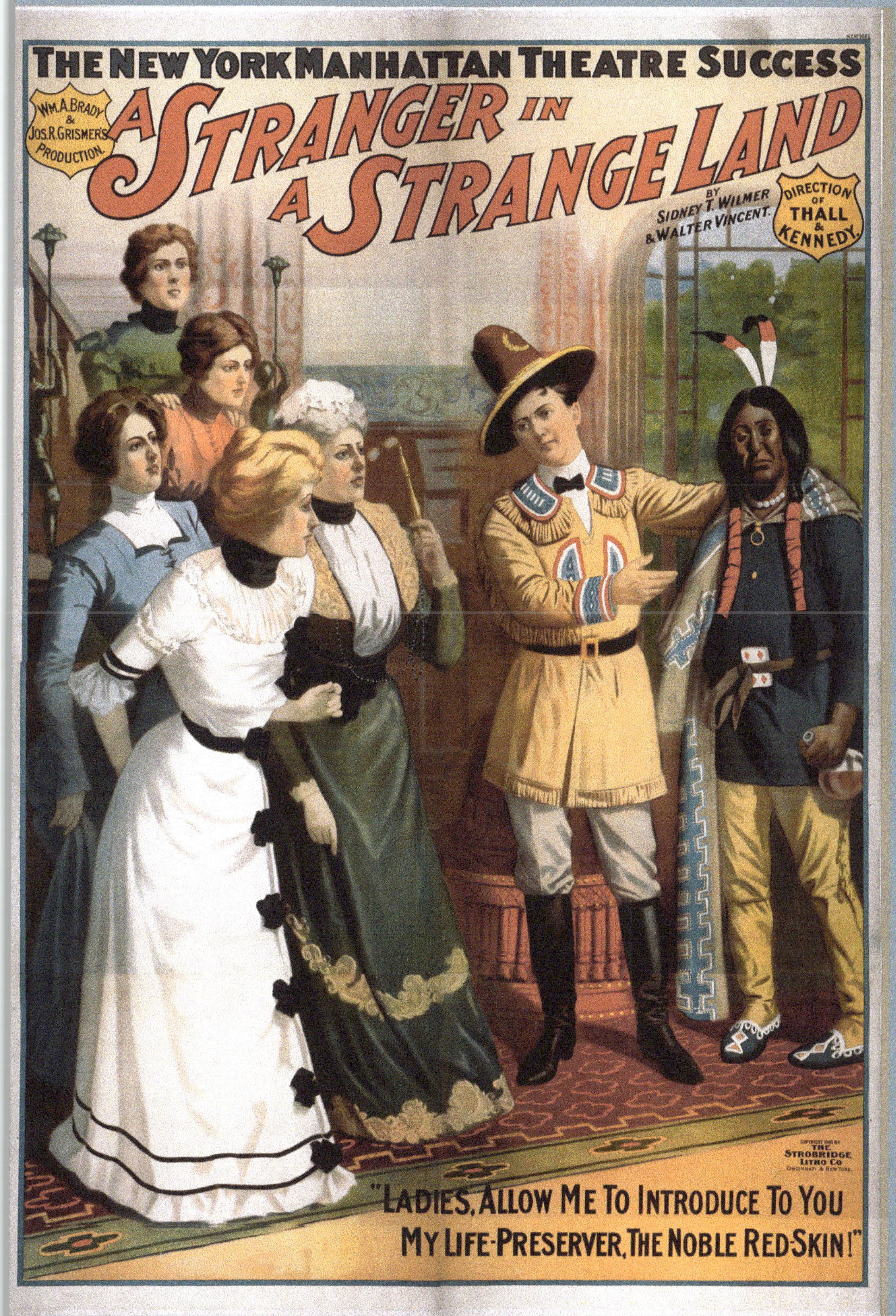

Stranger in a Strange Land poster. Image courtesy Library of Congress.

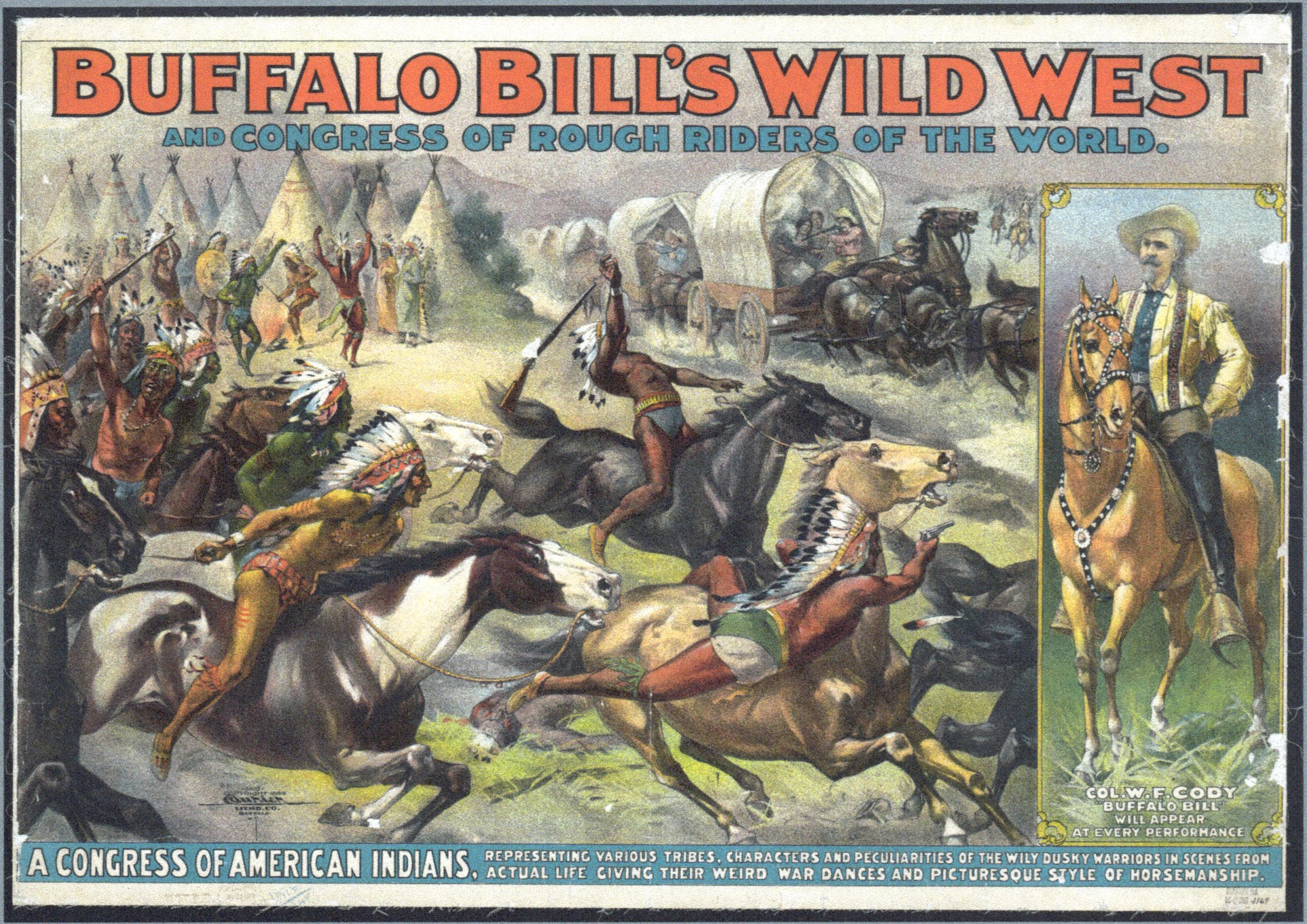

Buffalo Bill's Wild West and Congress of Rough Riders of the World: A Congress of American Indians, circa 1899. Image public domain.

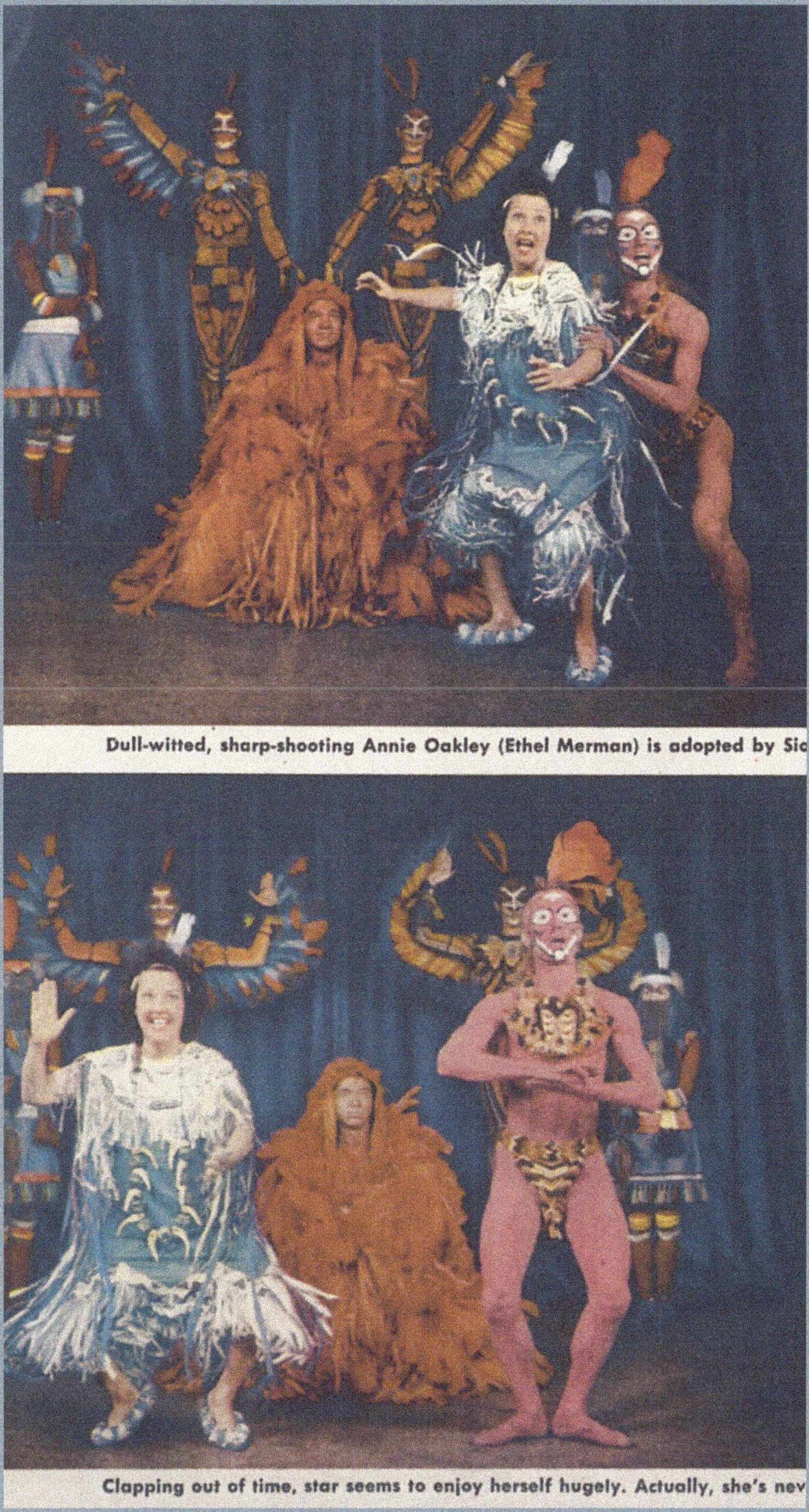

Ethel Merman as Annie, Harry Bellaver (*sitting*) as Sitting Bull, Daniel Nagrin as Wild Horse. Photos by Frank Bauman for *Look* magazine, from author's collection.

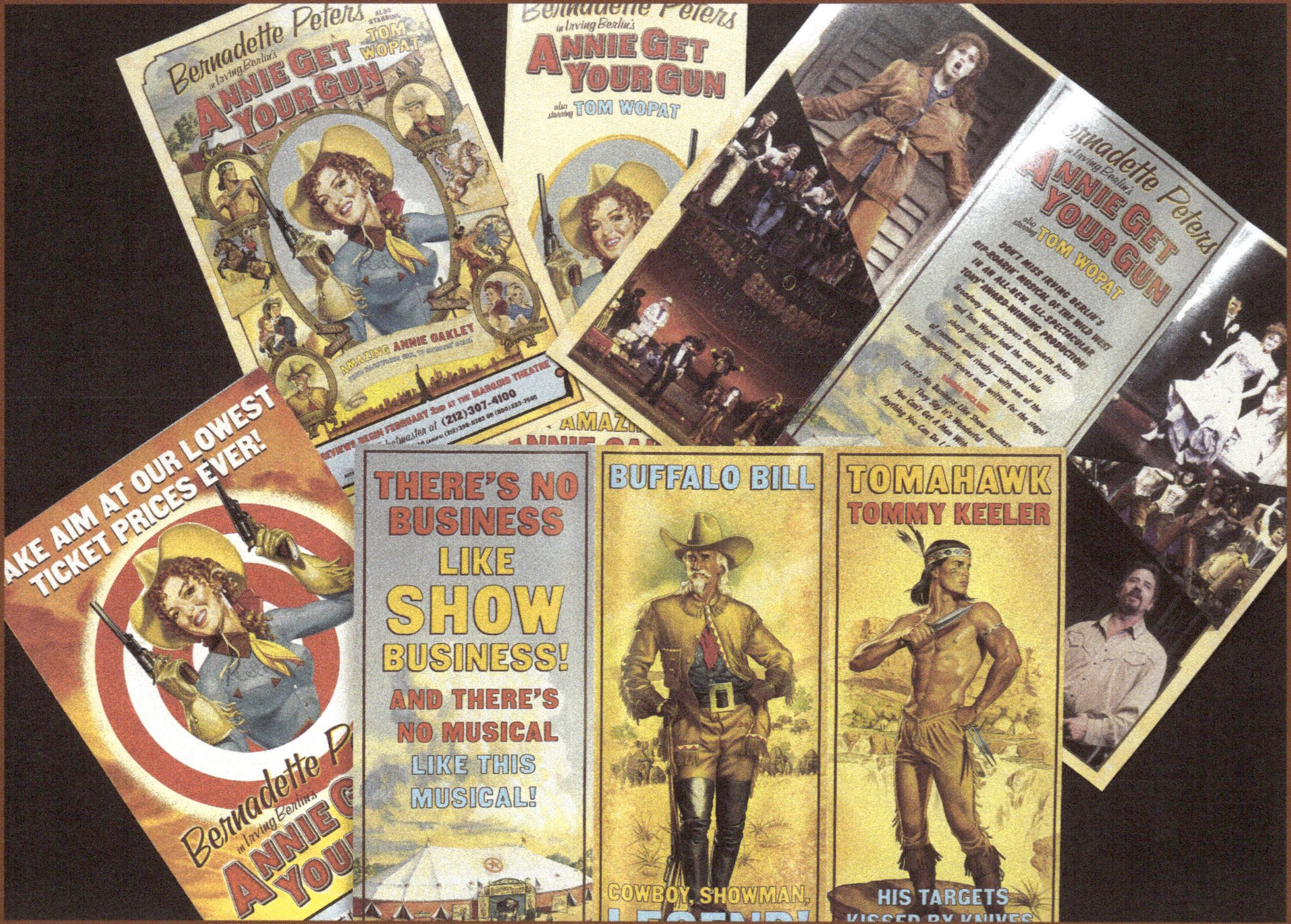

Selection of *Annie Get Your Gun* advertisements from author's collection.

on the criteria of personal reputation. Cody chose performers based on their audition performances, but also on their "reputations as fierce fighters and great horsemen."[118] Cody was invested in connecting the visuality, physicality, and racial essence of the (savage but vanishing) Indian to specific individuals whose participation in historically or culturally significant events further solidified their (defeated) Indian identity. This linkage created the conditions for the Lakota warrior to be attached to the Stage Indian, quickly becoming the primary legible Indian in the United States.

Because of Cody's preference for these impressive qualities (visual, kinetic, and historical), he also, whether intentionally or unintentionally, excluded women from the category of legible Stage Indian. If the markers of ideal Indianness were something practiced or possessed only by male Oceti Sakowin, then Indianness became synonymous with masculinity. To be an Indian woman in *Buffalo Bill's Wild West*—and there were many of these women performing and living in the Indian Village with their husbands—was to be less than the Stage Indian. To be a Stage Indian woman in the show was to be not quite Indian enough. Cody's focus on displaying and advertising male Indians did not actively support the hypersexualization of female Native Americans, which remains rampant in the United States, but did actively exclude female Native Americans from being part of the racialized (and romanticized) Stage Indian, which was so expertly produced in *Buffalo Bill's Wild West.* In a production intent on advertising the most spectacular, the most hair-raising, the most (controlled) threatening Indians (figure 3.6), female Indians were conspicuously absent.

Cody's decisions about who was onstage, when, and doing what, created not just material performances of Indianness but also immaterial standards of Indianness that became culturally diffuse. Real Indians were part of a racial group, but with specific gendered and cultural markers that morphed into racial markers (e.g., men in feathered headdress). *Buffalo Bill's Wild West* supported its claims to authenticity through hiring primarily Oceti Sakowin performers and then heavily advertising their presence, typically through images of male Indians with feathered headdresses. The performers' personal regalia, their dance skills, and their personal reputation all were factors in their se-

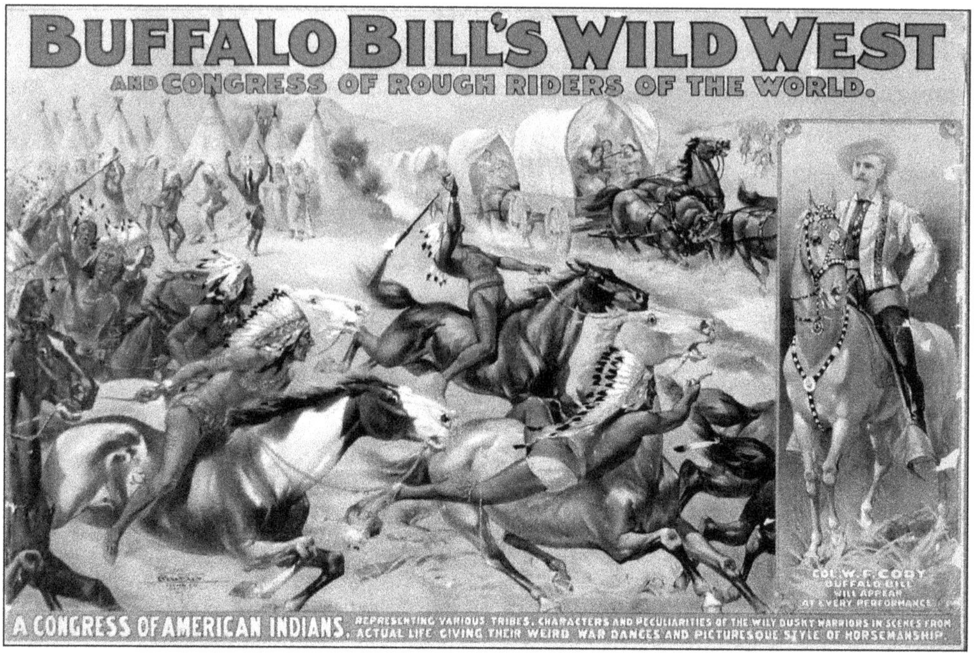

Figure 3.6. Buffalo Bill's Wild West and Congress of Rough Riders of the World: A Congress of American Indians, circa 1899. Image public domain.

lection to work in the show. Cody wanted his employees to be seen as real and not as performers.

However, in *Buffalo Bill's Wild West,* audiences never encountered a noncurated, unmediated version of the Indian. The "Grand Entry," the beginning sequence of every show, explicitly demonstrates this fact. During the "Grand Entry," all the performers rode horses in an elaborate pattern crisscrossing the performance space, giving the audience a chance to see who and what was coming. In the "Grand Entry" (titled "Grand Introduction" in figure 3.2), Native American performers were introduced as members of four different tribes. To distinguish these tribes and help audiences read the Indians as legibly distinct rather than homogenous, each tribe rode horses of a different color. A 1902 film of a parade advertising *Buffalo Bill's Wild West* depicts this grouping of Native Americans by horse color.[119] This would be an unremarkable and effective visual tool if it were not a blatant mislabeling of tribal belonging. Among the show's Native American performers and historians, it was common knowledge that the performers were not actually from the four tribes they played onstage. Employee Luther Standing Bear explained that at least for the 1887 tour of England, "all the Indians belonged to the Sioux tribe" but "were supposed to represent four different tribes, each tribe to ride animals of one color."[120] Vine Deloria Jr. noted more generally that while "some of the Sioux chiefs were listed as chiefs of the Cheyenne and Arapaho tribes . . . in fact they were almost all from the Pine Ridge reservation in South Dakota."[121] He went on to explain that the Native American performers knew they were being mislabeled in performance but that it did not bother them.[122] The performers understood that they were being hired to play a role. The audience believed they were witnessing the truth. *Buffalo Bill's Wild West* touted the authenticity of the Indians in the entertainment, while knowingly mislabeling their tribal membership.

While the "Grand Entry" horse-color trick is not more deceptive than Edwin Forrest's claim to know Choctaw chief Pushmataha, it is similar. The show heavily advertised authentic Indians as one of the ways in which audiences would encounter the real history of the West. But the "real history" was heavily mediated in both the preferences for hiring male Oceti Sakowin who were sufficiently impressive visually, kinetically, and reputationally and the dramatic and character shaping force of the show's teleological drama. Even though *Buffalo Bill's Wild West* advertised real Indians, what it actually provided was a Stage Indian that gave audiences a spectacular figure, a defeated foe easily identifiable and dependent on the whim of Cody/Salsbury/Burke/MacKaye for its tribal membership. And by providing the Stage Indian, the show narrowed and sharpened the criteria used to determine who was Indian.

BUT IT'S EDUCATIONAL

Buffalo Bill's Wild West claimed to present the authentic Indian doing authentic Indian things and instead represented the Stage Indian as it carefully constructed audience interaction with Indian characters and imagery. It used two main methods of controlling the Indian and reshaping the Stage Indian. The first was touting itself and being recognized as a legitimate source of educational information about history and Indians. The second was carefully monitoring, creating, and publicizing its presentation of Indian characters. It mediated the Stage Indian while advertising the authentic Indian. These twinned strategies were implemented early in the history of *Buffalo Bill's Wild West*, showing up in The Drama of Civilization. These strategies were deployed simultaneously by the show to increase audience attendance and profit through ticket sales. Showing an Indian and shaping the Stage Indian were part of an extractive economic practice of utilizing Native American resources to benefit non-Native American entities. This practice connects *Buffalo Bill's Wild West* to other national projects of the time, like the imposition of allotment on Native American nations from 1887 to 1934, which drastically reduced the Native land base (from 147 million acres to 55 million acres) and resulted in bursts of settler development and settler profit across the continent.[123] *Buffalo Bill's Wild West* extracted and profited from its Native American employees' identities and used those identities to assure audiences of the educational nature of the production. The show did not just passively become known as an educational experience. It actively pursued this reputation.

In January 1887, thirty Indians performing in The Drama of Civilization went to Public School 40 in New York City to visit school children and sing for them.[124] By offering or agreeing to perform in a school, the show was agreeing to the interpretation of its entertainment as an educational experience. In turn, schools sent crowds of students to watch matinee performances and witness history. On February 6, 1887, the *New York Times* reported that "every school in the city nearly" sent their students to "witness the battle of the Little Big Horn."[125] The Drama of Civilization had made the transition from an outdoor entertainment held at an amusement grounds to an upstanding, educational experience, enriching the lives of public school students by showing them recent historical events. It was also seen as an educational tool for adults. As one New York journalist noted, The Drama of Civilization drew "statesmen, teachers, writers, musicians, business men, politicians, artisans, mechanics, and others who desire to know as much as possible about the history of their country."[126] The show educated audiences young and old, prominent and obscure, and in doing so, reinforced both its middle-class reputation and its role as an arbiter of historical fact. In advertising itself as educational and being received as such by audiences, *Buffalo Bill's Wild West* presented authentic history with authentic Indians.

Audiences took advantage of the educational performances of American history and Indianness both onstage and off. In addition to the show, audiences could visit the Indian encampment, sometimes called the Indian Village. This was where Native American employees lived while performing. They would erect their dwelling places, often tipis, and live with their families.[127] This community campsite was then on display to the audience, offering an educational and up-close look at how Indians actually lived. Guests and audience members could wander through the Indian Village and see the Indians who had attacked a stage coach in performance "in modern dress reading the newspaper, playing ping pong, or eating Cracker Jack."[128] During The Drama of Civilization's run, the encampment was located on Staten Island away from Madison Square Garden.[129] Audiences liked these up-close experiences with Indians as much as the staged performances.[130] They could inspect the living arrangements of Native Americans and a few hours later see the very same Native Americans viciously attack settlers. The truth of the performance onstage was echoed by the truth of the everyday lives of the Native American performers offstage. It is unclear whether audiences understood these as competing truths or complementary. What is clear is that in advertising itself as educational and in being received as such by audiences, The Drama of Civilization relied on an understanding of authenticity that rested on its didactic capabilities.

However, the line between education and publicity was very fluid. Employees of *Buffalo Bill's Wild West* were often called upon to be displayed at public events to advertise for the show, and the Indians were a special draw. A week before The Drama of Civilization opened, Steele MacKaye invited guests to witness a special "spectacle so unique" provided by Cody.[131] "The Chiefs of the Pawnee and Cheyenne Tribes of Indians . . . will meet for the first time, off the war path" to perform a ceremony required of them "to go into camp together."[132] These "Ancient Aboriginal Ceremonies of the Nappay-oboloose-poppay, which means 'the Burial of the Hatchet,'" allowed members of the two tribes who had "never in their whole history made a treaty of peace" to live among one another.[133] The invitation states that the recipient will "meet a few friends" at this event, which was held in Madison Square Garden at 10:30 p.m. on a Friday evening.

There are several pieces of evidence that support the interpretation of this event as a staged publicity stunt. First, the ceremony was described in the invitation as something that had to happen before the two tribes could live among one another. The Drama of Civilization had a six-week preparation process with only three of those weeks in Madison Square Garden.[134] Native American performers in the show largely comprised performers from the summer season at Erastina and therefore had been living in New York for months already and had been working together on the production for weeks. It seems most likely that they had worked together for weeks if not months before this supposedly essential ceremony would occur.

Given the reputation of John Burke, Cody's press agent, for extravagant and elaborate advertisements (and sometimes embellished truths), a late-night performance for a privately invited audience appears much more likely. Cody regularly gave private dinners for invited guests, often reporters, as a method of advertisement.[135] A private performance of an Indian ceremony aligns with the publicity practices of Cody and *Buffalo Bill's Wild West*. There are mixed reports of whether all the performers in The Drama of Civilization were Oceti Sakowin only or also included Northern Cheyenne. But scholars agree that Cody stopped hiring Pawnees by 1886.[136] It would seem that the Northern Cheyenne and Pawnees would have been an unlikely combination in November of 1886. The publicity performance of the "Burial of the Hatchet" was likely a staged event in which either Oceti Sakowin or Cheyenne individuals were intentionally misidentified as Pawnee in the invitation and the subsequent event. Given that the Native American performers were divided into four tribes for the performance, perhaps it is these tribal "roles" they performed in the publicity event. The invitation's language suggests that the reason for the event was the Indians' own cultural demands for ceremony, which could then be witnessed by white audience members. However, given the lack of evidence that the Native American performers required or demanded such a time for ceremony, the circumstantial information regarding their employment tenure and living arrangements in the Indian Village, and the obvious misidentification of tribal affiliation, it appears that the ceremony was nothing more than a publicity stunt. Given the desire for representing itself as historical fact and educational display, the manipulation of Native American tribal affiliation and ceremonial needs to stir up media coverage suggests The Drama of Civilization was more invested in creating a compelling advertisement than presenting an educational, cultural event.

Through publicity events, the Indian Village, educational performances, and more, *Buffalo Bill's Wild West* shaped expectations of authentic Indianness by proclaiming who was an Indian, what was an Indian, and where an Indian lived. In doing so, it created just another iteration of the Stage Indian, one as deeply invested in race as that of earlier iterations and as interested in proving its own authenticity and asserting its own authority. *Buffalo Bill's Wild West* turned to regalia, dancing, and masculine warrior reputations to hire Native American performers, creating a revised set of criteria for being legibly Indian (Not just feathers! Headdresses! And horses!). They deployed these criteria in the creation of events, both educational and publicity focused, to assure audiences that what they were seeing was the real Indian—this despite the fact that the "real" in the real Indian was heavily curated and mediated if not outright manipulated. Despite the holes in the show's façade so obvious to twenty-first-century readers, the processes and mechanisms it used in presenting the Stage Indian remain clear. Show an audience an Indian. Tell an audience how that Indian is real. Demand that Indigenous people match those criteria for realness. For without "good wigs and good costumes," even an Indigenous person cannot get hired to be a Stage Indian.[137]

AGENTIAL OR COMPLICITOUS?

It is perhaps controversial to make the claim that Oceti Sakowin performers wearing their own clothes, doing the dances they knew, living with their families under the watchful eye of audiences strolling through the Indian Village, and speaking their own language were performing in redface. In the second decade of the twenty-first century, the word *redface* grew to mean any Native American role played by a non-Native American actor. However, I argue that to limit the word's definition in that way is imprecise and doing so conceals redface's actual practices and impact. The role of Native American performers in the production and circulation of the Stage Indian is a simple and complex one. Native Americans contributed to the circulation and modification of the Stage Indian before and after *Buffalo Bill's Wild West*. The show itself is just a hypervisible example of how Indigenous performers were part of a collaborative, curatorial process that resulted in a legible Stage Indian. Their complicity in the reductive, racializing depiction of Indians is not inexplicable because it was also advantageous.

The Indian as a featured figure in live entertainment was ubiquitous across many performance genres at the time. During the nineteenth century, there were at least two hundred different performances in New York City alone that purported to show paying audiences real Indian dances, songs, speeches, or sometimes just real Indians on display.[138] These were not plays as such but exhibitions and performances for audiences at circuses, museums, theaters, amphitheaters, and pleasure gardens of all kinds. Some of these performers were likely Indigenous, and some were likely not. For instance, "Five Indian Chiefs" were advertised at the City Hotel in 1808, while in 1829, the "Indian Chief Red Jacket" gave a speech at the Park Theatre.[139] A "Band of Chippewa Indians" were at the New York Museum in fall of 1843, while in 1860, the Great North American Indian Troupe appeared at the Polytechnic Hall in Brooklyn.[140] In the 1870s, Donald McKay, a Warm Springs (Apache) leader, established a touring company that traveled across the United States, appearing at the Old Bowery Theatre in New York City in 1874 and eventually touring Europe with a different company.[141] These performances and many more like them were in addition to the numerous Indian plays (discussed in chapter 1) that continued in legitimate theaters throughout the nineteenth century and the dozens of vaudeville Indians circulating at the turn of the twentieth century. Indigenous and non-Indigenous performers had performed as Indian for decades. The performer Lillian Smith, for example, performed as a sharpshooter in The Drama of Civilization (billed as the "California Girl" between the third and fourth epoch, visible in figure 3.3) and later as Wenona, an Indian princess sharpshooter, in *Miller Brothers 101 Ranch Wild West*.[142] It is unclear whether New York audiences of the time could discern the difference between Indigenous performers presenting culturally accurate demonstrations and non-Indigenous performers practicing racial/ethnic fraud, nor is it clear if audiences would have cared about the difference. What is clear is that Indigenous performers had many opportunities to participate in the American theater and entertainment industry for the entirety of the nineteenth century.

Indigenous performers made the decision to pursue economic opportunities through performance for diverse reasons and to diverse ends. In some cases, their situations were not exploitative, financially or otherwise. In *Buffalo Bill's Wild West*, Native American employees earned a respectable wage, anywhere from $25 to $90 a month. If they earned on the higher end of that range, they could earn the equivalent of two-thirds of the annual salary of an Indian agent from one season's employment.[143] However, other Wild West productions did not pay as well. In 1911, *The Miller Brothers 101 Ranch*, a Wild West show headquartered in Oklahoma, corresponded with Native Americans about employment opportunities, listing a weekly salary of five dollars for Native American men and four dollars for Native American women. This sixteen- to twenty-dollar gendered monthly salary range is significantly lower than the top earning potential in Buffalo Bill's production. Dance studies scholar Jacqueline Shea Murphy has discussed the positive contributions that employment in Wild West shows held for Native Americans, such as possibilities for free movement, continuation of cultural practices banned or made illegal on reservations, and lucrative employment with which to support families both nuclear and extended.[144] Employment in Wild West shows could be a lucrative, desirable, or agential choice for Native Americans. Despite the positive personal impact, Native American Wild West performers were also enmeshed in a larger cultural project that worked to essentialize them as a racial minority. This book does not attempt to critique or condemn

Indigenous performers for their personal choices, but it also does not attempt to absolve them of the impact of those choices. The Stage Indian has both helped and hurt Native Americans. That is the simple and complicated truth.

The hundreds of Indian performances across the nineteenth and early twentieth century offered artists, entertainers, and audiences alike the opportunity to racialize, repeat, modify, standardize, and interpret just what an Indian was, could be, and should be. I contend that the word *redface* should be reserved for the process by which a body is understood as legibly Indian. Redface, as Pocahontas has shown us, carries racial and gendered meaning while maintaining a relationship with historical fact. It also, as Forrest and *Buffalo Bill's Wild West* have shown us, depends on claims of authenticity that are built on reductive and demeaning racial logics of erasure and inferiority. Redface is more than who is on the stage; it is how the Indian is brought to life in/through a racialized body. But it is not the body exclusively that carries the racial meaning; it is the collaborative curatorial process that does. Redface is not on the surface. It is the space between actor and audience, created through performance and shaped by settler colonialism's desire for Indigenous death and dominion.

CONCLUSION

The question of Indian authenticity is not ontological; it is epistemological. And the epistemology offered by *Buffalo Bill's Wild West* reveals much about the nation enacting it and the people pledging allegiance to it. It is not actually self-evident that all Indians wear feathered headdresses. It is not actually self-evident that all Indians have red skin. It is not actually self-evident that Indianness resides in blood or DNA. These are markers, embodied and essential, that have been actively, though not always intentionally, knit together with the idea of the Indian. Feathers and face paint do not fundamentally possess Indianness. It is the repeated interpretation of them as Indian markers that make Indianness stick to them. The American national (read, settler colonial) project calls Indians into being even as it claims to be merely recognizing them. The criteria used to determine and recognize

Indianness are the key to revealing the racializing project of redface. They are key to understanding that the right question to ask is not, What is true about Indians?, but, How do we recognize truth about Indians?

This is precisely why redface should be located not in the individual actor but in the system that constructs and perpetuates it. Forrest's actions make perfect sense if you know that all Indians are alike, that is, if you subscribe to an essentialized, racialized definition of Native Americans. The depiction of Indians in *Buffalo Bill's Wild West* is perfectly authentic if you know that Indians are a racial group that presented obstacles to US expansion and settlement and that the way to recognize Indians is to listen to those who "conquered" them. The solution to Forrest's reductive and racist portrayal of Metamora is not to get rid of feathers and face paint. The solution to the curation of Oceti Sakowin markers in *Buffalo Bill's Wild West* is not to add other nation's characteristics, and neither is adding more historical details to a play or changing the plot so that the Indians win or the audience is sympathetic when they lose. The solution is no longer to consider Indians as a homogenous race and a subservient category to American identity and nationhood. However, to do that, US theater artists, audiences, and institutions would have to accept Indigeneity and sovereignty, self-determination, complexity, nuance, diversity, and the responsibilities and obligations to Native Americans so long forfeited, ignored, and actively refused by US government and society.

What, then, can be done with this theatrical practice that knits together popularity, embodiment, history, myth, authenticity, and power? It can be modified, as we have seen. Its dramaturgy can be shifted in service of new narratives. But can we excise the underlying assumptions shaping redface? Can we remake the Stage Indian into a figure that speaks to a nation's need to understand, make amends, and inhabit the diverse bodies it comprises? Maybe. Or maybe we need to choreograph a new dance.

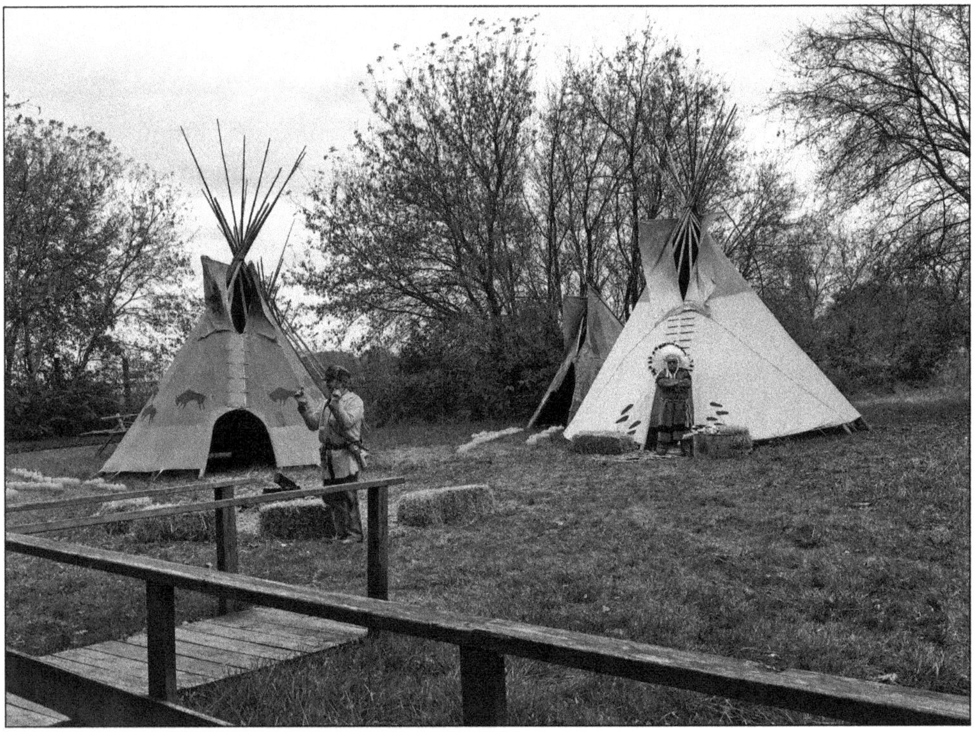

Figure 4.1. Chief Big Eagle's campground. Photo by author.

CHAPTER FOUR

FIXING REDFACE

In October 2017, I took my family to the Fall Festival at Donley's Wild West Town, a small, privately owned amusement park and museum in northern Illinois.[1] First opened in 1974, the park, which permanently closed in 2022, was geared toward elementary school children. It offered hands-on activities and rides and a museum loosely based on the late nineteenth-century American West. There were typical amusement park rides like a roller coaster and water, carousel, and train rides, but at a kid-friendly scale. There were also places to pan for gold, throw a tomahawk, and watch a stunt show, and in the fall, guests could trade beads for a pumpkin. This last activity is the reason we went. Children who visited Wild West Town during the Fall Festival received a strand of beads, specifically the cheap kind colloquially known as Mardi Gras beads, boarded a small train, and rode to Chief Big Eagle's campground (figure 4.1). The campground comprised three tipis and the skeleton of a fourth. Each tipi had a few decorative touches like buffalo or circles painted on the sides. There was a small fire burning and a handful of hay bales around the fire.

As my family disembarked from the train, a man in what I can only describe as a nineteenth-century western-wear costume greeted us. The man welcomed the train travelers and gathered the children to the makeshift benches of hay. He instructed the children that the chief, waiting in the tipi in the back, might be open to trading his pumpkins for beads. He went on to explain that the chief did not speak English, so he would be speaking in Plains Indian Sign Language and serving as a translator for the trades. He taught the children how to sign "thank you" and then welcomed the chief to the gathering. The chief strode out of his tipi wearing a dark red robe, with a painted face and a feathered headdress. He struggled a bit with the headdress as the windy day pushed it forward into his face more than once. The black face paint that ringed his eyes like a pair of glasses was missing a part near his right eye. It had clearly been applied hours before and either not been set correctly with powder or had accidentally been rubbed off. He sat in front of the light-colored tipi on a bale of hay, and the children lined up to trade with him. One by one, the children, including mine, stepped up, gave their beads to the chief, and waited for his assessment of their offering (figure 4.2). The chief carefully inspected each necklace, sometimes pausing to eye the child who gave it to him, sometimes handing it to the interpreter who, in the case of my son, bit on the beads to check if they were real gold (the beads passed the test). The chief ultimately signed his assent to every trade. The children signed their gratitude and walked to the rows of pumpkins on the ground to select which one they would take home.

After all trades had been made and the train had arrived to return the various families to the main area of the park, some of the parents began speaking with our interpreter. He excitedly told them about the Plains Indian Sign Language he had taught their children and showed them some other words. I noticed that his gloves had a circular design beaded on their backs and that his costume was clearly put together with attention to detail. I surmised that this actor was enthusiastic about historical accuracy and approached his "trader" encounters with audience members as an opportunity to educate youth on history. Enthusiastic in my incredulity that this kind of redface performance was still accessible in the second decade of the twenty-first century, I naturally insisted that we have a family photo with Chief Big Eagle before we boarded the train back to the main park grounds. The "trader" kindly offered to take the picture for us.

I left that park, three pumpkins the richer, wondering about the implications of an embodied interaction between children and an Indian. I had told my children that they had to trade beads because I could not access this redface performance without them. They dutifully though cautiously obliged as my research assistants/cover story. But what exactly had they experienced? The park had framed their experience as one belonging to the Wild West, a temporality and location of mythical proportions. The train trip from the park proper to this outpost of an

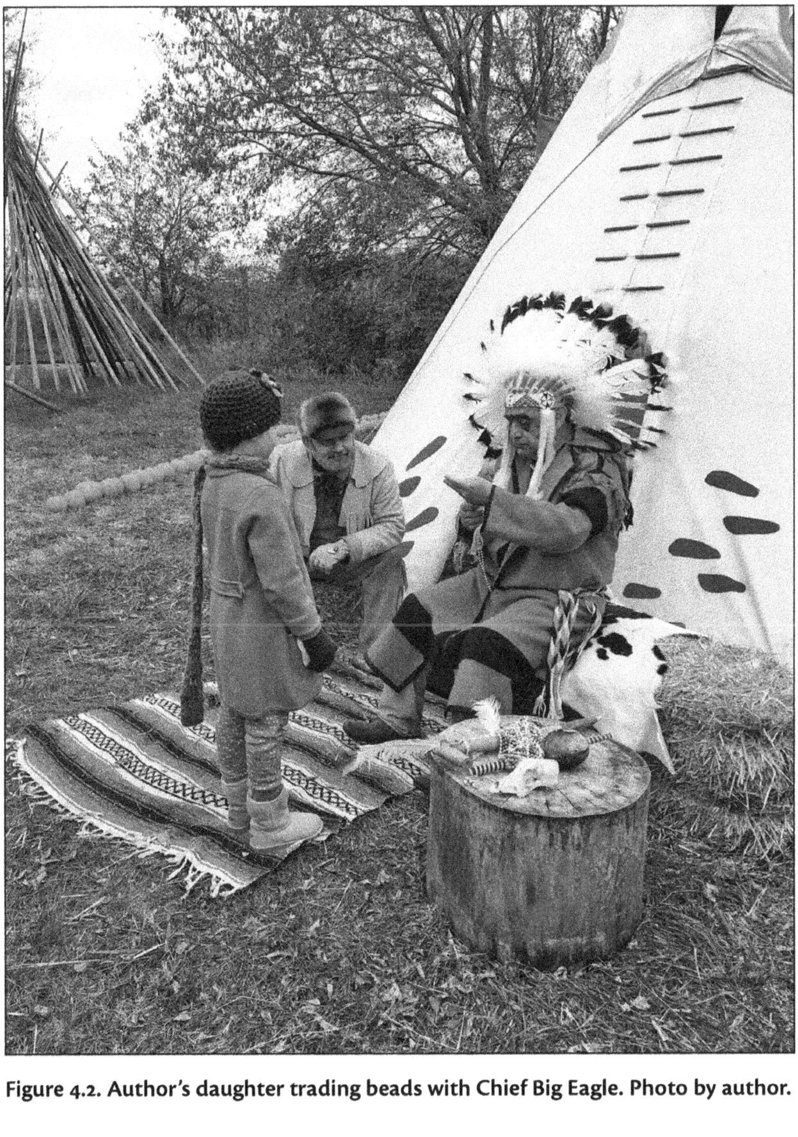

Figure 4.2. Author's daughter trading beads with Chief Big Eagle. Photo by author.

Indian village suggested that Indians were peripheral to the Wild West but could be approached with the help of a guide or interpreter. Their interaction with a person announced as and visually marked as Indian was silent and brief. Yet they participated in an imaginative interaction with him that included material objects, one of which they would decorate and bring home. They had performed in an Indian play, and I had taken pictures.

This short Indian play relied on verbal, contextual, visual, and material markers of Indianness to communicate which character should be legible as a Stage Indian. The feathered headdress and the framing location connected the performance to the long history of Wild West shows and the ubiquity of the Plains Indian as the visual standard of Indianness par excellence. The educational talk by the translator linked us to the facts of history and the force of historical authority. And we left having had a taste of something akin to an authentic essence rather than a factually accurate encounter. We had also participated in the collaborative process of redface, assenting to the roles we played (bead-trading child, parent on a fun family outing) in an interaction that placed the Indian in an imagined past and reinforced the racialization of Indigenous people.

This kind of interaction is growing increasingly rare in the United States. Instead, there is a widespread desire to correct the long history of Native Americans being misrepresented, often motivated by genuine concern and a sense of justice. A shift to sympathetic, rather than antagonistic, depictions of Native American characters occurred in American popular culture during the last decades of the twentieth century. Suddenly, it was not cowboys versus Indians or cavalry versus Indians. Indians were wise, funny, thoughtful, and impactful characters, revealing deep truths about white America and its past. From Arthur Kopit's Pulitzer-nominated play *Indians* in 1968 to Disney's *Pocahontas* in 1995 to the 1999 revival of a 1946 Broadway musical *Annie Get Your Gun*, US entertainment culture was interested in how the Indian condemns the United States and reveals its failures and foundational vices. It was also interested in righting the wrongs of previous racist caricatures and distancing itself from those past indiscretions. But how exactly can redface be fixed?

* * *

This chapter takes seriously the challenge of changing Native American representation in theater so that it no longer damages Indigenous peoples and nations. This, as I will demonstrate, is very hard to do because first, you have to diagnose the problem correctly. By tracing the original Broadway production of the musical *Annie Get Your Gun* and its significantly revised 1999 revival, I argue that shifting from antagonistic to sympathetic interpretations of the Stage Indian does not actually correct the misrepresentation, racialization, and depoliticization of Indigenous peoples. It merely makes cosmetic changes that cover over or refresh but never touch the foundations. Redface is difficult to excise because the process of achieving legibility is wrapped in the materiality of the familiar and the ideology of a raced, gendered, "historically real" Indian. It is always imbricated in assertions of power over Indigenous identity and nationhood. In short, the Stage Indian of redface persists because it is still effective. It is effective because American audiences still identify Indians by feathers and face paint, still understand Indians as a vanished/vanishing race not as enduring polities, and still assume that they hold ultimate authority over Indigenous identity. Without feathers and face paint, we would just be trading beads for pumpkins with a random stranger in an Illinois field, which is maybe the truth that redface conceals in the first place. If you do not want to admit to the situation you are in (settler-colonial expansion and conquest), you can always imagine that you are in a different situation (benevolent dominion over friend/foe).

ANNIE GET YOUR GUN

One beloved Broadway musical illustrates the persistence of redface better than any other. Irving Berlin's *Annie Get Your Gun* appeared when the Wild West show Indian had been thoroughly incorporated into American popular culture and its cartoonish iteration was widely accepted and utilized. A late twentieth-century revival of the musical on Broadway demonstrates how well-intentioned but cosmetic changes were made to try to solve the problem of redface. Together, these two productions, produced decades apart, and the show itself, performed routinely into the twenty-first century by professional and amateur theaters alike, tell a story of inattentiveness and hyperattentiveness to Native American representation. Both extremes, while forwarding differing interpretations of Native American characters, one comedic and the other sympathetic, rely on culturally legible markers of the Stage Indian and diffuse racialized knowledge of Indigenous peoples.

Both create a cosmetically enhanced Stage Indian, one attuned to mid-century tastes, the other using a palette more suited to the turn of the twenty-first. Both speak to the foundations of redface, a foundation that cannot be washed away or covered over.

In 1946 the musical *Annie Get Your Gun* opened on Broadway with a scene set in Cincinnati, Ohio. Employees of *Buffalo Bill's Wild West* parade through the town, advertising their upcoming performance in song. Charlie Davenport, the show's manager, introduces the show's exciting components with a word now widely accepted as a racial slur for an Indigenous woman. (Many readers will possess strong opinions about the necessity of excluding or including the slur on this page. To provide readers some choice in the matter, I will not use the word on this page but will make it available in an endnote.)[2]

> Who's got the show that gets the most applause?
> Five hundred Indians and fifty s----s
> Ten feature acts, and there's the special feature still
> Colonel Buffalo Bill.[3]

While the word "s----" can denote a Native American woman, it also carries negative and racist connotations. The *Merriam-Webster Dictionary* states it is "often offensive" and "usually disparaging."[4] Thirty-three years later, in 1999, a revival of *Annie Get Your Gun* opened with neither the offensive word nor the opening number. Instead, it began with a single actor onstage singing the most famous song of the show's score, "There's No Business Like Show Business." Following the solo, Buffalo Bill introduced a new framework for the musical.

> You are now going to see my own personal version of the tempestuous and romantic story of Annie Oakley and Frank Butler, featuring my celebrated troupe of western actors and—my fabulous Cowboy Band—and all of it exactly as I've presented it over the years, right here under my big top![5]

The musical had been transformed into a self-aware piece of theater, a show within a show. The show's new book writer, Peter Stone, charged with fixing what writer John Lahr calls the musical's "unwitting but breathtaking racism," utilized this new framing device to soften the dramatic structure deemed clunky by decades of evolution of the American musical.[6] It now overtly claimed temporal historicity (by announcing it as performed "over the years") and distanced itself from factual historicity ("my own personal version"). This tension between past event and present depiction, between personal account and public history, and between fact and fiction is vividly refracted through the Native American characters in the musical. They are put in service of denying an offensive historical past (redface in the original production) and creating a fictionalized, sanitized version of the past (a pro-Indian, anti-racist Wild West show). Yet *Annie Get Your Gun*, the revised version, is dependent on tropes, markers, and techniques that evoke and reinforce the Stage Indian at the dawn of the twenty-first century.

How the *Annie Get Your Gun* revival interacts with, modifies, and ultimately reifies stereotypical depictions of Native American characters reveals that while artists and audiences desire change, countering racialized performance tropes, particularly in live, theatrical performance, is incredibly difficult. Admirably, the revival carefully excised dialogue and music that portrayed Native Americans as a stereotypical, uniform racial category. However, the strategies chosen to remediate the perceived problem of racist representation—such as significant changes to characters, intentional casting of Native American actors, and dramaturgical and musical revision—show that redface exists not just on the surface of the skin. It is deeply embedded in production and performance practices. In what follows, I will investigate the specific revision strategies used to address plot, character, dialogue, dance, music, costumes, and casting. In doing so, I show how redface is multiply located and difficult to excise because it relies on and activates the Stage Indian, even with overt attempts to subvert it.

In May 1946, thirty-three years after *Buffalo Bill's Wild West* closed for good but only eight years after the most recent attempt at a grand Wild West show sputtered to a close in 1938, a new musical opened on Broadway bringing the Wild West roaring back to life.[7] With music and lyrics by Irving Berlin, book by Herbert and Dorothy Fields, producers named Richard Rodgers and Oscar Hammerstein II, and a powerhouse star in Ethel Merman, *Annie Get Your Gun* was unsurprisingly a hit and ran for over a thousand performances (almost three years).[8] Opening three years after *Oklahoma!* took Broadway by storm and initiated the era of integrated musicals (those in which story, song, and dance are integrated to present a unified narrative), *Annie Get Your Gun* is considered an old-fashioned musical comedy. The songs mostly provide fun and funny explorations of various moments rather than functioning as windows into character psyches and narrative development. The exceptional Berlin score is filled with songs that could be removed and sung anywhere and still retain their excellence: "There's No Business Like Show Business," "I've Got the Sun in the Morning and the Moon at Night," and "Anything You Can Do, I Can Do Better." Written to feature the dynamic and exceptionally resonant actress Ethel Merman, the musical highlighted her belting, her humor, and her star power. It told a brash, romantic tale with catchy tunes, an engaging star, and quite a few Indians.

The original Broadway *Annie Get Your Gun* follows Annie Oakley, a historical figure (1860–1926) and arguably the best female sharpshooter of the Wild West show era.[9] The musical traces her discovery as an unsophisticated but talented backwoods young woman to her success as a star of *Buffalo Bill's Wild West*. Annie is discovered by Buffalo Bill when his show stops to perform in Ohio. She wins a match against Cody's sharpshooter, Frank Butler, and is persuaded to join Cody's show. One advantage of joining the show is remaining near Butler, with whom Oakley has fallen instantly in love. However, Butler makes it clear to her that her uncouth and unkempt ways make her undesirable to him. Never one to back down from a challenge, Oakley sets out to transform herself into Butler's ideal woman. Butler is eventually taken with her newly feminized appearance, and they begin a romance. However, he remains invested in retaining his ranking as the best sharpshooter in the show. When it becomes clear that Oakley is preferred over him, he quits both the show and the romance with Oakley. To win him back, Oakley travels with the show to Europe, thanks to the financial backing of Sitting Bull, the Sioux leader. On her return to the United States, she attempts to reunite with Butler, but they get bogged down in yet another argument over who is the best shot. A final shooting match against Butler wins her the man of her dreams, but only after she throws the match (on the advice of Sitting Bull) to let Butler keep thinking he is better than she. For those who have not seen the show, this brief summary might suggest that Oakley is blown about by the force of the narrative, but *Annie Get Your Gun* has always been a vehicle for a female star. The women who have played Annie on Broadway dominate the performance, even if the character does not dominate the plot. *Annie Get Your Gun* is above all else a show about making a star that requires a star performance. Yet that star is supported by a range of characters drawn from history, amply embellished and shaped by mid-twentieth-century sensibilities.

Several of the most prominent characters in the show are historical figures: Annie Oakley, Buffalo Bill Cody, Frank Butler, Sitting Bull, and Pawnee Bill. Other secondary characters are not, such as Frank Butler's assistant, Dolly Tate, *Buffalo Bill's Wild West* show manager Charlie Davenport, Dolly's younger sister, Winnie Tate, and Winnie's love interest, Tommy Keeler. However, even the historically based figures are only loose interpretations, with many liberties taken for dramatic and aesthetic purposes. For example, the rivalry between Butler and Oakley is an invention of the show's creators. Although the initial shooting match where Oakley was discovered purportedly occurred in 1881 and Butler and Oakley did marry, several other crucial aspects of their relationship in the show were entirely fictitious. Butler met Oakley around 1881, when she went by her given name, Annie Moses, married her in 1882, and only in 1883 teamed up with her in a shooting act.[10] Her excellence in shooting was quickly realized by Butler, who became more like her manager than her show business rival.

The intense rivalry between the two depicted in the show aids the creation of a narrative arc, given that obstacles and complications are necessary for dramatic action. However, it morphs Butler from an admirer and partner to a shallow and conceited womanizer. In addition, it changes Oakley from a determined, talented, and savvy woman into a simpering, foolish girl, so eager to please a man she finds attractive that she spends an entire show changing, hiding, and denying herself. It is likely that the show's creators determined that this plot structure revealed the superiority of Oakley, given that she outsmarts Butler, beating him at his own game by being a better shot, becoming conventionally attractive, and when necessary, tricking him into being in a relationship with her. Feminine wiles and wiliness are on full display in this show and were undoubtedly connected to the centrality of the lead character and the lead actress, Ethel Merman. Merman would not be on the receiving end of anything. Her Oakley would be the one calling the shots and taking the shots. Whether a generous or skeptical interpretation of the plot is more persuasive is a subject for a different book. What is clear is that in *Annie Get Your Gun*, historical figures inspire but do not constrain the story, and any character can be modified in service to the show.

The famed Hunkpapa Lakota leader Sitting Bull is one of those significantly modified figures. Sitting Bull appears throughout *Annie Get Your Gun* and plays an important role in plot events, although it is considered a supporting or featured role rather than a leading one. Born in the 1830s and killed in 1890 during an attempt to arrest him, Sitting Bull did in fact work with William Cody for a time.[11] He was hired in 1885 to perform in *Buffalo Bill's Wild West*, and his employment in the show did overlap with that of Annie Oakley. They both joined the show in 1885 and had met previously in Minnesota.[12] Sitting Bull was hired in 1884 by Colonel Alvaren Allen to appear at the opening of the Northern Pacific Railroad in Bismarck, North Dakota, and to then join a fifteen-city tour of America.[13] While in St. Paul, Minnesota, on tour, he attended a performance by Annie Oakley and was impressed. It is claimed that he asked to meet her and "promptly christened Annie *Wantanya Cicilia*, or 'Little Sure Shot,' and adopted her as his daughter."[14] Although the veracity and implications of this anecdote have been questioned, they did become colleagues for a brief time in 1885 while both were employed by the show. This adoption scenario was included in act 1 of *Annie Get Your Gun* and becomes a pivotal moment in the plot. As with Oakley, the show's creators were inspired by the historical record of Sitting Bull but did not feel constrained by it. The presence of a legibly Indian supporting role, extensive imaginative modifications of historical figures and events, and a plot dependent on Indian financing (discussed shortly) means that *Annie Get Your Gun* was primed for depicting the Stage Indian.

(*Continued from page 222*)

In the land currently known as Canada, an Indigenous/Aboriginal theater movement began in the 1970s and has resulted in a decades-long, robust, and innovative network of artists, theater companies, and organizations supporting Indigenous creative practices and output. Indigenous artists founded theater schools, began festivals, wrote plays, and formed theater companies, among them the Centre for Indigenous Theatre, Native Earth Performing Arts, Debajehmujig Theatre Group, Weesageechak Begins to Dance, and the *wîcêhtowin* Theatre program.[5] An early breakout success in the development of Aboriginal/First Nations/Inuit/Métis theater was Tomson Highway's (Cree) 1986 play *The Rez Sisters*.[6] Generations of Indigenous playwrights, actors, and artists have now followed suit. Artists like Yvette Nolan (Algonquin), Drew Hayden Taylor (Ojibwe), Daniel David Moses (Delaware), and Marie Clements (Métis) are respected for their expertise and invention. A more recent symbolic development occurred in the 2019–20 inaugural season of the Indigenous Theatre at Canada's National Art Centre/Centre National des Arts (NAC). The "first National Indigenous theater department in the world," it joined the NAC English Theatre and the NAC French Theatre as a co-equally recognized generator of Canadian theater.[7] Books like Nolan's *Medicine Shows* and anthologies like *Performing Indigeneity* are beginning to look at the late twentieth and early twenty-first centuries to describe and assess just how Indigenous/Aboriginal theater in contemporary Canada has grown and continues to develop.[8] While scholar/artists such as Lindsay Lachance (Algonquin Anishinaabe) are working to develop and articulate Indigenous praxis in theater making.[9] The last fifty years of Indigenous theatrical work has resulted in opportunity, innovation, and institutionalization in Canada.

In the place now called the United States of America, Native American theater follows a similar temporal trajectory to Canadian Indigenous/Aboriginal theater. Haugo explains that the Native theater movement began "in the early 1970s by Kiowa/Delaware playwright Hanay Geiogamah with the formation of the American Indian Theater Ensemble."[10] Shortly

---

5 Centre for Indigenous Theatre, https://www.indigenoustheater.com; Native Earth Performing Arts, https://www.nativeearth.ca; Debajehmujig Theatre Group, www.debaj.ca; Weesageechak Begins to Dance https://www.nativeearth.ca; *wîcêhtowin* Theatre Program, https://artsandscience.usask.ca.

6 Highway, *The Rez Sisters*.

7 Lachance, "About: NAC Indigenous Theatre."

8 Nolan, *Medicine Shows*; Nolan and Knowles, *Performing Indigeneity*.

9 Lachance, "Tiny Sparks Everywhere."

10 Haugo, "Native American Drama."

thereafter, theater companies and training institutions appeared across the country, such as Thunderbird Theatre, Spiderwoman Theater, and theater training at the Institute of American Indian Arts.[11] Not all the companies and programs survived the ensuing decades, but some persisted. In the twenty-first century, more companies and organizations arrived to support Native American plays and playwrights, like the Yale Indigenous Performing Arts Program, the New Native Theatre in St. Paul, Minnesota, and the Oklahoma Indigenous Theatre Company.[12] Beyond theater companies, plays themselves have been disseminated through anthologies dedicated specifically to Native American playwrights.[13] Among those who shaped the field and found their work anthologized include Hanay Geiogamah (Kiowa/Delaware), Diane Glancy (Cherokee descent), William S. Yellow Robe (Assiniboine), the ensemble company members of Spiderwoman Theater (Kuna/Rappahannock), and the third-generation theater artist Monique Mojica (Kuna/Rappahannock). In the twenty-first century, Native American theater has also been increasingly featured at prominent regional theaters such as the Oregon Shakespeare Festival, Arena Stage, La Jolla Playhouse, the Guthrie, and even on Broadway.[14]

The constellation of Indigenous artists at work in the third decade of the twenty-first century glimmers with creativity and possibility. Coming from different Native nations and theatrical backgrounds and creating many kinds of performing arts, some use dance and movement, like Ty Defoe (Oneida/Ojibwe), Shaun Taylor Corbett (Blackfeet), and Rosy Simas (Seneca). Playwright Mary Kathryn Nagle's (Cherokee) work explores Native people's relationship with American law and jurisprudence. The 1491s, a sketch comedy troupe, create works for comedy shows, theaters, television, and online venues. Music is the medium for composer Jerod Tate (Chickasaw), whose work spans theater, classical, chamber, and choral music. Still other Native theater artists, like Randy Reinholz (Choctaw) and Madeline Sayet (Mohegan), have grappled with the Western canon

11 Thunderbird Theatre is no longer active, but for more information on Spiderwoman Theatre and IAIA, see www.spiderwomantheater.org and https://iaia.edu.

12 See https://theautry.org. Yale Indigenous Performing Arts Program, https://yipap.yale.edu. New Native Theatre https://newnativetheater.org, and Oklahoma Indigenous Theatre Company, https://okindigenoustheater.com.

13 See Geiogamah and Darby, *Stories of Our Way*; Geiogamah, *New Native American Drama*; Darby and Fitzgerald, *Keepers of the Morning Star*); Yellow Robe, *Where the Pavement Ends*; D'Aponte, *Seventh Generation*; Two-Rivers, *Briefcase Warriors*; Knowles and Mojica, *Staging Coyote's Dream*.

14 Oregon Shakespeare Festival, https://www.osfashland.org; Arena Stage, https://www.arenastage.org; La Jolla Playhouse, https://lajollaplayhouse.org, guthrietheater.org.

(*Continued on page 110*)

REVISING *ANNIE*

Annie Get Your Gun's success on the Broadway stage was quickly repeated on screen and stage. Just a year after the musical closed on Broadway, MGM premiered its 1950 Technicolor movie musical *Annie Get Your Gun*.[15] The film starred Betty Hutton as Annie Oakley, replacing Judy Garland, who was originally cast as the lead.[16] It revised the musical, adding a new song, "Old Fashioned Wedding," and cutting the weak juvenile lead subplot (Winnie Tate and Tommy Keeler) but still remaining largely faithful to the stage version. In 1966, a short-lived revival of the show opened in September on Broadway, with Ethel Merman again playing the title role.[17] The show was and continues to be produced in theaters across the United States, appearing in professional regional theater seasons, colleges, community theaters, children's theaters, and various educational theater settings, like high schools.[18] While not an outrageously popular or faddish musical, it has been something of a workhorse for nearly three-quarters of a century. Its familiarity to audiences perhaps contributed to a 1999 Broadway revival, this time starring another Broadway powerhouse, Bernadette Peters.[19] The 1999 revival won two Tony awards, for Best Actress in a Musical and Best Revival of a Musical.[20] Running for over a thousand performances, it was the second longest Broadway run for *Annie Get Your Gun,* closing just ten days before the events of 9/11. Through these versions and the many amateur and professional productions across the country, this musical has lived in the American cultural conscious for decades, but it has not stagnated. Many changes were introduced across the years, the most extensive for the heavily revised 1999 Broadway revival. However, its Stage Indian stayed remarkably the same.

While the 1966 Broadway revival hewed closely to the 1950 film with relatively minor changes from its original iteration, the 1999 version created something markedly different. The song "Old Fashioned Wedding" remained, but Butler's solo turn in the first act, "Bad, Bad Man," had disappeared. Gone were the substantial Indian numbers at the end of act 1 ("Wild Horse Ceremonial Dance," "Adoption Dance," and "I'm an Indian, Too"). Instead, the adoption ceremony happened in a brief dialogue scene between Oakley and Sitting Bull. The juvenile lead subplot was reinserted, but this time, Tommy Keeler was not the nephew of Cody but a mixed-race (Indian and white) knife thrower kept from his love, Winnie Tate, by her racist older sister, Butler's assistant, Dolly Tate. The revival also drastically reframed the musical and the final scene. Now, *both* Oakley and Butler throw the shooting match to prove their love for one another. Thus, the 1999 revival was reworked, reconfigured, and reimagined enough that it can be called a revisal, a term widely used in the twenty-first century to describe Broadway musicals that have undergone extensive rewrites before being revived (produced again) on Broadway. Scholar Bruce Kirle has argued cogently for musicals as works in process that are a product of the "text, performance and reception" within a specific time period.[21] Historical context influences the text *and* the reception of the musicals. The 1999 revisal of *Annie Get Your Gun* sought to adapt to its cultural moment and its audiences. However, adapting is often challenging, as musical theater scholar Bryan Vandevender has shown.[22] Updating and not updating are equally fraught strategies. In this chapter, I will use the terms *revival* and *revisal* interchangeably when discussing the 1999 production and will attend to what changed as well as what remained the same in the updated version.

The revisal of *Annie Get Your Gun* at the turn of the twenty-first century worked to address components some people had identified as racist and sexist within the original version. The benevolent interpretation of Annie Oakley as the one who outsmarts and outshines everyone else, even and especially the boys, was no longer culturally acceptable. Instead, Oakley must be in a relationship of equals. More pertinent to this chapter, the stereotypical depiction of Native Americans in the show was substantively changed. No longer did Sitting Bull speak in the "telegraphic style of stereotyped 'Indian' stage dialect," linguistic anthropologist Barbra Meek's "Hollywood Injun English."[23] Instead, he spoke with a syntax akin to any other character in the show. Gone was the song bearing "ridiculous-sounding Indian names" and the "tribal" dance accompanying it.[24] Also excised were the jokes at the expense of Indians and the aforementioned slur against Native American women. The revisal creators worked diligently to cut away all elements that could be deemed racist or stereotypical, keep elements that seemed respectful, and insert new elements that could bolster the show's positive depiction of Native Americans. What they cut, what they kept, and what they added provide an instructive snapshot of how redface changes and stays the same in the American theater. The revisal's attempt to excise redface and, as I will show, its eventual inability to do so show that trying to depict Native Americans using the tools of Indian legibility results in the presence, not the absence, of redface. In *Annie Get Your Gun* at the turn of the twenty-first century, redface remained materially and ideologically present. The material presence of redface can be seen by tracing the costuming of the Indians in *Annie Get Your Gun*. Costuming is a strong tool for articulating character identity, and both the original and the 1999 revival relied on it to communicate exactly who was Indian in the show. The revival removed some of the most overtly stereotypical costume pieces but still relied on tropes of Indianness.

Given that Ethel Merman was already a star by 1946, coverage of her in a new musical appeared widely. *Life*, *Look*, and *Collier's* all featured articles on her, her career, and her upcoming show, accompanied by vivid production photos. Several images included in the *Look* article reveal some of the costumes from the Indian sequence at the end of act 1.[25] Although Indians appear throughout the show, the photos in the article and others like it focus on what I call the Indian sequence at the end of act 1 of the 1946 version.[26] After Sitting Bull witnesses Oakley's superlative sharpshooting performance, he insists on meeting and adopting her immediately. The meeting sequence begins with a ceremonial chant, followed by a dance featuring a male dancer and ensemble performers, an adoption ceremony, Oakley's number "I'm an Indian, Too," and finally, a more lighthearted dance closing out the act (figure 4.3). Photos of the Indian sequence illustrate just exactly what mid-century artists and audiences agreed was legibly Indian.

The character Sitting Bull appears in the Indian sequence, but the focus is primarily on the visual and kinetic spectacle of Indians dancing. Sitting Bull was costumed in a red feathered robe and matching headdress.[27] His entire body was hidden by the voluminous robe. He also wore dark stage makeup for the role; he was literally in redface. Merman as Oakley wore a blue dress with fringe around the hem and

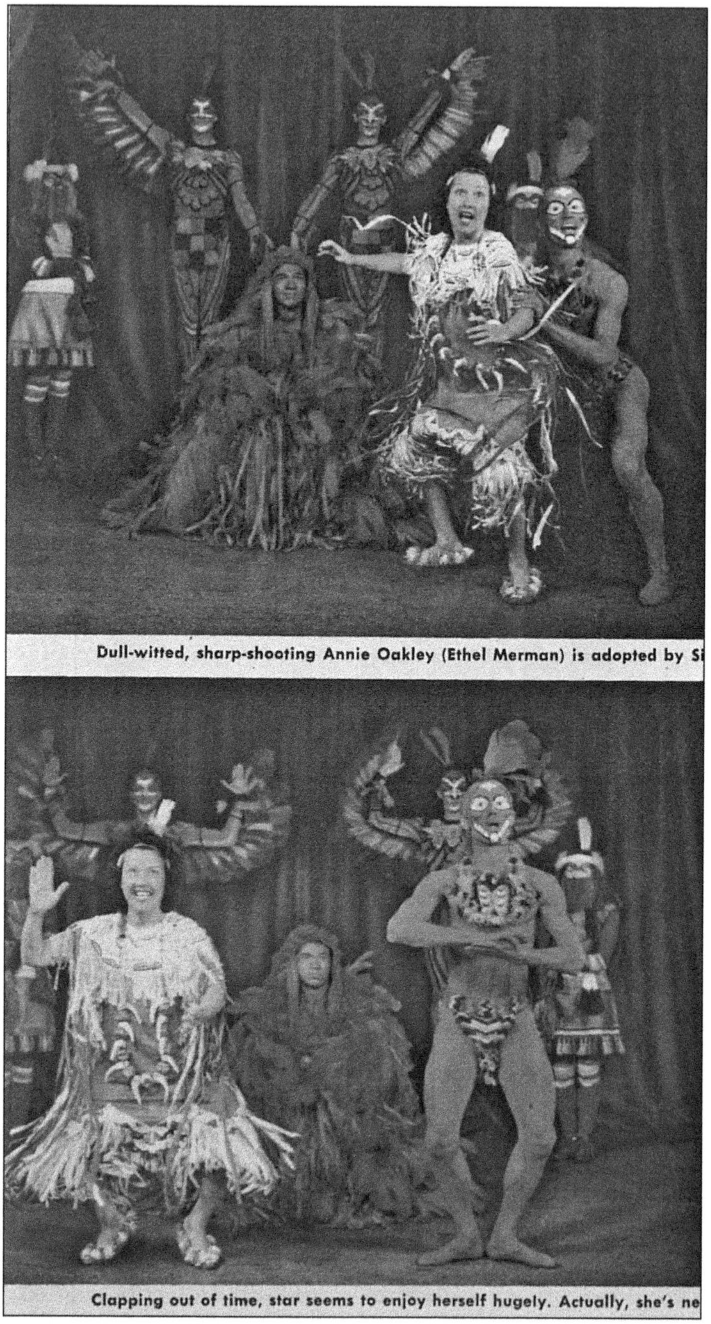

Figure 4.3. Ethel Merman as Annie, Harry Bellaver (*sitting*) as Sitting Bull, Daniel Nagrin as Wild Horse. Photos by Frank Bauman for *Look* magazine, from author's collection.

collar. The collar was decorated with horse designs, and the hem of the dress above the fringe was edged in a zigzag design and decorated with triangles. A blue headband and blue fringed moccasins completed the costume. From the back of her headband, a single feather stood up. There were three different costume categories for the Indian men onstage; two of these appear in the *Look* magazine photos along with the costume for the chorus women. The most prominent male Indian dancer, a principal male dancer named Daniel Nagrin in the role of Wild Horse, dances next to Ethel Merman in the foreground. He wears a loincloth, a necklace, flesh colored dance shoes, a wig cap, and an orange and red feathered headdress consisting of a single line of feathers traveling down the center of his skull, ending in a length of orange hair.[28] He has red full-body makeup, and his face is painted with striking white lines following his jaw line, around his eyes, and at the top of his forehead. Behind the seated Sitting Bull, there are two men and two women; the men are also featured dancers but wear full-body unitards with distinctly different designs on them. Both have feathers attached to the underside of their arms so that when they raise them, their arms look like wings. They were likely the "Eagle Dancers" noted in choreographer Helen Tamiris's papers, whose function was "to create suspense for entrance of the 'Wild Horse'" and who would use "frenetic and soaring movements."[29] They also wear wig caps and have two red feathers sticking up from the backs of their heads. Their faces are painted and highlighted with white lines that are, like the designs on their unitards, similar although not identical.

The women in the Indian sequence wore blue skirts with multicolored edging on the hem over what appear to be red bodysuits. The women's bodysuits have multicolor stripes on the elbows and knees and extend to their feet and over their hands. The top half of their faces are covered by a mask from which hangs a cloth veil covering the bottom half. The masks are part of headpieces that also include what appears to be dark wigs, decorative fringe around the sides of a headband circling their heads, and a few red feathers sticking up from the back of their head.

A third category of men's costuming appears on those who did not dance, likely members of the singing chorus. Men who were not dancing wore pants with fringe on the sides, long-sleeved tunics with fringe running down the arms, and feathered headdresses. The headdresses are the kind readily legible to audiences as Indian headdresses courtesy of the prominent presentation of Oceti Sakowin men in *Buffalo Bill's Wild West*. These costumes are made to look like recognizably but generically Sioux/Indian. Additionally, the headdresses are attached to a mask that covered the top half of the men's faces. Similar to the women's masks, there was a cloth veil that covered the lower half of their faces. Although no notes from the show give the reason for the veils, a reasonable speculation would be that they were deployed to prevent the chorus members from having to apply and remove redface makeup over the course of the show. There were at least thirty-two chorus members on the stage during the Indian sequence, and according to the playbill, there were only thirty-seven chorus members (singing and dancing combined) in the show.[30] Seven or eight of the male dancing chorus were costumed in unitards and individual makeup designs. Adding another twenty-five makeup changes might have been logistically impossible, economically unviable, or aesthetically undesirable. Indian costumes for the majority of the chorus were likely created as much to hide as to reveal.

Choreographic notes for the Indian sequence indicate that when the curtain rises, the singers appear in "Full Pow-Wow Regalia."[31] The questionable accuracy of the "regalia" aside, the Indian sequence costumes draw on almost cartoonish color and design in their representation of Native Americans. Feathers, painted bodies, suggested bare skin, geometric designs, and fringe are the repeated visual markers of Indianness in the scene. The movement vocabulary seemed also to be inspired by the Stage Indian of the Wild West show. Choreography notes describe a section of the dance in which they needed to "use women to build up terror," with another note suggesting that they "put bells on them" to do so.[32] In another section, "men enter in hunting movements of great agitation," with a side note that "thru out they always work in earthbound Indian movement." The men were hunting the Wild Horse and the notes indicate that later "Daniel" (Nagrin) goes "toward + almost touching in a terrifying impact with some of the men individually who react suddenly." This is followed by Nagrin doing "agonizing jumps"

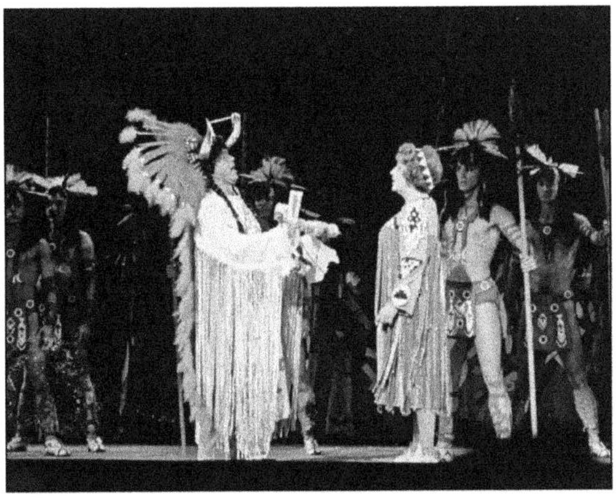

Figure 4.4. Harry Bellaver as Sitting Bull and Ethel Merman as Annie Oakley in the 1966 Broadway revival of *Annie Get Your Gun*. Image courtesy New York Public Library.

after which he "is surrounded—Does dying movement," and then a "Medicine Man in mask or Eagles" does something not recorded in the notes. At least in its planning stages, the dance contained elements of formality (powwow), threat ("terror"), hunting, horses (Wild Horse), and "earthbound" movements. Critics instantly admired it.[33] The *Boston Herald* called it an "elaborate ballet."[34] *Cue* magazine insisted, "Indeed, the Indian element gives *Annie Get Your Gun* the one exciting production sequence it can boast of. This is a ceremonial Indian dance, quite exciting to my taste."[35] In its review for the pre-Broadway production in New Haven, *Variety* said that Helen Tamiris's contribution "as terpsichorean creator is noteworthy" and noted that a "highlight is a stirring ceremonial dance."[36] Reviews of the Indian dances repeatedly referred to them as ceremonial rather than the aesthetic, commercial dances that they actually were. This is unsurprising given the deep need for connection between the Stage Indian and the "real thing."

For the 1966 Broadway revival, in which Merman and Bellaver reprised their roles as Annie and Sitting Bull, respectively, the Indian sequence costumes shifted slightly. Merman's costume had longer sleeves, longer fringe, and different patterned decoration. Bellaver had fewer feathers and more fringe, along with a different style of headdress. The headdress now had two horns and feathers of a different color than his clothing. The costumes of the chorus members underwent a more significant change. For instance, more than one male dancer had a costume primarily composed of his own skin. The men wore footwear reminiscent of gladiator sandals, briefs (no pants), and a loincloth decorated with geometric designs. Over their bare chests hung a necklace, and on their bare arms were leather wraps that coordinated with their sandals. They all wore dark, shoulder-length wigs with considerably less makeup than in the original production. On the back of their heads were small semicircular headdresses. Feathers, headdresses, geometric patterns, long dark hair, and bare skin continued to signal the Stage Indian in *Annie Get Your Gun*'s first revival.

By the 1999 revival, there were no cartoonish costume colors or designs or pretense at ceremonial or powwow dance. However, some of the same visual markers were retained. The male Indian characters of the chorus wore pants or chaps with fringe down the side, long dark hair with headbands or braids, and loose-fitting shirts or no shirts at all and just a vest.[37] The female Indian characters wore the same clothing as their non-Indian, female chorus counterparts: culottes, long-sleeve shirts, and bustiers over the shirts. Unlike the non-Indian chorus women, however, the Indian women wore their hair in two braids. The mixed-race character Tommy Keeler often wore fringed pants with beading or embroidery in triangular and rectangular shapes down the side, a vest decorated with triangular shapes (sometimes over a shirt, sometimes over his bare chest). When his arms were bare, he wore thin bands right above his biceps with a few three- or four-inch strands hanging from them. Occasionally, he wore only a shirt open to the sternum and no vest. He also routinely wore his dark hair long with a headband circling it. Sitting Bull wore dark pants, a loose shirt, and feathered headdress throughout the show. He did change costumes more than once and had more than one headdress, but these elements were always present. While the Indian characters in 1999 were dressed similarly to the non-Indian characters, the elements that set them apart as Indian were remarkably similar to the original production: feathers, bare skin, fringe, and long, braided hair with headbands. The only important addition was the cut of the men's shirts, which was looser than on the non-

Indian males, and at least once a female chorus member was indicated by braids and feathers sticking up from the back of her head.

The Indian characters' costuming in the revisal illustrates the difficulty in communicating Indian identity visually without relying on tropes that reify stereotype. Moving away from garish colors, cartoonish ornamentation, and actual red makeup was clearly a choice made to avoid stereotypical depictions of Native Americans. The show's creators did not want to further demean Native Americans by echoing the reductive cultural tropes that had appeared so easily in 1946. However, the challenge was that they still had to mark certain characters as Indian. Making matters worse, the Indian markers that remain legible and circulate into the twenty-first century are identical to those the production wanted to fight against. Hair color (black), length (long), and style (braided) are markers for both men and women—and not just the hair itself but the headbands surrounding the hair, for both men and women again. Although there were no dancers in loin cloths and painted red, there were Indian men showing more torso than any non-Indian man onstage. Even the romantic male lead of the show, Frank Butler, played by *The Dukes of Hazzard* actor Tom Wopat (who is no stranger to a little chest baring), never showed as much skin as Tommy Keeler or the nameless male Indian ensemble member who routinely appeared shirtless wearing a vest. Despite good intentions, theater artists at the turn of the twenty-first century still turned to the standardized and legible visual markers of the Stage Indian widely accepted for at least one hundred years. Making a character legible as an Indian still superseded the removal or modification of generic, racialized identity markers.

RETELLING A STORY

Making a heavily revised musical still legible as *Annie Get Your Gun* was writer Peter Stone's job. Known for his work on the musicals *1776*, *Titanic*, and *Curtains*, his book (the book is the dialogue of a musical) for the 1999 revival was part old and part new. It sought to keep the best parts, notably most of the Irving Berlin score and an outstanding leading role for a female performer, while jettisoning the unsavory bits. Butler's song extolling his serial romantic exploits, "I'm a Bad, Bad

Man," was cut. The song communicated that he was a man of the world, familiar with romance, or, in a less charitable reading of the song, a sexual predator. For an updated, more feminist, less racist iteration of the story, it was not deemed appropriate. The most important change to the Oakley/Butler romance, as noted previously, was that rather than Oakley's throwing the match to get her man, they both purposefully miss shots to prove their mutual love. This shift is part of what *New York Times* critic Ben Brantley called the production's intention "to transform a period piece, with a quaint, creaky book and a great score, into something acceptable to contemporary tastes."[38] And more pointedly, to address "what might be construed as antifeminist sentiment."[39] This more equitable, though perhaps equally as trite, ending is the primary place the revisal attempts to make clear that Oakley does not have to be subservient to a man in order to be loved. However, instead of making Oakley more confident in herself and unwilling to change for a man, the revisal makes him less of a conceited jerk. Sitting Bull still suggests that Oakley throw the match by using a rigged gun to ensure Butler's love for her.

> SITTING BULL: Better luck with this one.
> ANNIE: But that's the gun I missed with.
> SITTING BULL: Remember when you said—"can't get a man with a gun?"
> ANNIE: Shore I remember.
> SITTING BULL: You get a man with this gun.[40]

Only after Annie has missed five shots in a row does Butler choose to miss five of his shots, leading to a tie. The cyclical butting of heads between the lovers reappears immediately after their grand gestures of love, and they live, according to narrator Buffalo Bill Cody, "scrappily ever after."[41] For the purposes of a more feminist *Annie Get Your Gun,* or at least a differently feminist show, fixing Butler's character was seen as more effective than making any change to Oakley's. In contrast, the job of fixing the racism in the original required a bit more heavy lifting in the book.

A romantic subplot, originally between Buffalo Bill's nephew and the younger sister of Butler's assistant in 1946, reappears in the revisal to inject new appreciation for Native Americans into the show's ethos. It now follows a mixed-race couple who perform in the Wild West show, an Irish/Indian knife thrower, Tommy Keeler, and a young white woman, Winnie Tate. Although the young woman's older sister (Butler's assistant, Dolly Tate) opposes the relationship for racial reasons, the two eventually end up together with the notably vocal support of Annie Oakley. Dolly does not want Winnie to marry Tommy, because he is an Indian. Because Winnie is only seventeen, Dolly forces them to annul the marriage that Oakley supported. The reliance on the age of consent and legal adulthood being eighteen is but one anachronistic detail inserted into the show.[42] The young lovers are parted when Dolly forces Winnie to come with her when Butler leaves *Buffalo Bill's Wild West* and Tommy stays. The two young lovers are reunited in the second act and sing together, rekindling their love. This subplot appears not too different from the 1946 version, except for the constant reminders that Tommy is mixed race. His first entrance introduces the idea:

> WINNIE: Why do you always have to treat him like a bellboy? Tommy's a very important part of this show, and I happen to be his assistant, the same as you and Frank Butler.
>
> TOMMY: I don't mind, Winnie, honest.
>
> DOLLY: You hear that? Even an Indian has more sense than you do.
>
> WINNIE: He's half Indian, sis.
>
> DOLLY: And that's the half I was talking to.[43]

A conversation with Oakley later reinforces it:

> WINNIE: She's dead set against my seeing Tommy.
>
> TOMMY: On account of me bein' one half Indian.
>
> ANNIE: What's the other half?
>
> TOMMY: Irish.
>
> ANNIE: Well, ain't it a small world. I'm half Irish myself.
>
> TOMMY: No fooling!
>
> ANNIE: Shore am. Don't let Dolly get ya down, Tommy. Indians are real fine folks. It's the Irish I'm not too shore about.[44]

After their secret marriage, accomplished with Oakley's help, it comes up yet again:

> DOLLY: Husband?! Did I hear the word husband?! Don't tell me you actually married that redskin!
>
> WINNIE: Half-redskin!
>
> TOMMY: And it so happens she loves this half-redskin![45]

Only in the second act scene featuring Winnie and Tommy's reunion and the number "Who Do You Love?" is his race not discussed. Tellingly, this scene is the only one just between Winnie and Tommy. His race is important to articulate only when it clarifies the position of other characters and therefore who the audience should or should not sympathize with. Tommy is racially marked to demonstrate that racism is wrong. In the end, the romantic subplot adds little to the show, just as it did in the 1946 version, except for illuminating that those prejudiced against Indians are racist and that the central character is certainly not.

While the function of the revised Keeler character is most assuredly to telegraph racial lessons to the audience, it also introduces new complexity and problematic aspects. Rather than remaining the nephew of Buffalo Bill Cody, Keeler is transformed into the performer of a knife throwing act with a young, female assistant, Winnie Tate. In the musical, Winnie stands against a large board shaped and painted like a tipi as Keeler throws knives that come dangerously close to her body. Winnie is the target of both his knives and his affections. Changing Keeler from a nondescript juvenile male lead into a knife-throwing mixed-race Indian is an extraordinarily complex act revealing how the "Indian problem" and its solution were conceptualized by the production's creators. The production makes clear its antiracist stance by highlighting the racism of Dolly Tate, who openly disparages Tommy because he is an Indian. She confirms that her dislike of Keeler is because of his race when she declares that the Native American employees of Buffalo Bill are "nothing but a bunch of savages."[46] As noted previously, doing so presents Dolly as the foil to Annie's openness and moral superiority. Dolly is a racist, selfish, conniving woman presented in contrast to Annie's good-hearted, inclusive nature. Keeler provides the show's creative and production team an opportunity to demonstrate the antiracist views they espouse by passing judgement on those within the world of the play who do not share them. By changing Keeler into an Indian character, they were able to announce to audiences that this show was different from previous versions.

However, signaling turn-of-the-twenty-first-century virtue in the representation of Native Americans proved harder than they anticipated. For the virtuous aspects of the other characters and show makers to be understood by an audience, Keeler must be easily identified as Indian. To identify him as an Indian, the show relied on culturally suffuse and legible markers of Indianness. It relied on the Stage Indian. To assist the audience's interpretation of his character, the show chose to rely on long-circulated visual markers of Indianness: long dark hair, fringed pants, bare chest, weapon wielding. Advertisements for the musical showed leading characters as though in advertisements for a Wild West show. One of these, a flyer, had pictures in the style of nineteenth-century painted advertisements, with Annie Oakley on the front, Frank Butler on the back, and Buffalo Bill and Tommy Keeler inside (figure 4.5).

All images on the print advertisement were stylized and meant to emphasize attractive features. For example, the strategically placed arrows on Oakley's shirt emphasized her breasts. The images of Oakley and Butler used the likenesses of the show's stars, Bernadette Peters and Tom Wopat, to telegraph to audiences whom they would be seeing if they attended the show. The images of Cody and Keeler were less specific to the actors playing them and more specific to culturally legible markers of character identity. For Cody, this meant thigh-high boots, white shoulder length hair, fringed leather clothes, a cowboy hat, and a white mustache and goatee. These markers align with historical photographs and similar advertisements using the Cody image. These were the costume pieces that signaled his public persona as Colonel Buffalo Bill. The markers that signal cultural legibility for Keeler are decidedly less focused on a specific historical figure or a specific star actor able to attract audiences. Instead, they rely on visual tropes of Indianness coupled with attributes that invite a sexualized gaze.

Keeler's character is labeled "Tomahawk Tommy," and the flyer declares "His Targets Kissed By Knives But Never Cut!"[47] This hint at ro-

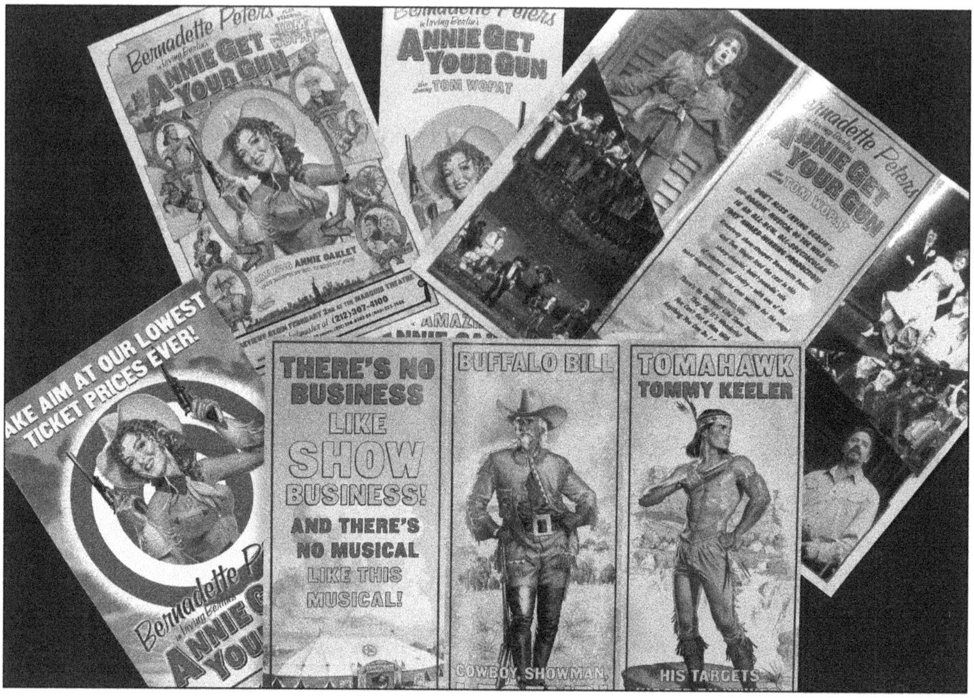

Figure 4.5. Selection of *Annie Get Your Gun* advertisements from author's collection.

mance, and possibly a Freudian suggestion of nonthreatening sexuality (phallic objects that kiss and never cut), is accompanied by an image of Keeler that could have easily appeared on the cover of a romance novel. The figure is shirtless with a chiseled physique: six-pack abs, toned biceps, and quadriceps visible through his tight-fitting pants. His bare chest glistens as if oiled, and he holds a knife to his (also chiseled) jaw. His right cheekbone has two small black stripes on it, as close to face paint as the advertising team was willing to go. His pants and boots are fringed.[48] While Butler's and Cody's pants are secured by a belt, Keeler's pants appear to have a drawstring waist. Almost miraculously, this drawstring creates a V-shaped dip just under his navel, which allows the viewer to better appreciate his lower abs, also chiseled. His flowing, shoulder-length, dark hair is encircled by a headband with two feathers tucked into the back. Feathers and face paint remained legible for the Indian at the turn of the twenty-first century. The headband is decorated with a colorful geometric pattern that echoes the one on his armband. The band is conveniently placed to further define his bicep from his deltoid. His right hand holds a knife to his left shoulder, creating a diagonal line and drawing the viewer's eye to the right of the image, following the gaze of the Keeler figure as he looks off to the viewer's right. His left hand holds two more knives at his hip. The background of Keeler's image also differs from those of the other images on the flyer. Oakley is in front of a light-blue background with white clouds. Cody stands at the foot of a rolling hill covered in buffalo and dotted with a few trees and small shrubs. Butler's background has mesas in the far distance and a saddled horse standing behind him. Keeler stands in front of an outdoor scene, but his does not have any sign of animal life. He stands on a stone outcropping at the end of a large waterfall. Behind the falls and the rocky rapids there are six tipis and a few trees. Behind this Indian village rises a small mountain. It is unclear whether this image suggests the chasm-like waterfall as the distance between him and his Indian roots or another Freudian image supplying a target for those knives, a churning watercourse. The combination of the sexualized figure with the decision not to base the image on a specific actor or historical image means that the image continues to draw on and construct the image of the Indian. In this case, an image that sexualizes the Stage Indian while connecting it to violence. It repurposes culturally legible markers of Indianness to create a desirable character that can entice audiences to buy a ticket.

The promises of the advertising campaign were only partially fulfilled onstage. The actor who originated Keeler in 1999, Andrew Palermo, was, as is typical of Broadway dancers, in remarkably good shape. Although his costume revealed considerably more skin than his counterparts, he was not actually paraded in front of the audience as eye candy. His character was too busy acting, singing, and dancing for that. However, he did throw knives at a young woman, reveal some torso, and make clear that though his intentions were honorable toward Winnie, they were also sexual. On meeting in the second act, after their marriage was annulled and they endured an extended separation, the couple attempts to navigate a reunion in which desire is at the forefront:

WINNIE: Oh, Tommy, Tommy! I'm so glad to see you!

TOMMY: Do you think I could get arrested for kissing a minor in public?

WINNIE: I turned eighteen last week. You can kiss me anywhere you want.

TOMMY: Now that's something I could get arrested for.[49]

Winnie matches his eagerness when they discuss whether Dolly will allow Winnie to marry him now that she is over eighteen:

WINNIE: Come on, we have to go.

TOMMY: I thought you said she might be ready to reconsider.

WINNIE: Who cares what she's ready to do? I'm eighteen now, Tommy, and I'm ready to get married again. And this time no one's going to stop it!

Rather than being an object of generic desire, Keeler shares with Winnie a mutual desire unanticipated by the flyer's iconography. In this, the Keeler promised by the flyer is not quite the Keeler delivered by the show.

The combination of stereotypical visual markers of Indianness, his profession as coded (sexual) violence against white women, and his racial mixing make Tommy Keeler an important character, despite his minor role. His work in *Buffalo Bill's Wild West* as a knife thrower is particularly interesting. Knife throwing acts were not a significant emphasis of the show.[50] The production team could have assigned him the job of a trick rider, a horseman, or even simply a performer of battle reenactments, all of which would have been historically accurate and easily verifiable roles played by Native American performers in *Buffalo Bill's Wild West*. But the revival's creative team chose knife thrower. The producers of *Annie Get Your Gun* tried to counteract racist stereotypes by inserting a sympathetic, half-Indian character but in doing so relied on racially stereotypical depictions in costuming and job choice. Although they did attempt to modify these markers to signal sexuality rather than terror or guilt, they still relied on a veiled threat of Indian violence against a white woman along with the old standard, feathers.

The choice to make him a half-Indian character is also intriguing. It gave producers the opportunity to both publicly denounce the racism of the musical's history and retain breadth in casting options. Andrew Palermo, who originated the role, is not Native American, unlike the actor who originated the role of Sitting Bull in the revival.[51] Palermo was aware that other actors who understudied the role or replaced him were Caucasian, Latino, and African American. (The first replacement for Gregory Zaragoza in the Sitting Bull role was not a Native American actor either. It was Larry Storch, most well-known for his work in the comedic Civil War period television show *F-Troop*.[52]) The half-Indian status of the Keeler role apparently was interpreted by the show's creators/producers as less Indian than the "full-blooded" Sioux chief. This understanding of Indianness as that which vanishes matches the logic of blood quantum, which appears within the show. In an interaction between Dolly, Winnie, and Tommy previously noted, blood quantum is overtly forwarded. The full interaction includes Winnie's suggestion of miscegenation's results as the increasing disappearance of Indianness:

> DOLLY: Husband?! Did I hear the word husband?! Don't tell me you actually married that redskin!
>
> WINNIE: Half-redskin!
>
> TOMMY: And it so happens she loves this half-redskin!
>
> WINNIE: And we plan on having a lot of little quarter-redskins![53]

In this brief exchange, the audience is assured of Dolly's ugly racism, the virtue of interracial relationships, and the construction of Indianness as a quality that disappears through admixture. At no point in the show is Keeler's tribe/nation mentioned. He is, above all, a generic Stage Indian. He is a legibly and racially identified Indian, the kind that disappears over time, the kind that is recognizable because of hair and fringe and feathers. In the great effort to make *Annie Get Your Gun* less racist, the revisal continued to rely on the racializing logics of the Stage Indian. This is why its efforts fell flat. This production explicitly advocated for a racialized understanding of Indianness and in doing so denied Indigenous persistence and nationhood. The role of

Tommy Keeler is simply an updated version of redface, a collaborative curatorial process of creating and perpetuating a body as legibly Indian. Keeler retains and deploys tropes of Indianness onstage, even as he is supposed to be redressing damage caused by them.

JOKES, SONGS, AND DANCES

The plot and a supporting character were not the only elements of *Annie Get Your Gun* that received focused attention in the revisal. The dialogue, music, and even the choreography were all revised to remove those parts deemed racist and to insert a more authentic and sympathetic depiction of Native Americans. A prominent strategy in accomplishing these goals was to change the target of the humor in the dialogue. For instance, this exchange between Charlie and Wilson, a hotel owner in Cincinnati, from the 1946 version was removed:

> CHARLIE: Wait a minute. I'll rent it from you. A hundred dollars for the afternoon.
>
> WILSON: No!
>
> CHARLIE: Will you take fifty dollars in cash, and two s—s?
>
> WILSON: No! No!
>
> CHARLIE: Will you take fifty s—s and two dollars in cash?[54]

Devaluing women in general, and Native American women specifically, coupled with the casual use of a derogatory slur, was no longer acceptable to artists and audiences in 1999. Instead, jokes demeaning men appeared. For example, in act 2, Sitting Bull and Charlie discuss Annie and Frank's final shooting match:

> SITTING BULL: But if Annie lose the match, she will win Frank Butler. Frank Butler, like all white men, cannot be shown up by woman!
>
> CHARLIE: You sayin' Indians are different?
>
> SITTING BULL: No. Indians just the same.[55]

The show attempts to display that it is on the side of women and minorities, but it does so by shifting the butt of stereotypical jokes rather than removing humor that only works by disparaging an entire group.

In another moment, Indians get to deliver the punch line and show their cleverness in the face of pejorative treatment. While traveling in a rail car with *Buffalo Bill's Wild West*, Dolly, complaining to Charlie Davenport, wants to know why there are Indians in the car with non-Indians:

> DOLLY: Didn't I tell you they were in here? Chief Eagle Feather, you know you people shouldn't be in this car.
> EAGLE FEATHER: We have permission to be here.
> DOLLY: Oh, really? Where's your reservation?
> EAGLE FEATHER: In South Dakota! [they laugh][56]

This interchange illustrates several key factors in the revisal's efforts to fix the problems they identified in the original production and reveals that their narrow understanding of what made them problems in the first place prevented a complete correction.

As noted previously, Dolly is the character chosen to display racist behavior and language. In singling out "you people," Dolly shows it is not a personal issue but a racial one. She believes that the car should not contain Indians. By bringing in the issue of permission, the show suggests that Dolly is enforcing not only her own desires but the expectations of either the railroad company or the Wild West show troupe. The Indians require permission to be in that particular car. Dolly shoots back at the Indian who responds, named Eagle Feather in the script but never called by name in the show, challenging the source of his permission and asking after his "reservation." She implies that there is a correct way to gain permission. Eagle Feather jumps on the double meaning of *reservation* and delivers a punch line: "In South Dakota!" This line makes Dolly look foolish, reinforcing the show's choice to concentrate all the racism in her character and disparage her for it. Instead of taking up her possibly historically realistic expectation that Indians and whites do not mix on a train, the show locates the problem in an individual's racist feelings and actions. Incidentally, the South Dakota punch line suggests the Indians' identity as Oceti Sakowin, given their historical and contemporary relationship to those lands. By delivering the punch line, Eagle Feather demonstrates the cleverness and sense of humor of Indians within a musical comedy, which elevates the race above Dolly's racist ideas. Dolly reiterates those ideas in her response, "They're nothing but a bunch of savages!" This short moment solidifies Dolly as the racist problem instead of offering a more systemic critique of racism. It also highlights the Indians as delivering sophisticated humor at the expense of Dolly, which signals to audiences that the revisal values Indians over Dolly. Dolly is a one-dimensional character who serves to locate socially unacceptable behavior and thought in the story and to relegate it to the butt of the joke.

The revisal also uses the character of Sitting Bull to update the humor. Sitting Bull is routinely used to comic effect in both the original and revisal productions. In the original production, the character relied on literal redface, as seen in the above photos. His dialogue also relied on "Hollywood Injun English." For example, in the original 1946 production, Sitting Bull declares three rules by which he lives his life: "Sitting Bull live by three rules—no red meat, no get feet wet, no put money in show business!" In the 1999 production, that line was changed to "Sitting Bull lives by three rules: don't eat red meat—don't get feet wet—and don't put money in show business!" He still refers to himself in the third person, another common marker of "Hollywood Injun English," but the revival has standardized the "no" to "don't."[57] This joke is about the foolishness of investing in show business, and it is effective, in part, because it is delivered by a character not typically represented as having insight into investment or show business. The justification for this joke is developed by explaining that Sitting Bull has just come from Washington, DC, and a meeting with the "Great White Father about Indian territory."[58] He explains the abundance of oil on his tribe's land and its negative impact on agriculture. When Charlie hears that the tribe sells fifty thousand barrels of oil a day, he asks what Sitting Bull plans to do with the money. Sitting Bull replies, "I'm planning to open a gambling hall on my reservation."[59] This is a punch line, an invitation for audiences to laugh, and they do. They laugh at the oil-rich Casino

(*Continued from page 43*)

the men's illness could be a plea for his son, his target audience, to heed warnings and protect his health. For modern readers who seek Indigenous interiority and resistance in the historical past, he gives us frustratingly few clues to his own thoughts and opinion of his employment situation. What he does offer us is how he wanted the public to understand him. Over only a handful of pages, Maungwudaus shows us a man who is interested in all manners of sights, sounds, and experiences that he encounters on his travels. He appreciates and notes kindness and generosity shown to him. He is careful to explain how he extended respect to all that he met, and he is thankful for his return to his homeland.

While he never fully addresses his job as a performer with Catlin, he does hint at what he thinks of being put on display and being mistreated. When a large group of young men mock the Ojibwe, he includes a lengthy quote by an unnamed bystander who scolds the young men by saying they are "foolish and ignorant." "You may consider yourselves better and wiser than those strangers [the Ojibwe], but you are very much mistaken. . . . Their little children have far better manners than you," the bystander says. It is impossible to know if this unnamed bystander actually existed or if it was what Maungwudaus wanted to say to the young men mocking him and his companions. But either way, by including this anecdote, Maungwudaus ensured that his readers would know what good manners and wisdom looked like and in whom they resided. He never presents himself as an ethnological object on display but as a man having new experiences, evaluating them based on his knowledge and values and recognizing kindness, competency, and hospitality when he sees it. What Maungwudaus offers his readers is not the diary of a Stage Indian but the travel accounts of a person encountering new places and people. The near absence of his job as an entertainer in his writing reveals that what he thought most important to tell his son and other readers was how he experienced the world and what he thought of it, not necessarily what his readers expected of him.

(*Continued on page 130*)

Indian, a familiar stereotype from the late twentieth century and anachronistic to the nondescript late nineteenth-century setting of the show. In its attempt to justify one joke about investing in show business, the revival reinforces a late twentieth-century trope in representations of Native Americans as rich "Casino Indians."[60]

By interpolating the Casino Indian into the revival, the show simultaneously presents commendation for and critique of Native Americans. Ostensibly, Sitting Bull's easy discussion of his tribe's wealth is meant to show his power and influence and to make sense of the fact that he invests a large amount of money in *Buffalo Bill's Wild West* later in the show. His investment in the show is a plot point on which the entire second act hinges, so it was necessary to keep it in the 1999 revisal. The reasoning behind it was never explained in the original production, so the 1999 attempt to include a reasonable explanation is admirable. However, it introduces a stereotype developed in the late twentieth century. Although the Supreme Court had only confirmed the right to gaming activities on tribal land in 1987 and the Indian Gaming Regulatory Act created guidelines and oversight in 1988, by 1999 Indian gaming had become a punch line.[61] Communication scholar Celeste Lacroix has shown that the Casino Indian is viewed as a threat because of their "changed economic, political, and social circumstances," since these improved circumstances activated "fear and anger" about the power that accompanied them.[62] Essentially, the Casino Indian makes white people afraid that Indians will take over. This late twentieth-century stereotype serves as a reminder of the flexibility of the Stage Indian and how modification over time occurs. Inserting the Casino Indian into the show also generalizes Native Americans and introduces inaccuracy by relying on a racial stereotype that all Indians are Casino Indians. Less than half of the federally recognized tribes/nation in the United States have casinos, and many of those are small-time operations or run by nations that do not disperse profits to individual citizens. That not all Indians are wealthy Casino Indians is a fact worthy of reiteration.[63]

In rewriting the dialogue and many of the jokes, book writer Stone created situations in which Indians were on the delivering end, not the receiving end, of the punch line. This well-intentioned effort to make the show less racist resulted in making other characters, like Dolly, and entire categories of people, like men, the new butts of the joke. In trying to make sense of why Sitting Bull would invest money in a Wild West show, Stone introduced a late twentieth-century trope about Indians into the production. It is unclear why the creators of the show decided that the best way to handle disparaging humor was to shift its target. Nor is it clear why they did not simply create a new source for funding Oakley's European tour and instead continued to rely on Indian money. Connecting Indians to oil, to South Dakota, and to male chauvinism do not appear to be strong moves away from culturally and racially reductive representational practices.

INDIAN SONGS

In addition to addressing humor, character, and plot, the revisal took aim at the musical representation of Native Americans. Three songs that depicted Indians in a negative light were cut for the 1999 revival. As mentioned previously, the opening number, "Colonel Buffalo Bill," was deleted, one assumes because of its stereotypical and negative depiction of Native Americans. The lyrics talk about Indians throwing spears and describe "very notable, cut your throatable Indians" who take "everyone by force" until Buffalo Bill arrives and shoots "till there's no one left to kill."[64] Given that it depicts Indians as violent and ultimately vanquished and that it uses a word commonly accepted as a racial epithet, the producers' unease with the song in the revival is perhaps self-explanatory. The changes made around the Indian sequence, while equally as self-evident, provide a more complex illustration of how the Indian problem in *Annie Get Your Gun* was addressed.

The end of act 1 underwent considerable cuts, with the removal of songs, the removal of one scene, and the revision of one scene that intriguingly remained. In the original production, Oakley performs a very complicated and impressive sharpshooting act that earns high praise from Sitting Bull. The sharpshooting occurs onstage, with Sitting Bull entering after to praise Oakley. As a result of Sitting Bull's admiration for Oakley, he insists on adopting her as his daughter. This process takes several minutes and results in the Indian sequence. Sitting Bull declares, "I have called Sioux tribe together. We have big Indian ceremony." This is quickly followed by two pieces of music, "Opening Chant" and "Indian Dance." These are performed by the "Braves and S—s" and showcase a dance that in the original production was choreographed by Helen Tamiris and highly praised. The dance leads into the next musical piece, "Ceremonial Chant," which begins the adoption ceremony, during which Oakley repeats non-English phrases, receives a necklace, and has a headband placed on her head by Sitting Bull. The ceremony is followed by one of the more famous songs in the musical, "I'm an Indian, Too." This comedic song extensively employs racially stereotypical language about Indians. Annie sings that just like "Battle-Axe, Hatchet-Face, Eagle-Nose—Like those Indians, I'm an Indian, Too, a Sioux." She continues to use disparaging names of fictitious Indians and discusses how she will have "totem poles, tomahawks, small papoose" while wearing "moccasins, wampum beads, feather hats, which will go to prove" that she is an Indian. The song includes a "tribal dance" in which Oakley joins and at the end of which declares, "Well now I'm an Indian." The Indian sequence relies on what musicologist Michael V. Pisani has marked as musical devices of Indianism. Indianism was a prominent musical genre in late nineteenth- and early twentieth-century compositions used to communicate Indianness through sound, not just lyrics.[65] These devices include the use of open fifths for brass to represent "nobility," woodwinds and high strings to suggest "savageness," and a pastoral moresca rhythm on open fifths (in 4/4, a half note followed by two quarter notes—long–short–short). The Indian sequence conjures up images of the Indian through musical and lyrical references, through costuming, and as I discussed previously, through choreography.

The parodic language of Indian names, tropes of musical Indianism, and depiction of what Sitting Bull calls a "big Indian ceremony" were distasteful to the revival's producers. The entire sequence of chant, dance, ceremony, and "I'm an Indian, Too" was cut for the 1999 revival. This removed a considerable source of the problem of Native American representation in the show. However, it did not remove all the problems. The Indian sequence at the end of act 1 occurs to emphasize the transformation of Oakley into a member of Sitting Bull's family. The formality of the adoption is necessary to legitimize Sitting Bull's decision to invest money in *Buffalo Bill's Wild West*. Sitting Bull, who had previously told Buffalo Bill and Charlie that one of the three rules he lives by is not to put money in show business, changes his mind after seeing Oakley's impressive shooting. Because he adopts her, he will financially support the Wild West show with money earned from oil on his land.[66] In both productions, Buffalo Bill, eager to get this influx of cash, rejoices over the news:

> Annie, Annie—we're made! With you and Sitting Bull, we'll go right to New York and Madison Square Garden. We'll tour Europe. We'll play before royalty. We'll make a fortune.

In the revival, Sitting Bull performs a ceremony of adoption immediately after declaring that he wants to adopt her. He shakes a rattle while chanting, names her, and gives her a bear-teeth necklace. She does not repeat after him or do anything more than witness and receive the gifts. The ceremonial adoption occurs in both versions, even though the production numbers were cut from the revival. It is required as a plot device because it is the reason Cody's show takes the European tour that separates Oakley from Butler. Additionally, it keeps Sitting Bull around for the second act to make jokes and use his influence to help Oakley get Butler back.

Although the adoption song was removed along with the spectacle of dancing Indians, the necessity of Sitting Bull's adoption of Oakley introduces a conception of Indianness that appears contradictory but presents no challenge to the racial logic of vanishing essentialism to which the revisal ascribes. A comparison between the two adoption scenes reveals how the revisal's version offers a narrower definition of Indianness and, taken with the blood quantum logic espoused with the Keeler character, further separates Indians from non-Indians. In the 1946 version, Annie is required to repeat phrases after Sitting Bull and expresses impatience to become an Indian:

SITTING BULL: Say after me. Ne taw waw kou.
ANNIE: Na taw waw kou.
SITTING BULL: Na traw wa key.
ANNIE: Na traw wa key.
SITTING BULL: Oh hein ya.
ANNIE: Oh hein ya.
SITTING BULL: Da Kot A.
ANNIE: Da Kot A.
SITTING BULL: Teeth of many bears. [places necklace on her]
ANNIE: Am I an Indian yet?
SITTING BULL: Shh! [puts feather in her headband] Now! (47)

This is likely a caricature of the Húŋka adoption ceremony.[67] It renders Dakota/Lakota languages poorly and incompletely. For example, "Ne taw waw kou," might be "Nitȟáwa ku," which means "I receive your pipe." Given that there is photographic evidence from the 1966 revival that Sitting Bull held a pipe during the Indian sequence as he stood facing Annie and the published script from 1966 version mentions him moving a pipe over Annie's head, this translation actually makes sense. However, the very next line, "Ne traw wa key," contains a sound, *r*, that does not exist in Lakota, the language of Sitting Bull. "Oh hein ya" is likely "Ohíya," which means to win or be victorious. And although Sitting Bull was a Hunkpapa Lakota leader, the musical has him pronounce Annie to be "Da Kot A," Dakota. However, she is not really an Indian until she wears a feather. This short scene is followed immediately by Oakley's song "I'm an Indian, Too." Some sort of consent or assent occurs in this scene as Oakley is eager to know when the adoption has occurred. Furthermore, she understands the adoption as a transformative experience that will imbue her with Indianness. She will be an Indian. Thus, her song celebrating her newfound Indianness, along with a discussion of how she had longed for such a transformation during her childhood, follows naturally. She has become Indian. The 1999 adoption scene is not only significantly shorter, but it also conceives of Indianness as a substance that cannot be shared, given, or accepted. There is no transformation.

BUFFALO BILL: You hear that, Annie? He wants to be your friend.

SITTING BULL: No! Not friend! Sitting Bull want to make Annie Oakley his daughter! (He removes his necklace.) Give you Indian name—Watanya Cecilla—"Little Sure Shot"—here are teeth of many bears. (He puts it over her heard.) And now, to help daughter, Sitting Bull will break lifelong rule—put money into show business![68]

There is no repeating anything. There is no anticipation of becoming an Indian. Oakley does not participate in the ceremony. She receives a necklace and an Indian name. The transformation occurs within Sitting Bull, who now feels fatherly affection for Oakley and wants to financially support her by supporting the show that employs her. The deletion of "I'm an Indian, Too" also reinforces this idea. Oakley has no song to celebrate becoming an Indian because she has not become an Indian. In this way, even though the original production was racially reductive in its depiction of Native Americans, it offered a glimpse of a different mode of Indianness, that of kinship creation. Falling far short of the complexity with which Native American nations created kinship networks and national identity, the adoption moment still suggested that there was an alternative to the racial logic of blood quantum.

While in the 1999 version, Oakley recognizes her newfound Indianness, she does not change because of it. Change in a character is an exceptionally common tool used by dramatists to demonstrate a narrative arc. Identifying the growth or change of a character is often the easiest way to identify the main character in realism-influenced plays that adhere to Aristotelian plot conventions. As such, the lack of substantive change in Oakley in the wake of her adoption ceremony demonstrates that it is not actually important to her character. It is an ornamentation. In the original production, it was the justification for a spectacle-filled production number and comedic song for the star. In the revisal, it was a momentary flourish before the plot moved forward. And because it forecloses the idea of kinship creation as a possibility, it also reifies the distance between Native Americans and white people. White people do not become Indians, because white people are not Indians. Thus, the revisal's well-intentioned attempt to remove offensive imagery and lyrics resulted in the reification of racialized essentialism and racial boundaries. The revisal reshaped the Stage Indian and connected it to centuries' long conceptions of blood that continue to delimit Indianness in many ways.

DANCE

When the Indian sequence at the end of act 1 was cut, most of the Indian dances were cut. By attending to their creation and reception, it becomes clear how these dances participated in the circulation of the Stage Indian. Only one brief dance interlude dedicated to Indian characters was created for the revival, revealing a different approach to how Indians dance, which was ultimately received by at least some audiences as illegible. The Indian sequence dances, referred to collectively at the time as a ballet, were, as previously noted, extremely well-received in the original production. The *New York Herald Tribune* referred to it as "a honey."[69] *Billboard* described choreographer Helen Tamiris's dances as packing "plenty of imagination, particularly the Indian ceremonial ballet which climaxes the first act."[70] In a June 1946 article on Tamiris's work, the *New York Herald Tribune* singled out the ceremonial Indian dances for special attention:

> "Wild Horse Ceremonial Dance" is, on the surface, an eye-filling production number put together with such splashes of scenic color that the first impression is one of spectacle rather than dance. But Tamiris has reflected much of this glitter in the dances themselves as her Indian braves, headed by Daniel Nagrin, turn to muscular warwhoops and succeed in drawing attention from the décor and costumes to the movement of dance.[71]

It goes on to describe the featured male dancer's ability to recreate the supposed spirituality of Native American dance within a musical comedy:

> Nagrin, clad in a paucity of covering, vibrates, stomps and cuts the air with frenetic-like leaps. In spite of its obvious musical-comedy accouterments,

> this dance manages to suggest the concentrated energy and the heightened spirits of a real dance incantation. Of course, such aspects of dance are not sustained for long, since Broadway dance, rather than ethnological dance, is the medium . . .[72]

The Indian dance was understood as not only an example of choreographic and technical expertise but an actual, though momentary, channeling of the power of an incantation. It is unclear from extant records whether Tamiris set this as her objective when choreographing the dance or if it was just an interpretation motivated by the critics' own familiarity with and expectations of the Stage Indian.

Instead of a Euro-American-choreographed dance meant to evoke Native American ceremonial dance, the revival inserted a brief dance based on modern Native American hoop dancing. The hoop dance is one of many dances regularly included at Native American powwow competitions, and in that form, it is considered an exhibition dance, not a sacred one. Its origins are in the southwestern Pueblo cultures, who perform it as a religious dance, according to ethnomusicologist and specialist in powwow music and dance Tara Browner.[73] The hoop dance in the 1999 revival lasts about forty seconds and is used as entertainment while a set change occurs. It is performed by a woman whose long dark hair is in two braids with a feather hanging down from a beaded decoration by her right ear. She wears a unitard with glow-in-the-dark or blacklight-visible stripes and uses five hoops to "ride" a horse and "fly" like a bird.[74] The music for this section is markedly different in tone and rhythm from the rest of the show. Like the music Pisani analyzed from the original production, it uses a moresca rhythm and distinct chord progressions to communicate musical Indianism. Beginning with bells and then drums, it is an arrangement of a few bars of "There's No Business Like Show Business" but with an Indianism flair. Even with this overt use of musical and visual tropes of Indianness, *New York Times* theater critic Ben Brantley still connected the hoop dance with "Mr. Calhoun's work on 'Grease!'"[75] Inserting a hoop dance was misread as influenced by a choreographer's earlier work on a musical set in the 1950s, rather than by contemporary Native American dance practices. This attempt to provide a more authentic movement vocabulary for Native American characters was hindered by its reliance on a contemporary powwow form rather than a stereotypical vocabulary of movement. Unlike the insertion of the Casino Indian joke, which also relied on late twentieth-century cultural knowledge, the insertion of actual late twentieth-century Native American dance practices was not immediately recognizable. The production removed stereotypical dance forms associated with Indians and replaced them with a dance form that was accurate but likely unrecognizable to the audience.

This brief dance demonstrates the difficulty of communicating Indianness to an audience without relying on decades-old visual and kinetic vocabularies that perpetuate reductive tropes. Adding to an existing trope, like the romance novel cover iconography of Tommy Keeler in the advertising campaign, appears to be an easier project than trying to create a new Indian marker. Furthermore, by removing nearly all places where Native American characters dance in a physical vocabulary distinct from the majority white characters, the revisal did not offer a robust response to the stereotypical and mythical dances included in the original production. Rather than address what was there and what needed to change, they simply cut it. This strategy is perhaps unsurprising since it is identical to the way the revisal cut the problematic, racist, and sexist aspects of the original production. Often, the revisal creative team decided that deletion was the most effective strategy for addressing past inaccuracies or harm. Unfortunately, this indicates that they also located the "problem" in the actions rather than the construction of the Indian as a racialized figure.

CASTING

The casting of the Native American roles in *Annie Get Your Gun* was another space where the production team attempted to rid itself of racist practices identified in previous productions. However, the solution they latched onto introduced other problems, including an underdeveloped understanding of Indianness. Records of the 1946 production do not indicate the racial identity of cast members. However, given that in 1946 it was not a typical casting practice to hire Native American actors for Native American roles, we can safely assume that the original cast of *Annie Get Your Gun* included few if any Native Americans.[76] In the original production, character actor Harry Bellaver played Sitting Bull. Bellaver earned special recognition from the *New York Times* for his performance in the show. Lewis Nichols complimented Mr. Bellaver's "comedy sense—and a flat nose Sitting Bull himself would admire."[77] Bellaver, a Euro-American actor, was marked as an excellent comedian and the possessor of a nose that looked Indian. His physicality was connected to his performance and gave him credibility as a Stage Indian. Rather than see the character of Sitting Bull as an Indian, Andrea Most has cogently argued that the character of Sitting Bull in the 1946 version is actually an American "who teaches the new immigrant how to behave in her adopted country."[78] Most argues that Sitting Bull is the character who helps Annie Oakley transition from backwoods girl to worldly and womanly entertainer. He has acclimated and assimilated to American culture and can support and show Oakley how to do so as well. In that, he "is an Indian who acts like a Jew."[79] Rather than a love song to the frontier and American West, Most claims that *Annie Get Your Gun* is a love song to Broadway, extolling and celebrating "the pleasures and power of the Broadway stage."[80] If Sitting Bull plays the role of the "Jewish comedian," so common across the Broadway and vaudevillian stages of the first half of the twentieth century, it is not surprising that the race of the actor playing the character was not prioritized as Native American.

The 1999 production approached casting quite differently. In the 1999 revisal, the role of Sitting Bull was originated by a Native American actor, Gregory Zaragoza (Pima). He was not a typical Broadway performer, having only one previous Broadway credit. The producers of the revival chose to hire an actor, not a star, presumably because he was Native American. This choice emphasized a particular definition of Native American identity, one that is racialized. The producers did not hire a Sioux actor.[81] It is not clear whether this was a purposeful choice. However, it is clear that the producers cast Zaragoza at least in part because of increasing cultural expectations that Native American roles be played by Native American actors. The success of the films *Dances with Wolves* and *Last of the Mohicans* earlier in the decade, with their emphasis on accuracy and sympathetic portrayals of Indians, may have primed audiences and artists alike to cast along racial lines. In hiring Zaragoza, the producers explicitly chose a Native American actor, an act that revealed their understanding of Indianness as essentially racial. By ignoring the fact that Zaragoza is Pima and not Sioux, the production accomplished their goal of not being racist in the casting of Sitting Bull. However, the production was still racializing Native Americans. Just like Edwin Forrest had nearly two hundred years earlier, they believed that one Indian was interchangeable with another Indian. This casting decision publicly claimed that Native Americans bring something to the performance of Indianness that non-Native Americans cannot, but that something is rooted in race, not in Indigeneity or sovereignty.

This critique of the racializing and essentializing logic of this casting choice is not meant to cast aspersions on the significant decision to hire a Native American actor. There is a long history in theater and film of casting non-Native American actors in Native American roles, which usually works to reduce employment opportunities for Native American actors.[82] However, it is important to separate the systemic issues of employment and access from the systemic issues of racialization, given that the solutions to these intertwining yet distinct systems may not be mutually applicable or effective. The problem of representation in American theatrical casting and its relationship to the construction of racialized depictions in American theater is beyond the scope of this book but is a subject in need of rigorous analysis and problem solving.

In an exceptionally revelatory act, the care that producers took to hire a Native American actor for the Sitting Bull character was not replicated with the mixed-race character Tommy Keeler. The commitment to a racially identifiable Indian actor for the "full-blood" character was not matched by a commitment to a racially identifiable Indian actor for the "mixed-blood" character. By prioritizing a Native American actor to play the full-blooded Native American role but not for the mixed-race character, the producers supported a conception of Native American identity that echoes the vanishing aspects of blood-quantum-based logic. To be a half-Indian character is to be a diminished Indian, a status that does not demand a Native American actor. The racial logic used in casting this production is further complicated by the fact that of the five understudies or replacements for Sitting Bull recorded by the Broadway League and available on their online database, none are identified as Native American.[83] This does not preclude any of them from actually being Native American by kinship or citizenship. However, it does suggest that the producers were not committed to hiring actors explicitly identified as Native American when it came time to hire replacements and understudies.

The production's ethical commitment to hiring Native American actors was constrained not only by the blood quantum of the character but also by the distance between the actor and the original cast. By grounding the casting choices in this racialized logic of blood quantum, the production perpetuated the practice of redface, demarcating a racial and gendered identity through a series of visual, aural, and kinetic markers (e.g., costuming, dialogue, knife-throwing act). The production admirably chose to break from theatrical tradition and prioritized casting a Native American actor for the role of Sitting Bull but fell back on a racialized concept of blood quantum to shape their casting of Tommy Keeler, and it eventually stopped prioritizing Native American identity in casting replacements. The revisal is actually remarkably consistent in its conception of Indians as Indian onstage and off, which illustrates how the Stage Indian is both reflective of and constitutive of the racialized Indian in America.

CONCLUSION

The 1999 revival of *Annie Get Your Gun* exposes the prevalence and persistence of the racial performance practices that mark characters as Indian in US theater. These markers of race are embodied, relying on the physicality and appearance of the characters and actors portraying them. However, these markers of redface are more than just red makeup applied to an actor's face. Redface comprises visual markers like feathers and fringe, aural markers like Hollywood Injun English and Indianism, kinetic markers like knife throwing and dancing, and dramaturgical and narrative markers like Indians used as a source of humor or important plot point or as mixed-race reminders of antiracist aspirations. But redface does not actually live in or through those markers. It is multiply located in the artists and audiences who collaborate on recognizing an Indian body, the Indian that is defined by American settler-colonial ideology and processes. The revisions *Annie Get Your Gun* undertook to address the problem of indelicate or offensive depictions of Native Americans were in fact attempts to address the problem of redface. The substantial revisions made to the musical to improve the show's racial politics ultimately fell short in many instances, which highlights the entrenched problems of performing racial identities within commercial theater. The methods used to revise the musical tried to remove, modify, or transform problematic elements. They included important steps like hiring Native American actors, a particularly welcome step to a routinely underutilized pool of actors working in the United States. However, hiring one Native American actor for one role that diminishes but does not demolish racially stereotypical tropes is ineffective in the overall goal of reducing the reliance on and tenacity of redface.

The 1999 revisal illustrates how difficult it is to fix redface. The difficulty comes not just in the analytical and creative effort to define, identify, and address the problem. It also comes in the challenge of reconceptualizing Native Americans as something other than a vanishing, blood-based race sharing common characteristics and experiences. Redface denies the complexity, heterogeneity, and sovereignty of Native American people and nations. Attempting to excise redface without excising those acts of denial results in the obvious state of racism just wearing a different costume. The fundamental settler-colonial idea of a racially inferior Indian who goes extinct in the face of superior white settlers/blood persists. *Annie Get Your Gun* fixed the makeup and kept the redface.

Although this production did not successfully accomplish its goals of removing all racist and sexist aspects of the musical, it did accomplish some things. It revealed the challenges of addressing perceived flaws in period musicals and plays. Attention must be paid to plot, character, costume, dialogue, casting, and more. And even then, it is remarkably easy to fall back on racial tropes that easily surface even in a culture that consciously identifies them as problematic. *Annie Get Your Gun* provides an example of how playing Indian onstage in the United States is always reliant on a repertoire of markers created through previous racialized performances and cannot fully escape the essentialist and reductive conceptions of the Indian identity already circulating. Thus, the production reveals that the constituent components of redface exceed the physical depiction of Native American characters. For redface is a collaborative process of making visible and decoding, of reading the stage and the actor. Remaking the practice cannot be done without first identifying what the actual problem is. The problem of redface is that America still wants Native Americans to be Indians. Recognizing that is the first step to understanding that if all you have been trained to look for is an Indian, and if an Indian is thus all you see, you might be missing out on something that has been staring you in the face all along.

PROVOCATION

The tension between fixing (repairing) and fixing (entrenching) redface is so fundamental to the project of representing Native Americans on the twenty-first-century stage that even the word confesses its confusion and competing alliances. Attempts to replace or correct images and embodied practices circulating in American culture are diffuse. From professional sports, television, and theater to the federal government, American institutions across the country are wrestling with how to respond to reductive and racist representational practices.

Professional sports has been a particularly visible space for the challenges of excising racist depictions of Native Americans. In 2020, the NFL Kansas City Chiefs banned those attending games at its stadium from wearing "ceremonial headdresses and American Indian-themed face paint."[1] However, the "arrowhead chop," a beloved fan ritual that includes an Indian-themed chant and a one-armed chopping motion (called the "tomahawk chop" in other sports venues) was still part of a "thorough review process."[2] Looking racist, the redface costume, was easily excised, but acting like an "Indian," the embodied redface practice, was not.[3] In 2022, Cleveland's MLB team took the field for the first time as the Guardians instead of its former name, the Indians.[4] That same year, the Washington, DC NFL team appeared as the Washington Commanders after going nameless for eighteen months while deciding on a new name after dropping their old one, the Redskins.[5] The controversial and difficult conversations that have occurred in sports demonstrate the competing investments teams, sponsors, fans, and Native American must navigate to make change happen.

Other kinds of entertainment like television, film, and theater opened up new opportunities and recognition for Native American–created work during the last several years as well. On the heels of the

2018 Reclaiming Native Truth project, which comprehensively researched how Americans learn and think about Native Americans, it was clear that American audiences were in need of better and more accurate Indigenous representation.[6] In 2021, NBC's first Native American–focused and Native American–created sitcom, *Rutherford Falls,* premiered on its Peacock streaming service.[7] In the show, Native American characters knowingly and openly interact with the Stage Indian and, importantly for more nuanced representation, do not all resolve the tension in the same way. Also in 2021, FX premiered the Sterlin Harjo and Taika Waititi creation *Reservation Dogs,* which follows a group of teens on an Oklahoma reservation. Receiving widespread accolades from critics and audiences, the show ran for three seasons, won a Peabody Award, and was nominated for dozens of other awards.[8] *Prey,* a 2022 addition to the *Predator* franchise, told the story of a Comanche woman protecting her tribe from a predacious otherworldly invader and became the first film to be dubbed in Comanche.[9] Martin Scorsese's 2023 film *Killers of the Flower Moon,* a story of murder and greed that descended on the Osage Nation, garnered Lily Gladstone (Niitsitapi [Blackfeet] and Nimiipuu [Nez Perce] descent) the Golden Globe and Screen Actors Guild awards for Best Actress (the first Native American to win them). American theater during the COVID-19 era joined in the project of offering alternatives to the caricatured Indians of the past, with companies like the Oregon Shakespeare Festival offering its 2018 production of Cherokee playwright Mary Kathryn Nagle's *Manahatta* as part of its digital 2021 season.[10] In 2023, the first known Broadway production of a play by a Native American woman opened, giving theater audiences a chance to see *The Thanksgiving Play* by Larissa FastHorse on the "Great White Way."[11] All these productions were heralded as momentous occasions for Native American representation and increased awareness of Native American contributions to American theater, film, and television.

Government institutions large and small have also taken steps to address their role in the depiction of Native Americans. In 2022, the US federal government began an initiative to recommend replacement of names of geographic features that included the racial slur s—. The Department of the Interior initiated tribal consultations and public commentary about the more than six hundred places that carry that name and sought recommendations for better naming options.[12] The state of California passed a law that same year to remove the word from the nearly one hundred places in the state that included it.[13] In 2023, the state of New York became the latest to declare, through a vote by the Board of Regents, that high schools must retire Native American–themed logos and mascots.[14] Schools that don't comply "risk losing their state funding."[15] These changes to imagery, logos, and names appear to be reflective of representational changes, but they are also reflective of the need for changes at the level of embodied performance. In a news story covering New York's law change, National Public Radio described a 2019 high school baseball game in which an opposing team relied on performances of "the most cliched Native American caricatures and stereotypes" to taunt their opponent, which had a Native American–identified team name.[16] These taunts included "hand-over-mouth war whoop," "tomahawk chop," and "twirling around in a circle like a war dance."[17] It turns out that racialized imagery of Native Americans and redface performances travel together. By targeting one, it seems that we could also be addressing the other.

These examples reveal efforts to contend with centuries of misrepresentation and to shift American understanding of what an Indian is or should be. Each of these American cultural institutions—sports, entertainment, government—is responding to the history and persistence of the racialized Indian and how its embodiment through performance has harmed Native Americans. Prohibiting visual markers of the Stage Indian, pushing back on reductive representation, and denying the power of the myths that prop it up, these attempts at correcting something understood as negative show not only that Americans understand the prevalence and power of the Stage Indian but also that they are ready to address its pernicious impact. Yet the tools with which they take on this project, as seen in the revisal of *Annie Get Your Gun*, often preclude them from fully addressing the complexity and the rhizomatic rootedness of redface in American culture. Only by fully understanding what redface is and, most importantly, how it works can American entertainment begin to dismantle and reconstruct the Stage Indian. And only when the United States stops racializing Native

Americans can the Stage Indian disappear. These tasks are not impossible, but they are arduous and imperative.

Because redface conceals as much as it reveals, it is exceedingly difficult to excise. Sympathy toward Native Americans does not change the function of redface. Removing or modifying objectionable visual markers does not change the project of redface. Only by uprooting its deepest intentions—to unmake Indigeneity and Indigenous sovereignty on the level of the body—can its message and impact be overturned. Redface theater practice has created a legibly Indian body that I have referred to in this book as the Stage Indian. Through a repertoire of material, dramaturgical, and sensorial components, artists and audiences together constructed the racialized, embodied figure. And together, we have repeated it, standardized it, modified it, and interpreted it as an Indian. The Stage Indian relies on history and dramatic license to carry its raced and gendered information that is extended outward from the stage into the quotidian lives of Native American people. Being labeled or categorized as a race (Indian) has had and continues to have real and material consequences for Indigenous people, most notably in curtailing legal rights and tribal sovereignty but also, among other things, in limiting access to economic and social resources.

The assertions of authenticity in redface performances elucidate how these claims are not appeals to objective standards that can accurately measure authenticity; instead, they are veiled attempts to delimit Indigenous identity and enforce settler-colonial boundaries around Indianness in service of Indigenous erasure. As cultural and political developments in the United States have shifted public understanding and perception of redface many steps have been taken to correct its inaccurate and demeaning attributes. However, defining the problem of redface has proved difficult. Some have understood it as a surface-level phenomenon and some as a character development issue, a problem solved in the costume shop or on the writer's page. As I have shown, it is actually a deeper and more invasive problem. Racializing Indigenous peoples into a category called the Indian is a colonial process intent on securing domination and dominion. It denies Indigenous peoples self-determination and erases Indigenous polities, nations, and governing systems. The Stage Indian is part of this high-stakes and large-scale assault on Indigeneity and Indigenous sovereignty. Sanitizing redface does not result in a radical reinvention of the relationship between Indigenous nations and the settler-colonial nations of the Americas. It just reduces the discomfort of settler-colonial guilt.

The desire to fix redface and the eventual turn to tools that reinforce it reveal that the true challenge is how American theater can kill off a character America needs to stay alive. Put another way, How will audiences know you are presenting a better representation of an Indian if they cannot read the character as Indian? This problem presents a double bind. Using existing markers of legibility reinforces those obviously deficient markers. Not using existing markers prevents audiences from connecting better representations to Native Americans/Indians. Despite the circularity of this problem, it is a distraction and about surface-level solutions.

As this book has argued, redface is not a surface-level phenomenon. Redface is an epistemology, not an ontology. Solving the problems redface generates is not about being better but about knowing better. In short, it is not a problem of seeing more clearly. It is a problem of seeing differently. Solving redface does not demand a better prescription or better-fitting frames but different cones and rods. American culture needs to be primed to see differently, not to apply external correction. Seeing the Stage Indian creates an audience unable to see the Indigeneity in front of them as much as it constructs a vision of Indians. Where might we turn to see differently?

Redface is the dominant way to see Native Americans in US theater, but it has never been the only way to see them. Redface, like all embodied performance practices, is ephemeral and iterative, a constant process of remaking, negotiating, and reconstructing. These are also the processes with which we can build something new. Understanding the possibilities and also the dangers of these processes helps us see how we might change, combat, or eliminate racialized representations that dehumanize Indigenous peoples. Through theater, we might teach ourselves and each other to see differently.

Seeing differently might lead us to understand Native American theater and performance as a recognizable theatrical genre and mode of public performance that functions as a tool and an outlet for Indigenous peoples. Commercial theater, experimental theater, activist theater, plays, comedies, musicals, you name it, Native American theater artists are already doing it. Native American theater is not a genre defined by conventions but a loose constellation of Indigenous artists tied together by shared experience, racialization, settler-colonial history, and telling stories for the peoples and nations they love.

Or we might find that our former inability to see fully, caused by redface's dominance, has prevented us from noticing Native American theatrical artists for years, decades, and even centuries. Our thorough training in recognizing the Stage Indian has made other modes of Indigenous performance illegible and unrecognizable. Identifying what we missed out on could be accompanied by regret and mourning and frustration, as the world *redface* has confined us to is incomplete and limiting. For redface has not only damaged the American understanding of Indigeneity but also damaged the American understanding of America. Seeing differently can bring anger as often as it brings relief. Working together to get to the other side of either emotional response will be imperative, for the work of creating is unceasing. Mourn and rejoice as is fitting, but keep moving forward toward a place where all flourish.

We might also find that refusing redface and relearning what is past and present in Indigenous performance is the key to creating that hoped-for future in which lofty goals like liberty, equality, reciprocity, and kinship are cultural practices rather than cultural ideals. Witnessing Native American theater and performance can transform audience understanding of how the past and present are intertwined in ways that reflect the danger of racialized logics, the stakes of Indigenous sovereignty, and the solutions possible for making a more just, peaceful, and humane world. All these potential scenarios—and countless others I cannot imagine or address— require labor.

This book invites you to rehearse this labor in "Hinushi Inla," an essay that briefly explores the long history of Indigenous theater and performance in the United States. Reading the essay will mean physically retracing your steps to pages you may have already read, skimmed, skipped over, or scrolled past. You will return to moments you have already lived to consider afresh what you encountered in that time and what else you needed in order to fully apprehend it. These moments are brief, just a few pages at a time, and will always include information on the next location you need to move to. You will not be blazing your own trail but traveling on a well-prepared surface. In choosing to read the essay, you will be rehearsing the incremental choices and changes, the labor, as well as the discomfort and unsettling sensation of reading differently. “Hinushi Inla” is simply an invitation to think and act intentionally. It will not by itself create substantive change in the world. But it can provide a space for embodied meditation on the limits and possibilities of reading practices that shape how we know, what we know, and most importantly, how we have come to recognize something as worth knowing.

HINUSHI INLA[1]

Two weeks after the heavily revised *Annie Get Your Gun* opened on Broadway in March 1999, a group of playwrights gathered at Miami University in Ohio for a conference celebrating over two decades of Native American Women's Theater.[2] The conference included performances of plays by Native American/First Nations women, among which was Vera Manuel's *The Strength of Indian Women*, a play about residential school survivors. Predating by twenty-three years Canada's Truth and Reconciliation Commission's final report and by thirty years the United States' investigative report into boarding schools, Manuel's 1992 play articulates an Indigenous perspective on intergenerational harm and the possibilities for healing.[3] Instead of seeing a fictional, mixed-race character throwing knives at a white woman, American audiences could have been watching stories that engaged with the past and present in Indigenous communities. To understand why an insightful and already decades-old theater movement celebrated in academic spaces was so disconnected from mainstream, commercial US theater is to understand the impact of redface. However, it is also an opening to understanding what Manuel and many other Indigenous theater artists have been creating despite the presence of the Stage Indian.

This essay is intent on introducing the scope of Indigenous theater and performance that has been obscured by the redface-shaped afterimage that American theater artists and audiences carry with them after

1 The title of this essay, "Hinushi Inla," is Chahta Anumpa (Choctaw) for "a different path." Pronunciations of the words and their definitions can be found at https://dictionary.choctawnation.com/word/.

2 A schedule of events is available online through the Native American Women Playwrights Archive (NAWPA) in Miami University's special collections. "A Celebration of Native Women's Theater," Miami University, Walter Havighurst Special Collections, The University Archives & Preservation, accessed November 21, 2023, https://spec.lib.miamioh.edu.

3 Many of Manuel's works, including *The Strength of Indian Women*, are included in a book honoring her contribution to Aboriginal literature. Manuel, *Honouring the Strength of Indian Women*.

years of staring at the bright light of the Stage Indian. This essay turns you away from that light, gives your eyes time to recover, and focuses on the rich, intriguing, complicated, and beautiful journey of Indigenous performance. *Illvppvt hinushi inla.* This is a different path.

First, I will briefly recount histories of North American Indigenous theater and performance pressing forward and backward from its 1970s origin story. Then I will introduce an early twentieth-century prolific and wildly popular Indigenous performer who was overwhelmingly read as white. A nineteenth-century Indigenous performer will offer a glimpse of his life touring Europe in exhibitions. Finally, I will close with a nineteenth-century performance that challenged the racialization of Indigenous peoples and political attacks against Indigenous nations. Native American theater has always coexisted alongside Euro-American theater. It is not the invention of twenty-first-century progressive desire for racial reconciliation, late twentieth-century desire for a multicultural valuing of difference, mid-twentieth-century fights for racialized peoples' rights, early twentieth-century longing for homegrown exoticism, late nineteenth-century need for spectacular nostalgia, or early nineteenth-century longing to capture a presumably vanishing race. It exists because Indigenous peoples have turned to performance as a tool and an art from time immemorial.

A brief history of Indigenous theater in the continent called North America will help reveal how decades of growth and development have produced a contemporary moment full of vibrant art despite minimal interaction with mainstream American theater. I am deeply indebted to the writing of theater historians and scholars Birgit Däwes, Henning Schäfer, and Anne Haugo for their work on this topic in the book *Indigenous North American Drama: A Multivocal History*, edited by Däwes. It offers a multifaceted account of Indigenous drama and performance across the Americas, asserting, "Indigenous drama and performance constitute—along with storytelling—the oldest literary genre in the Americas."[4] For these scholars, Indigenous theater and performance *is* American theater and performance.

4 Däwes, "Performing Memory."

(*Continued on page 175*)

ACKNOWLEDGMENTS

This book has benefited from research support from the Choctaw Nation of Oklahoma, Northwestern University, the Newberry Library, the American Indian Graduate Center, the Chahta Foundation, the Ford Foundation, and a University of Michigan SUCCEED grant. I owe a debt to the generous colleagues and teachers who have listened to, read, commented, challenged, and corrected me over the course of developing this project. Many thanks to Harvey Young, Susan Manning, Liz Son, Tracy Davis, Dassia Posner, Joshua Chambers-Letson, and David Márquez for the years they spent shaping my graduate education and my thinking. Thank you to Kelly Wisecup, Meredith McCoy, David Duty, Peggy McCracken, and Rose Bank for reading my work and providing feedback. Special thanks to the 2020–21 fellows at the Institute for the Humanities at the University of Michigan, who gave me a (Zoom) space to talk through the pandemic-necessitated revisions. Thank you to the communities I've found and the audiences who have patiently listened at the Native American and Indigenous Studies Association; Latinx, Indigenous and the Americas Focus Group at ATHE; American Society for Theatre Research; Mid-America Theatre Conference; NCAIS Graduate Conference in 2017; and the TDGSO Conference in 2014. Thank you to *Theatre Survey* for providing a space for an early version of part of chapter 3.

I am very grateful for the professional home and warm welcome I have found at the University of Michigan. Thank you for the conversation, the encouragement, and the advice Robin Beck, Dimitri Brown, Greg Dowd, Sherina Feliciano-Santos, Matthew Fletcher, Kayla Gonyon, Barbra Meek, Cherry Meyer, Sandra Momper, Susan Najita, Alphonse Pitawanakwat, Katie Schultz, Amy Stillman, David Temin, Arland Thornton, Gustavo Verdesio, and Michael Witgen. A special thanks to my colleagues in the Department of American Culture and especially to Anita Gonzalez, Colin Gunkel, and Laura Mielke for making time during lockdown in spring 2020 to read my draft and virtually attend my manuscript workshop. Thanks also to Andrew Reiter for organizing and to Mallory Whiteduck for taking notes. Special thanks to my research assistants Tuhin Chakraborty, Tia Folgheraiter, Solomon Milner, and Yufan Zhang.

Professional and personal networks also contributed to this book. Thank you to Gianna Mosser for the always incisive advice and to Elizabeth Hunter for the dependably smart, funny, practical, and encouraging thoughts. Brian Herrera, Robin Bernstein, and Stephanie Batiste deserve the credit for envisioning this book in the world in ways I would never have imagined without them. Yakoke to Theresa Struwe for translation assistance. Miigwech to Andrea Carlson for your recommendations and connections. I could not have written this book without Jenni, Emma, Evan, Destiny, Cheyenne, Alexis, Robin, Sheena, Tina, Rebekah, Kathy, and especially Michelle and Carolyn, who in caring for my children enabled the creation of this work. My greatest thanks go to my family and my family-in-law who give me joy and remind me who I am and who I want to be. I love you 5. Lastly, thank you Eric for half a life together, Gareth for being a test case, Amalia for the copyediting assistance, and Edlyn for making me tea. Chi hullo li.

NOTES

INTRODUCTION

1 For a fuller articulation of Indigeneity, see Justice, *Why Indigenous Literatures Matter*.

2 Taylor, *The Archive and the Repertoire*; Davis, "Nineteenth-Century Repertoire," 7.

3 Davis, "Nineteenth-Century Repertoire," 7.

4 King, *The Inconvenient Indian*.

5 For more on the English origins of blackface, see Vaughan, *Performing Blackness on English Stages*.

6 Lott, *Love and Theft*.

7 Johnson, *Burnt Cork*, 2.

8 Rhae Lynn Barnes's forthcoming work on amateur blackface performance in the twentieth century will argue for its continued saturation as an American theater form even though it was excluded from commercial theater spaces.

9 For a sampling of scholarship on blackface minstrelsy, see Lhamon, *Raising Cain*; Cole, *Ghana's Concert Party Theatre*; Johnson, *Burnt Cork*; Cole and Davis, "Routes of Blackface"; Lott, *Love and Theft*; Sammond, *Birth of an Industry*; Hoxworth, *Transoceanic Blackface*.

10 See Lee, *Made-Up Asians*.

11 "Redfacing" was coined by Michelle H. Raheja in *Reservation Reelism*, her book on Native Americans in film.

12 Google Books Ngram Viewer is a publicly available tool and is accessible at http://books.google.com/ngrams.

13 Jesse Green, "Review: 'An Octoroon,' a Branden Jacobs-Jenkins Comedy about Race," *New York Times*, June 1, 2018, www.nytimes.com.

14 Bird, *Dressing in Feathers*; Kilpatrick, *Celluloid Indians*; Aleiss, *Making the White Man's Indian*; Raheja, *Reservation Reelism*; Tahmahkera, *Tribal Television*; Black, *Picturing Indians*.

15 Kilpatrick, *Celluloid Indians*; Raheja, *Reservation Reelism*; Black, *Picturing Indians*.

16 Raheja, *Reservation Reelism*, xii, 20.

17 A recent study has shown that the perceived acceptability of redface is different from that of blackface. See Lopez, Eason, and Fryberg, "The Same, yet Different."

18 Deloria, *Playing Indian*.

19 Deloria, *Playing Indian*, 184, italics in the original.

20 Deloria, *Playing Indian*, 6.

21 Byrd, *The Transit of Empire*, xiii.

22 Ric Knowles's materialist semiotic analytical work introduces the scope of factors that should be taken seriously when analyzing theater. Knowles, *Reading the Material Theatre*.

23 Sandoval-Sánchez, *José, Can You See?*; Herrera, *Latin Numbers*.

24 Shimakawa, *National Abjection*; Burns, *Puro Arte*.

25 Dolan, *Utopia in Performance*; Muñoz, *Cruising Utopia*; Chambers-Letson, *After the Party*.

26 Dolan, *Utopia in Performance*, 2

27 Wolfe, "Settler Colonialism."

28 Wolfe, "Settler Colonialism," 388; Kauanui, "'A Structure, Not an Event.'"

29 Johnson, *Appropriating Blackness*; Manning, *Modern Dance, Negro Dance*; Brooks, *Bodies in Dissent*; Young, *Embodying Black Experience*; Bernstein, *Racial Innocence*; Chambers-Letson, *A Race So Different*.

30 Roach, *Cities of the Dead*; Nyongó, *The Amalgamation Waltz*; Khabeer, *Muslim Cool*.

31 Berkhofer, *The White Man's Indian*; Deloria, *Playing Indian*. Fryberg's work is extensive, but a starting point is Fryberg and Stephens, "When the World Is Colorblind."

32 O'Brien, *Firsting and Lasting*; Byrd, *The Transit of Empire*; TallBear, *Native American DNA*.

33 Coulthard, *Red Skin, White Masks*; Simpson, *Mohawk Interruptus*; Warrior, *Tribal Secrets*; Rickard, "Sovereignty"; Singer, *Wiping the War Paint off the Lens*; Robinson, *Hungry Listening*.

34 Vizenor, *Manifest Manners*; Howe, "Tribalography."

35 The pronunciation of the essay's title can be heard online at dictionary.choctawnation.com by searching for the individual words.

1. FEATHERS AND FACE PAINT

1 "Boston Tea Party Ships & Museum," Historic Tours of America, www.bostonteapartyship.com. Opened in 2012, the site offers a "museum experience" through a simulated town meeting, holographic reenactment, historical artifacts, and a life-size replica of an eighteenth-century ship. A café and a gift shop are also included at the site.

2 "Historic Tours," Historic Tours of America, www.historictours.com. "Historic Tours of America, Inc. is an entertainment company which provides historically oriented vacation experiences for our guests"; "Overview," Historic Tours of America, www.historictours.com. Historic Tours of America is headquartered in Key West, Florida, and operates properties in Florida, Massachusetts, California, Georgia, Tennessee, and Washington, DC.

3 Thank you, Andrew Gibb, for your act of care.

4 Deloria, *Playing Indian*.

5 I do not know why people chose not to wear their feather and instead carried it. My own conjecture leads me to think that there was a mixture of discomfort at racial performance, disdain for a seemingly childish dress-up game, inability to successfully affix the feather to their heads, or lack of interest, among any number of other possible reasons.

6 Deloria, *Playing Indian*, 12.
7 For a brief history of feathers' appearances in the iconography of the New World, America, and the United States from the sixteenth to the nineteenth centuries, see Fleming, "The American Image as Indian Princess 1765–1783"; and Fleming, "From Indian Princess to Greek Goddess." For discussion of nineteenth- and twentieth-century representations of Native Americans, consult editor Elizabeth Bird's aptly titled work *Dressing in Feathers*.
8 I use the term *Stage Indian* in this book similarly to how Tomáš Kačer configures it in his 2021 article, although I am less interested in the image and authenticity of an Indian figure than in how embodied performance creates and sustains a collaborative process of racial legibility with implications beyond the stage. Kačer, "The 'Stage Indian' in Early American Theatre Culture."
9 Omi and Winant, *Racial Formation in the United States*, 111.
10 See such recent works as Alfred, *Wasa'se*; Corntassel and Witmer, *Forced Federalism*; Coulthard, *Red Skin, White Masks*; Stark, "Nenabozho's Smart Berries"; Lerma, *Indigenous Sovereignty in the 21st Century*; and Moreton-Robinson, *The White Possessive*.
11 According to the Department of the Interior's Bureau of Indian Affairs, as of January 2022, there were 574 federally recognized Native American nations within the United States. "Indian Entities Recognized by and Eligible to Receive Services from the United States Bureau of Indian Affairs," 87 Fed. Reg. 4636 (Jan. 28, 2022).
12 Omi and Winant, *Racial Formation*, 111.
13 Vega, *The Discovery of the New World by Christopher Columbus*.
14 Chapman, *The Memorable Maske*, unnumbered pages.
15 Chapman, *The Memorable Maske*, unnumbered pages.
16 D'Avenant, *The Cruelty of the Spaniards in Peru*, unnumbered pages.
17 Review of Haymarket production in *World and Fashionable Advertiser*, August 6, 1787, reprinted in the online supplementary materials to Straub, Anderson, and O'Quinn, *The Routledge Anthology of Restoration and 18th Century Drama*, accessed May 23, 2023, https://routledgetextbooks.com. The "Inkle and Yarico" section is under the heading "Entertainment in an Age of Revolutions, 1760–1800."
18 Lescarbot, *The Theatre of Neptune in New France*, xiv.
19 Welch, "Performing a New France," 439.
20 Bray and Barker, *The Indian Princess*.
21 Berkhofer, *The White Man's Indian*.
22 Berkhofer, *The White Man's Indian*, 29.
23 Byrd, *The Transit of Empire*, xiii.
24 Byrd, *The Transit of Empire*, xx.
25 Byrd, *The Transit of Empire*, 136.
26 Davis, "Nineteenth-Century Repertoire," 7.
27 Davis, "Nineteenth-Century Repertoire," 7.
28 I take care to use the term *Indians* rather than *Native Americans* to draw a distinction between Indigenous peoples of this continent and the fictive creations of Euro-Americans. This distinction between real and fake will be a constant com-

panion and source of anxiety throughout this book. Assertions of accuracy and authenticity appear in redface performances well beyond the Indian plays era.

29 Bray and Barker, *The Indian Princess.*

30 Moses, *Representative Plays*, 570.

31 Moses, *Representative Plays*, 570.

32 See, for example, the rise of blackface performance in European performance traditions in Vaughan, *Performing Blackness on English Stages.*

33 As McConachie has noted, the shift from elite male theatergoers to family-friendly (read, appropriate for females and children) theater happened gradually over the first fifty years or so of the 1800s. See McConachie, *Melodramatic Formations.*

34 McConachie, *Melodramatic Formations*, 68 and 157–58.

35 Carlson, *The Haunted Stage.*

36 McConachie, *Melodramatic Formations*, 18.

37 Carlson, *The Haunted Stage*, 63.

38 Rourke, *American Humor.*

39 *The Cambridge Guide to American Theatre*, 2nd ed., ed. Don B. Wilmeth (Cambridge, UK: Cambridge University Press, 2007), s.v. "Support Services, theatrical."

40 A forthcoming companion website will be a repository of information on plays, theaters, playwrights, and timelines for redface performances in commercial theater settings of the United States.

41 See forthcoming companion website.

42 Bold, "*Vaudeville Indians,*" x.

43 A brief overview of the rise of these houses and their longevity can be found in the "Support Services, theatrical" entry in *The Cambridge Guide to American Theatre.* Special thanks to Rosemarie Bank for bringing this to my attention.

44 Rosemarie Bank first pointed this out to me.

45 Dazian est. 1842, Van Horn est. 1852, Eaves est. 1867. "Support Services, theatrical," *The Cambridge Guide to American Theatre.*

46 Medina, *Nick of the Woods*, 3.

47 Medina, *Nick of the Woods*, 3.

48 Medina, *Nick of the Woods*, 3.

49 Medina, *Nick of the Woods*, 3.

50 Hageman, *Hageman's Make-Up Book*, back cover.

51 Other racial and ethnic types are listed in "American Types," "Foreign Types," and "Character Types, Etc." Tellingly, "Hebrews" is the only minority/ethnic/religious group to be lumped in the "Character Types" list and briefly covered, since "the typical stage Jew is too well known to need any particular description." Clearly, the repertoire of Jew-face was legible by the late 1890s. Hageman, *Hageman's Make-Up Book*, 61. Heather S. Nathans has delved into the Jew as a figure of the nineteenth-century stage. in *Hideous Characters and Beautiful Pagans.*

52 Hageman, *Hageman's Make-Up Book*, inside front cover.

53 Hageman, *Hageman's Make-Up Book*, 54

54 Lake reds were utilized in fine art and fabric dying for centuries prior to this makeup application. See Martin, *A Treatise on the Art of Dyeing Woollen Cloth Scarlet, with Lac Lake,* a British wool dying guide from 1812, for an example of its uses.

55 Christy Minstrels, *The Original Christy's Minstrels.*

56 See Lott, *Love and Theft.*

57 Dumont, *Who's the Actor?.*

58 The costume list in the published script calls for an "Indian Chief" costume as the second needed for the character Bogus. Dumont, *Who's the Actor?*, 2.

59 Gill, *Parlor Tableaux and Amateur Theatricals.*

60 The exact color of an Indian's skin was hardly pinned down across the decades and centuries. Reddish, copperish, brownish; all were acceptable to communicate redface onstage.

61 Green, "The Tribe Called Wannabee," 35.

62 Sprague, "The Orator," 80.

63 Sprague, "The Orator," 80.

64 Drama League of America, *A List of Plays*, 8.

65 See Larissa FastHorse's recent play about school Thanksgiving plays called *The Thanksgiving Play*. FastHorse, *The Thanksgiving Play/What Would Crazy Horse Do?.*

66 See chapter 1 in Bank, *Theatre Culture in America.*

67 Carlson, *The Haunted Stage*, 2.

68 Sayre, *The Indian Chief as Tragic Hero*, 124–25.

69 Moody, *Edwin Forrest*, 98–99.

70 McConachie, *Melodramatic Formations*, 77.

71 McConachie, *Melodramatic Formations*, 70–71.

72 Matthew Rebhorn's article on Forrest and elocution cites *Hageman's Make-Up Book*, which mentions "burnt umber of balsamenia." Umber is a natural earth pigment originally extracted from the Umbria region of Italy. Rebhorn, "Edwin Forrest's Redding Up," 477.

73 Rebhorn, "Edwin Forrest's Redding Up," 477.

74 Harrison, *Edwin Forrest*, 38; Alger, *Life of Edwin Forrest*, 240.

75 This series is viewable online through the Smithsonian Institute's website, www.si.edu, and includes Forrest as Metamora, Coriolanus, Richard III, Virginius, Richelieu, Spartacus, Macbeth, Rolla, and Shylock.

76 Per his biographer, "Here he raised his figure to an additional height, lifted his right arm to the level of his shoulder, grasping his long bow." Harrison, *Edwin Forrest*, 41.

77 Metamora is described as wearing a "robe of fur" over his shoulder in act 1, scene 1. Stone, *Metamora.*

78 Oceana's description of Metamora in act 1, scene 1, includes mention of his "long, dark hair" with "an eagle's plume" over it like "a feather diadem." Stone, *Metamora.* The feathers and long dark hair are a constant across all images of Forrest as Metamora.

79 In various locations Sidney's name is recorded as Wilmer, Wilner, and Wilbur. *A Stranger in a Strange Land* traveled at least as far as Ogden, Utah, appearing there sometime after 1901. Browning, "History of Drama in Ogden," 17.

80 The *Oxford English Dictionary* notes that uses of "Blanket Indian" in American colloquial, governmental, and literary sources from 1859 to 2008 was "chiefly

depreciative or derogatory" and is "now historical." *Oxford English Dictionary*, s.v. "Blanket Indian (n.)," December 2023, https://doi.org/10.1093/OED/6556859105.

81 For more on the history of alcohol and Indigenous North America, see Mancall, *Deadly Medicine;* Frank, Moore, and Ames, "Historical and Cultural Roots of Drinking Problems among American Indians"; Martin, "'The Greatest Evil.'"

82 Meek, "And the Injun Goes 'How!'"

83 Sears, *A Pillar of Fire to Follow*, 8.

84 Doddridge, *Logan*, 8.

85 Doddridge, *Logan*, 10.

86 Doddridge, *Logan*, 10.

87 Doddridge, *Logan*, 13.

88 Doddridge, *Logan*, preface.

89 Doddridge, *Logan*, 16.

90 Doddridge, *Logan*, 19.

91 Doddridge, *Logan*, 21.

92 Doddridge, *Logan*, 22.

93 Doddridge, *Logan*, 34.

94 Doddridge, *Logan*, The Argument.

95 Letts, *August: Osage County*, prologue, act 2.

96 Letts, *August: Osage County*, act 3, scene 5.

97 Friedman, *Bloody Bloody Andrew Jackson*, song 6, page 6.

98 Young, *Embodying Black Experience*.

99 Bernstein, *Racial Innocence*, 12.

100 Bernstein, *Racial Innocence*, 246n10.

101 Alger, *Life of Edwin Forrest*, 245.

2. INDIAN PRINCESSES AND THE STAKES OF LEGIBILITY

1 Four months after my family's vacation, Disney opened the newly constructed world of Pandora in Animal Kingdom, a reproduction of a fictional alien world home to an indigenous people called the Na'vi. Pandora invites park guests to enter and experience life with and as Na'vi—and not incidentally to build the *Avatar* brand in preparation for more anticipated sequels to the massively successful 2009 film.

2 I hedge this statement in large part because we have more extant titles than scripts of Indian plays from this era.

3 German playwright August von Kotzebue began the Pizarro fad, with English-language versions written by Richard Heron, Thomas Durton, Matthew G. Lewis, Benjamin Thompson, Anne Plumptre, M. West, Charles Smith, William Dunlap, Arthur Murphy, Charlotte Smith, and, perhaps most famously, Richard Brinsley Sheridan.

4 Owen, *Pocahontas*, 10.

5 Owen, *Pocahontas*, 12.

6 Owen, *Pocahontas*, 13.

7 Owen, *Pocahontas*, 13.

8 Owen, *Pocahontas*, 13.

9 Owen, *Pocahontasa*, 13.
10 Owen, *Pocahontas*, 14.
11 Owen, *Pocahontas*, 14.
12 Owen, *Pocahontas*, 14.
13 Owen, *Pocahontas*, 14.
14 Owen, *Pocahontas*, 21.
15 Owen, *Pocahontas*, 21.
16 Owen, *Pocahontas*, 21.
17 Owen, *Pocahontas*, 21.
18 Owen, *Pocahontas*, 21.
19 Owen, *Pocahontas*, 22.
20 According to the unities, all events in a play should occur in one location over the course of twenty-four hours and should focus on one action. For the quote, see Owen, *Pocahontas*, 22.
21 See Victor Hugo's *Hernani* and the ensuing public uproar, called the Battle of *Hernani* (there were fisticuffs) that accompanied the premier, for a French response to violating dramaturgical structural conventions. For a brief overview of the event, see chapter 2 in Ziolkowski, *Scandal on Stage*.
22 Owen, *Pocahontas*, 22.
23 Owen, *Pocahontas*, 23.
24 Owen, *Pocahontas*, 23.
25 Barker, "The Indian Princess," 16, front matter.
26 Custis, *Pocahontas*, preface in front matter.
27 Thanksgiving was declared a national holiday in 1863 by President Abraham Lincoln.
28 Script available in Barnes, *Plays, Prose and Poetry*.
29 Barnes, *Plays, Prose and Poetry*, 147.
30 Barnes, *Plays, Prose and Poetry*, 147.
31 Barnes, *Plays, Prose and Poetry*, 147.
32 Barnes, *Plays, Prose and Poetry*, 147.
33 Barnes, *Plays, Prose and Poetry*, front matter.
34 Barnes, *Plays, Prose and Poetry*, 148.
35 Barnes, *Plays, Prose and Poetry*, 148.
36 The romance between Pocahontas and John Smith was possibly first told by John Davis in his 1805 novel *First Settlers of Virginia*. This ahistorical romantic tale circulated simultaneously with the more historically accurate plays discussed here, which deny any romance between Smith and Pocahontas and instead focus on the historically supported relationship between Pocahontas and John Rolfe. See also Davis, *Travels*. For a twenty-first-century continuation of this historically suspect but exquisitely dramatic narrative structure, see Malick, *The New World*.
37 For an analysis of Malik's film, see Goeman, *Settler Aesthetics*.
38 Barnes noted the "division of the interest" in the structure of her play, another nod to the hold the unities still had on American theater in the mid-nineteenth century. *Plays, Prose and Poetry*, 148.
39 Barker, *The Indian Princess*, 35.

40 Barker, *The Indian Princess*, 35.
41 Barker, *The Indian Princess*, 49.
42 Barker, *The Indian Princess*, 34.
43 Barker, *The Indian Princess*, act 3, scene 3.
44 Barker, *The Indian Princess*, 34–35.
45 In his biography of Edwin Forrest, Richard Moody explains that Forrest's summer supposedly spent among the Choctaw taught him "the simple values that governed the life of the red man: swift, stern revenge on the marauder, steady devotion to anyone who offered kindness and love." Moody, *Edwin Forrest*, 40.
46 Barker, *The Indian Princess*, 29.
47 Custis, *Pocahontas*, 44.
48 Owen, *Pocahontas*, 91.
49 *The Forest Princess* is included in Barnes, *Plays, Prose and Poetry*, 175.
50 Barker, *The Indian Princess*, 38.
51 Barker, *The Indian Princess*, 39.
52 As was seen in the Indian Removal Act of 1830 and the ensuing lawsuits, wars, and removals.
53 The first federal Office of Indian Affairs, established in 1824, was in the War Department. It was transferred to the Department of the Interior in 1849. Tellingly, the administrative arm of the federal government clearly saw Indian Affairs as inherently affairs of war during this time period. *Encyclopedia of United States Indian Policy and Law*, vol. 2, 2009 (Washington, DC: CQ Press), s.v. "War, U.S. Department of."
54 Assimilation projects through education and conversion began as soon as Europeans encountered the Americas but were particularly salient in what is now the United States from the seventeenth century on, coming to a head during the late nineteenth and early twentieth centuries in what is referred to as the Assimilation Era of Indian administration. For description and analysis of the era, commonly understood as between 1887 and 1934, see Ellinghaus, *Blood Will Tell.*
55 Blood quantum came in vogue for the US federal administration of Indian Affairs during the Assimilation Era as part of the intense effort and imagined goal of figuring out how to make Indians less Indian. The administrative logic of blood quantum, which has no material, physiological, or genetic basis, persists into the twenty-first century. See Ellinghaus, *Blood Will Tell*, 2017.
56 Prucha, *Documents of United States Indian Policy*, 33.
57 Kappler, "Treaty with the Choctaw, 1830," 311.
58 Barker, *The Indian Princess*, 14 (act 1, scene 3).
59 See Fleming, "The American Image," 65–81; Fleming, "From Indian Princess to Greek Goddess," 37–66. More recently, this has been taken up in Patel, "The 'Indian Queen' of the Four Continents."
60 Fleming, "The American Image as Indian Princess," 73.
61 Barker, *The Indian Princess*, 15.
62 Custis, *Pocahontas*, 10.
63 Custis, *Pocahontas*, 11.
64 Owen, *Pocahontas*, 148–49.

65 Owen, *Pocahontas*, 149.
66 Owen, *Pocahontas*, 150.
67 Owen, *Pocahontas*, 149.
68 Barnes, *Plays, Prose and Poetry*, title page.
69 Barnes, *Plays, Prose and Poetry*, 234.
70 Barnes, *Plays, Prose and Poetry*, 264.
71 Barnes, *Plays, Prose and Poetry*, 265.
72 Barnes, *Plays, Prose and Poetry*, 265.
73 Barnes, *Plays, Prose and Poetry*, 268.
74 For an optimistic interpretation of the Barnes play, see Jaroff, "Opposing Forces."
75 Detsi-Diamanti, "Burlesquing 'Otherness,'" 101; Brougham, *An Original Aboriginal*; Brougham, *La Belle Sauvage*.
76 Brougham, *Po-Ca-Hon-Tas*.
77 Detsi-Diamanti, "Burlesquing 'Otherness,'" 101.
78 Brougham, *Po-Ca-Hon-Tas*, front matter.
79 Brougham, *Po-Ca-Hon-Tas*, front matter.
80 Detsi-Diamanti, "Burlesquing 'Otherness,'" 114.
81 Italics in original. Brougham, *Po-Ca-Hon-Tas*, 18.
82 For example, see differences in Bancroft's articulation of the story between the early and later version of his *History of the United States*. "Smith had easily won the confiding fondness of the Indian maiden; and now the impulse of mercy awakened within her breast; she clung firmly to his neck, as his head was bowed to receive the strokes of the tomahawk." Bancroft, *History of the United States*, 131. By Bancroft's last revised version published in 1888, Pocahontas was described without the florid language of rescue but by a simple phrase: "the child, to whom in later days he [John Smith] attributed his rescue from death." Bancroft, *History of the United States*, 93–94.
83 Italics in original. Brougham, *Po-Ca-Hon-Tas*, 19.
84 Hendrick, *Pocahontas*.
85 Hendrick, *Pocahontas*, 2.
86 Hendrick, *Pocahontas*, 3.
87 Hendrick, *Pocahontas*, 2.
88 Hendrick, *Pocahontas*, 16.
89 Hendrick, *Pocahontas*, 17.
90 Hendrick, *Pocahontas*, 17.
91 Hendrick, *Pocahontas*, 16.
92 "About Us," Bureau of Indian Affairs, United States Department of the Interior, accessed August 20, 2019, www.bia.gov.
93 For example, a June 2019 publication listed American Indian and Alaska Native as one racial category and Native Hawaiian and Other Pacific Islander as a different race. US Census Bureau, "A More Diverse Nation," Census.gov, accessed November 21, 2023, www.census.gov.
94 Rothman, "Johnny Depp as Tonto: Is *The Lone Ranger* Racist?" *Time*, July 3, 2013, http://entertainment.time.com; Ted Berg, "Indians Look Great without Racist Wahoo Imagery in Toronto Series," *USA Today*, September 7, 2018, www.usatoday.com;

95 "Intergovernmental Affairs: Tribal Affairs," United States Census Bureau, accessed August 20, 2019, www.census.gov.

96 "About IHS," Indian Health Service, accessed August 20, 2019, www.ihs.gov.

97 Chickasaw theorist Jodi A. Byrd borrows this term in *The Transit of Empire*, xix, her work on the transit of empire.

98 For scholars and activists taking up the important work, see Alfred, *Wasa'se*; Stark, *Stealing Fire, Scattering Ashes*; Coulthard, *Red Skin, White Masks*.

99 Pulsipher, "Playing John White," 196.

100 Pulsipher, "Playing John White," 209.

101 Pulsipher, "Playing John White," 209.

102 Pulsipher, "Playing John White," 209.

103 Haney-López, "The Social Construction of Race."

104 Hudgins v. Wrights, 11 Va. 134 (1806).

105 Hudgins v. Wrights.

106 Hudgins v. Wrights.

107 Hudgins v. Wrights.

108 U.S. Reports: Johnson v. McIntosh, 21 U.S. (8 Wheat.) 543 (1823).

109 Johnson v. McIntosh.

110 U.S. Reports: Cherokee Nation v. the State of Georgia, 30 U.S. (5 Pet.) 1 (1831).

111 Cherokee Nation v. the State of Georgia.

112 United States ex rel. Standing Bear v. Crook, 25 F. Cas. 695 (1879).

113 M. M. Jobe (2004). Native Americans and the U.S. Census: A Brief Historical Survey. *Journal of Government Information, 30*(1), 75. Thanks to Arland Thornton for pointing me to Jobe's work.

114 Department of the Interior, Census Office, *Ninth Census, vol. 1, The Statistics of the Population of the United States* (Washington, DC: Government Printing Office, 1872), xiii, as quoted in Thornton and Young-DeMarco, "Federal Decennial Census Data for Studying American Indians," 8.

115 Department of the Interior, Census Office, *Eleventh Census of the United States. June 1, 1890. Instructions to Enumerators* (Washington, DC: Government Printing Office, 1890), 10, as quoted in Thornton and Young-DeMarco, "Federal Decennial Census Data for Studying American Indians," 8.

116 Thornton and Young-DeMarco, table 4 in "Federal Decennial Census Data for Studying American Indians," 39.

117 Thornton and Young-DeMarco, table 4 in "Federal Decennial Census Data for Studying American Indians," 39.

118 Thornton and Young-DeMarco, table 4 in "Federal Decennial Census Data for Studying American Indians," 39.

119 Thornton and Young-DeMarco, table 4 in "Federal Decennial Census Data for Studying American Indians," 39.

120 US Census Bureau, "Instructions to Enumerators" (Washington, DC: US Government Printing Office, 1919), 27.

121 US Census Bureau, "Measuring America: The Decennial Censuses from 1790 to 2000" (US Department of Commerce, 2002), 10.

122 US Census Bureau, "Measuring America," 20.

123 Rifkin, *When Did Indians Become Straight?*, 8.

124 Indigenous gender and sexuality is an ever expanding area of scholarship and beyond the scope of this book. However, for those interested in the subject, I suggest the following in addition to Rifkin's book: Slater, *Gender and Sexuality*; Barker, *Critically Sovereign;* Morgensen, *Spaces between Us*; Roscoe, *Changing Ones*; and Roscoe, *Living the Spirit*.

125 Rifkin, *When Did Indians Become Straight*, 8.

126 A copy of the act is available online through the Document Bank of Virginia, https://edu.lva.virginia.gov.

127 "The New Virginia Law to Preserve Racial Integrity," Virginia Department of Health, *Virginia Health Bulletin*, March 1924, 4.

128 "The New Virginia Law to Preserve Racial Integrity," 4.

129 "The New Virginia Law to Preserve Racial Integrity," 4.

130 Endo, "'The Word 'Mixed' without the 'Indian' Would Be Better, 92. See also Sherman, "'The Last Stand'"; and Sickels, *Race, Marriage and the Law*.

131 Maillard, "The Pocahontas Exception," 370.

132 See Wolfe, "Settler Colonialism and the Elimination of the Native."

133 For an in-depth look at Plecker's impact on the enforcement of the Racial Integrity Act, see Endo, "'The Word "Mixed" without the "Indian" Would Be Better.'"

134 "The New Virginia Law to Preserve Racial Integrity," 1.

135 "The New Virginia Law to Preserve Racial Integrity," 1.

136 "The New Virginia Law to Preserve Racial Integrity," 2.

137 Endo, "'The Word "Mixed" without the "Indian" Would Be Better,'" 100, 93.

138 As quoted in Endo, "'The Word "Mixed" without the "Indian" Would Be Better,'" 100.

139 Endo, "'The Word "Mixed," 103.

140 Endo, "'The Word "Mixed," 104.

141 Addie C. Rolnick as quoted in Ablavsky, "'With the Indian Tribes,'" 1029.

142 For a cogent analysis of the historical context and possible legal interpretations of Indians as race and nation, see Ablavsky, "'With the Indian Tribes.'"

143 Bold, "*Vaudeville Indians*," 136.

144 Bold, "*Vaudeville Indians*," 136.

3. AUTHENTIC INDIANS

1 A CDIB card is not automatically generated at birth; nor is tribal enrollment. Each new child born into my tribe must apply (or their parents must apply on their behalf) and submit proper documentation so that the child can be an official and legal member of the tribe.

2 For analyses and critique of the idea of Indian blood, see TallBear, *Native American DNA*; Pierce, "Adopted."

3 I use the verb *sires* intentionally. It is a colloquial truism that only dogs, racehorses, and Indians are tracked by the logic of fractions, sires, and dams.

4 Like many administrative logics, real blood quantum fractions are considerably messier than the tools used to measure them. Canadian blood quantum logic is a separate subject with different legal and political stakes from those in the United States, although there are echoes and resonances across the two.

5 For a brief time during this decade, Indians who were less than one-half Indian were automatically deemed competent to hold title to their own land, land they already owned. Those who were one-half or more, or those who were more Indian, were automatically incompetent. However, while being less Indian equaled competency, it did not necessarily equal agency. Competency was declared in service of ridding the federal government of trust responsibilities and resulted in tens of thousands of acres being removed (in legal and illegal ways) from Indian ownership. It was an attempt to speed up the process of getting rid of Indian land and Indians during what is called the Assimilation Era. Blood quantum fractions just helped accelerate the process because they easily measured the disappearance of Indianness.

6 See Hughes, "The Indispensable Indian."

7 Alger, *Life of Edwin Forrest*, 2:835.

8 Alger, *Life of Edwin Forrest*, 1:239.

9 Rees, *The Life of Edwin Forrest*, 97.

10 Harrison, *Edwin Forrest*, 36.

11 Moses, *The Fabulous Forrest*, 100.

12 Alger, *Life of Edwin Forrest*, 1:240.

13 Alger, *Life of Edwin Forrest*, 1:240.

14 Sabin, *Catalogue of the Library of Edwin Forrest*, 80.

15 Alger, *Life of Edwin Forrest*, 1:240.

16 Alger, *Life of Edwin Forrest*, 1:240.

17 Harrison, *Edwin Forrest*, 38.

18 Harrison, *Edwin Forrest*, 37.

19 Alger, *Life of Edwin Forrest*, 1:138.

20 Harrison, *Edwin Forrest*, 36–37.

21 Alger, *Life of Edwin Forrest*, 1:240.

22 Alger, *Life of Edwin Forrest*, 1:240.

23 He was engaged for a season in New Orleans with James H. Caldwell, making eighteen dollars a week. Barrett, *Edwin Forrest*, 32.

24 See Alger, *Life of Edwin Forrest*; Moses, *The Fabulous Forrest*; Moody, *Edwin Forrest*.

25 Moody, *Edwin Forrest*, 47.

26 Barrett, *Edwin Forrest*, 38.

27 Moody, *Edwin Forrest*, 47.

28 Rebhorn, *Pioneer Performances*, 35.

29 I have previously discussed this discrepancy between the historiographical claims surrounding Forrest and Pushmataha and the historical record. Hughes, "The Indispensable Indian."

30 "Mortuary Notice," *Alexandria Gazette* (Alexandria, Virginia), January 4, 1825, 1, Readex, America's Historical Newspapers, www.readex.com.

31 "Mortuary Notice," 1.

32 "Mortuary Notice," 1.

33 His grave is in section 1, range 31, and is listed as "Chief Push-Ma-Ta-Ha." You can view a satellite image of the graveyard and death and burial dates by searching for his name on the cemetery's website under "Records Search." "Chief Push-Ma-

Ta-Ha," Congressional Cemetery Records Search, accessed June 10, 2021, https://congressionalcemetery.org.

34 Alger, *Life of Edwin Forrest*, 1:126.

35 Moody, *Edwin Forrest*, 47.

36 For the earliest published account of Forrest's life, see E. T. W., *The Biography of Edwin Forrest*.

37 "Mortuary Notice," 1.

38 For a nineteenth-century, American-authored biographical sketch of Pushmataha, see Lanman, "Pushmatahaw."

39 The first description of Pushmataha was included by nineteenth-century Pushmataha biographer Gideon Lincecum, who lived in the Choctaw Nation between 1822 and 1825. Lincecum, *Pushmataha*, 101. Forrest biographer William Alger offered the second description. *Life of Edwin Forrest*, 1:126.

40 Alger, *Life of Edwin Forrest*, 1:127.

41 Amateur genealogical sources suggest that there could be more than one son of Pushmataha, but these are not corroborated by the historical record in the way that Johnson Pushmataha is.

42 Lewis, *Chief Pushmataha*; Cushman, *History of the Choctaw*.

43 McBee, *Mississippi County Court Records*, 61.

44 Goss, *The Choctaw Academy*, 144–5.

45 Goss, *The Choctaw Academy*, 144–5.

46 "Mortuary Notice," 1.

47 Alger, *Life of Edwin Forrest*, 1:138–39.

48 Alger, *Life of Edwin Forrest*, 1:138–39.

49 See chapter 6 of Moody, *Edwin Forrest*.

50 Lepore, *The Name of War*, 201.

51 Sarah E. Chinn has read *Metamora* as a warning tale directed at white males, urging them to "control your rage and unruliness." Chinn, "Masculinity and National Identity on the Early American Stage."

52 See Moody, *Edwin Forrest*.

53 There are two federally recognized Wampanoag nations in the twenty-first century, the Mashpee Wampanoag Nation and the Wampanoag Tribe of Gay Head (Aquinnah), both located in Massachusetts.

54 For more, see chapter 4 in Brooks, *The Common Pot*; and see the political writing of William Apess about Mashpee sovereignty in Apess, *Indian Nullification*.

55 For more, see Apess, *Indian Nullification*.

56 This idea is typically linked to work by eighteenth-century French writer Jean-Jacques Rousseau.

57 Stone, *Metamora*, 1996.

58 This is how Walter describes Metamora in act 1, scene 1. Stone, *Metamora*, (1996).

59 Walter describing Metamora's influence and power in act 1, scene 1. Stone, *Metamora*.

60 Oceana's turn to describe Metamora in act 1, scene 1. Stone, *Metamora*.

61 I am thinking alongside Harvey Young in this explanation. See Young, *Embodying Black Experience*.

62 Deloria, *Playing Indian*, 184.
63 For more on Cody's theatrical career, see Sagala, *Buffalo Bill on Stage*.
64 The coach used in *Buffalo Bill's Wild West* that is claimed to have been the original Deadwood coach is on display at the Buffalo Bill Center of the West in Cody, Wyoming. Buffalo Bill Center of the West, "Museum Minute: What the Deadwood Stagecoach Stands for in History," September 13, 2019, https://centerofthewest.org.
65 For more on Indians in Wild West shows, see Moses, *Wild West Shows*.
66 Russell, *The Wild West*, 25.
67 Authentic is in scare quotes for reasons developed in this chapter.
68 Warren, *Buffalo Bill's America*, 256.
69 Bridger, *Buffalo Bill and Sitting Bull*, 326.
70 Department of the Interior, *Report on Population*, lxvii, lx.
71 Department of the Interior, *Report on Population*, xi.
72 Blackstone, *Buckskins, Bullets, and Business*, 8.
73 The term *Show Indian* first appeared in correspondence from federal Indian Service employees during the 1890s. It has been used as a factual term referring to employment status as well as a pejorative against the stereotypical depictions it represented. See Moses, *Wild West Shows*.
74 Blackstone, *Buckskins, Bullets, and Business*, 13.
75 Names from Blackstone, *Buckskins, Bullets, and Business*.
76 Moses, *Wild West Shows*, 1.
77 Blackstone, *Buckskins, Bullets, and Business*, 8.
78 Moses, *Wild West Shows*, 291.
79 As described in the 1887 program. *Buffalo Bill's Wild West*, "A History of American Civilization," program, James Wojtowicz Collection 1880–1929, McCracken Research Library at the Buffalo Bill Center of the West. Obtained through personal email June 7, 2016 (hereafter cited as *Buffalo Bill's Wild West*, "A History of American Civilization").
80 McClintock, *Imperial Leather*, 37.
81 Warren, *Buffalo Bill's America*, 256.
82 MacKaye, *Epoch*, 2:77.
83 Moses. *Wild West Shows*, 1.
84 According to a 1907 program, twenty years later, *Buffalo Bill's Wild West* still included Indian attacks on settlers in wagon trains, a town, and a stagecoach. Buffalo Bill, *Buffalo Bill's Wild West*.
85 Helen M. Bannan's article explains Morgan's influence on Indian policy of the nineteenth century. Bannan, "The Idea of Civilization," 788.
86 Morgan, *Ancient Society*, v–vi.
87 Bannan, "The Idea of Civilization," 788.
88 Conn, *History's Shadow*, 6.
89 Simpson, *Mohawk Interruptus*, 70.
90 Simpson, *Mohawk Interruptus*, 70.
91 Simpson, *Mohawk Interruptus*, 74.
92 See Magelssen and Nees, "'Real Live Indian.'"
93 Reddin, *Wild West Shows*, 61.

94 Severely impacted by the Indian wars of the late nineteenth century, the Oceti Sakowin currently comprise twelve federally recognized tribes and many citizens living within and outside of reservation boundaries.
95 Moses's book *Wild West Shows* is an excellent starting point for understanding the constraints, benefits, and objections to Native Americans working in *Buffalo Bill's Wild West*. Rosemarie K. Bank's article also offers helpful insight and information; see Bank, "'Show Indians.'"
96 The Hunkpapa are Lakota-speaking Oceti Sakowin and are considered "the anchor of the Lakota organization." Dakota Department of Education Office of Indian Education, "Oceti Sakowin Essential Understandings and Standards," accessed February 21, 2017, https://indianeducation.sd.gov.
97 Magelssen and Nees, "'Real Live Indian,'" 26.
98 He was also reimbursed for travel to and from the reservation. Magelssen and Nees, "Real Live Indian,'" 26.
99 As quoted in Magelssen and Nees, 26.
100 For more on the often-tense relationship between Cody and the Bureau of Indian Affairs, see chapter 5, "American Indian Performers in the Wild West," in Kasson, *Buffalo Bill's Wild West*.
101 Moses, *Wild West Shows*, 31.
102 Moses, *Wild West Shows*, 34.
103 See Moses, *Wild West Shows*, 25.
104 Standing Bear, *My People the Sioux*, 252.
105 Bank, "'Show Indians,'" 151.
106 Reddin, *Wild West Shows*, xv.
107 Standing Bear, *My People the Sioux*, 270.
108 DeMallie, *The Sixth Grandfather*, 245.
109 Moses, *Wild West Shows*, 150.
110 Letter from *Miller Brothers 101 Ranch* to Native American leader in Calumet, Oklahoma, 1911, box 1, folder 10, Miller Brothers 101 Ranch Collection, Western History Collections, University of Oklahoma, Norman, Oklahoma.
111 Smithsonian National Museum of the American Indian, introduction to "Infinity of Nations: Art and History in the Collections of the National Museum of the American Indian," http://nmai.si.edu.
112 Standing Bear, *My People the Sioux*, 270.
113 *New York Times*, "Buffalo Bill in Drama: Four Wild West Epochs at Madison-Square Garden," November 25, 1886, ProQuest Historical Newspapers: *New York Times* (1857–1922).
114 Blackstone, *Buckskins, Bullets, and Business*, 17.
115 Blu Wakpa, "From Buffalo Dance to Tatanka Kcizapi Wakpala."
116 Shea Murphy, *The People Have Never Stopped Dancing*, 60.
117 Shea Murphy, *The People Have Never Stopped Dancing*, 63.
118 Blackstone, *Buckskins, Bullets, and Business*, 78.
119 Armitage, *Buffalo Bill's Wild West Parade*.
120 Standing Bear, *My People the Sioux*, 252.
121 Deloria, "The Indians," 52.

122 Deloria "The Indians," 52.

123 McLaughlin, "The Dawes Act," 65. https://doi.org/10.17953/aicr.20.2.j8u2308u37818m45.

124 Moses, *Wild West Shows*, 37.

125 "The Fascinating Wild West," *New York Times*, February 6, 1887, p. 3, col. 7, ProQuest Historical Newspapers, accessed January 18, 2021. This choice to send school children to entertainment deemed historically educational was echoed in the twenty-teens by the City of New York, which sent high school students to see the wildly popular and award-winning musical *Hamilton* on Broadway.

126 Warren, *Buffalo Bill's America*, 280.

127 Native American employees were often married and traveled with wife/wives and children. Luther Standing Bear recounted the story of his daughter's birth in Birmingham, England, during the 1887 tour. Standing Bear, *My People the Sioux*, 266.

128 Bank, "'Show Indians,'" 155.

129 Percy MacKaye was eleven when his father directed The Drama of Civilization and recalled visiting the encampment. MacKaye, *Epoch*, 91.

130 Moses, *Wild West Shows*, 57.

131 MacKaye, Epoch, 2:83.

132 MacKaye, Epoch, 2:82.

133 MacKaye, Epoch, 2:82.

134 In his 1915 memoir, Louis E. Cooke, general representative for the Madison Square Garden lessee in 1887, recalled the six-week preparation period with only three weeks in Madison Square Garden. As quoted in MacKaye, *Epoch*, 2:78.

135 Reddin, Wild West Shows, 64.

136 L. G. Moses indicates that Oceti Sakowin from Pine Ridge were hired during the summer 1885 season, with another contingent hired during the summer 1886 season. He states that "most returned to the show by early November," after briefly returning home to Pine Ridge. Additional Oceti Sakowin and Cheyenne were hired in December 1886. The last season that Pawnee were hired appears to have been 1885. Moses, *Wild West Shows*, 33–34.

137 Letter from *Miller Brothers 101 Ranch* to Native American leader in Calumet, Oklahoma, 1911, box 1, folder 10.

138 For more information, refer to Odell, *Annals of the New York Stage*.

139 Odell, *Annals of the New York Stage*, 3:318, 420.

140 Odell, *Annals of the New York Stage*, 5:71, 7:402.

141 Cothran, *Remembering the Modoc War*, 84–85. Odell, *Annals of the New York Stage*, 9:629.

142 For more on Smith's career, see Julian Bricklin, "The On-Target 'California Girl': Young Lillian Smith Was Annie Oakley's Rival as a Trick-Shot Artist, but Her Most Astonishing Act Was Her Transformation at Age 30 into 'Princess Wenona,'" HistoryNet, November 25, 2014, www.historynet.com.

143 Moses, *Wild West Shows*, 8.

144 For more, see Shea Murphy, *The People Have Never Stopped Dancing*.

4. FIXING REDFACE

1 It changed ownership and was called Onesti's Wild West Town for a brief time before it closed permanently.

2 The offensive word in this line and in other parts of the show discussed later in the chapter is *squaw*.

3 Berlin, Fields, and Fields, *Annie Get Your Gun*. Unless otherwise noted, all the lyrics and dialogue are from this script.

4 *Merriam-Webster's Unabridged Dictionary*, s.v. "squaw," accessed December 18, 2021, https://unabridged.merriam-webster.com.

5 *Annie Get Your Gun*, June 10, 1999, Theatre on Film and Tape Archive, New York Public Library, New York.

6 Lahr, "Irving Berlin," 154.

7 *Col. Tim McCoy's Wild West* played for one month in the spring of 1938 before it was shut down for insolvency. "Wild West Show Bites the Dust; 400 Employees to Get Part Pay," *Washington Post*, May 5, 1938, ProQuest Historical Newspapers: Washington Post (1923–1954), X1.

8 Information on the original Broadway production of *Annie Get Your Gun* is available at the Internet Broadway Database, the Broadway League's online archive. "Annie Get Your Gun—Broadway Musical—Original," *IBDB*, accessed February 22, 2021, www.ibdb.com.

9 For more on Annie Oakley, see Kasper, *Annie Oakley*.

10 See chapter 3, "Butler and Oakley," in Kasper, *Annie Oakley*.

11 For more on Sitting Bull, see Utley, *The Lance and the Shield*.

12 Russell, *The Wild West*, 21, 22.

13 Bridger, *Buffalo Bill and Sitting Bull*, 314–15.

14 Bridger, *Buffalo Bill and Sitting Bull*, 315.

15 Sidney, *Annie Get Your Gun*.

16 Some footage filmed before Judy Garland left the production is included on the DVD release of the film. Sidney, *Annie Get Your Gun*.

17 The revival was nominated for two Tony awards—Best Choreography and Best Direction of a Musical—though won neither. Internet Broadway Database, "Annie Get Your Gun—Broadway Musical—1966 Revival," accessed February 23, 2021, www.ibdb.com.

18 Current license holding company Concord Theatricals has a map built into their page where you can see current or planned productions. "Irving Berlin's Annie Get Your Gun," Concord Theatricals, accessed February 23, 2021, www.concordtheatricals.com.

19 Internet Broadway Database, "Annie Get Your Gun."

20 Internet Broadway Database, "Annie Get Your Gun."

21 Kirle, *Unfinished Show Business*, 1.

22 Vandevender, "Splitting Hair."

23 Magee, *Irving Berlin's American Musical Theater*, 230; Meek, "And the Injun Goes 'How!'"

24 Knapp, *The American Musical*, 211.

25 Amy Porter, "Sureshot Merman," *Collier's*, August 10, 1946.

26 This section draws on additional images from the following: Scrapbook, box 557, book 32, Irving Berlin Collection, Library of Congress; "'Annie Get Your Gun': Ethel Merman Plays Annie Oakley in a New Musical Smash Hit," *Life*, June 3, 1946; "Ethel Merman-She Turns Brass into Gold," *Look*, September 3, 1946.

27 Description of costumes are drawn from clippings in Irving Berlin scrapbook, *Life*, *Look*, and *Collier's* articles as well as photographs held by the New York Public Library for the Performing Arts. Billy Rose Theatre Division, "Musical comedies. Annie get your gun/[Photographs]," Special Collections, New York Library for the Performing Arts.

28 A photo of Nagrin is available online through the Library of Congress's website. "Annie Get Your Gun," image, Library of Congress, accessed November 21, 2023, www.loc.gov.

29 Billy Rose Theatre Division, Helen Tamiris Collection, New York Public Library, "Notes for Annie Get Your Gun" F# 53, 1946, Special Collections, New York Library for the Performing Arts.

30 Billy Rose Theatre Division, New York Public Library, "Musical Comedies. Annie Get Your Gun [Programs]," 1946, Special Collections, New York Library for the Performing Arts.

31 These notes, from the Helen Tamiris collection, are viewable online through the Library of Congress's website. "Annie Get Your Gun [Choreographic Notes]," image, Library of Congress, accessed November 21, 2023, www.loc.gov.

32 Billy Rose Theatre Division, Helen Tamiris Collection, New York Public Library, "Notes for Annie Get Your Gun" F# 53, 1946, Special Collections, New York Library for the Performing Arts.

33 Critical responses drawn from Billy Rose Theatre Division, New York Public Library. "Annie Get Your Gun (Musical: Berlin): Clippings, Special Collections, New York Library for the Performing Arts.

34 *Boston Herald*, April 3, 1946. Annie Get Your Gun (Musical: Berlin): Clippings, Special Collections, New York Library for the Performing Arts.

35 *Cue*, May 25, 1946, 66. Annie Get Your Gun (Musical: Berlin): Clippings, Special Collections, New York Library for the Performing Arts.

36 *Variety*, "Legitimate: Play out of Town-Annie Get Your Gun," April 3, 1946, 60.

37 Descriptions of costumes are drawn from the few available production photos online and from production film held at the Theatre on Film and Tape Archive, New York Public Library, *Annie Get Your Gun*, 1999.

38 Ben Brantley, "Everything The Traffic Will Allow: Annie Get Your Gun Reprising Everything The Traffic Will Allow," March 5, 1999, sec. Weekend, ProQuest Historical Newspapers: New York Times.

39 Brantley, "Everything the Traffic Will Allow."

40 *Annie Get Your Gun*, Theatre on Film and Tape Archive.

41 *Annie Get Your Gun*, Theatre on Film and Tape Archive.

42 Given the vague temporality of the revisal but the presence of Oakley and Sitting Bull, one can guess that it is set in the last decades of the nineteenth century, during which the age of consent varied from around seven to around sixteen, not

universally eighteen as the show implies. For a history of the age of consent in the United States, see Cocca, *Jailbait*.

43 *Annie Get Your Gun*, Theatre on Film and Tape Archive, act 1, scene 1.

44 *Annie Get Your Gun*, Theatre on Film and Tape Archive, act 1, scene 2.

45 *Annie Get Your Gun*, Theatre on Film and Tape Archive, act 1, scene 3.

46 *Annie Get Your Gun*, Theatre on Film and Tape Archive, act 1, scene 2.

47 Flyer from author's personal collection.

48 Flyer from author's personal collection.

49 *Annie Get Your Gun*, Theatre on Film and Tape Archive

50 For an excellent description of *Buffalo Bill's Wild West* and its production practices, see Blackstone, *Buckskins, Bullets, and Business*.

51 Andrew Palermo, email message to author, December 2, 2013.

52 Ben Brantley, writing for the *New York Times*, reviewed the revisal in February 2001 after country singer Reba McEntire assumed the role of Annie. Brantley called Storch's performance "a cross between Diana Vreeland and Calvin Coolidge" but insisted that "on its own wacky terms it works." Ben Brantley, "Annie's Got Her Gun Again, and Hits the Clay Pigeons," *New York Times*, February 9, 2001.

53 *Annie Get Your Gun*, Theatre on Film and Tape Archive, act 1, scene 3.

54 Berlin, *Annie Get Your Gun*.

55 *Annie Get Your Gun*, Theatre on Film and Tape Archive.

56 *Annie Get Your Gun*, Theatre on Film and Tape Archive.

57 Meek, "And the Injun Goes 'How!'"

58 *Annie Get Your Gun*, Theatre on Film and Tape Archive.

59 *Annie Get Your Gun*, Theatre on Film and Tape Archive.

60 For the development of this late twentieth/early twenty-first century stereotype, see Lacroix, "High Stakes Stereotypes."

61 California v Cabazon Band of Mission Indians, 480 U.S. 202 (1987). Public Law 100–497-Oct. 17, 1988 100th Congress Sec. 2701.102 Stat. 2467.

62 Lacroix, "High Stakes Stereotypes," 3.

63 A December 2020 press release by the National Indian Gaming Commission indicated their analysis of 2019 figures based on 245 tribes' records. National Indian Gaming Commission, "209 Indian Gross Gaming Revenues of $34.6B Set Industry Record and Show a 2.5% Increase," December 8, 2020, www.nigc.gov. There were 573 federally recognized tribes in 2019, according to a notice published by the Indian Affairs Bureau in the *Federal Register*. Indian Affairs Bureau, "Indian Entities Recognized by and Eligible to Receive Services from the United States Bureau of Indian Affairs," *Federal Register*, February 1, 2019, www.federalregister.gov.

64 Berlin, Fields, and Fields, *Annie Get Your Gun*.

65 Pisani, "'I'm an Indian Too,'" 243–91.

66 The historical inaccuracy of this plot point is unquestionable. Sitting Bull never invested in *Buffalo Bill's Wild West*. He did not financially support the show and was an employee of the show for only one season. Additionally, Sitting Bull did not have great wealth. For more, see Bridger, *Buffalo Bill and Sitting Bull*.

67 Translation efforts of the adoption ceremony for this book were done by Dakota language learner and instructor Heather Menefee. Menefee indicated that some

of the adoption ceremony is based on Dakota words, some words are likely fabricated or caricatured, while others are unidentifiable as Dakota. This interpretation of the text as garbled or fictive but also containing components of Dakota language was corroborated by Christopher Pexa (Spirit Lake Dakota) and Sara Pillatzki-Warzeha (Sisseton-Wahpeton Dakota).

68 Stone, *Annie Get Your Gun* (1999).

69 Howard Barnes, "Bull's Eye," review of *Annie Get Your Gun, New York Herald Tribune*, May 18, 1946, ProQuest Historical Newspapers: *New York Herald Tribune* (1926–62), 8.

70 "Broadway Openings: Annie, Get Your Gun," *Billboard*, May 25, 1946.

71 Waller Terry, "Helen Tamiris Wins Acclaim for 'Annie Get Your Gun' Ballet," *New York Herald Tribune*, June 16, 1946, D4, ProQuest Historical Newspapers: *New York Herald Tribune* (1926–62).

72 Terry, "Helen Tamiris Wins Acclaim," D4.

73 Browner, *Heartbeat of the People*, 61–62.

74 On at least one occasion, the hoop dance was performed by a male dancer. Program with performer notification insert from author's personal collection.

75 Brantley, "Everything the Traffic Will Allow," E1.

76 There were Native American performers throughout the twentieth century, and at least one appeared in a Broadway musical around the same time that *Annie Get Your Gun* premiered on Broadway. Choctaw Nation of Oklahoma citizen Ridge Bond played the lead role of Curly in the long-running 1940s musical *Oklahoma!* as a replacement actor. He played the role on Broadway and on tour in Germany in 1951. Sheila Kirven, "Choctaw Legend Still Remembered" *Biskinik*, April 2023, 12, www.choctawnation.com.

77 Lewis Nichols, "Merman at Work Experts All," review of *Annie Get Your Gun, New York Times*, May 26, 1946, Arts & Leisure, ProQuest Historical Newspapers: *New York Times* (1923–current file), X1.

78 Most, *Making Americans*, 140.

79 Most, *Making Americans*, 140.

80 Most, *Making Americans*, 122.

81 I do not have access to records of auditions for the production, so I cannot say whether the producers auditioned a Sioux actor and chose not to hire that person.

82 For a brief overview of one of the most recognizable Indian character actors of the mid-twentieth century and his decades of racial fraud, see Aleiss, "Iron Eyes Cody."

83 See the tabs for "Opening Night Cast" and "Replacements." "Annie Get Your Gun—Broadway Musical—1999 Revival," *IBDB*.

PROVOCATION

1 "A Statement from The Kansas City Chiefs," Kansas City Chiefs, accessed November 21, 2023, www.chiefs.com.

2 "A Statement," Kansas City Chiefs.

3 Unsurprisingly, this exact chant and chop is used by the Atlanta, Georgia, MLB baseball team, the Braves, and the Florida State University football team, the Seminoles. Same exact chant, same exact movement.

4 Joe Harrington, "How to Watch the Cleveland Guardians Opening Day Game vs. Kansas City Royals," *Akron Beacon Journal*, April 1, 2022, www.beaconjournal.com.

5 John Keim, "Washington Chooses Commanders as New Name," ESPN.com, February 2, 2022, www.espn.com.

6 The complete findings of Reclaiming Native Truth are available for download at illuminative.org.

7 *Rutherford Falls* was created by Ed Helms, Michael Schur, and Sierra Teller Ornelas, featuring Ed Helms, Michael Greyeyes, and Jana Schmieding. It premiered April 22, 2021, www.peacocktv.com.

8 Internet Movie Database, "Reservation Dogs," Comedy, Crime, IMDb, 2021, www.imdb.com.

9 Roxana Hadadi, "The Historic Power of Prey Is in Your Ears," *Vulture*, August 11, 2022, www.vulture.com.

10 "Manahatta 2021—Shows on O!," Oregon Shakespeare Festival, 2021, www.osfashland.org.

11 Talaura Harms, "The Thanksgiving Play Officially Opens Broadway Premiere April 20," *Playbill*, April 20, 2023, https://playbill.com.

12 Department of the Interior, "Interior Department Announces Next Steps to Remove 'Sq___' from Federal Lands," February 22, 2022, www.doi.gov.

13 Louis Sahagun, "New Law Will Remove the Word 'Squaw' from California Place Names," *Los Angeles Times*, September 25, 2022, www.latimes.com.

14 Scott Neuman, "As Schools Face Calls to Drop Native American Mascots, Some Could Lose State Money," *NPR*, April 19, 2023, sec. Race, www.npr.org.

15 Neuman, "As Schools Face Calls to Drop Native American Mascots."

16 Neuman, "As Schools Face Calls to Drop Native American Mascots."

17 Neuman, "As Schools Face Calls to Drop Native American Mascots."

BIBLIOGRAPHY

ARCHIVES AND COLLECTIONS

Berlin, Irving. Irving Berlin Collection. Library of Congress, Washington, DC.

McBee, May Wilson. May Wilson McBee Papers. Mississippi County Court Records, 1958. Greenwood, MS. https://i-share-nby.primo.exlibrisgroup.com.

Miller Brothers 101 Ranch Collection. Western History Collections, University of Oklahoma, Norman, Oklahoma.

Native American Women Playwright Archive. Walter Havighurst Special Collections, University Archives & Preservation, Miami University, Oxford, Ohio. https://spec.lib.miamioh.edu.

Rogers, Will. Will Rogers Archive. Will Rogers Museum and Archive, Claremore, Oklahoma.

Tamiris, Helen. Helen Tamiris Collection. Billy Rose Theatre Division. New York Public Library for the Performing Arts, New York, New York.

Theatre on Film and Tape Archive. New York Public Library for the Performing Arts, New York, New York.

Wojtowicz, James. James Wojtowicz Collection 1880–1929. McCracken Research Library, Buffalo Bill Center of the West, Cody, Wyoming.

SECONDARY SOURCES

Ablavsky, Gregory. "'With the Indian Tribes': Race, Citizenship, and Original Constitutional Meanings." *Stanford Law Review* 70, no. 4 (2018): 1025–76.

Aleiss, Angela. "Iron Eyes Cody: Wannabe Indian." *Cinéaste* 25, no. 1 (January 1, 1999): 30–31.

———. *Making the White Man's Indian: Native Americans and Hollywood Movies.* Westport, CT: Praeger, 2005.

Alfred, Taiaiake (Gerald). *Wasa'se: Indigenous Pathways of Action and Freedom.* Peterborough, Ontario: Broadview, 2005.

Alger, William Rounseville. *Life of Edwin Forrest, the American Tragedian.* 2 vols. Philadelphia: J. B. Lippincott, 1877.

Alsultany, Evelyn. *Arabs and Muslims in the Media: Race and Representation after 9/11.* New York: New York University Press, 2012.

Apess, William. *Eulogy on King Philip: As Pronounced at the Odeon, in Federal Street, Boston.* Boston: William Apess, 1836.

———. *Indian Nullification of the Unconstitutional Laws of Massachusetts, Relative to the Marshpee Tribe: Or, the Pretended Riot Explained.* Boston: Jonathan Howe, 1835.

Apess, William, and Barry O'Connell. *A Son of the Forest and Other Writings.* Amherst: University of Massachusetts Press, 1997.

Armitage, F. S. *Buffalo Bill's Wild West Parade*. New York: American Mutoscope and Biograph Company, 1901. www.loc.gov.

Bancroft, George. *History of the United States from the Discovery of the American Continent*. 8 vols. London: G. Routledge, 1853.

———. *History of the United States of America, from the Discovery of the Continent*. New York: D. Appleton, 1888.

Bank, Rosemarie K. "'Show Indians'/Showing Indians: Buffalo Bill's Wild West, the Bureau of Indian Affairs, and American Anthropology." *Journal of Dramatic Theory and Criticism* 26, no. 1 (2011): 149–58. https://doi.org/10.1353/dtc.2011.0016.

———. *Theatre Culture in America, 1825–1860*. New York: Cambridge University Press, 1997.

Bannan, Helen M. "The Idea of Civilization and American Indian Policy Reformers in the 1880s." *Journal of American Culture* 1, no. 4 (1978): 787–99. https://doi.org/10.1111/j.1542-734X.1978.0104_787.x.

Barker, James Nelson. *The Indian Princess; or La Belle Sauvage An Operatic Melo-Drama in Three Acts*. New York: Da Capo, 1972.

Barker, James Nelson, and John Bray "The Indian Princess; or, La Belle Sauvage an Operatic Melo-Drame, in Three Acts." In *Dramatic Works*, 16:7–74. New York: David Longworth at the Dramatic Repository Shakespeare Gallery, 1808.

Barker, Joanne, ed. *Critically Sovereign: Indigenous Gender, Sexuality, and Feminist Studies*. Durham, NC: Duke University Press, 2017.

Barnes, Charlotte Mary Sanford. *Plays, Prose and Poetry*. Philadelphia: E. H. Butler, 1848.

Barrett, Lawrence. *Edwin Forrest*. Boston: J. R. Osgood, 1882.

Berkhofer, Robert F., Jr. *The White Man's Indian: Images of the American Indian from Columbus to the Present*. New York: Knopf, 1978.

Berlin, Irving, Dorothy Fields, and Herbert Fields. *Annie Get Your Gun*. New York: Irving Berlin Music Company, 1967.

Bernstein, Robin. *Racial Innocence: Performing American Childhood from Slavery to Civil Rights*. New York: New York University Press, 2011.

Bird, S. Elizabeth, ed. *Dressing in Feathers: The Construction of the Indian in American Popular Culture*. Boulder, CO: Westview, 1996.

Black, Liza. *Picturing Indians: Native Americans in Film, 1941–1960*. Lincoln: University of Nebraska Press, 2020.

Blackstone, Sarah J. *Buckskins, Bullets, and Business: A History of Buffalo Bill's Wild West*. Westport, CT: Greenwood, 1986.

Blu Wakpa, Tria. "From Buffalo Dance to Tatanka Kcizapi Wakpala, 1894–2020: Indigenous Human and More-Than-Human Choreographies of Sovereignty and Survival." *American Quarterly* 74, no. 4 (2022): 895–920.

Bold, Christine. *"Vaudeville Indians" on Global Circuits, 1880s-1930s*. New Haven, CT: Yale University Press, 2022.

Bridger, Bobby. *Buffalo Bill and Sitting Bull: Inventing the Wild West*. 1st ed. Austin: University of Texas Press, 2002.

Brooks, Daphne. *Bodies in Dissent: Spectacular Performances of Race and Freedom, 1850–1910*. Durham, NC: Duke University Press, 2006.

Brooks, Lisa. *The Common Pot: The Recovery of Native Space in the Northeast*. Minneapolis: University of Minnesota Press, 2008.

Brougham, John. *La Belle Sauvage; Burlesque in Four Scenes*. 2nd ed. London: R. Wilson, 1870.

———. *An Original Aboriginal Erratic Operatic Semi-Civilized and Demi-Savage Extravaganza, Being a Per-Version of Ye Trewe and Wonderrefulle Hystorie of Ye Rennownned Princesse, Po-Ca-Hon-Tas: or, The Gentle Savage*. New York: Samuel French, 1856.

Browner, Tara. *Heartbeat of the People: Music and Dance of the Northern Pow-Wow*. Urbana: University of Illinois Press, 2002.

Browning, Beth. *History of Drama in Ogden*. Master's thesis, Brigham Young University, 1947.

Buffalo Bill. *Buffalo Bill's Wild West and Congress of Rough Riders of the World: Official Programme*. Cover title: *Buffalo Bill's Wild West: Historical Sketches and Daily Review*. Buffalo, NY: Courier, 1907.

Burns, Lucy Mae San Pablo. *Puro Arte: Filipinos on the Stages of Empire*. New York: New York University Press, 2012.

Byrd, Jodi A. *The Transit of Empire*. Minneapolis: University of Minnesota Press, 2011.

Carlson, Marvin A. *The Haunted Stage: The Theatre as Memory Machine*. Ann Arbor: University of Michigan Press, 2001.

Chambers-Letson, Joshua Takano. *After the Party: A Manifesto for Queer of Color Life*. New York: New York University Press, 2018.

———. *A Race So Different: Performance and Law in Asian America*. New York: New York University Press, 2013.

Chapman, George. *The Memorable Maske of the Two Honorable Houses or Inns of Court; the Middle Temple, and Lyncolns Inne*. Cambridge, UK: Chadwyck-Healey, 1995.

Chinn, Sarah E. "Masculinity and National Identity on the Early American Stage." *Literature Compass* 9, no. 2 (2012): 106–17. https://doi.org/10.1111/j.1741-4113.2011.00872.x.

Christy Minstrels. *The Original Christy's Minstrels: Complete Repertoire of Plantation Melodies*. London: Christy's Minstrels, 1860.

Cocca, Carolyn. *Jailbait: The Politics of Statutory Rape Laws in the United States*. Albany: State University of New York Press, 2004.

Cole, Catherine M. *Ghana's Concert Party Theatre*. Bloomington: Indiana University Press, 2001.

Cole, Catherine, and Tracy C. Davis, eds. "Routes of Blackface." *TDR: The Drama Review* 57, no. 2. Special issue (Summer 2013): 7–12.

Conn, Steven. *History's Shadow: Native Americans and Historical Consciousness in the Nineteenth Century*. Chicago: University of Chicago Press, 2004.

Corntassel, Jeff, and Richard C. Witmer. *Forced Federalism: Contemporary Challenges to Indigenous Nationhood*. Norman: University of Oklahoma Press, 2008.

Cothran, Boyd. *Remembering the Modoc War: Redemptive Violence and the Making of American Innocence*. Chapel Hill: University of North Carolina Press, 2014.

Coulthard, Glen. *Red Skin, White Masks: Rejecting the Colonial Politics of Recognition*. Minneapolis: University of Minnesota Press, 2014.

Croy, Homer. *Our Will Rogers*. New York: Duell, Sloan, & Pearce, 1953.

Cushman, H. B. (Horatio Bardwell). *History of the Choctaw, Chickasaw, and Natchez Indians*. Norman: University of Oklahoma Press, 1999.

Custis, George Washington Parke. *Pocahontas, or, The Settlers of Virginia: A National Drama in Three Acts*. Philadelphia: C. Alexander, 1830.

Dakota Department of Education Office of Indian Education. "Oceti Sakowin Essential Understandings and Standards." https://indianeducation.sd.gov.

D'Aponte, Mimi, ed. *Seventh Generation: An Anthology of Native American Plays.* 1st ed. New York: Theatre Communications Group, 1999.

Darby, Jaye T., and Stephanie J. Fitzgerald, eds. *Keepers of the Morning Star: An Anthology of Native Women's Theater.* Los Angeles: UCLA American Indian Studies Center, 2003.

D'Avenant, William. *The Cruelty of the Spaniards in Peru. Exprest by Instrumentall and Vocall Musick, and by Art of Perspective in Scenes, &c. Represented Daily at the Cockpit in Drury-Lane, at Three after Noone Punctually.* London: Henry Herringman, 1658.

Davis, John. *First Settlers of Virginia.* 2nd ed. New York: I. Riley, 1806.

———. *Travels of Four Years and a Half in the United States of America During 1798, 1799, 1800, 1801, and 1802.* New York: Henry Holt, 1909.

Davis, Tracy C. "Nineteenth-Century Repertoire." *Nineteenth Century Theatre & Film* 36, no. 2 (December 2009): 6–28.

Däwes, Birgit, ed. *Indigenous North American Drama: A Multivocal History.* Albany: State University of New York Press, 2013.

———. "Performing Memory, Transforming Time: History and Indigenous North American Drama." In Däwes, *Indigenous North American Drama,* 1.

Deloria, Philip. *Playing Indian.* New Haven, CT: Yale University Press, 1998.

Deloria, Vine, Jr. "The Indians." In *Buffalo Bill and the Wild West. Exhibition catalogue, Brooklyn Museum, Brooklyn, NY,* 45–56. Pittsburgh: University of Pittsburgh Press, 1981.

DeMallie, Raymond J., ed. *The Sixth Grandfather: Black Elk's Teachings Given to John G. Neihardt.* Lincoln: University of Nebraska Press, 1984.

Department of Commerce Bureau of the Census. "Instructions to Enumerators." Washington, DC: Government Printing Office, 1919.

Department of the Interior. *Report on Population of the United States at the Eleventh Census, 1890.* Part 1. Washington, DC: Government Printing Office, 1895.

Detsi-Diamanti, Zoe. "Burlesquing 'Otherness' in Nineteenth-Century American Theatre: The Image of the Indian in John Brougham's Met-a-Mora; or, The Last of the Pollywogs (1847) and Po-Ca-Hon-Tas; or, The Gentle Savage (1855)." *American Studies* 48, no. 3 (2007): 101–23.

Doddridge, Joseph. *Logan: The Last of the Race of Shikellemus Chief of the Cayuga Nagion.* Buffalo Creek: Soloman Sala, 1823.

Dolan, Jill. *Utopia in Performance: Finding Hope at the Theater.* Ann Arbor: University of Michigan Press, 2005.

Drama League of America. *A List of Plays for High School and College Production.* Chicago: Drama League of America, 1916.

Dumont, Frank. *Who's the Actor? An Ethiopian Farce.* Chicago: Dramatic Publishing, 1876.

Ellinghaus, Katherine. *Blood Will Tell: Native Americans and Assimilation Policy.* Lincoln: University of Nebraska, 2017.

Endo, Mika. "'The Word "Mixed" without the "Indian" Would Be Better': Virginia's Racial Integrity Act and the Destruction of Indian Race in the Early Twentieth Century." *Native South* 7, no. 1 (2014): 92–107.

FastHorse, Larissa. *The Thanksgiving Play/What Would Crazy Horse Do?* New York: Theatre Communications Group, 2019.

Fleming, E. McClung. "The American Image as Indian Princess 1765–1783." *Winterthur Portfolio* 2 (January 1, 1965): 65–81.

———. "From Indian Princess to Greek Goddess the American Image, 1783–1815." *Winterthur Portfolio* 3 (1967): 37–66.

Foster, Tol. "Of One Blood: An Argument for Relations and Regionality in Native American Literary Studies." In *Reasoning Together: The Native Critics Collective*, edited by Craig S. Womack, Daniel Heath Justice, and Christopher B. Teuton, 287–88. Norman: University of Oklahoma Press, 2008.

Frank, John W., Roland S. Moore, and Genevieve M. Ames. "Historical and Cultural Roots of Drinking Problems among American Indians." *American Journal of Public Health* 90, no. 3 (2000): 344–51. https://doi.org/10.2105/ajph.90.3.344.

Friedman, Michael, and Alex Timbers. *Bloody Bloody Andrew Jackson*. NewMusicalTheatre.com, 2010.

Fryberg, Stephanie A., and Nicole M. Stephens. "When the World Is Colorblind, American Indians Are Invisible: A Diversity Science Approach." *Psychological Inquiry* 21, no. 2 (May 28, 2010): 115–19. https://doi.org/10.1080/1047840X.2010.483847.

Geiogamah, Hanay. *New Native American Drama: Three Plays*. 1st ed. Norman: University of Oklahoma Press, 1980.

Geiogamah, Hanay, and Jaye T. Darby, eds. *Stories of Our Way: An Anthology of American Indian Plays*. Los Angeles: UCLA American Indian Studies Center, 1999.

Gill, William F. *Parlor Tableaux and Amateur Theatricals*. Nineteenth-Century American Drama: Popular Culture and Entertainment, 1820–1900. Boston: J. E. Tilton, 1868.

Goeman, Mishuana. *Settler Aesthetics: Visualizing the Spectacle of Originary Moments in the New World*. Lincoln: University of Nebraska Press, 2023.

Goss, Joe R., ed. *The Choctaw Academy: Official Correspondence 1825–1841*. Conway, AR: Oldbuck Press, 1992.

Green, Rayna. "The Tribe Called Wannabee: Playing Indian in America and Europe." *Folklore* 99, no. 1 (1988): 30–55. https://doi.org/10.1080/0015587X.1988.9716423.

Gura, Philip F. *The Life of William Apess, Pequot*. Chapel Hill: University of North Carolina Press, 2015.

Hadadi, Roxana. "The Historic Power of Prey Is in Your Ears." *Vulture*, August 11, 2022. www.vulture.com.

Hafen, P. Jane. "A Cultural Duet Zitkala Sa and the Sun Dance Opera." *Great Plains Quarterly* 18, no. 2 (Spring 1998): 102–11.

Hageman, Maurice. *Hageman's Make-Up Book*. Chicago: Dramatic Publishing, 1898.

Haney-López, Ian F. "The Social Construction of Race: Some Observations on Illusion, Fabrication, and Choice." *Harvard Civil Rights-Civil Liberties Law Review* 29, no. 1–62 (1994): 1–62.

Harrison, Gabriel. *Edwin Forrest: The Actor and the Man*. Brooklyn, NY: Brooklyn Eagle Book Printing Department, 1889.

Haugo, Ann. "Native American Drama: A Historical Survey." In *Indigenous North American Drama: A Multivocal History*, edited by Birgit Däwes, 39. Albany: State University of New York Press, 2013.

Hendrick, Welland. *Pocahontas, a Burlesque Operetta in Two Acts*. Chicago: T. S. Denison, 1886.

Henry, George. *An Account of the Chippewa Indians*. Boston: printed by the author, 1848.

Herrera, Brian Eugenio. *Latin Numbers: Playing Latino in Twentieth-Century U.S. Popular Performance*. Ann Arbor: University of Michigan Press, 2015.

Highway, Tomson. *The Rez Sisters: A Play in Two Acts*. Saskatoon: Fifth House, 1988.

Howe, LeAnne. "Tribalography: The Power of Native Stories." *Journal of Dramatic Theory and Criticism* 14, no. 1 (Fall 1999): 117–25.

Hoxworth, Kellen. *Transoceanic Blackface: Empire, Race, Performance*. Evanston, IL: Northwestern University Press, 2024.

Hughes, Bethany. "The Indispensable Indian: Edwin Forrest, Pushmataha, and Metamora." *Theatre Survey* 59, no. 1 (2018): 23–44.

Jaroff, Rebecca Dunn. "Opposing Forces: (Re)Playing Pocahontas and the Politics of Indian Removal on the Antebellum Stage." *Comparative Drama* 40, no. 4 (2006): 483–504. https://doi.org/10.1353/cdr.2006.0005.

Johnson, E. Patrick. *Appropriating Blackness: Performance and the Politics of Authenticity*. Durham, NC: Duke University Press, 2003.

Johnson, Stephen, ed. *Burnt Cork: Traditions and Legacies of Blackface Minstrelsy*. Amherst: University of Massachusetts Press, 2012.

Justice, Daniel Heath. *Our Fire Survives the Storm: A Cherokee Literary History*. Minneapolis: University of Minnesota Press, 2006.

———. *Why Indigenous Literatures Matter*. Waterloo: Wilfrid Laurier University Press, 2018.

Kačer, Tomáš. "The 'Stage Indian' in Early American Theatre Culture." *Ostrava Journal of English Philology* 13, no. 2 (2021): 5–15.

Kappler, Charles J. "Treaty with the Choctaw, 1830." In *Indian Affairs, Laws and Treaties*. 2nd ed. Vol. 2. Serial Vol. 4624, document # S.doc.319. Washington, DC: Committee on Indian Affairs Senate, 1903.

Kasper, Shirl. *Annie Oakley*. Norman: University of Oklahoma Press, 1992.

Kasson, Joy S. *Buffalo Bill's Wild West: Celebrity, Memory, and Popular History*. 1st ed. New York: Hill and Wang, 2000.

Kauanui, J. Kehaulani. "'A Structure, Not an Event': Settler Colonialism and Enduring Indigeneity." *Lateral Journal of the Cultural Studies Association* 5, no. 1 (Spring 2016).

Khabeer, Su'ad Abdul. *Muslim Cool: Race, Religion, and Hip Hop in the United States*. New York: New York University Press, 2016.

Kilpatrick, Jacquelyn. *Celluloid Indians: Native Americans and Film*. Lincoln: University of Nebraska Press, 1999.

King, Thomas. *The Inconvenient Indian: A Curious Account of Native People in North America*. Minneapolis: University of Minnesota Press, 2013.

Kirle, Bruce. *Unfinished Show Business: Broadway Musicals as Works-in-Process*. Carbondale: Southern Illinois University Press, 2005.

Knapp, Raymond. *The American Musical and the Performance of Personal Identity*. Princeton, NJ: Princeton University Press, 2006.

Knowles, Ric. *Reading the Material Theatre*. Cambridge, UK: Cambridge University Press, 2004.

Knowles, Ric, and Monique Mojica, eds. *Staging Coyote's Dream: An Anthology of First Nations Drama in English*. 1st ed. Toronto: Playwrights Canada Press, 2003.

Lachance, Lindsay. "About: NAC Indigenous Theatre." National Arts Centre/Centre National Des Arts. https://nac-cna.ca.

———. "Tiny Sparks Everywhere: Birchbark Biting as Land-Based Dramaturgies." *Canadian Theatre Review* 186 (Spring 2021): 54–58.

Lacroix, Celeste C. "High Stakes Stereotypes: The Emergence of the 'Casino Indian' Trope in Television Depictions of Contemporary Native Americans." *Howard Journal of Communications* 22, no. 1 (2011): 1–23. https://doi.org/10.1080/10646175.2011.546738.

Lahr, John. "Irving Berlin." In *Show and Tell: New Yorker Profiles*, 145–57. Woodstock, NY: Overlook, 2000.

Lanman, Charles. "Pushmatahaw." *Appletons' Journal: A Magazine of General Literature*, August 6, 1870.

Lee, Esther Kim. *Made-Up Asians: Yellowface during the Exclusion Era*. Ann Arbor: University of Michigan Press, 2022.

Lepore, Jill. *The Name of War: King Philip's War and the Origins of American Identity*. New York: Alfred A. Knopf, 1998.

Lerma, Michael. *Indigenous Sovereignty in the 21st Century: Knowledge for the Indigenous Spring*. Gainesville: Florida Academic Press, 2014.

Lescarbot, Marc. *The Theatre of Neptune in New France: Presented upon the Waves of Port Royal the Fourteenth Day of November, Sixteen Hundred and Six, on the Return of the Sieur de Poutrincourt from the Armouchiquois Country*. Translated by Harriette Taber Richardson. Boston: Houghton Mifflin, 1927.

Letts, Tracy. *August: Osage County*. New York: Theatre Communications Group, 2008.

Lewis, Anna. *Chief Pushmataha: American Patriot, the Story of the Choctaws' Struggle for Survival*. 1st ed. New York: Exposition, 1959.

Lhamon, W. T. *Raising Cain: Blackface Performance from Jim Crow to Hip Hop*. Cambridge, MA: Harvard University Press, 1998.

Lincecum, Gideon. *Pushmataha: A Choctaw Leader and His People*. Tuscaloosa: University of Alabama Press, 2004.

Lopenzina, Drew. *Through an Indian's Looking-Glass: A Cultural Biography of William Apess, Pequot*. Amherst: University of Massachusetts Press, 2017.

Lopez, Julisa J., Arianne E. Eason, and Stephanie A. Fryberg. "The Same, yet Different: Understanding the Perceived Acceptability of Redface and Blackface." *Social Psychological and Personality Science* 13, no. 3 (2022): 698–709. https://doi.org/10.1177/19485506211039906.

Lott, Eric. *Love and Theft: Blackface Minstrelsy and the American Working Class*. New York: Oxford University Press, 2013.

MacKaye, Percy. *Epoch; The Life of Steele MacKaye, Genius of the Theatre*. 2 vols. New York: Boni & Liveright, 1927.

Magee, Jeffrey. *Irving Berlin's American Musical Theater*. Broadway Legacies. Oxford: Oxford University Press, 2012.

Magelssen, Scott, and Heidi L. Nees. "'Real Live Indian': Sitting Bull's Performance of Self in Buffalo Bill's Wild West." *Popular Entertainment Studies* 2, no. 1 (March 31, 2011): 22–40.

Maillard, Kevin Noble. "The Pocahontas Exception: The Exemption of American Indian Ancestry from Racial Purity Law." *Michigan Journal of Race & Law* 12, no. 2 (2007 2006): 351–86.

Malick, Terrence, dir. *The New World*. Burbank, CA: New Line Home Entertainment, 2006.

Mallett, Mark E. "'The Game of Politics': Edwin Forrest and the Jackson Democrats." *Journal of American Drama and Theatre* 5, no. 2 (1993): 31–46.

Mancall, Peter C. *Deadly Medicine: Indians and Alcohol in Early America*. Ithaca, NY: Cornell University Press, 1995.

Manning, Susan. *Modern Dance, Negro Dance: Race in Motion*. Minneapolis: University of Minnesota Press, 2004.

Manuel, Vera. *Honouring the Strength of Indian Women: Plays, Stories, Poetry*. Edited by Michelle Coupal, Emalene A. Manuel, Deanna Reder, and Joanne Arnott. Winnipeg: University of Manitoba Press, 2019.

Martin, Jill E. "'The Greatest Evil': Interpretations of Indian Prohibition Laws, 1832–1953." *Great Plains Quarterly* 23, no. 1 (2003): 35–53.

Martin, William. *A Treatise on the Art of Dyeing Woollen Cloth Scarlet, with Lac Lake*. London: Gale and Curtis, 1812.

McClintock, Anne. *Imperial Leather: Race, Gender, and Sexuality in the Colonial Conquest*. New York: Routledge, 1995.

McConachie, Bruce A. *Melodramatic Formations: American Theatre and Society, 1820–1870*. 1st ed. Iowa City: University of Iowa Press, 1992.

McCracken, Harold. *George Catlin and the Old Frontier*. New York: Bonanza Books, 1959.

McLaughlin, Michael R. "The Dawes Act, or Indian General Allotment Act of 1887: The Continuing Burden of Allotment. A Selective Annotated Bibliography." *American Indian Culture and Research Journal* 20, no. 2 (January 1, 1996): 59–105. https://doi.org/10.17953/aicr.20.2.j8u2308u37818m45.

Medina, Louisa H. *Nick of the Woods*. New York, 1868.

Meek, Barbra A. "And the Injun Goes 'How!': Representations of American Indian English in White Public Space." *Language in Society* 35, no. 1 (2006): 93–128.

Moody, Richard. *Edwin Forrest: First Star of the American Stage*. New York: Alfred A. Knopf, 1960.

Moreton-Robinson, Aileen. *The White Possessive: Property, Power, and Indigenous Sovereignty*. Minneapolis: University of Minnesota Press, 2015.

Morgan, Lewis Henry. *Ancient Society: Or, Researches in the Lines of Human Progress from Savagery through Barbarism to Civilization*. New York: H. Holt, 1878.

Morgensen, Scott Lauria. *Spaces between Us: Queer Settler Colonialism and Indigenous Decolonization*. Minneapolis: University of Minnesota Press, 2011.

Moses, L. G. *Wild West Shows and the Images of American Indians, 1883–1933*. 1st ed. Albuquerque: University of New Mexico Press, 1996.

Moses, Montrose Jonas. *The Fabulous Forrest; The Record of an American Actor*. Boston: Little, Brown, 1929.

———. *Representative Plays by American Dramatists*. New York: E. P. Dutton, 1918.

Most, Andrea. *Making Americans: Jews and the Broadway Musical*. Cambridge, MA: Harvard University Press, 2004.

Muñoz, José Esteban. *Cruising Utopia: The Then and There of Queer Futurity*. New York: New York University Press, 2009.

Nathans, Heather S. *Hideous Characters and Beautiful Pagans: Performing Jewish Identity on the Antebellum American Stage*. Ann Arbor: University of Michigan Press, 2017.

Nolan, Yvette. *Medicine Shows: Indigenous Performance Culture*. Toronto: Playwrights Canada Press, 2015.

Nolan, Yvette, and Ric Knowles. *Performing Indigeneity: New Essays on Canadian Theatre*. Vol. 6. 1st ed. Toronto: Playwrights Canada Press, 2016.

Nyongó, Tavia. *The Amalgamation Waltz: Race, Performance, and The Ruses of Memory*. Minneapolis: University of Minnesota Press, 2009.

O'Brien, Jean M. *Firsting and Lasting: Writing Indians out of Existence in New England*. Minneapolis: University of Minnesota Press, 2010.

Odell, George C. *Annals of the New York Stage*. 13 vols. New York: Columbia University Press, 1942.

Omi, Michael, and Howard Winant. *Racial Formation in the United States*. 3rd ed. New York: Routledge, 2015.

Owen, Robert Dale. *Pocahontas: A Historical Drama, in Five Acts; with an Introductory Essay and Notes*. New York: G. Dearborn, 1837.

Patel, Shaista. "The 'Indian Queen' of the Four Continents: Tracing the 'Undifferentiated Indian' through Europe's Encounters with Muslims, Anti-Blackness, and Conquest of the 'New World.'" *Cultural Studies* 33, no. 3 (May 4, 2019): 414–36. https://doi.org/10.1080/09502386.2019.1584906.

Pierce, Joseph M. "Adopted: Trace, Blood, and Native Authenticity." *Critical Ethnic Studies* 3, no. 2 (2017): 57. https://doi.org/10.5749/jcritethnstud.3.2.0057.

Pisani, Michael V. "'I'm an Indian Too': Playing Indian in Song and on Stage, 1900–1946." In *Imagining Native America in Music*, 243–91. New Haven, CT: Yale University Press, 2006. https://doi.org/10.12987/9780300130737-011.

Price, Lawrence Marsden. *Inkle and Yarico Album*. Berkeley: University of California Press, 1937.

Prucha, Francis Paul. *Documents of United States Indian Policy*. Lincoln, Nebraska: University of Nebraska Press, 2000.

Pulsipher, Jenny. "Playing John White: John Wompas and Racial Identity in the Seventeenth-Century Atlantic World." In *Native Acts: Indian Performance, 1603–1832*, edited by Joshua David Bellin and Laura L. Mielke, 206–31. Lincoln: University of Nebraska Press, 2012.

Raheja, Michelle H. *Reservation Reelism: Redfacing, Visual Sovereignty, and Representations of Native Americans in Film*. Lincoln: University of Nebraska Press, 2010.

Rebhorn, Matthew. "Edwin Forrest's Redding Up: Elocution, Theater, and the Performance of the Frontier." *Comparative Drama* 40, no. 4 (2006): 455–81. https://doi.org/10.1353/cdr.2006.0004.

———. *Pioneer Performances: Staging the Frontier*. Oxford: Oxford University Press, 2012.

Reddin, Paul. *Wild West Shows*. Urbana: University of Illinois Press, 1999.

Rees, James. *The Life of Edwin Forrest with Reminiscences and Personal Recollections*. Philadelphia: T. B. Peterson & Brothers, 1874.

Rickard, Jolene. "Sovereignty: A Line in the Sand." *Aperture*, no. 139 (July 1, 1995): 50–59.

Rifkin, Mark. *When Did Indians Become Straight?: Kinship, the History of Sexuality, and Native Sovereignty*. Oxford: Oxford University Press, 2011. https://doi.org/10.1093/acprof:oso/9780199755455.001.0001.

Roach, Joseph. *Cities of the Dead: Circum-Atlantic Performance*. Social Foundations of Aesthetic Forms. New York: Columbia University Press, 1996.

Robinson, Dylan. *Hungry Listening: Resonant Theory for Indigenous Sound Studies*. Minneapolis: University of Minnesota Press, 2020. https://doi.org/10.5749/j.ctvzpv6bb.

Rogers, Betty Blake. *Will Rogers: His Wife's Story*. Indianapolis, IN: Bobbs-Merrill, 1941.

Rogers, Will. *The Papers of Will Rogers*. Edited by Arthur Frank Wertheim and Barbara Bair. 5 vols. Norman: University of Oklahoma Press, 1996.

———. *Will Rogers' Weekly Articles*. Edited by James Smallwood and Steven K. Gragert. Stillwater: Oklahoma State University Press, 1980.

Roscoe, Will. *Changing Ones: Third and Fourth Genders in Native North America.* New York: St. Martin's, 1998.

———, ed. *Living the Spirit: A Gay American Indian Anthology.* New York: St. Martin's, 1988.

Rourke, Constance. *American Humor: A Study of the National Character.* New York: Harcourt, Brace, 1931.

Russell, Don. *The Wild West Or, A History of the Wild West Shows, Being an Account of the Presitgious, Peregrinatory Pageants Pretentously Presented before Citizens of the Republic, the Crowned Heads of Europe, and Multitudes of Awe-Struck Men, Women, and Children around the Globe, which Created a Wonderfully Imaginative and Unrealistic Image of the American West.* Fort Worth, TX: Amon Carter Museum of Western Art, 1970.

Sabin, Joseph, ed. *Catalogue of the Library of Edwin Forrest.* Philadelphia: Collins, 1863.

Sagala, Sandra. *Buffalo Bill on Stage.* Albuquerque: University of New Mexico Press, 2008.

Sammond, Nicholas. *Birth of an Industry: Blackface Minstrelsy and the Rise of American Animation.* Durham, NC: Duke University Press, 2015.

Sandoval-Sánchez, Alberto. *José, Can You See?: Latinos on and off Broadway.* Madison: University of Wisconsin Press, 1999.

Sayre, Gordon M. *The Indian Chief as Tragic Hero: Native Resistance and the Literatures of America, from Moctezuma to Tecumseh.* Chapel Hill: University of North Carolina Press, 2005.

Sears, Priscilla. *A Pillar of Fire to Follow: American Indian Dramas, 1808–1859.* Bowling Green, OH: Bowling Green University Popular Press, 1982.

Shea Murphy, Jacqueline. *The People Have Never Stopped Dancing: Native American Modern Dance Histories.* Minneapolis: University of Minnesota Press, 2007.

Sherman, Richard B. "'The Last Stand': The Fight for Racial Integrity in Virginia in the 1920s." *Journal of Southern History* 54, no. 1 (1988): 69–92. https://doi.org/10.2307/2208521.

Shimakawa, Karen. *National Abjection: The Asian American Body Onstage.* Durham, NC: Duke University Press, 2002.

Sickels, Robert J. *Race, Marriage and the Law.* Albuquerque: University of New Mexico Press, 1972.

Sidney, George, dir. *Annie Get Your Gun.* Burbank, CA: Warner Home Video, 2000.

Simpson, Audra. *Mohawk Interruptus: Political Life across the Borders of Settler States.* Durham, NC: Duke University Press, 2014.

Singer, Beverly R. *Wiping the War Paint off the Lens: Native American Film and Video.* Minneapolis: University of Minnesota Press, 2001.

Slater, Sandra, ed. *Gender and Sexuality in Indigenous North America, 1400–1850.* Columbia: University of South Carolina Press, 2022.

Sprague, Charles. "The Orator: The American Indians." *Oliver Optic's Magazine. Our Boys and Girls,* February 16, 1867.

Standing Bear, Luther. *My People, the Sioux.* Edited by E. A. Brininstool. Boston: Houghton Mifflin, 1928.

Stark, Heidi Kiiwetinepinesiik. "Nenabozho's Smart Berries: Rethinking Tribal Sovereignty and Accountability Indian Tribes and Human Rights Accountability." *Michigan State Law Review* 2013, no. 2 (2013): 339–54.

———. *Stealing Fire, Scattering Ashes: Anishinaabe Expressions of Sovereignty, Nationhood, and Land Tenure in Treaty Making with the United States and Canada, 1785—1923.* Minneapolis: University of Minnesota Press, 2008.

Sterling, Bryan B., ed. *The Best of Will Rogers*. New York: Crown, 1979.

Sterling, Bryan B., and Frances N. Sterling, eds. *A Will Rogers Treasury: Reflections and Observations*. New York: Crown, 1982.

Stone, John Augustus. *Metamora, Or, The Last of the Wampanoags*. Brooklin, ME: Feedback Theatrebooks & Prospero Press, 1996.

Tahmahkera, Dustin. *Tribal Television: Viewing Native People in Sitcoms*. Chapel Hill: University of North Carolina Press, 2014.

TallBear, Kimberly. *Native American DNA: Tribal Belonging and the False Promise of Genetic Science*. Minneapolis: University of Minnesota Press, 2013.

Taylor, Diana. *The Archive and the Repertoire: Performing Cultural Memory in the Americas*. Durham, NC: Duke University Press, 2003.

Thornton, Arland, and Linda Young-DeMarco. "Federal Decennial Census Data for Studying American Indians." Sociological Studies of American Indians Working Paper 2021–01, March 2021. https://ssai.isr.umich.edu.

Two-Rivers, E. Donald. *Briefcase Warriors: Stories for the Stage*. Norman: University of Oklahoma Press, 2001.

United States Census Bureau. "Intergovernmental Affairs: Tribal Affairs." Census.gov. www.census.gov.

———. "Measuring America: The Decennial Censuses from 1790 to 2000." Washington, DC: US Department of Commerce, 2002.

———. "A More Diverse Nation." Census.gov. www.census.gov.

Utley, Robert M. *The Lance and the Shield: The Life and Times of Sitting Bull*. 1st ed. New York: Henry Holt, 1993.

Vandevender, Bryan. "Splitting Hair: Reviving the American Tribal Love-Rock Musical in the 1970s." *New England Theatre Journal* 29 (2018): 31–53.

Vaughan, Virginia Mason. *Performing Blackness on English Stages, 1500–1800*. Cambridge, UK: Cambridge University Press, 2005.

Vega, Lope de. *The Discovery of the New World by Christopher Columbus: A Comedy in Verse*. Translated by Frieda Fligelman. Berkeley, CA: Gillick, 1950.

Vizenor, Gerald. *Manifest Manners: Postindian Warriors of Survivance*. Hanover: University Press of New England, 1994.

Ware, Amy M. *The Cherokee Kid Will Rogers, Tribal Identity, and the Making of an American Icon*. Lawrence: University Press of Kansas, 2015.

———. "Unexpected Cowboy, Unexpected Indian: The Case of Will Rogers." *Enthohistory* 56, no. 1 (2009): 1–34. https://doi.org/10.1215/00141801-2008-034.

Warren, Louis S. *Buffalo Bill's America: William Cody and the Wild West Show*. 1st ed. New York: Alfred A. Knopf, 2005.

Warrior, Robert. *Tribal Secrets: Recovering American Indian Intellectual Traditions*. Minneapolis: University of Minnesota Press, 1995.

Welch, Ellen R. "Performing a New France, Making Colonial History in Marc Lescarbot's Théâtre de Neptune (1606)." *Modern Language Quarterly* 72, no. 4 (2011): 439–60. https://doi.org/10.1215/00267929-1382217.

Wilmeth, Don B. *The Cambridge Guide to American Theatre*. 2nd ed. Cambridge, UK: Cambridge University Press, 2007.

W. E. T. *The Biography of Edwin Forrest, the Distinguished American Tragedian*. Philadelphia: Turner and Fisher, 1835.

Wolfe, Patrick. "Settler Colonialism and the Elimination of the Native." *Journal of Genocide Research* 8, no. 4 (December 1, 2006): 387–409. https://doi.org/10.1080/14623520601056240.

Yagoda, Ben. *Will Rogers: A Biography*. 1st ed. New York: Knopf, 1993.

Yellow Robe, William S. *Where the Pavement Ends: Five Native American Plays*. Norman: University of Oklahoma Press, 2000.

Young, Harvey. *Embodying Black Experience: Stillness, Critical Memory, and the Black Body*. Ann Arbor: University of Michigan Press, 2010.

Ziolkowski, Theodore. *Scandal on Stage: European Theater as Moral Trial*. Cambridge, UK: Cambridge University Press, 2009. https://doi.org/10.1017/CBO9780511635502.

INDEX

Page numbers in *italics* indicate illustrations.

ABOUT THE AUTHOR

BETHANY HUGHES is Assistant Professor at the University of Michigan in the Department of American Culture and a core faculty member in the Native American Studies Program.

www.ingramcontent.com/pod-product-compliance
Lightning Source LLC
Chambersburg PA
CBHW041109280526
45792CB00011B/2354
* 9 7 8 1 4 7 9 8 2 9 3 9 2 *